"Mr. Taggert, Are You Quite Serious About Your Marriage Proposal to Me?"

Houston Chandler stood in the doorway of Kane Taggert's office. "You think I got the time to waste doin' all the courtin' I been doin' if I wasn't serious?" Kane stared appreciatively at her.

"I don't know if you're serious, Mr. Taggert," Houston replied stiffly. "But I *do* know men who work in coal mines who are better dressed than you are. And your language is atrocious, as well as your manners. So, you will have to agree to some kind of instruction from me."

"Come 'ere," Kane said, motioning her around his desk.

Thinking he wanted something, she did as he bid. Roughly, he caught her wrist and pulled her into his lap. "If you get to be my teacher, I guess I'm gonna have to teach you about some things too." He began nuzzling her neck with his face, his lips caressing her skin. She was about to protest his treatment of her, but then parts of her body began to melt. . . .

Books by Jude Deveraux

The Velvet Promise
Highland Velvet
Velvet Song
Velvet Angel
Sweetbriar
Counterfeit Lady
Lost Lady
River Lady
Twin of Ice
Twin of Fire
The Temptress
The Raider
The Princess
The Awakening
The Maiden
The Taming
A Knight in Shining Armor

Published by POCKET BOOKS

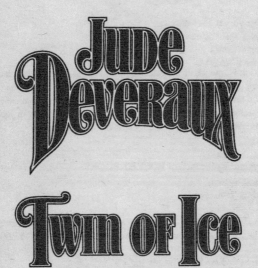

JUDE DEVERAUX

TWIN OF ICE

POCKET BOOKS

New York　London　Toronto　Sydney　Tokyo　Singapore

An *Original* Publication of POCKET BOOKS

POCKET BOOKS, a division of Simon & Schuster Inc.
1230 Avenue of the Americas, New York, NY 10020

Copyright © 1985 by Deveraux Inc.
Cover art copyright © 1985 Harry Bennett

ISBN: 0-671-72646-3

First Pocket Books printing June 1985

15 14 13 12 11 10 9

POCKET and colophon are registered trademarks of Simon & Schuster Inc.

Printed in the U.S.A.

My Twins are for Claude because one day he suggested that I write something like the Alexandria Quartet. When I'd picked myself off the floor, where I'd fallen from laughing so hard, I thought about it. . . .

Twin of Ice

Prologue

The fat old woman, gray hair scraggling from beneath a battered hat, teeth blackened, was surprisingly agile as she hoisted herself onto the seat of the big wagon. Behind her lay a variety of fresh vegetables covered with a dampened canvas.

"Sadie."

She looked to her left to see Reverend Thomas, tall, handsome, his brow furrowed in concern.

"You'll be careful? You won't try anything foolish? Or call attention to yourself?"

"I promise," Sadie said in a soft, young-sounding voice. "I'll be back in no time." With that, she clucked to the horses and set off at a lumbering pace.

The road out of the town of Chandler, Colorado, and into the coal mine that was Sadie's domain was long and rutted. Once, she had to wait for a train to pass on one of the spur lines of the Colorado and Southern Railroad. Each of the seventeen coal camps outside Chandler had its own train line into the camp.

Outside the turnoff to the Fenton mine Sadie passed another huckster wagon with another old woman sitting on the seat. Sadie halted her four horses, scanning the landscape as far as she could see.

"Any trouble?" Sadie quietly asked the other old woman.

"None, but the union talk is stronger. You?"

Sadie gave a curt nod. "There was a rumble in tunnel

number six last week. The men won't take the time to shore up as they dig. Do you have any peppermint?"

"Gave it all away. Sadie," the woman said, leaning closer, "be careful. The Little Pamela is the worst one. Rafe Taggert scares me."

"He scares a lot of people. Here comes another wagon." Her voice deepened as she hijahed to the horses. "See you next week, Aggie. Don't take no wooden nickels."

Sadie drove past the men on the approaching wagon and raised her hand in greeting. Moments later, she was turning down the long road into the Little Pamela mine camp.

The road was steep as she travelled up into the canyon and she didn't see the guard post until she was in front of it. In spite of herself, her heart began pounding.

"Mornin', Sadie. You got any turnips?"

"Big, fat ones." She grinned, showing her wrinkles and rotted teeth.

"Save me a sackful, will ya?" he said, as he unlocked the gate. There was no question of payment. Opening the gate to allow an outsider into the closed camp was payment enough.

The guards were posted there to make sure no union organizers got inside. If they suspected anyone of trying to organize the miners, the guards shot first and asked questions later. With that kind of power, all the guards had to do was say whomever they'd killed was a unionist and both the local and state courts freed them. The mine owners had a right to protect their property.

Sadie had to work to maneuver the big four-horse wagon through the narrow, coal-littered streets. On each side of her were frame boxes that the mine owners called houses, four or five tiny rooms, with a privy and coal shed out back. Water was drawn by buckets from a coal-infested community well.

Sadie moved the horses past the company store and coolly greeted the store owner. They were natural enemies. The miners were illegally paid in scrip so a family could purchase what it needed only from the company store. Some people said the mine owners made more money off the company store than they did from the coal.

To her right, between the railroad tracks and the steep mountainside, was Sunshine Row—a straggling line of double houses painted a ghastly yellow. There were no yards and only fifteen feet between houses and privies. Sadie knew too well the combination of train smoke and noise combined with the other smells. This was where the new mine workers lived.

Sadie halted her horses before one of the larger mine houses.

"Sadie! I thought you weren't coming," a pretty young woman said as she came out of the house, drying her wet hands and arms on a thin towel.

"You know me," Sadie said gruffly, as she laboriously dismounted. "I slept late this mornin' and my maid forgot to wake me. How you been, Jean?"

Jean Taggert gave a grin to the old woman. Sadie was one of the few outsiders allowed into the camp, and each week Jean was afraid the mine police would search her wagon.

"What did you bring?" Jean asked in a whisper.

"Cough medicine, liniment, a little morphine for Mrs. Carson, a dozen pairs of shoes. There's not much I can hide inside a head of cabbage. And lace curtains for Ezra's bride."

"Lace curtains!" Jean gasped, then laughed. "You're probably right. Lace will do more for her than anything else. Well, come on, let's get started."

It took Jean and Sadie three hours to distribute the vegetables, the townspeople paying Sadie in scrip—which Jean would later return to them in secret. The mine owners nor the camp police nor even most of the miners themselves had any idea that Sadie's vegetables and secret goods were free. The miners were proud and wouldn't have liked taking charity—but the women would take anything they could get for their children and their tired husbands.

It was late when Sadie and Jean returned with the empty wagon to Jean's house.

"How's Rafe?" Sadie asked.

"Working too hard, as is my father. And Uncle Rafe is stirring up trouble. You have to go. We can't risk your getting into trouble," she said, taking Sadie's hand. "Such a young hand."

"Trouble . . . ?" Sadie began, confused. She jerked away, making Jean laugh.

"Next week then. And Sadie, don't worry about me. I've known for a long time."

Confused into speechlessness, Sadie climbed into the wagon and clucked to the horses.

An hour later, she was parked at the back of the old rectory in Chandler. In the twilight evening, she ran through the unlocked door, down a short hall, and into the bathroom where clean clothes hung from a hook.

Quickly, she tore the wig from her head, washed the theatrical makeup from her face, scrubbed the black gum from her teeth. In another quick motion, she slipped out of the hot, padded clothes that made her look fat, and pulled on drawers and petticoats of fine lawn, a white linen corset that she laced in front, and stepped into a tailored skirt of blue serge edged with jet beads. A pale green silk blouse was covered with a jacket of blue serge trimmed with the new green looking glass velvet.

As she was fastening her dark blue leather belt, a knock sounded.

"Come in."

Reverend Thomas opened the door and stood for a moment gazing at the woman before him. Miss Houston Chandler was tall, slim and beautiful, with dark brown hair highlighted with red glints, wide-set blue-green eyes, a straight, aristocratic nose and a small, perfectly-shaped mouth.

"So, Sadie has gone for another week." The reverend smiled. "Now, Houston, you must go. Your father—."

"Stepfather," she corrected.

"Yes, well, his anger is the same whatever his title."

"Did Anne and Tia make it back with their wagons?"

"Hours ago. Now get out of here."

"Yes, sir." She smiled. "See you next Wednesday," she called over her shoulder as she left by the front door of the rectory and began to walk briskly toward home.

Chapter 1

May 1892

Houston Chandler walked the block and a half to her house as sedately as she could manage, halting before a three-story, red brick French Victorian house that the town called the Chandler Mansion. Composing herself, smoothing her hair, she mounted the steps.

As she put her parasol in the porcelain holder in the little vestibule, she heard her stepfather bellowing at her sister.

"I'll not have language like that in my house. You may think that because you call yourself a doctor you have a right to indecent behavior, but not in my house," Duncan Gates shouted.

Blair Chandler, as like her twin sister as another person can be, glared at the man, who was a few inches shorter than she was and built as solidly as a stone building. "Since when is this *your* house? My father——."

Houston stepped into the family parlor and put herself between her sister and her stepfather. "Isn't it time for dinner? Perhaps we should go in." With her back to her stepfather, she gave a pleading look to her sister.

Blair turned away from them both, her anger obvious.

Duncan took Houston's arm and led her past the staircase and toward the dining room. "At least I have one decent daughter."

Houston winced as she heard the often repeated remark. She hated being compared to Blair, and worse, hated being the winner.

They were barely seated at the big, mahogany table, each setting laid with crystal, porcelain and sterling, Duncan at the head, Opal Gates at the foot, the twins across from each other, when he started again.

"You'd think you'd want to do something to please your mother," Duncan said, glaring at Blair, as an eleven-pound roast was set before him. He picked up carving utensils. "Are you too selfish to care about anybody else? Doesn't your mother mean anything to you?"

Blair, her jaw clenched, looked at her mother. Opal was like a faded copy of her beautiful daughters. It was obvious that what spirit she'd ever had was either gone or deeply buried. "Mother," Blair said, "do you want me to return to Chandler, marry some fat banker, have a dozen children and give up medicine?"

Opal smiled fondly at her daughter as she took a small helping of eggplant from the platter held by a maid. "I want you to be happy, dear, and I believe it's rather noble of you to want to save people's lives."

Blair turned triumphant eyes toward her stepfather. "Houston's given up her life in order to please you. Isn't that enough for you? Do you have to see me broken too?"

"Houston!" Duncan thundered, clutching the big carving knife until his knuckles were white. "Are you going to allow your sister to say such things?"

Houston looked from her sister to her stepfather. Under no circumstances did she want to side with either one of them. When Blair returned to Pennsylvania after the wedding, Houston'd still be in the same town with her stepfather. With joy, she heard the downstairs maid announce Dr. Leander Westfield.

Quickly, Houston stood. "Susan," she said to the serving maid, "set another place."

Leander walked into the room with long, confident strides. He was tall, slim, dark, extremely good-looking—with green eyes to die for, as a friend of Houston's once said—and exuded an air of self-assurance that made women stop on the street and stare. He greeted Mr. and Mrs. Gates.

Leander leaned across the edge of the table and gave Houston a quick kiss on the cheek. Kissing a woman, even

6

your wife, and certainly your fiancée, so publicly was outrageous, but Leander had an air about him that allowed him to get away with things other men couldn't.

"Will you have dinner with us?" Houston asked politely, indicating the place set next to her.

"I've eaten, but maybe I'll join you for a cup of coffee. Good evening, Blair," he said as he sat down across from her.

Blair only glanced at him in answer as she poked at the food on her plate.

"Blair, you'll speak to Leander properly," Duncan commanded.

"That's all right, Mr. Gates," Leander replied pleasantly, but looking at Blair in puzzlement. He smiled at Houston. "You're as pretty as a bride today."

"Bride!" Blair gasped, standing and nearly upsetting her chair before she ran from the room.

"Why, that—," Duncan began, putting down his fork and starting to rise.

But Houston stopped him. "Please don't. Something's upsetting her badly. Perhaps she misses her friends in Pennsylvania. Leander, didn't you want to talk to me about the wedding? Could we go now?"

"Of course." Leander silently escorted her to his waiting buggy, clucked to the horse and drove her up the steep end of Second Street and parked on one of the many dead ends in Chandler. It was beginning to get dark and the mountain air was growing cold. Houston moved back into the corner of the carriage.

"Now, tell me what's going on," he said as he tied the horse's reins, put on the brake, and turned to her. "It seems to me that you're as upset as Blair."

Houston had to blink back tears. It was so good to be alone with Lee. He was so familiar, so safe. He was an oasis of sanity in her life. "It's Mr. Gates. He's always antagonizing Blair, telling her she's no good, reminding her that even as a child he thought there was no hope for her, and he's always demanding that she give up medicine and remain in Chandler. And, Lee, he keeps telling Blair how perfect I am."

"Ah, sweetheart," Lee said, pulling her into his arms, "you *are* perfect. You're sweet and kind and pliable and—."

7

She pulled away from him. "Pliable! You mean like taffy?"

"No," Lee smiled at her, "I just meant that you're a pretty, sweet woman, and I think it's good of you to be so worried about your sister, but I also think Blair should have been prepared for some criticism when she became a doctor."

"*You* don't think she should give up medicine, do you?"

"I have no idea what your sister should do. She's not my responsibility." He reached for her again. "What are we talking about Blair for? We have our own lives to live."

As he spoke, his arms tightened around her and he began to nuzzle her ear.

This was the part of their courtship Houston always hated. Lee was so easy to be around, someone she knew so well. After all, they'd been a "couple" since she was six and he was twelve. Now, at twenty-two, she'd spent a great deal of time near Leander Westfield, had known forever that she was going to be Mrs. Westfield. All her schooling, everything she'd ever learned was in preparation for the day she'd be Lee's wife.

But a few months ago, after he'd returned from studying in Europe, he'd started this kissing, pushing her into the buggy seat, groping at her clothes, and all she'd felt was that she wished he'd stop fumbling at her. Then Lee'd get angry, once again call her an ice princess, and take her home.

Houston knew how she was supposed to react to Lee's touch. For all its appearance of staidness, Chandler, Colorado, was an enlightened town—at least its women were—but for the life of her Houston felt nothing when Lee touched her. She'd cried herself to sleep with worry many times. She couldn't imagine loving anyone more than she loved Leander, but she was just not excited by his touch.

He seemed to sense what Houston was thinking and drew away from her, his anger showing in his eyes.

"It's fewer than three weeks," she said with hope in her voice. "In a short time we'll be married and then . . ."

"And then what?" he said, looking at her sideways. "The ice princess melts?"

"I hope so," she whispered, mostly to herself. "No one hopes so more than I do."

They were silent for a moment.

"Are you ready for the governor's reception tomorrow?"

Lee asked, pulling a long cheroot from his pocket and lighting it.

Houston gave him a trembling smile. These few minutes after she'd turned him down were always the worst. "My Worth gown's steamed and ready."

"The governor will love you, you know that?" He smiled at her, but she sensed he was forcing the smile. "Someday I'll have the most beautiful wife in the state at my side."

She tried to relax. A governor's reception was a place she felt confident. This was something she was trained for. Perhaps she should have taken a course in how not to be a cold, sexless wife. She knew that some men thought their wives shouldn't enjoy sex, but she also knew Leander was like no one else. He'd explained to her that he expected her to enjoy him and Houston'd told herself she would, but mostly she felt annoyed when Leander kissed her.

"I have to go to town tomorrow," he said, interrupting her thoughts. "Want to come along?"

"I'd love to. Oh! Blair wanted to stop by the newspaper office. I believe someone sent her a new medical journal from New York."

Houston leaned back in the carriage as Leander clucked to the horse and wondered what he'd say if he knew his "pliable" intended was, once a week, doing something that was quite illegal.

Blair lounged against the end of the ornate, canopied, walnut bed, one knee bent, showing the separation of her Turkish pants. Her big blue and white room was on the third floor, with a beautiful view of Ayers Peak out the west window. She'd had a room on the second floor with the rest of the family, but after she'd left Chandler when she was twelve, Opal'd become pregnant and Mr. Gates had made her room into a bath and a nursery. Opal lost the child and the little room stood unused now, filled with dolls and toy soldiers Mr. Gates had bought.

"I really don't see why we have to go with Leander," Blair said to Houston who sat quite straight on a white brocade chair. "I haven't seen you in years and now I have to share you."

Houston gave her sister a little smile. "Leander asked us to accompany him, not the other way around. Sometimes I think you don't like him. But I can't see how that could be possible. He's kind, considerate, he has position in the community and he—."

"And he completely owns you!" Blair exploded, jumping up from the bed, startling Houston with the strength of her outburst. "Don't you realize that in school I worked with women like you, women who were so unhappy they repeatedly attempted suicide?"

"Suicide? Blair, I have no idea what you're talking about. I have no intention of killing myself." Houston couldn't help drawing away from her sister's vehemence.

"Houston," Blair said quietly, "I wish you could see how much you've changed. You used to laugh, but now you're so distant. I understand that you've had to adjust to Gates, but why would you choose to marry a man just like him?"

Houston stood, putting her hand on the walnut dresser and idly touching Blair's silver-backed hairbrush. "Leander isn't like Mr. Gates. He's really very different. Blair"—she looked at her sister in the big mirror—"I love Leander," she said softly. "I have for years, and all I've ever wanted to do is get married, have children and raise my family. I never wanted to do anything great or noble like you seem to want to do. Can't you see that I'm happy?"

"I wish I could believe you," Blair said sincerely. "But something keeps me from it. I guess I hate the way Leander treats you, as if you were already his. I see the two of you together and you're like a couple who've lived together for twenty years."

"We have been together a long time." Houston turned back to face her sister. "What should I look for in a husband if it isn't compatibility?"

"It seems to me that the best marriages are between people who find each other interesting. You and Leander are too much alike. If he were a woman, he'd be a perfect lady."

"Like me," Houston whispered. "But I'm not *always* a lady. There are things I do—."

"Like Sadie?"

"How did you know about that?" Houston asked.

"Meredith told me. Now, what do you think your darling

Leander is going to say when he finds out that you're putting yourself in danger every Wednesday? And how will it look for a surgeon of his stature to be married to a practicing criminal?"

"I'm not a criminal. I'm doing something that's good for the whole town," Houston said with fire, then quieted. She slipped another hairpin invisibly into the neat chignon at the back of her head. Carefully arranged curls framed her forehead beneath a hat decorated with a spray of iridescent blue feathers. "I don't know what Leander will say. Perhaps he won't find out."

"Hah! That pompous, spoiled man will forbid you to participate in anything dealing with the coal miners and, Houston, you're so used to obeying that you'll do exactly what he says."

"Perhaps I should give up being Sadie after I'm married," she said with a sigh.

Suddenly, Blair dropped to her knees on the carpet and took Houston's hands. "I'm worried about you. You're not the sister I grew up with. Gates and Westfield are eating away at your spirit. When we were children, you used to throw snowballs with the best of them but now it's as if you're afraid of the world. Even when you do something wonderful like drive a huckster wagon, you do it in secret. Oh, Houston—."

She broke off at a knock on the door. "Miss Houston, Dr. Leander is here."

"Yes, Susan, I'll be right down." Houston smoothed her skirt. "I'm sorry you find me so much to your distaste," she said primly, "but I *do* know my own mind. I want to marry Leander because I love him." With that, she swept out of the room, and went downstairs.

Houston tried her best to push Blair's words from her mind but she couldn't. She greeted Leander absently and was vaguely aware of a quarrel going on between Lee and Blair, but she really heard nothing except her own thoughts.

Blair was her twin, they were closer than ordinary sisters and Blair's concern was genuine. Yet, how could Houston even think of not marrying Leander? When Leander was eight years old, he'd decided he was going to be a doctor, a surgeon who saved people's lives, and by the time Houston met him, when he was twelve, Lee was already studying textbooks borrowed from a distant cousin. Houston decided to find out how to be a doctor's wife.

Neither wavered from his decision. Lee went to Harvard to study medicine, then to Vienna for further study, and Houston went to finishing schools in Virginia and Switzerland.

Houston still winced whenever she thought of the argument she and Blair'd had about her choice of schools. "You're going to give up an education just so you can learn to set a table, so you can learn how to walk into a room wearing fifty yards of heavy satin and not fall on your face?"

Blair went to Vassar, then medical school, while Houston went to Miss Jones's School for Young Ladies where she was put through years of rigorous training in everything from how to arrange flowers to how to stop men from arguing at the dinner table.

Now, Lee took her arm as he helped her into the buggy. "You look as good as always," he said close to her ear.

"Lee," Houston said, "do you think we find each other . . . interesting?"

With a smile, his eyes raked down her body, over the dress that glued itself to her tightly corseted, exaggerated hourglass figure. "Houston, I find you fascinating."

"No, I mean, do we have enough to talk about?"

He raised one eyebrow. "It's a wonder I can remember how to talk when I'm around you," he answered as he helped her into his buggy, and drove them the six blocks into the heart of Chandler.

Chapter 2

Chandler, Colorado, was a small place, only eight thousand inhabitants, but its industries of coal, cattle, sheep, and Mr. Gates's brewery made it a rich little town. It already had a telephone system and electricity, and, with three train lines through town, it was easy to reach the larger cities of Colorado Springs and Denver.

The eleven blocks comprising downtown Chandler were covered with buildings that were almost all new and built of stone from the Chandler Stone Works. The greenish gray stone was often carved into intricate patterns for use as cornices for the Western Victorian style buildings.

Scattered outside the town were houses in varied styles of Queen Anne and High Victorian. At the north end of town, on a small rise, was Jacob Fenton's house, a large brick Victorian structure that until a few years ago had been Chandler's largest house.

At the west end of town, just a short distance from the Fenton house, on the flattened top of what most citizens had once considered part of the mountains, was Kane Taggert's house. Fenton's house would have fit into the wine cellar of the Taggert house.

"The whole town still trying to get inside the place?" Blair asked Houston as she nodded toward the house barely visible behind the trees. That "barely visible" part was large enough to be seen from almost anywhere in town.

"Everyone," Houston smiled. "But when Mr. Taggert

13

ignored all invitations and extended none of his own, I'm afraid people began spreading awful rumors about him."

"I'm not so sure all the things people say about him are rumors," Leander said. "Jacob Fenton said—."

"Fenton!" Blair exploded. "Fenton is a conniving, thieving—."

Houston didn't bother to listen but leaned back in the carriage and gazed at the house through the window at the back of the buggy. Lee and Blair continued arguing while he halted the carriage to wait for one of the new horse-drawn trolley cars to pass.

She had no idea whether what was said about Mr. Taggert was true or not, but it was her own opinion that the house he'd built was the most beautiful thing she'd ever seen.

No one in Chandler knew much about Kane Taggert, but five years ago over a hundred construction workers had arrived from the East with an entire train loaded with materials. Within hours, they'd started what was soon to become the house.

Of course everyone was curious—actually, a good deal more than curious. Someone said that none of the construction workers ever had to pay for a meal because all the women of Chandler fed them in an attempt to get information. It didn't do any good. No one knew who was building the house or why anyone'd want such a place in Nowhere, Colorado.

It took three years to complete, a beautiful, white U-shaped building, two stories, with a red tile roof. The size of it was what boggled people's minds. One local store owner liked to say that every hotel in Chandler could be put on the first floor, and considering that Chandler was a crossroads between north and south Colorado, and the number of hotels in town, that was saying a great deal.

For a year after the house was completed, trainloads of wooden boxes were delivered to the house. They had labels on them from France, England, Spain, Portugal, all over the world.

Still, there was no sign of an owner.

Then one day, two men stepped off the train, both tall, big men, one blond and pleasant looking, the other dark, bearded, angry. They both wore the usual miner's garb of

14

canvas pants, blue chambray shirt, and suspenders. As they walked down the street, women pulled their skirts aside.

The dark one went up to Jacob Fenton, and everyone assumed he was going to ask for a job in one of the mines Fenton owned. But instead, he'd said, "Well, Fenton, I'm back. You like my house?"

It wasn't until he had walked through town and onto the land of the new house and then through its locked front door that anyone had had any idea he mean *that* house.

For the next six months, according to Duncan Gates, Chandler was the site of a full-fledged war. Widows, single women and mothers of young women made an all-out attack for the hand in marriage of the man they'd swept their skirts aside for. Dressmakers by the dozen came down from Denver.

Within a week, the women'd found out his name and Mr. Taggert was besieged. Some of the attempts to get his attention were quite ordinary; for instance, it was amazing how many women fainted when near him, but some attempts were ingenious. Everyone agreed that the prize went to Carrie Johnson, a pregnant widow who climbed down a rope and into Mr. Taggert's bedroom while she was having labor pains. She thought he'd deliver her baby and of course fall passionately in love with her and beg her to marry him. But Taggert was away at the moment, and all the assistance she got was from a passing laundress.

After six months, nearly every woman in town'd made a fool of herself with no success, so they began to talk sour grapes. Who wanted a rich man who didn't know how to dress properly? And his grammar was that of the lowest cowboy. They started asking questions about him. What had he meant when he'd said, "I'm *back*"?

Someone located an old servant of Jacob Fenton's who remembered that Kane Taggert had been the stable lad until he started dallying with Pamela Fenton, Jacob's young daughter. Jacob kicked him off his property—and rightly so.

This gave the town something new to talk about. Who did Taggert think he was, anyway? What right did he have to build that outlandish, garish house overlooking the peaceful, pretty little town of Chandler? And was he planning revenge on dear Jacob Fenton?

Once again, women started sweeping their skirts aside when he passed.

But Taggert never seemed to notice any of it. He stayed in his house most of the time, drove his old wagon into town once a week and bought groceries. Sometimes, men would arrive on the train and ask directions to his house, then leave town before sundown. Other than these men, the only people to enter or leave the big house were Taggert and the man he called Edan, who was always with him.

"That's Houston's dream house," Leander said when the trolley car had passed, bringing Houston back to the present. He'd finished—or stopped—his argument with Blair. "If Houston didn't have me, I think she'd have joined the line of women fighting for Taggert and that house of his."

"I *would* like to see the inside," she said with more wistfulness than she meant to reveal, then, to cover herself, she said, "You can drop me here, at Wilson's, Lee. I'll meet you at Farrell's in an hour."

Once out of the buggy, she realized she was glad to get away from their constant bickering.

Wilson's Mercantile was one of four large, all-purpose dry-goods stores in Chandler. Most people shopped at the newer, more modern store, The Famous, but Mr. Wilson had known Houston's father.

The walls were lined with tall, walnut, glass-doored cases, interspersed with marble-topped counters covered with goods.

Behind one counter sat Davey Wilson, Mr. Wilson's son, a ledger open before him, but his fountain pen was unmoving.

In fact, neither the three customers nor the four clerks seemed to be moving. Everything was unnaturally quiet. Instantly, Houston saw the reason why: Kane Taggert stood at one counter, his back to the few people in the store.

Silently, Houston went to a counter to look at a selection of patent medicines, which she had no intention of buying, but she sensed something was happening.

"Oh, Mamma," Mary Alice Pendergast wailed in her high voice, "I *couldn't* wear that, I'd look like a coal miner's bride. People would think I was a no-'count . . . servant, a scullery maid, who thought she was a big cheese. No, no, Mamma, I couldn't wear that."

Houston gritted her teeth. Those two women were baiting Mr. Taggert. Since he'd turned all the women in town down, they seemed to think it was open season for their nasty games. She glanced toward him and, when she did, she saw his face in an advertising mirror behind the counter. There was so much hair surrounding his face that his features could barely be seen, but Houston could see his eyes. He most certainly was hearing Mary Alice's nasty little comments and, what's more, they were bothering him. There was a furrow between his eyes.

Mary Alice's father was a gentle rabbit of a man who never raised his voice. But Houston knew, from living with Mr. Gates, what an angered man could say and do. She didn't know Mr. Taggert, but she thought she saw anger in those dark eyes.

"Mary Alice," Houston said, "how do you feel today? You look a little pale."

Mary Alice looked up in surprise, as if she'd just seen Houston. "Why, Blair-Houston, I feel fine. Nothing's wrong with me."

Houston examined a bottle of liver activator. "I was just hoping you wouldn't faint—again," she said pointedly, her eyes boring into Mary Alice's. Mary Alice had fainted in front of Taggert twice when he'd first come to town.

"Why you—! How dare—!" Mary Alice sputtered.

"Come along, dear," her mother said, pushing her daughter toward the door. "We know who our friends are."

Houston felt quite annoyed with herself after Mary Alice and her mother had left. She'd have to apologize later. Impatiently, she tugged at her kid gloves, preparing to leave the store, when she again glanced toward Mr. Taggert and saw, in the mirror, that he was watching her.

He turned to face her. "You're Houston Chandler, ain't you?"

"I am," she said coolly. She had no intention of having a conversation with a man she didn't know. What in the world had made her take this stranger's side against someone she'd known all her life?

"How come that woman called you Blair? Ain't that your sister?"

From a few feet away, Davey Wilson gave a little snort.

17

There were only the four clerks in the store now besides Houston and Kane, and each one was nailed to his place.

"My sister and I are identical twins and, since no one can tell us apart, the townspeople call us Blair-Houston. Now if you'll excuse me, sir." She turned to leave.

"You don't look like your sister. I seen her and you're prettier."

For a moment, Houston paused to gape at him. *No* one had *ever* been able to tell them apart. When her momentary shock was over, she again turned to leave.

But as her hand touched the doorknob, Taggert bounded across the room and grabbed her arm.

All her life, Houston had lived in a town filled with coal miners, cowboys and inhabitants of a part of town she wasn't supposed to know existed. Many women carried a good strong parasol which they found useful for cracking over men's heads. But Houston could give looks that could freeze a man.

She gave one to Mr. Taggert now.

He withdrew his hand from her arm but he stayed close to her, the size of him making her feel small.

"I wanted to ask you a question," he said, his voice low. "If you don't mind, that is," he added, with laughter in his voice.

She gave him a curt nod, but she wasn't going to encourage his speaking to her.

"I was wonderin' about somethin'. If you, bein' a lady an' all, was gonna make curtains for my house, you know, the white one on the hill, which one of these here materials would you pick?"

She didn't bother to look at the shelves of bolts of fabric to which he was pointing. "Sir," she said with some haughtiness in her voice, "if I had your house, I'd order the fabric specially woven in Lyons, France. Now, good day." As quickly as possible, she left the store to emerge under the striped awnings which covered the southern side of the street, her heels clicking on the wide boardwalk. The town was busy today and she nodded and spoke to several people.

As she turned the corner of Third and Lead, she opened her parasol against the brilliant mountain sun and started toward Farrell's Hardware Store. She could see Lee's buggy parked in front.

Just past Freyer's Drugs, she began to relax and to muse on her encounter with the elusive Mr. Taggert.

She could hardly wait to tell her friends about the meeting, and how he'd asked if she knew which house was his. Perhaps she should have volunteered to measure his windows and order his curtains. That way she'd get to see the inside of his house.

She was smiling to herself when a hand suddenly caught her upper arm and roughly pulled her into the shadowy alleyway behind the Chandler Opera House. Before she could scream, a hand clamped down on her mouth, and she was pushed against the stone wall. With frightened eyes, she looked up at Kane Taggert.

"I ain't gonna hurt you. I just wanted to talk to you, and I could see you wasn't gonna say nothin' in front of them others. You ain't gonna scream?"

Houston shook her head, and he dropped his hand but he stayed close to her. She wanted to be calm, but she was breathing quite hard.

"You're prettier up close." He didn't move but glanced down over her snug green wool suit. "And you look like a lady."

"Mr. Taggert," she said with all the calmness she could muster, "I very much resent being pulled into an alley and held against a wall. If you have something to say to me, please do so."

He didn't move away from her but put one hand on the wall beside her head. There were little lines beside his eyes, his nose was small, and the lower lip visible under his mass of beard was full.

"How come you stood up for me in that store? How come you reminded that woman about when she fainted in front of me?"

"I . . ." Houston hesitated. "I guess I don't like anyone hurting another person. Mary Alice was embarrassed because she'd made a fool of herself in front of you and you hadn't noticed."

"I noticed all right," he said, and Houston saw that lower lip stretch into a smile. "Me and Edan laughed at all of 'em."

Houston stiffened. "That wasn't very polite of you. A gentleman should not laugh at a lady."

He gave a little snort into her face and Houston found herself thinking that he had especially sweet-smelling breath, and wondered what he looked like when he wasn't under so much hair.

"The way I figure it, all them women was carryin' on so because I'm rich. In other words, they was makin' whores of themselves, so they wasn't ladies, so I didn't have to act like no gentleman and pick 'em up."

Houston blinked at his vocabulary. No man had ever used such a word in front of her.

"How come you didn't try to get my attention? Ain't you wantin' my money?"

That snapped Houston out of her lethargy. She came to attention and realized she'd been almost lounging against the wall. "No, sir, I do *not* want your money. Now, I have places to go. Do not ever accost me like this again." With that she turned on her heel and, as she left him in the alley, she heard him chuckling behind her.

She realized she was angry when she crossed the wide, dusty street and narrowly missed being run down by a smelly wagon loaded with hides. No doubt Mr. Taggert thought her action this morning was another play for his money.

Lee said something to her as a greeting but she was too distracted to hear him.

"I beg your pardon," Houston said.

Lee took her elbow and escorted her to the carriage. "I said that you'd better get home now so you can start getting ready for the governor's reception tonight."

"Yes, of course," she said absently as he led her to his waiting buggy.

Houston was almost glad when Blair and Lee started arguing again because it gave her time to think about her encounter this morning. It sometimes seemed that all her life she'd been Miss Blair-Houston. Even when Blair was away, out of habit, the name stayed. Yet today someone'd told her she wasn't at all like her sister. Of course, surely, he was just bragging. He couldn't actually tell them apart.

As they were driving west, out of town, she found herself straightening her spine as she saw Mr. Taggert and Edan about to pass them in their dilapidated old wagon.

Kane pulled the horses to a halt and shouted, "Westfield!" at the same time.

Startled, Lee halted his horse.

"I wanted to say good mornin' to the ladies. Miss Blair," he said to Blair on the far side. "And Miss Houston," he said, his voice softening as he looked at her directly. "Mornin' to you," he said, then cracked a whip over the heads of his four horses to set them into motion.

"What in the world was that about?" Leander asked. "I didn't know you knew Taggert."

Before Houston could answer, Blair said, *"That* was the man who built that house? No wonder he doesn't ask anyone to it. He knows they'd turn him down. By the way, how could he tell us apart?"

"Our clothes," Houston answered too quickly. "I saw him in the mercantile store."

Blair and Leander continued talking, but Houston didn't hear a word that was said. She was thinking about her encounter that morning.

Chapter 3

The Chandler house was set on one-half acre of land, with a brick carriage house in back and a latticed grape arbor just off the deep porch that surrounded three sides of the house. Over the years, Opal'd turned the land into a jewel of a garden. Elm trees that she'd planted when the house was new were now mature and shaded the lush lawns and flowers from the moisture-stealing Colorado sun. There were narrow brick pathways, stone statues and birdbaths hidden in the orderly tangle of flowers. Between the house and coach house was a cutting garden, and Opal always kept every room in her house filled with fresh, lovely flowers.

"All right," Blair said as Houston bent over a rosebush in the garden at the northwest corner of their property. "I want to know what's going on."

"I have no idea what you're talking about."

"Kane Taggert."

Houston paused for a moment, her hand on a rose. "I saw him in Wilson's Mercantile and later he said good morning to us."

"You're not telling me everything."

Houston turned to her sister. "I probably shouldn't have involved myself, but Mr. Taggert looked as if he were getting angry and I wanted to prevent a quarrel. Unfortunately, it was at Mary Alice's expense." She told Blair about Miss Pendergast's nasty remarks.

"I don't like your getting mixed up with him."

"You sound like Leander."

"For once, he's right!"

Houston laughed. "Perhaps we should mark this day in the family Bible. Blair, after tonight I swear I'll never even mention Mr. Taggert's name."

"Tonight?"

Houston pulled a piece of paper from inside her sleeve. "Look at this," she said eagerly. "A messenger brought it. He's invited me to dinner at his house."

"So? You're supposed to go somewhere with Leander tonight, aren't you?"

Houston ignored the remark. "Blair, you don't seem to realize what a stir that house has caused in this town. *Everyone* has tried to get an invitation to see the inside of it. People have come from all over the state to see it, but no one has been invited in. Once, it was even put to Mr. Taggert that an English duke who was passing through should be allowed to stay in the house, but Mr. Taggert wouldn't even listen to the committee. And now *I've* been invited."

"But you have to go somewhere else. The governor will be there. Surely he's more important than the inside of any old house."

"You couldn't understand what it was like," Houston said with a faraway look in her eyes. "Year after year we watched the train unload its goods. Mr. Gates said the owner didn't build a spur line to the house site because he wanted everyone to see everything going all the way through town. There were crates of goods from all over the world. Oh, Blair, I know they must have been filled with furniture. And tapestries! Tapestries from Brussels."

"Houston, you cannot be in two places at once. You promised to go to the reception and you must go."

Idly, Houston toyed with a rose. "When we were children, we could be in two places at once."

It took Blair a minute to understand. "You want us to trade places?" she gasped. "You want *me* to spend an evening with Leander, pretending I like him, while you go see some lecherous man's house?"

"What do you know about Kane to call him lecherous?"

"Kane, is it? I thought you didn't know him?"

"Don't change the subject. Blair, please trade places with

me. Just for one night. I'd go another night but I'm afraid Mr. Gates would forbid it, and I'm not sure Leander would want me to go either, and I'll never get another opportunity like this. Just one last fling before I get married."

"You make marriage sound like death. Besides, Leander would know I wasn't you in a minute."

"Not if you behaved yourself. You know that we're both good actresses. Look at how I pretend to be an old woman every Wednesday. All you have to do is be quiet and not start an argument with Lee, and refrain from talking about medicine and walk like a lady instead of looking like you're running to a fire."

Blair took a long time before she answered, but Houston could see she was weakening. "Please, please, Blair. I hardly ever ask you for anything."

"Except to spend months in the house of our stepfather whom you know I detest. To spend weeks in the company of that self-congratulating man I think you intend to marry. To—."

"Oh, Blair, please," Houston whispered. "I really do want to see his house."

"It's just his house you're interested in, not Taggert?"

Houston knew she'd won. Blair was trying to act reluctant, but for some reason of her own, she was going to agree. She hoped Blair wouldn't try to get Lee to take her to the Infirmary.

"For Heaven's sake!" Houston said, "I've been to hundreds of dinner parties and I haven't yet been swept off my feet by the host. Besides, there'll be other people there." At least, she hoped there would be. She didn't want to be held against a wall again.

Blair suddenly smiled. "After the wedding, would you mind if I told Leander he spent an evening with me? Just to see the look on his face would be worth everything."

"Of course you may. Lee has a very good sense of humor, and I'm sure he'll enjoy the joke."

"I somehow doubt that, but at least I'll enjoy it."

Houston threw her arms about her sister. "Let's go get ready. I want to wear something befitting that house, and you'll get to wear the blue satin Worth gown," she said enticingly.

"I should wear my knickerbockers, but that would give it away, wouldn't it?" Blair said as she followed her sister into the house, a light dancing in her eyes.

What followed was an orgy of indecision. Houston went through her entire extensive trousseau that had been made for her wedding, in an attempt to find just the right dress.

At last she settled on a gown of mauve and silver brocade, the low square neck and hem edged with ermine, the short, puffed sleeves made of mauve chiffon. She would hide the dress in a leather valise—Blair was always carrying bags full of oddly-shaped medical instruments—and change at Tia's.

She didn't want to use the telephone for fear someone'd hear her, so she paid a penny to one of the Randolph boys to deliver a message to her friend Tia Mankin, whose house was near the foot of Kane's drive, that asked her to say Blair was there, should anyone ask.

Blair started complaining again, acting as if Houston were sending her on an impossible quest. And she wailed for twenty minutes about the tightness of the corset that forced her waist small enough to wear the Worth gown. But when Blair looked in the mirror, Houston saw the sparkle in her eyes and knew she was pleased with how she looked.

The few minutes they spent in the parlor with their mother and Mr. Gates were a joy to Houston. Blair's comfortable clothes made her feel quite the tomboy, and she antagonized Mr. Gates to no end.

And when Leander came, she enjoyed baiting him too. Lee's reserved coolness, the way nothing she said to him penetrated his superior attitude, began to make her angry and, by the time they reached Tia's, she was glad to get away from both Lee and Blair.

She met Tia in the dense shadow of a cottonwood tree and followed her up the back stairs to her room.

"Blair," Tia whispered, as she helped Houston to dress, "I had no idea you knew our mysterious Mr. Taggert. I wish I could go with you tonight, and I bet Houston wanted to go too. She loves that house. Did she ever tell you about the time she . . . ? Maybe I'd better not tell."

"Maybe you shouldn't," Houston said. "Now, I must go. Wish me luck."

"Tell me about it tomorrow. I want to hear about every

stick of furniture, every floor, every ceiling," Tia said, following her friend down the stairs.

"I will," Houston called as she ran up the drive leading to the Taggert house. She hated arriving without a carriage, on foot, like a runaway or a beggar, but she couldn't risk being denied this opportunity.

The circular drive led to the front of the house, tall white wings radiating out like arms on each side of her. Around the roof was a railing and she wondered if there were terraces above.

The front door was white, with two long glass panels in it, and as she peered inside and smoothed her dress, she tried to calm her pounding heart and knocked. Within minutes, she heard heavy footsteps echoing through the house.

Kane Taggert, still wearing his coarse clothing, grinned as he opened the door for her.

"I hope I'm not early," Houston said, keeping her eyes on his face and forcing herself not to gawk at her surroundings.

"Just in time. Supper's ready." He stepped back and Houston had her first look at the interior of the house.

Directly in front of her, sweeping from both sides, was a magnificent double staircase, a black iron, brass-railed bannister gracefully curving along it. Supporting it, white columns topped with intricately carved headers rose to the high, panelled ceiling. It was a study in white and gold, with the soft electric lights drenching everything in their golden haze.

"You like it?" Kane asked and was obviously laughing at her expression.

Houston recovered herself enough to close her gaping mouth. "It's the most beautiful thing I've ever seen," she managed to whisper.

Kane puffed up his big chest in pride. "You wanta look around some or eat?"

"Look," she said, even as her eyes tried to devour every corner of the hall and stairwell.

"Come on, then," Kane said, setting off quickly.

"This little room is my office," he said, throwing open the door to a room as large as the downstairs of the Chandler house. It was beautifully panelled in walnut, a marble fireplace along one wall. But in the center of the room was a cheap oak desk, two old kitchen chairs beside it.

Papers littered the top of the desk, fell onto the parqueted floor.

"And this is the library."

He didn't give her time to look longer but led her to a vast, empty room, with golden colored panelled walls inset with empty bookcases. Three large bare areas of plastered wall interrupted the panelling.

"Some rugs go there but I ain't hung 'em up yet," he said as he left the room.

"And this is what's called the large drawing room."

Houston only had time to look into a large white room, completely empty of furniture, before he showed her a small drawing room, a dining room painted the palest green, then led the way down a hallway to the service area.

"This is the kitchen," he said unnecessarily. "Have a seat." He nodded toward a big oak table and chairs that must have come from the same place as the desk in his office.

As she took a seat, she saw that there was grease on the table edge. "Your table and desk seem to match," she said cautiously.

"Yeah, I ordered 'em all from Sears, Roebuck," he said as he filled bowls from a huge pot on the cast-iron stove. "I got some more stuff upstairs. Real pretty, too. One of the chairs is red velvet with yellow tassels on it."

"It sounds like an interesting piece."

He put before her a bowl of stew with enormous pieces of meat swimming in grease, and sat down. "Eat it before it gets cold."

Houston picked up her big spoon and toyed with the stew. "Mr. Taggert, who designed your house?"

"A man back East, why? You like it, don't you?"

"Very much. I was just curious, though."

"'Bout what?" he asked, mouth full of stew.

"Why it's so bare. Why is there no furniture in the rooms? We, the people of Chandler that is, saw crates delivered after the house was finished. We all assumed they contained furniture."

He was watching her as she moved the meat around in her bowl. "I bought lots of furniture, and rugs, and statues. Actually, I paid a couple of men to buy it for me and it's all in the attics now."

"Stored? But why? Your house is so lovely, yet you live here, I believe, alone, with only one employee, and not even a chair to sit on. Except what you bought from Sears, Roebuck, of course."

"Well, little lady, that's why I invited you here. You gonna eat that?" He took her bowl away and began to eat the stew himself.

Houston had her elbows on the table, leaning forward in fascination. "Why did you invite me, Mr. Taggert?"

"I guess you know that I'm rich, real rich, and I'm good at makin' money—after the first five million the rest is easy—but the truth is, I don't know how to spend money."

"Don't know how . . . ?" Houston murmured.

"Oh, I can make an order from Sears all right but when it comes to spendin' millions, I have to hire other people. The way I got this house was I asked some man's wife who I should get to build me a house. She gave me a man's name, I called him to my office and told him I wanted somethin' that'd be beautiful and he built me this place. He hired those two men I told you about to buy furniture for it. I ain't even seen what they bought."

"Why didn't you have the men arrange the furniture?"

"Because my wife might not like what they did and she'd want it rearranged, and I didn't see no reason to do it twice."

Houston leaned back in her chair. "I didn't know you were married."

"I ain't, yet. But I got her all picked out."

"Congratulations."

Kane smiled at her through his beard. "I can't have just any woman in this house. She has to be a real, true, deep-down lady. Somebody once told me that a *real* lady was a leader, that she'd fight for causes and stand up for the underdog and still keep her hat on straight. And a real lady could freeze a man with a look. That's what you done today, Houston."

"I beg your pardon."

He pushed the second empty bowl out of the way and leaned toward her. "When I first come back to this town, all them women made fools of themselves over me, and when I ignored 'em they started actin' like the bitches they was. The men all stood back and laughed, or some of 'em got mad, but they never said nothin' to me. And not one of 'em was ever just plain nice to me. Except you."

"Surely, Mr. Taggert, other women——."

"None of 'em defended me like you done today, and the way you looked at me when I touched you! Near froze me to death."

"Mr. Taggert, I believe I should go." She didn't like the turn this conversation was taking. She was alone with this huge, half-civilized man; no one even knew where she was.

"You can't leave yet. I got somethin' to say."

"Perhaps you could send me a letter. I really must go."

"Come outside with me. I got lots of plants outside," he said in a little-boy pleading way.

She hoped she wouldn't regret this, but then maybe his "lots of plants" was a garden.

It was a garden: acres of fragrant, flowering shrubs and perennials, roses and trees.

"It's as beautiful as the house," she said, wishing she could explore the pathways she saw outlined in the moonlight. "What else did you have to say to me, Mr. Taggert? I really must leave soon."

"You know, I used to see you when you was a little girl. You used to play with Marc Fenton. Course you never noticed me. I was just the stable boy," he said tightly, then relaxed. "I always wondered what you'd turn out like, what with bein' a Chandler and playin' with the Fentons, but you turned out real good."

"Thank you." She was puzzled by this talk and wondered where it was leading.

"What I got to say is that I'm thirty-four years old, I got more money 'n I know what to do with, I got a big empty house and an attic full of furniture that needs movin' downstairs, and I wish somebody'd hire me a cook so me and Edan don't have to eat our own food. What I need, Miss Houston Chandler, is a wife and I decided I want you." He said the last triumphantly.

It took Houston a moment before she could speak. "Me?" she whispered.

"Yes, you. I think it's fittin' that a Chandler should live in this, the biggest house Chandler, Colorado, will ever see and, too, I had somebody do a search on you. You been to some real fine schools and you know how to buy things. And you know how to give parties, like the ones Jay Gould's wife used to give. I'll even buy you some real gold plates if you want 'em."

Houston was recovering herself, and the first thing she did was turn on her heel and start walking.

"Wait a minute," he said, walking beside her. "What about a date for the weddin'?"

She stopped and glared at him. "Mr. Taggert, let me make myself perfectly clear. First of all, I am already engaged to be married. Second, even if I weren't engaged, I know nothing about you. No, I will *not* marry you, even if you ask me properly instead of making a lordly decree." She turned away again.

"Is that what you want? Courtin'? I'll send you roses every day until the weddin'."

She stopped again, took a deep breath, and faced him. "I do *not* want you to court me. In fact, I'm not sure I ever want to see you again. I came to see your house and I thank you for showing me. Now, Mr. Taggert, I want to go home, and if you want a wife perhaps you should look at one of the many unattached women in this town. I'm sure you can find another so-called true, deep-down lady." With that, Houston turned, and if she didn't quite run toward the front of the house, she certainly didn't collect any dust.

"Damn!" Kane said when she was gone, and he made his way upstairs.

Edan stood in the upstairs hallway. "Well?"

"She told me no," Kane said in disgust. "She wants that penniless Westfield. And don't you say nothin' about I-told-you-so. I ain't done yet. Before I'm through, I'm gonna have 'Lady' Chandler as my wife. I'm hungry. Let's go find somethin' to eat."

Chapter 4

Houston crept quietly into the Chandler house, making sure the stairs didn't creak as she tiptoed up them. Mr. Gates trusted Leander completely and Houston was quite unsupervised when she went out with him.

As she slipped into her room, she smiled at her mother, whose frowning face was peeping through her bedroom door. Once inside, the door closed, Houston smiled as she realized that her mother was probably frowning because Houston was supposed to be Blair yet she'd just entered Houston's room. No doubt her mother'd guessed their game and not liked it.

With a shrug, Houston dismissed her mother's disapproval. Opal Gates loved her daughters, indulged them, and wouldn't question what they'd done, or betray them to Mr. Gates.

As Houston began to undress, she thought of her evening. That beautiful house, so empty, so uncared for. And the owner had offered it to her! Of course, he was part of the package, but then every worthwhile gift had some strings attached.

Sitting down at her dressing table, wearing her corset and drawers, she absently applied cold cream to her face. No man had ever treated her as Kane Taggert had tonight. All her life she'd lived in this little town, and everyone knew she was the last of the founding family. She'd grown up being aware that she was some sort of possession to be acquired, as in "no party is complete without one of the Chandlers." When the prominent, rich Westfields came here from the East when Houston was a child, it seemed to be taken for granted that a Chandler and a Westfield would marry.

And Houston always did as she was told. Blair stood up to people but Houston never did. Over the years Houston had learned to do exactly what was expected of her. Everyone around her thought she should marry Leander Westfield so she set out to do so. Since she was a Chandler, she was expected to be a lady, so she was one.

Dressing like a fat old woman and going into the coal camps was the only unladylike thing she'd ever done, and that was in secret.

Looking into the mirror, she saw fear enter her face as she thought of what Leander would have to say if he found out about Sadie. Leander liked things his own way. He knew exactly what he wanted in a wife: one without surprises.

Standing, she began to unfasten her corset. Tonight had been an adventure, a one-time happening before she gave up all adventures and became Mrs. Leander Westfield.

Taking a few deep breaths once her corset was off, she allowed an irreverent thought to flash through her mind: what would a man like Kane Taggert do if he found out his wife was the driver of a huckster wagon every Wednesday?

"Well, honey," Houston said aloud, deepening her voice, "just make sure you keep your hat on straight. Real ladies do, you know."

Trying to cover her laughter, Houston fell back onto her bed. Wouldn't all of Chandler be surprised, she thought, if she decided to accept Mr. Taggert's offer?

She sat upright. What in the *world* would he wear to the wedding? Perhaps a red suit with gold tassels on it?

Still laughing to herself, she finished undressing and put on her nightgown. It had been quite nice to receive another marriage proposal, to find out that at least not everyone took it for granted that she was Leander's personal property. Everyone, including Houston, knew what her future was going to be. She and Lee had been together so long that she knew what he ate for breakfast, how he liked his shirts done.

The only unknown question was the wedding night. Well, perhaps after that one night Leander wouldn't expect her to do it again for a long time. It wasn't that she didn't like men, especially after what happened the night before her friend Ellie got married, but sometimes touching Leander seemed, well . . . incestuous. She loved Leander, knew she'd have no difficulty living with him, but the thought of lying with him . . .

She climbed into bed, pulled a quilt over her and prepared for sleep. I wonder how Blair did with Leander, she thought briefly. No doubt he'll be in a bad mood tomorrow because, of course, he and Blair must have had a quarrel. They couldn't possibly spend hours together and not be at each other's throats.

With a sigh, she drifted into sleep. Today had been an adventure; tomorrow she would be back to her humdrum everyday existence.

Houston had to ward off Leander's advances as he helped her into his carriage, and again she thought how oddly everyone was behaving. All morning Blair had been evading her, and she looked as if she'd been crying. Houston hoped Blair and Lee hadn't had a serious argument last night, and that Lee hadn't found out they'd traded places. Houston had tried to talk to Blair about last night, but Blair had just looked at her as if her life were over and run from the room.

At eleven, Lee had arrived to take her on a picnic, a pleasant surprise, and Houston had heard Blair shouting at him on the front porch. To further confuse her, Lee had been quite forward with her physically in the middle of the street and Houston had thought she was going to have to slap his wayward hands.

Now, feeling as if she'd walked into the middle of a play and understood nothing about what was going on, she sat beside Lee in the buggy. He just drove, saying nothing, but he was smiling. Houston began to relax. Nothing too bad could have happened last night if he was smiling.

He drove her to a place of big rocks and tall trees that she'd never seen before, miles out of town, secluded and enclosed.

He had barely helped her out of the carriage, in such a hurry that she nearly fell, when he grabbed her in a smothering embrace. She was fighting so hard to breathe that at first she didn't hear him.

"I thought about nothing else but you last night," he said.

"I could smell your hair on my clothes, I could taste your lips on mine, I could—."

Houston managed to pull away from him. "You what?" she gasped.

He began disarranging her hair and looking at her strangely. "You aren't going to be shy with me today, are you? You aren't going to be the way you were before last night, are you?"

While he was talking, Houston was thinking, but she didn't believe what she thought could be the only answer to his bizarre words. Blair couldn't have . . . Couldn't have made herself available to Lee? Could she? Impossible.

"Houston, you've proven to me that you can be different, so there's no need to go back to being the ice princess. I know what you're really like now, and I can tell you that if I never see that cool woman again, I'll be even happier. Now come here and kiss me like you did last night."

Houston suddenly realized what else he was saying besides telling her how wonderful Blair was. He'd not only enjoyed Blair last night, but he never wanted the cool woman he was engaged to to return. She pushed free of him. "Are you saying that I wasn't like I usually am last night? That I was . . . better?"

He smiled in an idiotic way and continued raving about how wonderful Blair was.

"You know you were. You were like I've never seen you. I didn't know you could be like that. You'll laugh at this but I was beginning to believe that you were incapable of any real passion, that beneath your cool exterior was a heart of ice. But, if you can have a sister like Blair who starts fires at the least provocation, surely some of it had to rub off."

He grabbed her again before she could say a word and gave her an unpleasant, lip-grinding kiss, and when Houston managed to escape, she saw that he was angry.

"You're carrying this game too far," he said. "You can't be wildly passionate one minute and frigid the next. What are you, two people?"

Houston wanted to scream at him that he was lusting after the wrong sister, that he was engaged to the cold, frigid one and not the fiery one he seemed to prefer.

It was as if Lee read her thoughts, because his face changed.

"That's an impossibility, isn't it, Houston?" he said. "Tell me that what I'm thinking is wrong. No one can be two people, can she?"

Houston knew that what had been a simple game was becoming serious now. How could Blair have done this to her?

Lee walked away and sat down heavily on a rock. "Did you and your sister trade places last night?" he asked softly. "Did I spend the evening with Blair and not with you?"

Somehow, she managed to whisper, "Yes."

"I should have known from the first: how well she handled that suicide and she didn't even know it was the house I'd bought for her—you. I don't think I wanted to see. From the moment she said she wanted to go on the case with me to see if she could be of any help, I was so stupidly pleased that I never questioned anything after that. I should have known when I kissed her . . .

"Damn both of you! I hope to hell you enjoyed making a fool of me."

"Lee," Houston said, her hand on his arm. She didn't know what she could say to him, but she wanted to try.

The face he turned to her was frightening. "If you know what's good for you, you won't say a word. I don't know what possessed either of you to play such a dirty little trick, but I can tell you that I don't like being the butt of such a joke. Now that you and your sister have had a good laugh at my expense, I have to decide what to do about last night."

Leander took her home and nearly shoved her from the carriage before driving away.

Blair was standing on the porch.

"We need to talk," Houston said to her sister, but Blair only nodded, following her sister mutely into the little rose garden, away from the house.

"How could you do this to me?" Houston began. "What kind of morals do you have that you can go out with a man once and sleep with him? Or am I assuming too much? You did sleep with him?"

Mutely, Blair nodded.

"After one evening?" Houston was incredulous.

"But I was *you!*" Blair said. "I was engaged to him. I assumed you always . . . After he kissed me like that, I thought for sure that the two of you . . ."

"We what?" Houston gasped. "You mean you thought we repeatedly . . . made love? Do you think I would have asked you to trade places if that had been true?"

Blair hid her face in her hands. "I didn't think. I couldn't think. After the reception, he took me to his house, and—."

"*Our* house," Houston said. "The one I've spent months decorating, preparing for *my* marriage."

"There were candles and caviar and roast duck and champagne, lots of champagne. He kissed me and I kept drinking champagne and there were the candles and his eyes and I couldn't stop myself. Oh, Houston, I'm sorry. I'll leave Chandler. You'll never have to see me again. Leander will forgive us after a while."

"No doubt he kissed you and you saw red," she said in a voice heavy with sarcasm.

"With little gold and silver sparks." Blair was quite serious.

Houston was gaping at her sister. What in the world was she talking about? Champagne and candles? Had Lee tried to seduce his fiancée? Had he planned something that had backfired so that he'd spent the night with the wrong sister? Or *was* Blair the wrong sister?

"What was his kiss like?" Houston asked softly.

Blair looked shocked. "Don't torture me. I'll try to make it up to you, Houston, I swear I will, no matter what I have to do. I'll—."

"What was his kiss like?" she asked louder.

Blair sniffed and her sister handed her a handkerchief. "You know what they're like. I don't need to describe them."

"I don't think I *do* know."

Blair hiccupped. "It was . . . It was wonderful. I never thought a man as cool as Lee could have so much fire. When he touched me . . ." She looked up at her sister. "Houston, I'll go to Lee and explain that it was all my fault, that it was my idea to trade places and that you were entirely innocent. I don't see why anyone but the three of us should ever know what happened. We'll sit down together and talk and he'll understand what happened."

Houston leaned forward. "Will he? How will you explain that I wanted to spend the evening with another man? Will you tell Lee that his mere touch enflamed you so that you couldn't control yourself? That will certainly be a contrast to the frigid Miss Houston Chandler."

"You're not frigid!"

Houston was silent for a moment. "All Lee could talk about was how magnificent you were last night. He's not going to like someone inexperienced after you . . ."

Blair's head came up. "I'd never made love to anyone before. Lee was the first."

Houston wasn't sure whether to laugh or be overcome with admiration. She was scared to death of her wedding night, and she was sure there wasn't enough champagne in the world to make her react as Blair had done. Lee's kisses had never made her forget anything.

"Houston, do you hate me?" Blair asked softly.

She considered this. It was odd, but she wasn't even jealous. Her main thought was that now Lee was going to want the same thing from her, and how could she live up to what Blair had done? Maybe Blair had learned how in medical school but at Miss Jones's School for Young Ladies in Virginia, they taught that a woman's place was in the parlor, and no mention was made of what went on in the bedroom.

"You're looking at me strangely."

It was on the tip of Houston's tongue to ask Blair for details of last night but she couldn't. "I'm not angry. I just need time to adjust," she said. "You're not in love with Lee, are you?"

Blair looked up in horror. "No! Never! That's the last thing I am. Did . . . did he say much about me today?"

Houston ground her teeth together, remembering how he had said Houston was usually so frigid, but last night . . . "Let's forget this if we can. I'll talk to Lee when he's over his anger and we'll keep it between the three of us. This may make things awkward for a while, but I'm sure we can work out a satisfactory solution. Let's not allow something like this to come between us. Our sisterhood is more important than this."

"Thank you," Blair said, impulsively hugging her sister. "No one ever had a sister like you. I love you."

Blair seemed to feel better, but Houston had some nagging

doubts which she told herself were absurd. She loved Lee, had always loved him, had planned to marry him since she was a child. This one little thing, this one night with the wrong sister wouldn't change anything, would it?

"Of course not," she said aloud, smoothed her skirt and went toward the house. One night wasn't going to erase years together.

Chapter 5

At four o'clock, Houston, Blair and their mother were sitting in the parlor, Blair reading her medical journal, the other two women sewing, when the front door was opened, followed by a jamb-jarring slam.

"Where is she?" Duncan Gates bellowed, making the chandelier above their heads rattle. "Where is that immoral harlot? Where is the Jezebel?"

Mr. Gates burst into the room, his stout body puffed with fury. He grabbed Blair's arm, pulled her out of her chair, dragging her toward the door.

"Mr. Gates!" Opal said, on her feet at once. "What is the meaning of this?"

"This . . . this daughter of Satan has spent the night with Leander and, in spite of the fact that she's unclean, he plans to make an honest woman of her."

"What?!" the three women gasped.

"Leander is going to marry the harlot, I said." With that he half-dragged a protesting Blair out of the house.

Houston sat down heavily, not able to comprehend what was happening around her.

"Houston," her mother said. "You and Blair traded places last night, didn't you?"

Houston only nodded silently and picked up her sewing as if nothing had happened.

The sun set, the room darkened, and the maid switched on the electric lights, but still mother and daughter didn't speak.

Only one thought went through Houston's mind: It's over. Everything is over.

At midnight, the front door opened and Duncan pushed Blair into the parlor ahead of him.

"It's settled," he said in a voice hoarse with overuse. "Blair and Leander will be married in two weeks. It will be announced in church on Sunday."

Quietly, Houston stood.

"Daughter," Duncan said with feeling, "I'm sorry about this."

Houston merely nodded as she started toward the stairs.

"Houston," Blair said from the foot of the staircase. "Please," she whispered.

But at the moment, Houston had no compassion to give her sister and, even when she heard Blair at last break into weeping, she didn't look back.

In her room, she still seemed to be numb. Her whole life over, turned around in one single night. Everything lost.

On the wall hung a framed diploma from Miss Jones's School for Young Ladies. With violence, she tore the diploma from the wall and flung it across the room, feeling no relief when the glass shattered.

With steady fingers, she began to unbutton her dress. Moments later she was standing in her nightgown, just standing, not moving, not aware of when her mother entered the room.

"Houston?" Opal said, her hand on her daughter's shoulder.

"Go to her," Houston said. "Blair needs you. If she stays here and marries Leander, she's going to give up a great deal."

"But you have, too. You've lost a lot tonight."

"I lost it long before tonight. Really, go to her. I'll be all right."

Opal picked up the broken diploma. "Let me see you in bed."

Obediently, Houston climbed into bed. "Always obedient, aren't I, Mother? I always obey. If not my parents, then Leander. I've always been such a good little girl and what has it gotten me? I'm a true, deep-down lady and my sister with her knickers and her kisses is getting everything I've worked for since the first grade."

"Houston," Opal pleaded.

"Leave me alone!" Houston screamed. "Just leave me alone."

With a shocked look on her face, Opal left the room.

Sunday morning dawned bright and beautiful, the sun highlighting Ayers Peak that graced the western side of Chandler. There were many churches in town, covering every denomination, and nearly all were full of people.

But even the sun couldn't melt the coldness inside the Chandler twins, who walked on opposite sides of their stepfather. Their mother had suddenly been attacked with a mysterious ailment that kept her from witnessing her daughters' public humiliation.

Leander waited in the pew for them, his eyes looking toward Houston, and when they neared the bench, he put his hand out to her. "Houston," he whispered.

Now he can tell us apart, she thought, but said nothing as she moved aside to keep from touching him.

Duncan nearly pushed Blair toward Lee and at last they were seated, Blair beside Lee, then Duncan and Houston on the end.

The service seemed to pass in seconds because Houston knew that at the end of it *the* announcement was going to be made.

It came much too soon.

Unfortunately, Reverend Thomas wasn't conducting the service today but was replaced by Reverend Smithson who could have been more tactful.

"Now I have an announcement to make," he said with an amused tone. "It seems that our own Leander has changed his mind about which twin to marry and is now engaged to Blair. I don't believe I could make up my mind between them, either. Congratulations again, Lee."

For a moment the church was thunderstruck. Then, men began to chuckle, and women gasped in astonishment. Everyone rose to leave.

"Houston, you must listen to me," Lee said, catching her arm. "I must explain."

"You have explained," she hissed at him. "When you told me how wonderful Blair was, and how you hoped the ice princess would never return, *that's* when you did your explaining. Good morning," she smiled at a passerby.

"Hello, Houston, or are you Blair?" someone asked.

"Congratulations, Lee." A man slapped him on the shoulder and went away laughing.

"Houston, let's go somewhere."

"You can go to . . . your bride." She glared at him in anger.

"Houston," Lee pleaded. "Please."

"If you don't take your hand off me I'll scream, for surely I can suffer no more embarrassment than you have caused me already."

"Leander!" Duncan said. "Blair is waiting for you."

Lee reluctantly turned away from Houston, clutched Blair's arm, shoved her into his buggy and drove away much too fast.

The minute Houston was alone, women descended on her, edging her away from Duncan's protection. The many faces were concerned, curious, some sympathetic. Mostly, the women seemed to be puzzled.

"Houston, what happened? I thought you and Lee were so happy."

"How could Leander want Blair? They argue constantly."

"When was the decision made?"

"Houston, is there someone else?"

"You're damned right there is, ladies," came a booming voice from behind them, and they all turned to look up at Kane Taggert. No one in town had ever heard him say much and he had certainly never seemed to be aware of what any of the townspeople were doing.

The women gaped openly at this big man in his rough clothes, with his unkempt beard, as he made his way through them. No one was more surprised than Houston.

"I'm sorry I didn't make the service today or I could a sat with you," he said as he reached her. "Don't look so surprised, sweetheart. I know I promised to keep our secret a little longer, but I couldn't keep quiet after ol' Lee told ever'body."

"Secret?" one of the women prompted.

Kane put his arm around Houston. They were an incongruous pair, him hairy, rumpled, her perfect. "Houston broke her engagement to Leander because she fell right smack in love with me. Ladies, she just couldn't help herself."

"When did this happen?" one of the women recovered herself enough to ask.

Houston was beginning to breathe again. "It started when Mr. Taggert and I had dinner together at his house," she whispered, knowing she was going to regret every word later, but now it was nice not to have to admit she'd been jilted.

"But what about Leander?"

"Leander consoled himself with the love of Houston's dear sister, Blair," Kane said sweetly. "And now, ladies, we got to be goin'. I hope all of you will come to the weddin'—a double weddin'—in two weeks." He put his hand on the small of Houston's back, and pushed her toward his old wagon.

As he drove away, Houston sat rigidly on the edge of her seat.

He halted the wagon at the edge of his own property. Before them spread his acres of garden and in the background was his house. He put up his arms to help her down. "You and me gotta talk."

Houston was too numb to do anything but obey.

"I woulda come to church to sit with you, but I had some work to do. It looks like I got there just in time. Another minute and them ol' biddies would of eaten you alive."

"I beg your pardon." Houston was only vaguely listening. Until this morning she'd hoped it was all a bad dream, that she'd wake up and Leander and she would still be engaged.

"Are you listenin' to me at all? What's wrong with you?"

"Other than public humiliation, Mr. Taggert, nothing is wrong with me." She stopped. "I apologize. I didn't mean to burden you with my problems."

"You ain't heard a word I've said, have you? Didn't you hear me tell 'em you and me was gonna get married? I invited 'em all to a double weddin'."

"And I thank you for it," Houston said, managing a smile. "It was very kind of you to come to my rescue. You would make a splendid knight. Now, I think I should leave."

"You're the damnedest woman I ever met! If you don't marry me, what else you gonna do? You think any of the so-called society men are gonna have you? They're afraid of the whole Westfield clan. You think Marc Fenton wants you?"

"Marc Fenton?" she asked, puzzled. "Why should Marc, as you put it, 'want me'?"

"I was just wonderin', that's all." He stepped closer to her. "How come you don't wanta marry me? I'm rich and I gotta big house and you just got jilted and you ain't got nothin' else to do."

She looked up at him, his size making her a little uneasy, but she wasn't really afraid of him. Suddenly, all thought of Leander and Blair was gone. "Because I don't love you," she said firmly. "And I know nothing about you. For all I know, you could have been married ten times before and have locked all your wives away in the cellar. You look like you're capable of such a trick," she said as she looked down her nose at his hairy face and heavy shirt that was torn at the shoulder.

For a full minute, Kane stared at her in open-mouthed astonishment. "Is that what you think of me? Listen, lady." He took a step closer to her. "I ain't had *time* to marry anybody. Since I was eighteen and Fenton tossed me out on my ass, I've done nothin' but make money. There was three years when I didn't even sleep. And here you're tellin' me I might of had time to marry ten women."

By the time he finished, Houston was leaning backward, Kane bending over her.

"I think perhaps I was in error," she said with a gentle smile.

Kane didn't move. "You know, you're the prettiest woman I ever seen in my life."

With that, he slipped one arm around her back, pulled her to him, as he buried his right hand in her carefully pinned coiffure, and kissed her.

Houston had kissed Leander hundreds of times. He was familiar to her, nothing unexpected—but Kane's kiss was unlike anything she'd ever experienced before. His mouth was demanding on hers, not the refined kiss of a gentleman with a lady, but more like how she'd imagine a stableman would kiss.

He released her so abruptly she nearly fell, and for a moment they looked at each other. "Lady, if you can kiss me like that when you love that Westfield, I'll manage to do without your love."

Houston could say nothing.

He took her elbow. "I'm gonna take you back now, and you can start plannin' for our weddin'. Buy yourself whatever you need. I'll put some money in the bank for you. I want lots of flowers at the weddin' so get some sent here. Have 'em sent from California if you want or come look at what I got in my glasshouse. And we'll be married in my house. There's chairs in the attic. I want ever'body in town to come."

"Wait! Please," she said, repinning her hair as he propelled her along. "I haven't agreed yet. Please, Mr. Taggert, give me some time. I haven't yet recovered from losing my fiancé." She put her hand on his arm, could feel the muscles of his forearm under his heavy shirt.

He lifted her hand and for a moment she thought he was going to kiss it.

"I'll buy you a ring. What do you like? Diamonds? Emeralds? What are those blue ones?"

"Sapphires," she said absently. "Please don't buy me a ring. Marriage is a lifetime commitment. I can't rush into this too quickly."

"You take your time. You got two whole weeks before the weddin' to get used to the idea of bein' my wife."

"Mr. Taggert," she said with exasperation, "do you *ever* listen to what other people say?"

He grinned at her from beneath his beard. "No, never. That's the way I got rich. If I saw somethin' I wanted, I went after it."

"And I'm next on your list of things you want?" she asked softly.

"At the very top. Right up there with an apartment buildin' in New York that Vanderbilt owns and I want. Now, I'll take you home so you can tell your family about me and you can put me in Westfield's place. He's gonna be sorry! He got a Chandler all right but I'm gettin' the lady one." He flipped the reins to the horses so suddenly

Houston fell back into her seat before she could say a word.

At the door to her house, he jumped from the wagon and nearly pulled her to the ground. "I got to get back now. You tell your parents about me, will ya? And I'll send a ring over to you tomorrow. Anything you need, you let me or Edan know. I'll try to see you tomorrow." He gave a quick look over her shoulder toward her house, then said again, "I got to go," and bolted into the wagon.

Houston stood before the little stone fence in front of her house and watched him speed away, dust almost obscuring the buggy from view. She felt as if she'd just weathered a tornado.

Inside the house, both Duncan and Opal were waiting for her, Opal in a chair, her eyes red from crying, while Duncan, arms folded, was pacing the floor.

Houston braced herself before entering the room. "Good afternoon, Mother, Mr. Gates."

"Where have you been?" Duncan seethed.

"Oh, Houston," Opal cried, "you don't have to marry him. You'll find someone else. Just because Leander made a mistake doesn't mean you should, too."

Before Houston could speak, Duncan started on her. "Houston, you've always been the sensible one. Blair never did have any sense. Even as a little girl she'd rush off head first into trouble, but you always had as much sense as a woman is capable of. You were going to marry Leander and—."

"Leander is no longer going to marry me," Houston pointed out.

"But not Kane Taggert!" Opal wailed and buried her face in her damp handkerchief.

Houston began to feel protective of Kane. "What in the world has the man done to deserve so much hostility? I have not agreed to marry him, but I don't see why I shouldn't."

Jumping up from her seat, Opal ran to her daughter. "He's a monster. Look at him. You can't live with that great smelly bear of a man. Every friend you ever had would desert you. And there are terrible stories about him."

"Opal!" Duncan commanded and, meekly, she went back

to her seat to continue sobbing. "Houston, I'm going to address you as I would a man. I couldn't care less if the man'd never had a bath in his life. That doesn't bother me. He can certainly afford a bathtub. But there are things . . ." He gave her a hard look. "There are stories, among the men, that Taggert has had a couple of men killed in order to make his fortune."

"Killed?" Houston whispered. "Where did you hear that?"

"It doesn't matter where—."

"It *does* matter!" she snapped. "Don't you see? The women of this town were angry because he ignored them, so they made up stories about him. Why would the men be any different? Leander told me of several men in town who tried to sell Mr. Taggert things such as worn-out gold mines. Perhaps one of them began the rumors."

"What I heard comes from a very reliable source," Duncan said darkly.

Houston was quiet for a moment. "Jacob Fenton," she said softly and saw by the expression on Duncan's square face that she was right. "From the gossip I've heard," Houston continued, "Mr. Taggert dared to make advances to Jacob Fenton's precious daughter Pamela. When I was a girl, I remember people whispering about the disgraceful way Mr. Fenton spoiled her. Of course he'd hate a man who'd once been his stable boy and who had the audacity to want to marry his spoiled daughter."

"Are you saying Fenton's a liar?" Duncan accused. "Are you choosing this newcomer over a family you've known all your life?"

"If I do marry Kane Taggert—and I mean *if*—yes, I will believe in him over the Fentons. Now, if you'll excuse me, I suddenly feel very tired and I think I'll lie down."

She swept out of the room with more grace than she actually felt and, once in her room, she collapsed onto the bed.

Marry Kane Taggert? she thought. Marry a man who talked and acted worse than any River Street ruffian? Marry a man who treated her without respect, one who hauled her in and out of carriages as if she were a sack of potatoes? Marry a man who kissed her as if she were a scullery maid?

She sat upright. "Marry a man who, as Blair says, when he kisses me makes me see red with little sparks of gold and silver?" she said aloud.

"I just might," she whispered, leaned back against the bed, and for the first time began to consider becoming Mrs. Kane Taggert.

Chapter 6

By morning Houston had convinced herself that she couldn't possibly, under any circumstances, marry Mr. Taggert. Her mother'd sniffed throughout breakfast and cried repeatedly, "My beautiful daughters, what will become of them?" while Blair and Duncan'd argued about how Blair'd ruined Houston's life. Houston wasn't sure it was an argument, since they seemed to be agreeing with one another.

Houston entered the discussion when it was said that Kane Taggert was her means of punishing herself for losing Leander. But no one seemed to hear what Houston said, and nothing made any difference to Blair's misery, so Houston stopped listening to them. But being the cause of so much weeping made her decide she couldn't marry Mr. Taggert.

Immediately after breakfast, people began "dropping by."

"I was just starting to bake an apple pie and knew how much you liked them, Opal, so I baked two and brought you one. How are the twins?"

By midmorning, the house was full of food and people. Mr. Gates stayed in his brewery office, having one of the maids bring him his lunch, so Houston, Blair and Opal had to fend off the questions by themselves.

"Did you really fall in love with Mr. Taggert, Houston?"

"Have another piece of pie, Mrs. Treesdale," Houston answered.

At eleven, Blair managed to slip away, leaving Opal and Houston alone to cope, and Blair didn't return until three o'clock. "Are they *still* here?" she gasped, looking at the crowd on the lawn.

At three thirty, a man pulled up in front of the Chandler house driving a beautiful carriage such as no one in Chandler had ever seen. It was painted white, with white wheels, a cream-colored collapsible hood on top with shiny brass detailing. There was a seat in front upholstered in red leather and a smaller seat in back for an attendant.

The group of people on the lawn, on the deep porch, and spilling into the garden, stopped their questions and gawked.

A man, crudely dressed, stepped down and walked straight into the midst of the people. "Who's Miss Houston Chandler?" he asked into the silence.

"I am," Houston said, stepping forward.

The man reached into his pocket, pulled out a slip of paper and began to read. "This here carriage is from the man you're gonna marry, Mr. Kane Taggert. It's a lady's drivin' carriage, a spider phaeton, and the horse is a good 'un."

He folded the paper, put it back into his pocket and turned away. "Oh yeah." He turned back. "Mr. Taggert sent you this, too." He tossed a small parcel wrapped in brown paper toward Houston and she caught it.

The man went down the path, whistling. Everyone watched him until he was out of sight around a corner.

"Well, Houston," Tia said, "aren't you going to open your gift?"

Houston wasn't sure she should open the package because she knew what she'd find inside, and if she accepted his ring, it would mean she accepted him.

Inside the box was the biggest diamond she'd ever seen, an enormous, breathtaking chunk of brilliance surrounded by nine square-cut emeralds.

The combined intake of breath from the women around her was enough to stir the tree leaves.

With resolution, Houston snapped the blue velvet box shut, and walked straight down the path toward the carriage. She didn't hesitate or answer any questions thrown at her but snapped the reins and the lovely brown horse moved briskly.

She drove straight up Sheldon street, across the Tijeras River that separated the north and south sections of town, and up the steep drive to the Taggert house. Since pounding on the front door brought no answer, she strode inside, took a left and stopped in the doorway of Kane's office.

He sat hunched over his desk, puffing away on a vile cigar, making notes and giving quick orders to Edan, who was leaning back in a chair, his feet on the desk, smoking an equally awful cigar.

Edan saw her first and the big blond man stood at once and punched Kane on the shoulder.

Kane looked up with a frown.

"You must be Edan," Houston said, going forward, her hand outstretched. She wasn't sure if he was a servant or a friend. "I'm Houston Chandler."

"Houston," he said. He was not a servant, not with that air of confidence.

"I'd like to talk to you," Houston said, turning to Kane.

"If it's about weddin' plans, I'm real busy right now. If you need money, tell Edan, he'll write you a check."

Waving smoke away from her face, she went to a window and opened it. "You shouldn't sit in this smoke. It isn't good for you."

Kane looked up at her with cold eyes. "Who are you to give me orders? Just because you're gonna be my wife, don't—."

"As far as I can recall, I haven't yet agreed to be your wife and if you can't find time to talk to me—in private—I don't think I *will* be your wife. Good day, Mr. Taggert, and Edan."

"Good day, Houston," Edan said with a slight smile.

"Women!" she heard Kane say behind her. "I told you a woman'd take a lot of my time."

He caught up with her at the front door. "Maybe I was a little hasty," he said. "It's just that when I'm workin' I don't like no interruptions. You got to understand that."

"I wouldn't bother you if it weren't important," she said coolly.

"All right," he said. "We'll go in here an' talk." He pointed to the echoing emptiness of the library. "I'd offer you a chair, but the only ones I got are in my bedroom. You wanta go up there?" He gave her a grinning leer.

"Definitely not. What I want to talk about, Mr. Taggert, is whether or not you are quite serious about your marriage proposal to me."

51

"You think I got the time to waste doin' all the courtin' I been doin' if I wasn't serious?"

"Courting?" she said. "Yes, I guess you could call Sunday morning courting. What I want to ask you, sir, is, well, have you ever killed or hired someone to kill for you?"

Kane's mouth dropped open and his eyes grew angry, but then he began to look amused. "No, I ain't never killed nobody. What else you wanta know about me?"

"Anything you care to tell me," she said seriously.

"Ain't much. I grew up in Jacob Fenton's stable"—a muscle twitched in his cheek—"I got tossed out for messin' with his daughter and I been makin' money since then. I ain't killed nobody, robbed nobody, cheated nobody, never beat up no woman and only knocked out an average number of men. Anythin' else?"

"Yes. When you proposed, you said you wanted me to furnish your house. What do I get to do with you?"

"With me?" With a grin, he looped his thumbs in the empty belt loops on his trousers. "I ain't gonna hold nothin' back from you if that's what you mean."

"I do *not* mean whatever you're implying, I'm sure," she said stiffly. "Mr. Taggert," she said, as she began walking around him. "I know men who work in coal mines who are better dressed than you are. And your language is atrocious, as well as your manners. My mother is scared to death of my marrying a barbarian like you. Since I cannot spend my life frightening my own mother, you will have to agree to some instruction from me."

"Instruction?" he said, narrowing his eyes at her. "What can you teach me?"

"How to dress properly. How to eat—."

"Eat? I eat plenty."

"Mr. Taggert, you keep mentioning names like Vanderbilt and Gould. Tell me, were you ever invited to the homes of any of those families when the women were present?"

"No, but—," he began, then looked away. "I was once, but there was an accident and some dishes got broke."

"I see. I wonder how you expect me to be your wife, to run a magnificent house like this, to give dinner parties like you want while you sit at the head of the table eating peas from a knife. I assume you do eat peas with a knife."

"I don't eat peas at all. A man needs meat, and he don't need a woman to tell him——."

"Good day, sir." She turned on her heel and took two steps before he grabbed her arm.

"You ain't gonna marry me if I don't let you teach me?"

"And dress you, and shave you."

"Anxious to see my face, are you?" he grinned, but stopped when he saw how serious Houston was. "How long I got to decide this?"

"About ten minutes."

He grimaced. "Who taught you how to do business? Let me think about this then." He walked toward a window, and stood there for several long minutes.

"I got some requests of you," he said when he came back to her. "I know you're marryin' me for my money." He put up his hand when she began to speak. "Ain't no use denyin' it. You wouldn't consider marryin' me with my knife-eatin' ways if I didn't have a big house to give you. A lady like you wouldn't even talk to a stableboy like me. What I want is for you to pretend, and to tell ever'body, that you . . ." He looked down at the parqueted floor. "I want people to think you did, uh, fall in love with me and that you ain't just marryin' me 'cause your sister jumped the gun and I just happened along. I want even your sister"—he said this with emphasis—"to think you're crazy for me, just like I said in front of the church. And I want your mother to think so, too. I don't want her to be afraid of me."

Houston had expected anything but this. So this was the big, fearsome man who stood aloof from the whole town. How awful it must be to not be able to do the smallest social thing. Of course women wouldn't put up with having him in their houses when there were "accidents" and china was broken. Right now, he didn't fit into any world, neither the poor one where his manners and speech placed him, nor the rich one where his money placed him.

He needs me, she thought. He needs me as no one ever has before. To Leander, I was something extra, nice but not necessary. But to this man, the things I've learned are vital.

"I will pretend to be the most loving of wives," she said softly.

"Then you *are* gonna marry me?"

"Why, yes, I believe I am," she said with a feeling of surprise.

"Hot damn! Edan!" he bellowed as he ran out of the room. "Lady Chandler's gonna marry me."

Houston sat down on a window ledge. *He* was going to marry "Lady" Chandler. Who in the world had *she* agreed to marry?

It was evening before Houston drove back to her own home. She was exhausted, and at the moment she wished she'd never heard of Kane Taggert. He seemed to think he would be able to stay at his house and work, and his fiancée could attend all the engagement parties alone, tell everyone she was in love with him, and all would be well.

"Unless they see us together, no one will believe we even know each other," she said to him across his littered desk. "You *have* to attend the garden party the day after tomorrow, and before then we have to make you a proper suit of clothes and shave you."

"I'm tryin' to buy some land in Virginia and a man's comin' tomorrow. I got to stay here."

"You can talk business during your fittings."

"You mean, have one of them little men put his little hands all over me? I ain't havin' that. You have somebody send over some suits and I'll pick one out."

"Red or purple?" she asked quickly.

"Red. I seen some red plaid ones once——."

Houston's half scream stopped him. "You *will* have a tailor make a suit for you and *I* will choose the fabric. And you *will* attend the garden party with me, and you will also attend several other functions with me within the next few weeks before our marriage."

"You sure real ladies are this bossy? I thought real ladies never raised their voices."

"They don't raise their voices to real gentlemen, but to men who want to wear red plaid suits they are allowed to use blunt instruments."

Kane had looked sulky at that, but he'd given in. "All right then, I'll have a suit made like you want, and I'll go to your dam . . . your lovely, dainty tea party," he changed it to, making her smile, "but I don't know about them other parties."

"We'll do one day at a time," she said, suddenly feeling exhausted. "I must return home. My parents will be worried."

"Come 'ere," he said, motioning her around his desk.

Thinking he wanted to show her something, she did as he bid. Roughly, he caught her wrist and pulled her into his lap. "You get to be my teacher, I guess I'm gonna have to teach you about some things, too."

He began nuzzling her neck with his face, his lips nibbling her skin. She was about to protest his treatment of her, but then parts of her body began to melt.

"Kane," Edan said from the doorway. "Excuse me."

Without ceremony, Kane pushed her off his lap. "You'll get more of that later, honey," he said, as if she were a street trollop. "Go on home now, I got to work."

Houston swallowed what she wanted to say and, with a face red from embarrassment, murmured a good night to both men and left the house.

Now, driving home at last, tired, hungry, still suffering from an emotion that was half anger, half embarrassment, she faced telling her family that she'd agreed to marry the notorious Mr. Kane Taggert.

Why, she asked herself as she slowed the horse to the barest walk. Why in the world was she agreeing to marry a man she didn't love, who didn't love her, a man who made her furious every other minute, a man who treated her like something he'd bought and paid for?

The answer came to her quickly.

Because he made her feel alive. Because he *needed* her.

Blair had said that when they were children, Houston had thrown snowballs with the best of them, but Duncan and Leander had taken away her spirit. Long ago she'd learned that it was easier to give in to the men, to be the quiet, ladylike, spiritless woman they wanted.

But there were times, at receptions, at dinner gatherings, when she felt as if she were a painting on a wall—pretty and nice to have around, but completely unnecessary to anyone's day-to-day well-being. She'd even said something like this to

Leander once and he'd talked about the quality of life changing without art objects.

But in the end, Lee had traded Houston's quiet, serene beauty for a woman who set his body on fire.

Never had a man made her feel as Kane Taggert did. Lee's taste in clothing and furniture was impeccable. Easily, he could have done the interiors of the house he'd had built for them by himself. But Mr. Taggert was at such a loss about what to do that, without her, he couldn't even arrange his furniture, much less buy it.

Houston thought of all the years of work she'd gone through at school. Blair seemed to think her sister had done little but drink tea and arrange flowers, but Houston remembered the strict discipline and Miss Jones's ruler slapping on tender palms when a girl failed.

When she was with Lee, she had to make a conscious effort to put all her schooling into effect because Lee would know when she was wrong. But with Mr. Taggert, she felt free. Today she'd screeched at him. In fourteen years of knowing Lee, never once had she raised her voice to him.

She took a breath of cool, night air. All the work ahead of her! Arranging the wedding, the surprise of exploring the attics and putting the furniture where *she* wanted it. And the challenge of trying to turn Mr. Taggert into some form of gentleman!

By the time she reached home, she was bursting with excitement. She was going to marry a man who *needed* her.

She left the horse and carriage with the groom, straightened her shoulders, and prepared herself to face the storm that was her family.

Chapter 7

Much to her surprise—and relief—the house was quiet when Houston entered through the kitchen, only the cook and Susan washing up.

"Has everyone gone to bed?" she asked, her hand on the big oak table that nearly filled the room.

"Yes, Miss Blair-Houston," Susan answered as she cleaned the coffee grinder. "More or less."

"Houston," she said automatically, ignoring the maid's last comment. "Will you bring me something on a tray and come to my room, Susan?"

As she walked through the house to the stairs, she noticed several large bouquets of freshly cut flowers, not flowers from her mother's garden. She saw a card attached:

To my wife to be, Blair, from Leander.

Leander had never sent her flowers in all the months they were engaged.

She held her head high and went upstairs.

Houston's bedroom was papered in a subtle cream and white design, the woodwork was painted white and the windows were hung with handmade Battenberg lace. The low tables and the backs of the two chairs were also adorned with the airy lace. The underside of her bed canopy was of gathered silk in a light tan and the bedspread was intricately quilted, all in white.

When Houston had undressed down to her underwear, Susan came with the tray. While eating, Houston began giving orders.

"I know it's late but I need you to send Willie on some errands. He's to take this note to Mr. Bagly, the tailor on Lead Avenue. I don't care if Willie has to drag the man out of bed, he is to make sure Mr. Bagly personally gets this. He must be at the Taggert house at eight o'clock tomorrow."

"At the Taggert house?" Susan asked, as she put away Houston's clothes. "Then it's true, Miss, you're going to marry him?"

Houston was sitting at her tiny mahogany desk and she turned around. "How'd you like to work for me? To live in the Taggert house?"

"I'm not sure, Miss. Is Mr. Taggert as bad as people say?"

Houston considered this. It was her experience that servants often knew much more about a man than his peers. Even though Kane lived alone, no doubt the servants knew things about him that no one else did. "What have you heard about him?"

"That he has a violent temper and he yells a fierce lot and nothing ever pleases him."

"I'm afraid that's all probably true," Houston sighed, turning around again, "but at least he doesn't beat women or cheat people."

"If you're not afraid to live with him, Miss Houston, then I'll do it. I don't guess this house'll be a fit place to live after you twins are gone."

"I don't imagine it will be either," Houston said absently, as she made a note to herself to call the barber, Mr. Applegate on Coal Avenue, and request that he arrive at nine o'clock. She thought how much time it'd save if everyone in town were on the telephone system.

"Susan, don't you have a couple of brothers?"

"Yes, Miss."

"I'll need six brawny men for all day tomorrow. They'll be moving furniture downstairs. They'll be paid well and fed well and they're to arrive at eight thirty. Do you think you can find six men?"

"Yes, Miss."

Houston wrote another note. "Willie must deliver this to

Mrs. Murchison. She's staying with Reverend Thomas while the Conrads are in Europe. I want her to come and cook at the Taggert house until they return. I hope she'll be glad to have something to do. Willie will have to wait for a reply because I've told her the kitchen is bare and she's to stock it with whatever she needs and to send Mr. Taggert the bill. Willie may have to meet her in the morning with a wagon. If so, I'm sure he can borrow the Oakleys' big wagon."

She leaned back in the chair. "There, that should take care of tomorrow. I have Mr. Taggert dressed and shaved, the furniture moved, and everyone fed."

Susan began to unpin Houston's hair and brush it.

"That feels lovely," she said, closing her eyes.

Minutes later she was in bed and, for the first night in days, she didn't feel like crying herself to sleep. In fact, she felt quite happy. She'd bargained with her sister so she could have one night of adventure, but it looked as if she were going to have weeks of adventure.

When Susan knocked on her door at six the next morning, Houston was already half dressed for work in a white cotton blouse, a black cord skirt that cleared the floor and a wide leather belt. A little jacket and matching hat completed the outfit.

Tiptoeing downstairs through the silent house, she placed a note on the dining table for her mother explaining where she'd be all day, then ate a hurried meal in the kitchen and went to the carriage house where she made a sleepy Willie harness the horse to the beautiful new buggy Kane had sent her.

"Did you give out all the messages, Willie?"

"All of them. Mrs. Murchison was right glad to get busy. I'm to meet her with a wagon at six thirty and meet Mr. Randolph at the grocery store. Mrs. Murchison called him late last night with a long list of things she wanted. And then we're goin' out to the Conrad place and raid their garden. She wanted to know how many she's to feed."

"There'll be about a dozen people but most of them are men so tell her to cook for thirty. That should do it. And tell her to bring pots and pans. I don't imagine Mr. Taggert has any. Come as soon as you can, Willie."

Everything was silent at the Taggert house as Houston unhitched her horse and tied it in the shade. She knocked at a side entrance but no one heard her so she tried the door, found it open and entered the kitchen. Feeling a bit like a thief, she began opening cabinets. If this house was to prepare a feast for a large number of wedding guests within two weeks, she needed to know what resources she had.

The cabinets were empty except for cases of canned peaches—no cookware except the cheapest enamelware.

"Sears again," she murmured as she decided to explore the rest of the service area. A large butler's pantry separated the dining room from the kitchen, and behind the kitchen was an L-shaped wing with pantry, scullery, quarters with a bath for three servants, the housekeeper's room and, beside it, the housekeeper's office.

In the corridor outside the kitchen was a stairway and Houston took it. Pausing at the second floor, she peeped down a hallway but could see only shadows on oak floors and panelled walls. She continued toward the attics.

As she'd already guessed, the attics were actually servants' quarters that were now being used for storage. There were two bathrooms, one male, one female, and the rest of the space was divided into small rooms. And each room was stacked to the ceiling with crates and boxes; some had furniture hidden under dust covers.

Tentatively, she lifted a dust sheet. Beneath it were two gilded chairs covered in tapestries of cherubs. A tag was attached. Holding her breath, she read the tag:

> *Mid-eighteenth century*
> *tapestries woven at Gobelin works*
> *believed to have belonged to Mme. de Pompadour*
> *one of set of twelve chairs, two settees*

"My goodness," Houston breathed, allowing the cover to fall back into place.

Against the wall was a rolled carpet. Its tag read:

> *Late seventeenth century*
> *made at Savonnerie factory for Louis XIV*

A crate, obviously holding a painting, was merely labelled "Gainsborough." Beside it stood one with the word "Reynolds" painted on it.

Slowly, Houston removed the cover from the Mme. de Pompadour chairs, lifted off the top chair and sat down. She needed a moment to collect her thoughts. Looking about her, she could see gold feet protruding from beneath the sheeted furniture, and without further exploring, she knew that all the furniture and works of art were museum quality. Absently, she lifted a sheet beside her. Beneath it sparkled a chandelier that looked as if it were made of diamonds. Its tag read: 1780.

She was still sitting, a bit stunned at the prospect of living daily with the treasures around her when she heard a carriage below. "Mr. Bagly!" she said as she flew down the stairs and managed to arrive at the front door just as he and his assistant were leaving their carriage.

"Good morning, Blair-Houston," he said.

Mr. Bagly was a tiny, white-faced little man who somehow managed to be a tyrant. As Chandler's premier tailor, Mr. Bagly received a great deal of respect.

"Good morning," she answered. "Do come in. I'm not sure what you've heard, Mr. Bagly, but Mr. Taggert and I are to be married within two weeks and he'll need an entire wardrobe. But right now, he needs one good afternoon suit for a reception tomorrow, something in vicuña, three buttons, gray trousers and a vest of cashmere. That should do it. Do you think you can have it ready by two o'clock tomorrow?"

"I'm not sure. I have other customers."

"I'm sure no one is in as much need as Mr. Taggert. Put as many seamstresses on it as possible. You will be paid."

"I think I can arrange it. Now, if I could begin measuring Mr. Taggert, I could start the suit."

"He is upstairs, I believe."

Mr. Bagly looked at her steadily: "Blair-Houston, I've known you all your life, and I'm willing to put aside all my other work to do a job for you, and I'm willing to come here this early in the morning in order to measure your fiancée, but I will *not* go up those stairs and search for him. Perhaps we should come back when he's awake."

"But you won't have time to make the suit! Please, Mr. Bagly."

"Not if you went on your knees to me. We will wait in here for one half-hour. If Mr. Taggert is not downstairs by then, we will leave."

Houston was almost glad there were no chairs for them in the large drawing room where they planned to wait. Courage, she told herself and started up the stairs.

The second floor was as beautiful as the first, with white painted panelling, and directly in front of her was a wide, open room with a green tiled area in back. "An aviary," she whispered with delight.

With a sigh, she knew she must get down to business. Around her were many closed doors and behind one of them was Kane.

She opened one door and, in the dim light, she saw a blond head in the midst of a rumpled bed. Quietly, she closed the door again, not wanting to wake Edan.

She went through four rooms before she found Kane's bedroom at the back of the house. Suspended from picture wires from the ceiling mold were crude curtains blocking out the morning sun. The furniture consisted of an oak bed, a little table littered with papers, an earthenware water pitcher on it, and a three-piece set of upholstered furniture covered in a ghastly red plush with bright yellow tassels at the bottom.

Houston looked toward the attics. "Forgive him, Mme. de Pompadour," she whispered.

With resolution, she pulled back the curtains, tied them in a fat knot so they'd stay in place, and let the sunlight in.

"Good morning, Mr. Taggert," she said loudly, as she stood over his bed.

Kane roused, turned over, but continued sleeping.

He was exposed from the waist up, nude, and, she suspected, nude the rest of the way down, too. For a moment she stood still, looking at him. It was few times that she'd seen a man's bare chest before and Kane was built like a prizefighter —big, muscular, his chest very hairy. His skin was dark and warm-looking.

One minute she was standing beside the bed and the next minute a great hand caught her thigh and she was pulled across him and into the bed.

"Couldn't wait for me, could you?" Kane said, as he began hungrily kissing her neck and throat as his hands energetically ran over her body. "I've always been partial to a good romp in the mornin'."

Houston struggled against him for a moment, saw it was useless and began looking for other ways to stop his attack on her. Her groping hand came in contact with the handle of the pitcher on the table, and she swiftly brought it down on his head.

The thin chalkware broke, and water and pieces of the pitcher cascaded down as Houston jumped out of the bed, moving safely to the foot of it.

"What the hell—," Kane began, sitting up, rubbing his head. "You could a killed me."

"Not likely," Houston said. "I correctly assumed your taste in quality toiletries would match your taste in furniture."

"Listen, you little bitch, I'll—."

"No, Mr. Taggert, you listen to me. If I am to be your wife, you will treat me with the respect due a woman in that position. I will not be treated as some hussy you've . . . you've hired for the evening." Her face turned red but she continued. "I did *not* come to your bedroom because, as you say, I couldn't wait to share your bed. I was in a sense blackmailed into this. Below, I have a tailor waiting to measure you for a suit, I have furniture movers arriving any minute, a cook is coming with a wagonload of food and, in less than an hour, a barber will remove that mass of hair you're sporting. If I am going to prepare both you and this house for a wedding, I will unfortunately need your presence, and therefore you cannot be allowed to loll about in bed, sleeping the day away."

Kane just looked at her while she delivered her speech. "Is my head bleedin'?" he asked.

With a sigh, Houston went to him and examined his head, until he caught her about the waist and pressed his face against her breast. "Any of that paddin'?" he asked.

Houston pushed him away in disgust. "Get up, get dressed and come downstairs as quickly as possible," she said before turning on her heel and leaving the room.

"Damned bossy female," she heard him say behind her.

Downstairs, everything was chaos. The six men Susan'd

hired were strolling through the house as if they owned it, shouting comments to one another. Willie and Mrs. Murchison were waiting to ask her questions and Mr. Bagly had decided to leave.

Houston set to work.

By nine o'clock, she was wishing she knew how to use a whip. She had immediately fired two of the furniture movers for insolence and then asked who wanted to earn a day's pay.

Kane didn't like Mr. Bagly touching him and didn't like Houston deciding what he could and could not wear.

Mrs. Murchison was beside herself, trying to cook in the bare kitchen.

When the barber arrived, Houston slipped out the side door and nearly ran for the privacy of the big glasshouse that for days she'd been wanting to explore. She closed the door and gazed with pleasure down the three-hundred-foot-long expanse of flowering plants. The fragrance and the peace were what she needed.

"Noise get too much for you?"

She turned to see Edan, as he set down a big pot of azaleas. He was nearly as large as Kane, handsome, blond, and, she guessed, younger than Kane. "I guess we woke you," she said. "There seems to have been a great deal of shouting this morning."

"If Kane's around, people usually shout," he said matter-of-factly. "Could I show you my plants?"

"This is yours?"

"More or less. There's a little house past the rose garden where a Japanese family lives. They take care of the outside gardens, but in here is mine. I have plants from all over the world."

She knew she had no time, but she also knew she wanted a few minutes of quiet.

With pride, Edan showed her the many plants in the glasshouse: cyclamen, primroses, tree ferns, orchids, exotic things she'd never heard of.

"You must enjoy it in here," she said, touching a cymbidium orchid leaf. "I broke a pitcher over his head this morning."

For a moment, Edan's mouth dropped open, then he gave a

snort of laughter. "I've gone after him with my fists more than once. Do you really mean to try to civilize him?"

"I hope I can. But I can't keep on striking him. There must be other ways." Her head came up. "I know nothing about you, or how you relate to him."

Edan began repotting an overgrown passionflower. "He found me in an alleyway in New York where I was staying alive by eating from garbage cans. My parents and sister had died a few weeks before from smoke inhalation in a tenement fire. I was seventeen, couldn't hold a job because I kept fighting," he smiled in memory, "starving, and had decided to turn to a life of crime. Unfortunately, or perhaps fortunately, the first person I chose to rob was Kane."

Houston nodded. "Perhaps his size was a challenge to you."

"Or maybe I was hoping I'd fail. Kane flattened me onto the street, but instead of sending me to jail, he took me home with him and fed me. I was seventeen, he was twenty-two, and already on his way to becoming a millionaire."

"And you've been with him ever since."

"And earning my keep," Edan added. "He made me work for him all day and sent me to accounting school at night. The man doesn't believe in sleep. We were up till four this morning, so that's why we were still in bed when you arrived.

"Ah!" Edan said suddenly, grinning broadly as he looked through the glass walls. "I think the barber's been here."

With much curiosity, Houston looked through the glass. Coming down the path was a big man wearing Kane's clothes, but instead of the long dark hair and beard, he was clean-shaven.

Houston looked at Edan in wonder, and he laughed as Kane walked through the door.

"Houston!" he bellowed. "You in here?"

She stepped from behind an elephant's-foot tree to look at him.

"Ain't bad, is it?" he said happily, rubbing his clean jaw. "I ain't seen myself in so long I'd forgotten how good-lookin' I was."

Houston had to laugh, for he was indeed handsome, with a big square jaw, fine lips, and with his eyes with their dark brows, he was extraordinary.

"If you're through lookin' at Edan's plants, come on back to the house. There's a lady in the kitchen cookin' up a storm and I'm starvin'."

"Yes," she said, walking out of the glasshouse ahead of him.

Once outside, he caught her arm. "I got somethin' to say to you," he said softly, looking at his boot toe, then at some place to the left of her head. "I didn't mean to jump on you this mornin'. It was just that I was asleep, and I woke up to see a pretty gal there. I wouldn't a hurt you. I just guess I ain't used to ladies." He rubbed his head and grinned at her. "But I imagine I'll learn real quick."

"Sit down here," she said, pointing to a bench under a tree. "Let me look at your head."

He sat quite still while she searched his hair for the lump and examined it. "Does it hurt very much?"

"Not at the moment," he said, then caught both her hands. "You still gonna marry me?"

He's much better looking than Leander, she suddenly thought, and when he looked at her like this, odd things happened to her knees. "Yes, I'm still going to marry you."

"Good!" he said abruptly and stood. "Now, let's go eat. Me and Edan got work to do and I got a man waitin' for me. And you got to watch them idiots with the furniture." He started back toward the house.

Houston had to half run to keep up with him. He certainly does change moods quickly, she thought, as she held her hat on and scurried.

By afternoon, she had rugs down in three rooms and had two of the attic rooms cleared. The furniture that was downstairs was in no order and she had yet to decide where each piece went. Kane and Edan closeted themselves in Kane's office with their visitor. Now and again she heard Kane's voice over the movers' noise. Once he looked into the library at the gilded chairs and said, "Them little chairs gonna hold up?"

"They have for over two hundred years," she'd answered.

Kane snorted and went back to his study.

At five o'clock, she knocked on the study door and, when Edan answered it, she looked through the blue haze of cigar smoke to tell Kane she was leaving but would return tomorrow. He barely looked up from his paperwork.

Edan walked out with her. "Thank you so much for all you've done today. I'm sure the house will be what it should be when you finish."

She stopped at the doorway. "Please tell him I'll be here at noon tomorrow with his new suit, and we'll attend the garden party at two."

"I hope he'll go."

"He will," she said with more assurance than she felt.

Chapter 8

Breakfast at the Chandler house was a solemn affair, only Duncan and Houston doing justice to the steak, ham, eggs, peach pie, and buckwheat cakes. Opal looked as if she'd lost five pounds overnight, Blair's jaw was set in a hard line of anger, while Duncan seemed to range from anger to bewilderment and back again.

Houston thought about what Susan had told her this morning concerning Blair and Leander. Yesterday, Blair had been canoeing on the lake in Fenton Park with a handsome blond stranger when Leander had rowed up beside them, and the next thing anyone knew, the stranger was thrashing about in the water while Lee hauled Blair into his canoe and rowed them to shore. While everyone was laughing, Blair used a paddle to shove Lee into the mud, rescued her stranger from drowning, and rowed him back to the boat rental area.

Houston knew she should be jealous of their love play, angry at how publicly Leander was telling everyone that he preferred Blair, and jealous of all the flowers Lee was sending, but her mind kept racing to things like where she was going to place that little Jacobean desk and whom she could get to help her hang the curtains she'd found in carefully-labelled packages. And then there was Mr. Taggert. She hoped he wouldn't give her too much trouble today.

"I'd like to speak to you, Houston," Duncan said after breakfast, startling Houston so much that she jumped. He led

68

the way into the front parlor, the one used for guests—and serious discussions.

Quietly, she took a seat. This man had been her stepfather since she was a girl, and because she'd always done what he wanted and conducted herself perfectly in his image of what a lady should do, they'd never had a disagreement.

"I hear that you've agreed to marry him," he began, standing, his back to the window that faced the street.

"Yes," she answered, steeling herself for the coming storm. How was she going to plead her case? Could she say she'd asked Kane and he said he'd never murdered anyone? Or maybe she could try to explain about how much he needed her.

As if he weighed hundreds of pounds, Duncan sat down.

"Houston," he said, in a voice barely above a whisper, "I know this house hasn't been like it was when your father was alive, but I never thought you'd take drastic measures to get out of it."

She'd not expected this. "You think I'm marrying Mr. Taggert in order to leave your house?"

He stood. "That and a few other reasons." He moved to look out the window. "I know that what Leander did to you must be a humiliating experience, and at your age it must seem to be the end of the world."

He turned back to face her. "But believe me, Houston, it's *not* the end of the world. You're the prettiest young lady in town, maybe in the whole state, and you'll find someone else. If you'd like to, I'll take you to Denver and introduce you to some young men."

Rising, Houston went to him and kissed his cheek. Until this moment, she'd not known that he really cared for her. In spite of the fact that they lived in the same house, there was always a formality between them, and this was the first time she'd ever kissed him.

"I thank you so much for your kindness," she said when Duncan turned away in embarrassment. She stepped back. "I don't believe I am marrying Mr. Taggert merely because he's the one most available."

Duncan looked back at her. "Are you *sure?* Maybe you want to hold him up before the town to say, 'See, I can get another man any time I want.' You *can* get another man.

Maybe one not so rich or not one with a house like Taggert's, but a man whose family you know. For all you know, there could be insanity in Taggert's family. I hear that uncle of his is nothing but a troublemaker."

Houston's head came up. "Uncle?"

"Rafe Taggert in the coal mines. The man is a thorn in Jacob Fenton's side, but Jacob keeps him on no matter what he does."

Houston turned away to hide her face. The name Taggert was fairly common, and she'd never connected her friend Jean to Kane. Maybe Jean knew Kane. And if they were related, she could vouch for Kane's family being sane.

She turned back to Duncan. "I don't believe there's insanity."

A look of frustration crossed Duncan's face. "How can you change so completely in so short a time? You were so sensible with Leander, getting to know each other before you made the commitment of marriage, but you've known this man for only days, yet you've agreed to spend the rest of your life with him."

There was no answer to give him. He was completely right. Logically, Houston knew she couldn't marry this stranger. Except that she damn well wanted to! She covered the little smile that appeared on her lips with her hand. She couldn't adopt Mr. Taggert's language!

"Marriage is a serious matter," Duncan continued. "Think about what you're doing."

"I've already agreed to marry him," she said, as if it were an answer.

"Blair proved that until that ring is on a woman's finger, anything might happen," he said bitterly. "Don't let her . . . waywardness ruin your life. Find out about Kane Taggert. Talk to some people who know him. Talk to Marc Fenton; he might remember Taggert when he worked in the stables. I've tried to see Jacob but he can't bear to hear Taggert's name. It's your whole life, Houston; find out everything you can about the man before you commit yourself to him."

Houston knew his request was reasonable, but she hesitated before agreeing. Maybe she didn't want to find out about Kane, maybe she liked thinking of him as a mystery man who'd swept her off her feet.

Maybe she just wasn't ready for the adventure to end. But Duncan's words were sensible, and Houston was used to obeying. Briefly, she wondered what he'd do if he knew about Kane's attack on her yesterday morning and the subsequent pottery breakage. Lock her in her room no doubt. She sighed. "I will ask several people," she whispered. "I will find out all I can, and if there is nothing horribly wrong, I will marry him on the twentieth."

Duncan gave a heavy sigh. "That's all I can ask. Houston, tell me, have you always wanted money so badly? Have you considered your life in this house one of poverty?"

"Is his money one of the other reasons you think I'm marrying him?"

"Of course." He looked surprised. "Why else would you marry the great ugly thing? If it weren't for his money, no one would speak to him. He'd be just another coal miner like the rest of his family and no one would give him the time of day."

"Would he be just another miner?" she asked. "He started as a stable boy but he's earned millions. No one gave it to him. Perhaps what I like is the man inside, the one who can pull himself up from the stable filth to achieve something in life. All I've ever done is learn how to dress properly." And he needs that knowledge, she thought, feeling a little thrill run through her body.

"What else should a lady know?" Duncan asked.

"Women today are writing books, are—." She stopped, waving her hand to dismiss the subject. "I wonder why no one is asking why a man of Mr. Taggert's wealth is marrying a woman from the Colorado mountains? He could have a princess."

"You *are* a princess," Duncan snapped.

Houston smiled at him as she moved toward the door. "I must go. I have to visit Mr. Bagly and choose a wardrobe for my future husband, then I must order a second wedding dress identical to the first one. I'm sure Blair hasn't thought to do it."

"I doubt she has either," Duncan said, reaching into his pocket. "The bank president came by yesterday with this." He handed her a piece of paper.

It was a deposit slip stating that two hundred and fifty thousand dollars had been deposited in her name.

Houston's hand on the doorknob trembled a bit. "Thank you," she murmured. "Thank you for everything and I shall do as you ask." With a smile, she left the room.

She was on the stairs before she could breathe again. She stopped and looked again at the deposit slip. He said he was going to deposit "some" money for her. Whatever faults he had, lack of generosity was not one of them. Repressing the urge to laugh with delight, she hurried up the stairs to dress for the day's outing.

An hour later, she sat inside Mr. Bagly's little shop, fabric samples all about her. One of the things she'd learned in finishing school was how to dress a man—if for no other reason than so she could argue with her husband's valet.

"He'll need a dozen business suits," she was saying to Mr. Bagly as a clerk wrote furiously. "This light-colored wool, the Oxford gray check, the Angola, and that heavy blue Scottish wool . . . for now."

"And for evening?" Mr. Bagly asked.

"The black worsted with a white marseilles vest. Now, for riding."

She chose clothes for sports, pausing at, then rejecting, the golfing knickers and clothes for afternoon receptions. For his own wedding, she chose a black cutaway, then shirts, scarves, gloves. She then chose a large supply of underwear of lisle, linen handkerchiefs, and balbriggan socks.

"Shall we leave the hats until later?"

"Yes," Houston answered. "And the canes." She looked at the little gold watch pinned to her breast. "I must go now. May I have the completed suit?"

When Mr. Bagly had brought the new suit and a complete set of accessories, including shoes, from a storage room, Houston made arrangements for him to measure Edan for clothes for the wedding. "Good luck," he called after her, as Houston sped away in her elegant new carriage. "You'll need it," he muttered under his breath.

Two hours later, Houston was dressed for the garden party, wearing a formfitting gown of dotted white mousseline de soie over yellow satin, a wide yellow ribbon across the bodice, tying in a bow on her hip. Somehow, this morning, Susan had managed to pull Houston's corset a full three-quarters of an inch tighter. Breathing was done only in the upper half of her lungs, but what did a little discomfort matter? She wanted to look her best for her first official outing with her fiancé.

Sighing as she parked before the Taggert house, she realized she must hire servants soon. Now, she needed someone to help her from the carriage. Looking around to make sure no one was about, she pulled her dress up almost to the knees and stepped down.

A low whistle came from her left. "Prettiest thing I've seen all day," said Kane, walking around the side of the house. "In fact you got better legs 'n a dancer I seen in New Orleans."

Houston tried to control her blush. "I brought your suit, and you just have time to get ready."

"Ready for what?"

She still wasn't used to seeing him without his beard. His face was bristly this morning with dark, unshaven whiskers, but they didn't hide his extraordinary good looks. How fortunate, she thought, to agree to marry a grizzly bear and have him turn into a handsome prince.

"For the garden party at two," she answered.

"Oh, that," he said over his shoulder as he started toward the door, leaving her standing.

"Yes, that." She picked up her skirts and followed him inside and toward his office. "I thought perhaps we'd have time for a few lessons before we went, just enough so you'd feel comfortable, and of course you'll want time to dress."

He stopped behind his desk, picked up a piece of paper. "I'm real sorry, but I ain't got time to go. I got too much work to do. You go on, though. You're already dressed up and all. Maybe you can take some flowers from me."

Houston took a deep breath. "Perhaps I should just give them money."

He looked at her over the paper, his expression one of surprise. "They'd like that?"

"No," she said evenly, *"they* wouldn't but I'm sure you would. That way you wouldn't have to face them."

"Are you sayin' I'm afraid of a bunch of overdressed, tea-drinkin' snobs? Why, I could buy and sell—."

Her look cut him off.

"I ain't goin'," he said stubbornly and sat down.

She walked to stand near him, wanting very much to put her hand on his shoulder, but she didn't. "It won't be so bad.

You've only met the worst people of the town. I'd like to introduce you to my friends, and I promise you not one person will faint at your feet."

He looked up at her. "Not one lady'll faint when she sees me with my beard gone?"

With a smile, she moved away from him. "Are you trying to get me to say you'll be the most handsome man there?"

He made a grab for her hand, but she moved back too quickly. "Let's you and me stay here," he said. "We'll find somethin' to do together. I like that dress."

"Oh, no, Mr. Taggert," she laughed, wondering if she could tighten her corset another quarter inch. "I will not be seduced into . . . into whatever you have in mind. You must get dressed for the garden party." She'd backed up until she was pressed against the wall.

Kane moved very close to her, put both hands on the wall on either side of her head and leaned forward. "We haven't really gotten to know each other, have we? I mean, a couple should spend some time alone before they get married, shouldn't they?"

Houston deftly slid from under his arm. "Mr. Taggert," she said firmly, "I'll not be sweet-talked out of this party. I think you are afraid to go, and perhaps if you're the sort of man who lets a little gathering of people frighten him, I'm not sure you're the man I want to marry."

With an angry look, he went back to his desk. "You gotta mean streak in you a mile wide. I ain't afraid of no damn party."

"Then prove it by getting dressed and going with me." As she watched, he seemed to be fighting something inside himself, and she almost said she'd stay at home with him. Be firm, Houston, she told herself. This is what he wants you for.

He tossed the papers to his desk. "I'll go," he said in disgust. "And I hope you ain't gonna be sorry." He stormed past her and out the door.

"I hope so, too," she breathed, as she ran after him to get the suit that was still in the carriage.

While Kane dressed, Houston looked at the furniture scattered about the house and planned where it should go. After an hour and a half, when she'd begun to think Kane had left by a second-story window, she turned to see him standing in the doorway wearing the dark frock coat, white linen shirt, and slate gray trousers, a white cravat held in his hand.

"I don't know how to tie this."

Houston couldn't move for a moment. The well-tailored suit showed to advantage the extraordinary difference in width between his shoulders and his trim waist, and the dark cloth emphasized his brows and hair. With pride, she thought of appearing at the party on his arm. Maybe there was a part of her that wanted to show the town that she could get another man. She could certainly do worse than this man. Oh my, yes she could.

"Do you know how to tie this?" he persisted.

"Yes, of course," she said, coming to herself. "You'll have to sit down so I can reach your neck."

He sat on one of the little gilt chairs as if he were a condemned man.

As Houston worked on the Windsor tie, she began to talk to him. "The party is at the house of a friend of mine, Tia Mankin. There'll be long tables set with food and drink, and all you'll have to do is walk around and talk to people. I'll stay with you as much as I can."

Kane said nothing.

When the tie was done, she looked into his eyes. Was this the man on whose head she'd broken a pitcher? "It'll be over soon, then we'll come back here and have supper."

Suddenly, his arms tightened about her and he kissed her hard—as if he wanted courage from her. The next moment he was standing beside her. "Let's get this over with," he said, heading for the door.

Again, Houston was too stunned to move. Their few kisses seemed to mean nothing to him but each one left her breathless.

"Ain't you comin'?" he asked impatiently from the doorway.

"Yes, certainly," she said, smiling, and feeling very alive.

As Kane drove them the short distance to Tia's house, she gave him a few instructions. "If people are to believe our engagement, perhaps you should be attentive to me," she said cautiously. "Stay beside me, hold my arm, that sort of thing. And *please* help me out of the carriage."

He nodded without looking at her.

"And smile," she said. "Surely marriage isn't that bad."

"If I live through the engagement," he said grimly.

The people already gathered in the Mankin garden were more than curious about Kane and Houston. Trying their best to act politely, they practically ran toward the carriage, then stood back and gaped. The hairy coal miner had been replaced with a gentleman.

Kane didn't seem aware of the people's reactions but Houston was very aware of them, and, with pride, she put her hands on his big shoulders as he helped her from the carriage. Slipping her arm through his, she guided him toward the waiting people.

"May I introduce you to my fiancé, Mr. Kane Taggert?" she began.

Twenty minutes later, when he'd been introduced to everyone, she felt him begin to relax.

"It wasn't as bad as you thought, was it?"

"Naw," he said a bit smugly. "You want somethin' to eat?"

"I would love some punch. Would you excuse me for a moment? I need to speak to someone."

She watched him for a moment as he started toward the tables of food and noticed how many women stopped to look at him. Meredith Lechner walked over to talk to him, smiling first at Houston as if for permission.

Mine, Houston thought, my very own frog-turned-prince. And it took only one lump on his head. She coughed politely to cover what might have been a giggle.

While Kane was busy, she walked toward Reverend Thomas, who stood alone on the outskirts of the crowd.

"You've certainly changed him," Reverend Thomas said, nodding toward Kane, who now had three women near him.

"The outside perhaps," she said, and her voice lowered. "I want to talk to you. Last week, in the coal town, Jean Taggert said she knew about me. How much does she know?"

"Everything," the reverend answered.

"But how—?" Houston began.

"I told her. I had to. I wanted you to have a friend, a real friend, on the inside."

"But what if I'm caught? Jean could be in even more trouble if she knows who I am. It's bad enough as it is."

"Houston," the reverend said, his eyes on hers. "You can't take all the responsibility by yourself. Jean came to me months ago and wanted to know the truth. I was glad to tell her."

Houston was silent for a moment as she watched Kane laugh at something one of the women said, and she saw the women take a step closer. It's not just me he charms, she thought.

"Did you know that Kane and Jean are related?" she asked.

"First cousins." He smiled at her startled look. "As soon as I learned about your engagement, I went to Jean. Oh, the guards were reluctant to let me in, but I do have a higher boss than theirs. Neither Jean nor any of her family's met Kane. There's some secrecy about his birth, something about his mother. Jean's guess was that she was a . . . ah, lady of the evening and Kane's father had some doubt that the child was his. That would explain why Kane was put to work at Fenton's rather than being reared by the Taggerts."

"Do you know what happened to his parents?"

"Jean felt sure they were both dead. Houston," Reverend Thomas put his hand on her arm, "are you sure you want to marry this man? I know that what Leander did must have hurt you but—."

Houston didn't feel she could listen to another lecture, no matter how well-intended. "I'm sure," she said firmly. "Now, if you'll excuse me, I must see to my fiancé before he's stolen from me."

"All right, but, Houston, if you want to talk, I'll be here."

As Houston made her way toward Kane, one person after another stopped her.

"He looks quite nice, Houston. You've done wonders with him."

"Did you really fall in love with him while you were engaged to Leander?"

"Was Lee terribly heartbroken when you told him?"

"Did you sneak out of your house to meet Mr. Taggert?"

"Houston, you must tell us *everything!*"

Finally, she made her way to Kane's side and slipped her arm through his.

"You damn well took long enough," he said under his

breath. "Do you know what those women wanted to know?" he asked in a shocked tone.

"I can guess," she laughed. "Did you get something to eat?"

"Just a couple of those little sandwiches. A body could eat all of 'em and still be hungry. We have to stay here much longer? Who was that man you were talkin' to?"

"Reverend Thomas."

"Oh, yeah. You teach a class for him on Wednesdays." Smiling, he touched her nose with his fingertip. "Don't look so surprised. I know lots about you. Why don't you go sit down and I'll bring you a plate of food? That's what I seen the other men doin' for the women."

If she were with Lee now he'd know exactly what was proper to do, she thought. And they'd have to leave the party at 3:15 because on Thursdays he—.

"You wishin' you had a man that knew what to do?" Kane asked from above her, his big shadow blocking the sunlight, a plate of food in his hand.

"Why no, I wasn't," she answered, but said no more because a mass of very wet food came tumbling into her lap.

Kane didn't move but shown in his face was the knowledge that everything he'd feared had just happened.

It was when Houston heard a woman's smothered laugh—for the entire party had come to a halt—that she reacted.

Quickly, she stood, the food falling to the ground. "Pick me up," she whispered, but he only stared at her with bleak eyes. "Sweep me into your arms, carry me to the carriage and drive away," she commanded quietly.

Kane wasn't used to obeying orders blindly, but he did this one. With ease, he picked her up.

As he carried her toward the carriage, Houston snuggled against him. On Thursdays, Leander took fencing lessons, but Mr. Taggert's Thursdays were spent in sweeping his intended off her feet.

Kane was silent until they were in the carriage and driving toward the Chandler house. "Why?" he asked. "What good did my carryin' you do?"

"Because few of the men in there have backs strong enough to carry their wives, and I think any woman would trade a little spilled food for a man who could lift her."

"You don't weigh nothin'," he said.

With a smile, she leaned toward him and kissed his cheek. "I weigh nothing to you," she said softly.

He stopped the buggy and stared at her. "You're a real lady, ain't you, Miss Chandler? A real lady."

"I hope so," she murmured and thought that it could be possible that whatever Kane Taggert wanted her to be, she just might become.

Chapter 9

Houston burst into her mother's bedroom, where Opal sat quietly embroidering a pair of cuffs.

"Mother! You have to help me," Houston said.

"Look at your dress," Opal said, rising. "Do you think it'll come clean?"

"I don't know. Mother, he's downstairs waiting for me and you must entertain him while I change. If you don't talk to him, I'm afraid he'll leave."

Opal took a step backward. "You can't mean your Mr. Taggert? You have him downstairs?"

Houston took both her mother's hands in her own. "He is very upset. By accident, he spilled some food in my lap and, oh Mother, everyone started to laugh at him. If you'd seen his face! He was completely humiliated. Please go down and talk to him for a few minutes. Don't let him leave."

Opal felt herself softening. "No one should have laughed at him if it was an accident."

"Thank you," Houston said, quickly kissing her mother's cheek before rushing from the room. She ignored Opal's cry of, "What will I talk to him about?"

Susan was waiting for Houston and helped her with the back fastenings of the dress.

"It's just the front panel that's stained," Houston said, holding the dress up and examining it. "Susan, tell Mrs. Thomas to rub it with magnesia powder for the grease and—oh Heavens, every stain in the world is on it. Hold the

80

panel over a sulfur flame, and if it still doesn't come clean, I'll use naphtha on it. But I'll do it myself. The last thing I want is the kitchen exploding. Hurry now, before it sets any worse."

When Susan returned from her errand, Houston was sitting at her desk, writing. "When I finish this note, I want you to give it to Willie to take to Mrs. Murchison. I also want you to explain to him what I need, so there's no misunderstanding."

She wrote as she talked. "Tell Willie to take the stairs in the Taggert house, the ones by the kitchen, all the way to the attics, turn left and he'll see a long corridor. The second door on the left leads to a small room filled with furniture, and along the back wall is a small Soumak carpet—no, I'll write a red figured carpet—and a large muslin bag of decorative pillows. The bag is as tall as he is, so he can't miss it. Tell him to take the carpet and the pillows downstairs to the small drawing room. Mrs. Murchison will show him where it is. Have him unroll the carpet, put the pillows along the edges of the carpet, and then bring in the large, three-arm silver candelabra from the dining room next door and set it in the middle of the carpet."

She looked up. "Can you remember all that to tell Willie?"

"Oh, yes, Miss. A picnic indoors. Did Mr. Taggert really spill the whole table of food on people?"

"Where did you hear that?"

"Ellie, who works for the Mankins' neighbors, came by."

"Well, it's not true at all. Now, go downstairs, tell Willie, and have him give this to Mrs. Murchison. And quickly, please. I'll need help dressing. Oh yes, and have him tell Mrs. Murchison I'll delay as long as possible to give her time to cook."

Houston saw to her dismay, as soon as Susan had gone, that the spilled food had soaked all her undergarments. After a quick inspection, she thought boiling would cleanse them, and she hurriedly began to undress.

From her closet she chose a dress of soft, pale green lawn with short puffed sleeves, the bodice and high neckline made of cotton guipure lace. Unfortunately, the back was laced with thirty-six tiny green buttons. She was struggling with these when Susan returned.

"What do you hear from downstairs?"

"Nothing, Miss," Susan said, beginning to fasten the

buttons with a little brass hook. "Should I look? I think the parlor door's open."

"No," Houston said, but she was beginning to worry. Opal Gates was a woman who needed protection, a woman who was easily shocked. Houston had a vision of Kane using some of his vile language, of Opal fainting from shock and Kane feeling no obligation to "pick her up."

"There's no one else in the house, is there, Susan?"

"No, Miss."

"Good, because I'm going downstairs and look through the hinges. You can button me down there."

Houston tiptoed down the stairs, Susan behind her, and peeked through the parlor door.

Kane and Opal sat close to one another on the horsehair sofa, both peering together into a stereopticon.

"I've never seen the place myself," Opal was saying, "but I hear it's quite impressive."

"I lived in New York for years but I never heard of this place," Kane said. "What was that name again?"

"Niagara Falls."

Kane put the viewer down and looked at her. "You'd like to go see it, wouldn't you?"

"Why, yes, I would. In fact, Mr. Taggert, I've always had a secret dream to travel. I would like to hire my own private railroad car and travel all over the United States."

Kane took Opal's hand in his. "I'm gonna give you that dream, Mrs. Chandler. What color train would you like to have? I mean the inside. You like red?"

"I couldn't possibly—," Opal began.

Kane leaned closer to her. "I have a real weakness for ladies," he said softly. "And you, Mrs. Chandler, are as much a lady as your daughter."

There was silence for a moment between them and Susan, as she looked over Houston's shoulder, stopped her buttoning.

"Pink," Opal said. "I should like a train completely done in pink."

"You'll have it. Anything else you want?"

"I should like you to call me Opal. I'm afraid my husband, Mr. Gates, won't appreciate his wife being called by her former husband's name."

Houston held her breath to see how Kane would take the correction.

Kane took Opal's hand he was holding and kissed it heartily, not a gentleman's kiss. "No wonder you got a lady for a daughter."

"I think your mamma'll marry him if you won't," Susan said.

"Hush and finish the buttons."

"Done," Susan said, and Houston walked around the door to the front of the parlor.

"I hope I didn't take too long," she said sweetly. "You were comfortable, Mr. Taggert?"

"Yeah," Kane said, grinning. "Real comfortable. But I gotta be goin' now. I have work to do."

"Mr. Taggert," Houston said, "could you please drive me into town to the dressmaker's? I need to leave her some patterns."

A frown crossed Kane's face, but he agreed when Houston said her errand would take fifteen minutes at the most.

"Don't expect me back until evening," she whispered to her mother as she kissed her cheek good-bye and grabbed her parasol.

"You're in capable hands, dear," Opal said, smiling fondly at Kane.

When they were in Houston's carriage, she turned to Kane. "Did you and my mother have a pleasant chat?"

"You got a good mother," he said. "Where's this dress shop you want to go to? You sure you'll only take ten minutes?"

"Fifteen," she answered. "My . . . previous wedding dress was made in Denver, but I'm going to have an identical one made here."

"Identical? Oh, yeah, for the double weddin'. When is it, anyway?"

"Monday, the twentieth. I do hope you don't have to work that day and can come."

He gave her a sideways look, then smiled. "I'll be there on the weddin' day if you'll be there on the weddin' night." He laughed as her face pinkened and she turned away.

She directed him down Coal Avenue to the Westfield Block, a long, two-story, sandstone building that ran from

Second to Third Streets and contained retail stores below and offices above.

Kane tied the horse, and helped Houston out of the carriage. "I think I'll have a drink while I'm waitin'," he said, nodding toward one of the town's many saloons. "I hope bein' a husband is easier 'n bein' an intended."

Turning, he left her standing in the dusty street. There were times, Houston thought, when she missed Leander's manners.

Her business inside the dressmaker's took only seven minutes, and the woman threw up her hands in despair at the idea of being asked to make such an elaborate dress in so short a time. She sat down in shock when Houston asked her to also make a dress for Jean Taggert. In a flurry of movement, she pushed Houston from the shop, saying she needed every moment for work. Houston could tell she was thrilled at the prospect.

Now, Houston stood outside the shop, her green parasol open, and looked across the street toward the saloon where Kane was waiting for her. She hoped he didn't stay in there too long.

"Lookee here," came a man's voice. "You waitin' for us?"

Three young cowboys surrounded her and, by the smell of them, they had just come in from weeks on the trail.

"Come on, Cal," one of the cowboys said. "She's a lady."

Houston pretended the men weren't there, but silently prayed Kane would suddenly appear.

"I like ladies," Cal said.

Houston turned and put her hand on the doorknob of the Sayles Art Rooms.

Cal put his hand over hers.

"I beg your pardon," Houston said, drawing back, giving the man a look of contempt.

"Talks like a lady," Cal said. "Honey, how about you and me goin' over to the saloon and havin' a few beers?"

"Cal," one of the other cowboys said, with warning in his voice.

But Cal leaned closer to Houston. "I'll show you a real good time, honey."

"I'll show you a good time," came Kane's voice as he grabbed the back of the cowboy's shirt, and the waistband of his trousers, and sent the boy sailing to land face down in the dirty street.

When the cowboy, who was half Kane's size, lifted himself, shaking his head to clear it, Kane towered over him. "This here's a clean town," he growled. "You wanta free woman, you go to Denver, but here we take care of our women." He leaned closer to the boy. "And I damn well take care of *my* woman. You understand that?"

"Yes, sir," he mumbled. "I didn't mean no—," he began but stopped. "Yes, sir, I'm goin' to Denver right now."

"I like that idea," Kane said as he stepped back, grabbed Houston's arm and propelled her into the carriage seat.

He drove in silence to his house, then stopped. "Damn! I guess you wanted to go home." He picked up the reins again. "That kid didn't hurt ya, did he?"

"No," she said softly. "Thank you for coming to my rescue."

"Nothin' to it," he said, but he was frowning as if he were worried about something.

Houston put her hand on his arm. "Perhaps it was forward of me but I sent a message ahead to Mrs. Murchison to prepare us something to eat. That is, if you don't mind my dining with you."

He gave her a quick up-and-down look. "I don't mind, but I hope you got enough dresses to last you, since I seem to ruin 'em often enough."

"I have more than enough dresses."

"All right then," he said reluctantly, "but I got to work sometime today. You go on in and I'll put your horse away."

Once inside the house, Houston ran to the kitchen. "Is everything prepared?" she asked.

"Everything," Mrs. Murchison smiled. "And there's cold champagne waiting."

"Champagne?" Houston gasped, thinking of when Blair had drunk too much champagne and had ended up making love to Leander.

"And I've made all of Mr. Kane's favorites," Mrs. Murchison continued, her eyes softening.

"Buffalo steaks, no doubt," Houston muttered, "and another woman in love with him."

"What was that, Miss Houston?"

85

"Nothing. I'm sure everything will be perfect, as whatever you cook always is." Houston left the kitchen to go to the small drawing room. It was exactly as she'd envisioned it, with the candles already burning, champagne cooling, pâté and crackers set on a silver platter. The late sun coming through the windows made the room glow.

"You set this up?" Kane asked from behind her.

"I thought perhaps you'd be hungry," she began a bit nervously. The picnic had seemed a good idea, but now it looked like a setting for a seduction. "You said you'd like to talk, too," she whispered, eyes on her hands.

Kane gave a grunt and strode past her. "If I didn't know better, I'd say you wanted more than to talk. Come on and sit down here and let's eat. I—."

"Have to work," she interrupted, feeling a little hurt at his attitude. After all, she'd done this because he'd seemed so miserable when he'd dropped the food on her.

Kane walked closer to her, put his hand under her chin. "You ain't gonna cry, are you?"

"Certainly not," she said firmly. "Let's eat so I can go home. I have a great deal to do also and—."

Kane grabbed her wrist and pulled her into his arms.

Houston felt her body softening and her anger disappearing. Perhaps this was what she'd been after. She did so much like to be touched by him.

"You smell good," he said, nuzzling her neck, as his big body surrounded hers, protecting her, making her feel safe and unsafe at the same time.

"You were real nice today." He was placing little nibbling kisses along her neck. "You ain't gonna mind bein' married to a stableboy like me too much, are you?"

Houston didn't answer as she felt her knees giving way, but Kane easily held her upright as he began to make love to her left ear.

"You were the prettiest lady there today," he whispered, his soft breath sending chills down her legs. "And I liked carryin' you. In fact, I'd like to carry you upstairs to my bed right now."

Houston was tempted to say nothing and, in truth, wondered if it was possible for her voice to work.

"Eh-hem," came a loud sound from the doorway.

"Go away," Kane said, his teeth nipping along Houston's jawline.

But Houston was too steeped in years of training to continue. She pushed at Kane but didn't budge him. "Please," she pleaded, looking into his dark eyes.

With a look of disgust, he released her so suddenly she nearly fell.

Mrs. Murchison stood in the doorway, holding an enormous porcelain soup tureen. As she passed Houston on the way out, she gave her shaming looks which made Houston blush.

Trying to calm herself, Houston realized how close she'd come to blithely jumping into bed with her fiancé. But she'd promised her stepfather she'd ask questions about Kane before she married him. What if she found out he was a criminal? Would she marry him anyway? She would certainly have to if she'd been to bed with him.

Looking at him now, as he sat on the floor opening the champagne, his jacket off, the sleeves of his white shirt rolled to the elbows and showing strong, tanned forearms, she thought perhaps she should let him make love to her, then she'd have to marry him no matter what she found out about him.

But that would be cheating.

Carefully arranging her skirts, she sat on the pillows across from him. "I have a favor to ask of you," she began.

"Sure," he said, mouth full of pâté.

"I'd like to remain a virgin until my wedding."

Kane choked so badly Houston was worried about him, but he downed half a bottle of the champagne and managed to recover. "It's nice to hear you are one," he said at last, tears in his eyes. "I mean what with Westfield and all."

Houston stiffened.

"Now, don't go gettin' your back up. Here, have some of this." He held out a tulip glass of champagne. "It's good for you. So, you want to remain a virgin, do you?" he said, as he ladled creamy oyster stew into porcelain bowls. "I guess that means you want me to keep my hands off you."

He was watching her in an odd way, speculatively.

"Perhaps that would be better," she said, thinking that if he kept touching her as he had a minute ago, she'd never stay a virgin—nor want to remain one.

"All right," he said and there was coldness in his voice.

Houston's eyes widened. No doubt he thought it was because he was once a stableboy and she thought she was better than he was. "No, please," she began. "It's not what you think. I—." She couldn't tell him what she'd promised her stepfather, or that his hands made her feel far and away from being a lady. She put her hand on his bare forearm.

Kane moved away from her touch. "You made your point. Look, we have an agreement, a contract more or less, and I've been breakin' it. You said you'd pretend we were . . . in love, I guess, in public and you've done that. In private you don't have to put up with me. I'll keep my hands off you. In fact, I think it'd be better if I left now. You stay here 'n' eat and I'll go to work."

Before Houston could move, Kane had stood and was halfway across the room.

"Please don't go," she cried, leaping up to follow him, then tripping and falling on her long skirts.

He caught her before she hit the hard floor but swiftly released her once she was steadied.

"I didn't mean to insult you," she began. "It's not that I don't *like* your touch," she began, then stopped, blushed, and looked at her hands. "I mean I . . . It's just that I never . . . And I would like to remain . . . If possible," she concluded, looking up at him.

Kane was staring at her quite hard. "You don't make no sense. You want me to keep my hands off or what? All I asked for in this marriage was a lady in public. In private, this house is big enough you don't even have to look at my ugly face. It's your choice, lady."

A lady must be positive, Houston remembered from school. She put her chin in the air and her shoulders back. "I want to be your wife in private as well as in public, but I also want to remain a virgin until the wedding."

"Well, who's stoppin' you?" Kane glared at her. "Am I haulin' you upstairs by your hair? Am I forcin' you into my bed?"

"No, but you are a persuasive asker, Mr. Taggert," she shot back at him, then put her hand to her mouth.

Understanding lit Kane's eyes. "Well, I'll be damned," he said, with wonder in his voice. "Who would a thought? Oh well, maybe ladies like stableboys. Come on and sit down and eat," he said jovially. "A good asker, am I?" He grinned as she sat down across from him.

With all her heart, Houston wished she'd never brought the subject up.

The intimate little dinner Houston'd planned turned into controlled chaos. Edan came in before the soup was finished and handed Kane papers he had to read and sign. Kane invited him to eat with them, and they proceeded to talk business throughout the meal.

Houston silently watched the sun set through the long windows. Mrs. Murchison went in and out bearing great quantities of delicious food, which were consumed down to the last crumb.

Kane kept giving the woman compliments, which ranged from a mumbled "damned good" to, when she brought in an enormous baked Alaska, asking her to run away with him and live in sin. Mrs. Murchison giggled and blushed like a schoolgirl.

Houston, remembering the cook's remark that she was cooking all Mr. Kane's favorite foods, said, "What are your favorite foods, Mr. Taggert?"

He looked at her over the top of some papers. "Anything that tastes good and that includes pretty ladies."

With pinkened cheeks, Houston looked away.

At nine o'clock she rose. "I must leave now. Thank you so much for the dinner, Mr. Taggert." She really didn't think he'd notice whether she was there or not.

Kane caught the hem of her dress. "You can't leave yet. I want to talk to you."

Without yanking her skirt away, she couldn't leave, so she stood still, looking at a wall panel over the heads of the two men seated at her feet.

"I think I'm the one who should go," Edan said, beginning to gather papers.

"We ain't done yet," Kane said.

"Don't you think you should spend a little time alone with your bride?" Edan asked pointedly. "I'll tell Mrs. Murchison to go home." He stood. "Houston, thank you for dinner. I enjoyed it very much." Edan left the room, closing the door behind him.

Houston didn't move, but stood just where she was, not looking down at him.

He tugged on her skirt a few times, but when she didn't respond, he stood and looked at her. "I think you're mad at me."

Houston looked away. "That's utterly ridiculous. It's quite late, Mr. Taggert, and I must go home. My parents will be worried."

Kane put his hand on her cheek, cupping her face. "It was real nice of you to fix up this dinner with the candles an' all."

"I'm glad you were pleased. Now I must—."

He pulled her into his arms. "All night I've been thinkin' about what you said, about how I could talk you into things," he said, his lips against her neck.

"Please don't," she said, ineffectually pushing at him.

He moved his hand up to her carefully arranged hair, buried his fingers in it and slowly began to work his way through. Her thick, soft hair fell about her shoulders and Kane ran the fingers of both his hands through it.

"Pretty," he murmured, looking at her, their faces very close. The next moment he tilted her head to the side and began to kiss her in a way that made her feel as if she were dissolving. He played with her lips, pulling the lower one out with his teeth, touching the tip of his tongue to her lip.

Houston stood still as waves of feeling coursed through her body. Then, with abandon, she put her arms about his neck and pressed her body against his. Kane reacted instantly, pulling her close, bending her to fit the planes of his big body.

When he began to bend his knees and descend to the carpet and pillows, Houston didn't even consider protesting, but clung to him as if he were a life-giving force. His lips never left hers as they lay side by side on the carpet.

Kane ran his hand down her hip and thigh as his mouth travelled down her neck.

"Kane," she whispered, her head back, her leg pressed between his.

"Yes, sweetheart, I'm here," he whispered, his voice sending chills down her body.

His hand pulled her dress up to explore her legs, quickly finding the bare expanse of thigh above her gartered stockings and under her long, loose drawers.

Houston had no mind, no thoughts at all, but only felt the heavenly sensations of his hand on her skin, his lips on her face. Instinctively, she moved closer to him, wedged her leg between his even tighter.

With a groan, Kane pushed her away, lay beside her, looking at her for just a second, then stood.

"Get up," he said coldly and walked away, his back to her as he looked out the dark window.

Houston felt dirty, humiliated, cheated, as she lay on the rug, her skirts hiked about her waist. Swift tears came to her eyes as she slowly stood and tried to regain her composure.

"Go fix your hair," Kane said, not turning around. "Fix your hair and I'll take you home to your mother."

As quickly as she could, Houston fled the room, her hand to her mouth to prevent a sob coming out.

The two bathrooms downstairs were off the kitchen and in Kane's office. She didn't want to risk seeing either Edan or Mrs. Murchison so she ran upstairs to a bath near Kane's bedroom.

Once inside the marble-covered room, she gave herself over to tears. He'd wanted to marry a lady, and he was disgusted that she'd acted like a harlot. Yet this was what Blair had meant when she'd said she saw sparks when Leander kissed her. Never had Lee's kisses made her feel anything, but Kane's . . .

She looked at herself in the mirror, her eyes alive and sparkling, her mouth slightly swollen, her cheeks pink, her hair wild about her shoulders. This was not the lady he'd wanted. No wonder he pushed her away from him.

Again, the tears began to flow.

As soon as Houston left the drawing room, Kane made his way to his office, where Edan sat behind the desk, his nose in a pile of papers.

"Houston leave?" Edan asked absently. When Kane didn't answer, the blond man looked up to see Kane, with shaking hands, pour himself a water glass half full of whiskey.

"What have you done to her?" Edan asked, barely concealed anger in his voice. "I told you she wasn't like other women."

"What the hell do you know about her? And you should damn well ask what she's done to me. I want you to hitch up her buggy and take her home."

"What happened?"

"Women!" Kane said in disgust. "They never act the way they're supposed to. There's only one reason why I ever wanted to marry a lady and—."

"Fenton again," Edan said tiredly.

"You're damned right, Fenton!" Kane half shouted. "Everything I've ever done, all I've ever worked for, I've done in order to repay Fenton for what he did to me. All those years of work, the years I spent scrapin', I had one dream and that was that someday he'd come to dinner at my house. *My* house would be four times the size of his and sittin' at the foot of the table would be my wife, the woman he once denied me, his precious daughter Pamela."

"But you've had to make do with another woman," Edan said. "Isn't Houston to your liking?"

Kane took a deep drink of his whiskey. "She puts on a damn good act," he said. "She must want my money *real* bad."

"And what if she's not after your money? What if she wants a husband, children?"

Kane shrugged. "She can get 'em later. All I want is to show up Fenton. I want to sit in my own dinin' room with one of those Chandlers there as my wife."

"And what do you plan to do with Houston after this dinner? She's not a pair of shoes that you can throw away."

"I'm buyin' her some jewelry. She can keep it and, if I can't find a buyer, I'll give her this house."

"Just like that?" Edan asked. "You're going to tell her to go away, that you're through with her?"

"She'll be glad to get rid of me." He finished the whiskey. "And I don't have time for a woman in my life. Take her home, will you?" With that, he left the room.

Chapter 10

Houston cried herself to sleep that night. Her confusion was what made her so miserable. Most of her life she'd lived under the rule of her stepfather, and Duncan Gates had rigid ideas of what a lady should and should not do. Houston had always tried to live up to his ideas. Any time she'd broken rules she'd done so in secret.

With Leander, she'd conducted herself with absolute restraint. He needed a lady for a wife and Houston had become that lady. In public and in private, she'd been a lady. Her conduct was always perfect.

Yet Leander had actually wanted someone who was far and away from being a lady. The words he'd said about how wonderful Blair was were burned on her heart.

And then Kane came along, so different from Lee, with none of Lee's polish, none of Lee's sense of self-worth. But Kane'd wanted a lady, and when she wasn't one . . .

She'd never forget the look of disgust on his face after she'd rolled about on the floor with him.

How could she please a man? She'd thought Lee wanted a lady, but he hadn't. She had thought she'd learned from that experience that what men really wanted was a woman of passion. But Kane didn't. He wanted a lady.

The more she thought, the more she cried.

Later in the day, when Blair came to Houston's room, she saw her sister's red, swollen eyes and slipped into bed with her. For a while they didn't speak, but Houston began crying again.

"Is your life so awful?" Blair asked.

Sniffling, Houston nodded against Blair's shoulder.

"Taggert?" Blair asked.

Again Houston nodded. "I don't know what he wants from me."

"Anything he can get, most likely," Blair said. "You don't have to marry him. No one's forcing you to. If you'd make it clear that you want Leander, I think you could get him back."

"Leander wants you," Houston said, sitting up.

"He only wants me because I gave him what you wouldn't," Blair said. "Houston, you love Leander. Heaven only knows why, but you do, you have for years. Think what marriage to him would mean. You could live in the house he built for you, have your children and——."

"No," Houston said, taking a handkerchief from a bedside drawer. "Leander belongs to you in a way he never belonged to me. He'd much rather have you."

"No, he wouldn't! You don't know what you're saying. He doesn't like me at all. This morning at the hospital he said I was a puppet-doctor, that I did more harm than good and——." She buried her face in her hands.

"Maybe he doesn't like your doctoring but he *loves* your kisses," Houston said angrily. "Oh, Blair, I am sorry. I'm just tired and upset. Perhaps it's nerves before the wedding."

"What did Taggert do to you?"

"Nothing," Houston said, hiding her face in the handkerchief. "He's always been more than honest with me. I think perhaps I lie to myself."

"And what is that supposed to mean?"

"I don't know. I have work to do," she said as she got out of the bed. "There's so much to do to get ready for the wedding."

"You're still going to marry him?" Blair asked softly.

"If he'll have me," Houston whispered, her back to her sister. After last night, Houston thought, he may have changed his mind, and the prospect of life without Kane's moods—as well as his kisses—made a barren-looking future. She pictured herself sitting quietly in a rocker with her crochet hook.

"Do you want to help me with the wedding arrangements?" Houston asked, turning back to her sister. "Or would you rather leave everything to me?"

"I don't want to even think of marriage, not mine to Leander, and especially not yours to Taggert. Lee's just angry about what happened and I'm sure that if you—."

"Leander and I are dead to each other!" Houston snapped. "Can't I make you see that? Lee wants you, not me. It's Kane . . ." She turned away. "I'm going to marry Mr. Taggert in ten days."

Blair jumped out of the bed. "You may think that you failed with Leander, but you didn't. And you don't have to punish yourself with that overbearing oaf. He can't even handle a plate of food, much less—."

Blair stopped because Houston slapped her across the face.

"He's the man I'm going to marry," Houston said, anger in her words. "I'll not let you or anyone else denigrate him."

With her hand to her cheek, Blair's eyes filled with tears. "What I've done is coming between us," she whispered. "No man anywhere means more than sisters," she said before leaving the room.

For a moment, Houston sat on the bed. She wanted to comfort Blair but didn't know how. What was Kane doing to her that would make her slap her own sister?

And the next question was, did Kane still want to marry her?

With shaking hands, she sat down at her desk and wrote a note to her fiancé.

Dear Mr. Taggert,
    My behavior last night was unforgivable. I'd understand if you'd like the return of your ring.
                         Sincerely,
                         Miss Houston Chandler

She sealed the letter and had Susan give it to Willie to deliver.

When Kane received the letter, he snorted

"Bad news?" Edan asked.

Kane started to hand the letter to Edan but, instead, slipped it into his pocket. "It's from Houston. You know, I don't think I ever met anybody quite like her. Weren't you goin' into town later?"

Edan nodded.

"Stop by one of the jewelry stores and buy a dozen rings, all different colors, and send them over to Houston's house."

"Any message?"

Kane smiled. "No, the rings oughta be enough. Now, where were we?"

At four o'clock, Mr. Weatherly, of Weatherly's Jewels and Coronation Gifts, came rushing up the steps of the Chandler house.

"I have a package for Miss Houston," he said excitedly to Susan, who answered the door.

Susan led him into the parlor where Opal and a subdued Houston sat, surrounded by lists of wedding preparations.

"Good afternoon, Mr. Weatherly," Opal said. "Could I get you some tea?"

"No, thank you," he said, looking at Houston, lights dancing in his eyes. "This is for you." He thrust a large, thin black velvet box at her.

Puzzled, but with a glimmer of hope blossoming within her, Houston took the box. All day had been miserable as she tried to plan a wedding that might not happen. And to make things worse, at noon, Mr. Gates had come home for dinner and privately informed her that he'd made an appointment for her to meet with Marc Fenton tomorrow morning. He was holding her to her promise to ask questions about Kane.

When Houston opened the box and saw the rings, she had to blink back tears of relief. "How pretty," she said with outward calm as she looked at each one: two emeralds, a pearl, a sapphire, a ruby, three diamond rings, an amethyst, one ring with three opals, a ring of carved coral and one of jade.

"Could have knocked me over with a feather," Mr. Weatherly was saying. "That blond fella that follows Mr. Taggert around came in an hour ago and asked for a dozen rings, and they were all for Miss Houston."

"Mr. Taggert didn't choose them himself?" Houston asked.

"It was his idea; the blond man said so."

Very calmly, Houston stood, the closed box of rings in her

hand. "Thank you so much, Mr. Weatherly, for coming personally with the rings. Perhaps you'd like to see them, Mother," she said, handing the box to Opal. "I'm sure they need to be sized. Good day, Mr. Weatherly."

As Houston went upstairs to her room, her heart lightened. The rings themselves didn't matter, but he'd read her note and he meant to marry her. That was what was important. Of course, he hadn't asked to see her but soon they'd be married and he'd see her every day.

Upstairs, she began to dress for dinner.

Houston smiled at Marc Fenton, who sat across from her in Miss Emily's quiet, pink and white Tea Shop. Opal had taken a seat not far away, but she tried to leave them their privacy. Mr. Gates had insisted that Opal accompany Houston because he said he had no more faith in the morals of young Americans.

Marc was a good-looking man, short, stocky, blond, with wide-set blue eyes and an infectious grin.

"I hear you've made the catch of the season, Houston," Marc was saying, as he took another raisin tart onto his plate. "Everyone's whispering about how he's half barbarian and half knight-on-a-white-horse. Which one is the real Kane Taggert?" he asked, eyes twinkling.

"I thought perhaps you could tell me. Mr. Taggert used to work for you."

"He left when I was seven years old! I barely remember the man."

"But what do you remember?"

"He used to scare me to death," Marc laughed. "He ran that stable like his own private domain and nobody, including my father, trespassed."

"Even your sister, Pamela?" Houston asked, as she idly toyed with her teacup.

"So that's what you want to know about." He laughed again. "I knew nothing of what was going on. One day, both Taggert and my sister were gone. You know, to this day, I still get a little nervous when I take a horse and don't ask permission."

"Why did your sister leave?" Houston persisted.

"Father married her off immediately. I don't think he

wanted to take any more chances on his daughter falling in love with another stableboy."

"Where is Pam now?"

"I rarely see her. She moved to Cleveland with her husband, had a kid, and stayed there. He died a few months ago and her kid was very sick for a long time. She's had it rough in the last year."

"Is she—?"

Marc leaned forward in conspiracy. "If you want to know more about the man you're planning to marry, you ought to talk to Lavinia LaRue."

"I don't believe I know her."

Marc leaned back with a smile. "Of course you don't. She's Taggert's light skirt."

"His . . . ?"

"His mistress, Houston. I have to go now," he said, rising, leaving money on the table.

Houston also rose, put her hand on his arm. "Where do I find Miss Larule?"

"LaRue, Lavinia LaRue, and ask down on Crescent Street."

"Crescent Street?" Houston's eyes widened. "I've never been there."

"Send Willie. He knows his way around there. Meet her somewhere private. You don't want to be seen with the Lavinia LaRues of this world. Good luck on your wedding, Houston," he said over his shoulder as he left.

"Did you find out what you wanted?" Opal asked her daughter.

"I think I found out much more than I wanted to know."

Houston spent the rest of Friday and all day Saturday making arrangements for the double wedding, ordering flowers, planning for food to be cooked and served.

"You haven't seen Kane in how many days, dear?" Opal asked.

"A matter of hours," Houston answered, not letting her mother see her face. She was not going to throw herself at Kane again. She'd made a fool of herself already and she didn't need to do it again.

On Saturday, there were other matters to consider. Mr. Gates started yelling at five in the morning, waking everyone to announce that Blair had been out all night. Opal reassured him that Blair had been out with Lee, but that made Mr. Gates worse. He shouted that Blair would have no reputation left, and that Lee would have to marry her today.

Between Houston and Opal, they managed to get him to settle down enough to eat breakfast and it was while they were eating that Blair and Leander walked into the room.

And what a sight they were! Blair was wearing an odd garment of navy blue, the skirt barely to her ankles. Her hair was down about her shoulders and all of her was covered with mud, cockleburs, and what looked to be dried blood. Lee was as bad, wearing only a shirt and trousers, holes in his pants and his sleeve.

"Lee," Opal said breathlessly. "Are those bullet holes?"

"Probably," he said, grinning good-naturedly. "You can see that I brought her back safe and sound. I need to go home and get some sleep. I'm on duty this afternoon." He turned to Blair, caressed her cheek for a moment. "Good night, doctor."

"Good night, doctor," she said, and he was gone.

For a moment no one could move, as they all stared at the bedraggled figure of Blair. For all her appearance of looking as if she'd been through three catastrophes, there was a light in her eyes that was close to fire.

Houston rose from the table and, as she got closer to her sister, she could smell her.

"Whatever is in your hair?"

Blair grinned idiotically. "Horse manure I would imagine. But at least it's in my hair and not on his chin."

Houston could hear Mr. Gates starting to move behind her. She grabbed Blair's arm firmly. "Upstairs!" she ordered.

Houston led Blair to the bathroom, turned on the tub taps and began undressing her sister. "Wherever did you get this extraordinary suit?"

Once Blair started talking, she didn't seem able to stop. Houston unbuttoned her, unlaced a shoe while Blair got the other one, shampooed her sister's hair while Blair scoured the dirt off her skin—and all the while, Blair talked about what a wonderful day she'd had with Leander, telling the most horrifying stories about maggots, range wars, cut arteries and a wrestle with a woman. And in every story, Leander was there, saving one life after another, and at one point, even saving Blair's life.

Houston could barely believe that the Leander Blair was raving about was the remote man she'd known for years. According to Blair, Leander was close to magic when it came to being a doctor.

"Fourteen holes in that man's intestines! And Lee sewed them all," she said, as Houston rinsed her hair, then shampooed it again. "Fourteen."

And the more Blair talked, the worse Houston felt. Leander had never once looked at her as he'd looked at Blair this morning, nor had he taken her with him on his calls—not that she wanted to see the inner workings of a man's digestive system, but the sharing was what she wanted.

Blair had Leander, and after only a few days, he was hers in a way Houston had never had him. And now she didn't seem to have Kane either. Should she go to him? Eventually they'd have to see one another to talk about the wedding. Houston imagined showing up at his house. No doubt he'd say, "I knew you'd give in. You couldn't stay away too long."

All day Saturday, while Blair slept, she hoped Kane would visit her, but he didn't.

On Sunday morning, she dressed in a skirt of gray serge, a dark green blouse of plissé surah and a gray Figaro jacket, and went downstairs to join her family for church services.

When everyone was seated in the church and hymnals were open, a quiet settled on the people.

"Move over," Kane said to Houston.

Startled, she moved down so he could sit beside her. Throughout the service, he sat still, looking up at the Reverend Thomas with a bored expression. The instant the service was over, he caught Houston's arm. "I wanta talk to you."

He half pulled her from the church, oblivious to people's attempts to socialize with them, and lifted her to the seat of his old wagon. Once seated himself, he flicked the reins to the four horses and set off so quickly Houston had to hold her hat on.

"All right," he said when he'd stopped abruptly on the south edge of town under some cottonwood trees near the waterworks plant, "what were you doin' with Marc Fenton?"

No matter how Houston remembered Kane, he was, in life, more than she imagined.

"I have known Marc all my life," she said coolly, "and I may see any friend I care to. Besides, my mother was with me."

"You think I don't know that? At least your mother's a sensible woman."

"I have no idea what you mean." She began to toy with her parasol.

"What were you doin' with Marc Fenton?" He leaned toward her in a threatening way.

Houston decided to tell him the truth. "My stepfather has made me promise to ask as many people as possible about you. Mr. Gates arranged for me to meet Marc so I could ask him about you. I would have talked to Mr. Fenton, but he refused the request." She glared at him. "And I will probably speak to a Miss Lavinia LaRue."

"Viney?" he asked, then grinned. "Gates gave you this advice? Not bad. I wonder how come he never made any money? Wait a minute, what if you ask somebody and he—or she—says I'm no good?"

"Then I'll have to reconsider our marriage," she said primly.

She wasn't prepared for his explosion of anger.

"We're supposed to be married one week from tomorrow, yet you just might call it off at any minute!? Because somebody says he don't like the cut of my shirt? I'll tell you somethin', *Miss* Chandler, you can ask ever' man I ever dealt with and ever' woman I ever slept with about me and, if they're honest, you're gonna find I ain't cheated a man in my life."

He got out of the wagon and walked under a tree, looking at the distant horizon.

"Damnation, but Edan told me a lady'd cause me nothin' but trouble. He said, 'Kane, marry some farm girl, move to the country and raise horses.' He told me not to get mixed up with no lady."

Houston managed to climb down from the tall wagon by herself. "I didn't mean to upset you so badly," she said quietly.

"Upset me!" he bellowed into her face. "I ain't had any

101

peace since I met you. I'm rich, I ain't bad to look at, I offer you marriage and you turn me down flat. I don't hear nothin' from you, then I find out your sister's gonna marry the man *you're* so crazy in love with. But, still, you won't marry me. Then maybe you will. Then maybe you won't.

"For days you're at my house bossin' ever'body around, includin' me, and then you act like we got a bad case of measles and you don't come near the place. One mornin' I wake up and you're lookin' at me like you're starvin' and when I touch you, you break a water pitcher over my head and yell at me that I gotta respect you. But the next time I touch you, you pull me down on the floor and nearly tear my clothes off. But I respect you and I leave you a damn virgin, just like you wanted. But what do I get? Next thing I know, you're wonderin' if I want my ring back, an' it's back to maybe you ain't gonna marry me.

"This mornin' your mother come to me, told me the right suit to wear to church," he gave her a look of reproach, "and invited me to Sunday dinner."

He stopped and glared at her. "So here I am, all dressed up, with you tellin' me maybe you'll marry me, maybe you won't, and it all depends on what people say about me. Houston, I've had all this I'm gonna take. Right now you're gonna give me a yes or no and you're gonna stick to it. If you say yes now and no the day of the weddin', so help me, Houston, I'll drag you down the aisle by your hair. Now, what you got to say?"

"Yes," she said softly, and the amount of joy inside her was amazing.

"And what if somebody tells you I'm worthless? Or that I've killed people?" he asked with some hostility.

"I will still marry you."

He turned away. "You dreadin' it so much? I mean, I know you wanted to marry Westfield, and I ain't exactly been a gentleman all the time in our courtin', but so far you've done your part of the bargain. In public, you've always acted like you didn't mind marryin' me."

Houston's relief that he hadn't been repulsed by her was so great she began trembling. She wasn't going to spend her life crocheting but was going to live with this man who was unlike anyone else.

She moved to stand in front of him. "After Sunday dinner, most young couples go to Fenton Park to walk and talk and just spend time together. Perhaps you'd like to go with me."

"I need to . . . ," he began. "If you still want to be seen with me after dinner with your family, I'm willin'."

She slipped her arm through his. "Just watch me, don't talk with your mouth full, don't shout at anyone, and above all, don't curse."

"You don't ask much, do you?" he said grimly.

"Pretend that the purchase of Mr. Vanderbilt's apartment building depends on this dinner. Maybe that will help you remember your manners."

Kane looked startled. "That reminds me. I need to—." He glanced down at her. "You know, I think I'd rather spend the afternoon sittin' in the park. It's been a long time since I took a whole day off."

Kane seemed to enjoy himself immensely at Sunday dinner. Opal fawned over him, and Duncan asked his advice. Houston watched them. They'd expected a monster and found a pleasant man.

Blair had been silent through the meal, and Houston was glad she was meeting Kane at last and could see what a generous man he was. Kane even offered to allow Mr. Gates to buy some land with him, at what Houston suspected was a bargain price.

As they were leaving, Kane said, "Your sister ain't like you at all."

Houston asked him what he meant but he wouldn't explain.

At the park, she introduced Kane to other engaged couples. For once, Kane relaxed rather than worrying about the amount of work he was missing. When a woman referred to Kane's previous mishap of dumping the food in Houston's lap, Kane stiffened, but then, when she sighed at his romantic gesture of carrying Houston, Kane ostentatiously denied that he'd done anything extraordinary.

An ice-cream parlor across from the park was open for a few hours on Sunday and Kane treated everyone to sodas and Hire's root beer.

At the end of the day, Houston returned home with stars in her eyes. She'd had no idea he could be so charming.

"I never had time to do this kind of thing before. I always

thought it was a waste of time, but it's nice. You think I did all right with your friends? I didn't act too much like a stable-boy?"

"Not in the least."

"Can you ride a horse?"

"Yes," she said, hope in her voice.

"I'll pick you up in the mornin' and we'll ride. Like that?"

"Very much."

Without another word, Kane put his hands in his pockets and went down the walk of the Chandler house whistling.

Chapter 11

Kane showed up on Monday morning at five o'clock, before anyone was out of bed. As soon as Houston heard the movement downstairs, she knew it could be only one person. No one ever dressed faster in a riding habit in her life.

"You took long enough," Kane said, as he led the way to two horses loaded with heavy saddlebags.

"Food," was all Kane said before mounting.

It was a good thing she'd been telling the truth when she said she could ride, she thought, hours later, as she followed Kane's horse up the side of a mountain.

They rode west, past the Taggert estate, toward the tail of the Rocky Mountains that ran along one side of Chandler. They travelled across flat land covered with fierce little chamisa plants and on until they reached the hills.

Kane led the way up the piñon-dotted hills, up higher until they reached pines and rock formations. He weaved his horse through the spruce and fir to halt before a breathtaking view of Chandler far below them.

"How did you find this place?" she whispered.

"When you play, you ride bicycles and drink tea with other people. I come up here." As he dismounted, he nodded his head toward a steep rise above them. "I gotta cabin up there, but it's pretty rough goin', not for ladies."

He began unloading food from his saddlebags as Houston dismounted by herself.

As they ate, they sat on the ground and talked.

"How did you make your money?" she asked.

"When Fenton kicked me out, I went to California. Pam had given me $500 and I used it to buy a played-out gold mine. I was able to hack out a couple thousand dollars' worth of the gold, and I used the money to buy land in San Francisco. Two days after I bought the land I sold it for half again what I paid for it. I bought more land, sold it, bought a nail factory, sold it, bought a little railroad line . . . You get the idea."

"Did you know that Pamela Fenton is a widow now?" Houston asked as if she weren't interested in his answer.

"Since when?"

"I believe her husband died a few months ago."

Kane stared at Houston for several long minutes, as if seeing her for the first time. "It's funny how things work out, ain't it?"

"How do you mean?"

"If I hadn't asked you to my house, your sister wouldn't have gone out with Westfield and you'd be marryin' him now."

She drew in her breath. "And if you'd known Pamela was free, you'd not have asked me to your house. Mr. Taggert, you're free to break our engagement at any time. If you'd rather have—."

"You ain't gonna start that again, are you?" he said, rising. "Why don't you try sayin' somethin' different sometime?"

Relief flooded Houston as she stood. "I just thought perhaps—."

Kane turned and grabbed her against him. "Damned woman, please shut up," he said as he kissed her.

Houston obeyed.

Early on Tuesday, Willie informed Houston that Miss Lavinia LaRue would meet her by the bandstand in Fenton Park at nine that morning.

Houston was met by a garishly dressed woman, short, dark, with an enormous bosom. Wonder how much is paddin', Houston thought.

"Good morning, Miss LaRue. It was good of you to meet me so early."

"It's late for me. I ain't been to bed yet. So you're the one

Kane's marryin'. I told 'im he could buy hisself a lady if he wanted one."

Houston gave her an icy look.

"Oh, all right," Lavinia said. "You didn't expect me to hug you, did you? After all, you are takin' away a source of income to me."

"Is that all Mr. Taggert is to you?"

"He's a good lover, if that's what you mean but, truth to tell, he scares me. I never know what he wants from me. Acts like he can't bear me one minute, the next he can't get enough."

Houston knew she'd felt the same way but said nothing.

"What'd you wanta see me about?"

"I thought perhaps you could tell me something about him. I've really known him a very short time."

"You mean what he likes in bed?"

"No! Certainly not." She didn't like to think of Kane and another woman. "As a man. What can you tell me about the man?"

Lavinia stepped away, her back to Houston. "You know, one time I did think of somethin', but I know it was silly."

"And what was that?"

"Most of the time he acts like he don't care, but one time he saw that friend of his, Edan, out the window walkin' with a woman, and Kane asked if I liked him. If I liked him, Kane, I mean. He didn't wait for me to answer 'fore he left, but I thought then, he's a man no one's ever loved. 'Course that couldn't be true, a man with all his money must have lots of women in love with him."

"Do you love him? Not his money, but him. If he had no money—."

"If he had no money, I'd not get near 'im. I told you, he scares me."

Out of her pocketbook, Houston pulled a check. "The bank president has instructions to cash this only if he sees that you've purchased a train ticket to another state."

Lavinia took the check. "I'm takin' this because I wanta leave this two-bit town. But no money could buy me if I didn't wanta leave."

"Of course not. Again, Miss LaRue, thank you."

* * *

On Tuesday afternoon, just when Houston was getting tired of yet more wedding plans, Leora Vaughn and her fiancé, Jim Michaelson, stopped by the Chandler house on a tandem bicycle. They asked if Houston could possibly persuade Kane to rent another double bike and ride in the park with them.

After Houston had changed, borrowing Blair's Turkish pants, she rode on the handlebars up the hill to Kane's house.

"Goddamn Gould!" They could hear Kane's shouts through the open window.

"I'll ask him," Houston said.

"Do you think he'd mind if we waited inside?" Leora asked, her eyes greedily roaming over the front of Kane's house.

"I think he'd be pleased."

Houston never knew how Kane was going to greet her, but this time he seemed glad of the diversion. He was a little hesitant about the bicycle, since he'd never ridden one before, but he mastered it in minutes—then began challenging the other men in the park to races.

By late afternoon, when they returned the rented bicycles, Kane was saying he was going to buy a bicycle manufacturing plant. "Maybe I'll not make any money off it," he said, "but sometimes I like to gamble. Like recently I bought stock in a company that makes a drink called Coca-Cola. I'll probably lose ever'thing." He shrugged. "You can't always win."

In the evening they went to a taffy pull at Sarah Oakley's house.

Kane was the oldest person in the group, but all the games and diversions were new to him, and he seemed to have the most fun. He always seemed a little shocked that these young society people accepted him.

And it wasn't because he was easy to accept. He was outspoken, intolerant of any ideas he didn't agree with, and always aggressive. He told Jim Michaelson he was a fool to be content to run his father's store, that he should expand, get some business down from Denver if he insisted on staying in Chandler. He told Sarah Oakley she ought to get Houston to help her buy dresses because the ones she wore weren't as pretty as they should be. He got taffy on Mrs. Oakley's draperies and the next day had delivered to her fifty yards of silk velvet from Denver. He bent a wheel of a rented bicycle, then yelled for twenty minutes at the owner for having inferior merchandise. He told Cordelia Farrell she could get a better man than John Silverman, and that all John wanted was somebody to take care of his three motherless children.

Houston prayed for the floor to open up and swallow her when Kane invited everyone to his house for dinner on Wednesday night. "I ain't got any furniture downstairs," he said, "so we'll do it like Houston done for me one night—a rug, pillows to lay down on, candles, everything."

When three women dissolved into giggles at the look of pain and disbelief on Houston's red face, Kane said, "Did I miss somethin'?"

And Houston soon learned that everything connected with Kane involved an argument. He called it "discussin'" but it was more a verbal wrestle. On Tuesday evening, she asked him to sign some blank cards, beside her signature, which would be included in the little boxes of cake to be given away at the wedding.

"Like hell I will!" he said. "I ain't puttin' my name on somethin' blank. Somebody could write whatever they like above it."

"It's tradition," Houston said, "everyone puts autographed cards in the boxes of cake that people take home."

"They can eat cake at the weddin'. They don't need little boxes of it. It'll melt anyway."

"It's to dream on, to make wishes on, to—."

"You want me to sign blank cards for a dumb idea like that?"

Houston lost that bout, but she won about hiring men to help the ladies from their carriages and women to turn Kane's small drawing room into a cloakroom.

"How many people you plannin' on havin', anyway?"

She looked at her list. "At last count, 520. Most of Leander's relatives are travelling in from the East. Is there someone special you wanted to invite besides your uncles and cousins, the Taggerts?"

"My *what?*"

They were off again, and again Houston won. Kane said he'd never met his relatives and had no desire to meet them. Houston, who couldn't tell him she knew Jean, or he'd no doubt ask how, said she was inviting them whether he knew them or not. For some reason, Kane didn't want them there and, after several minutes of arguing, he said they'd show up in coal miner's clothes.

Houston called him a snob. She thought she might die rather than tell him she'd already arranged for clothes to be made for his relatives—at his expense.

Before Kane could reply, Opal walked into the room, bade them good evening and sat down with her embroidery.

Kane appealed to Opal, who said, "Well then, you shall have to buy them new clothes, won't you?"

By the time Kane left, Houston felt as if she'd survived a storm at sea, but Kane seemed unperturbed. He kissed her in the hallway and said he'd see her tomorrow.

"Will everything always be an argument?" she whispered, sitting down heavily beside her mother.

"I should think it will be," Opal said cheerfully. "Why don't you take a long, hot bath?"

"I need a three-day-long one," Houston muttered, rising.

Kane stood before the tall windows in his office, a cigar clamped between his teeth.

"Are you planning to work or daydream?" Edan asked from behind him.

Kane didn't turn around. "They're all just kids," he said.

"Who are?"

"Houston and all her friends. They've never had to grow up, to worry about where their next meal's comin' from. Houston thinks food comes out of the kitchen, clothes from her dressmaker's and money from the bank."

"I'm not sure you're right. Houston seems pretty sensible to me, and I think her being jilted by Westfield made her grow up some. Those things mean a lot to a woman."

Kane turned back to face his friend. "She's consoled herself well enough," he said, his gesture encompassing the house.

"I'm not so sure she's after just your money," Edan said thoughtfully.

Kane snorted. "No doubt it's the delicate way I handle a teacup. I want you to watch her."

"You mean spy on her?"

"She's engaged to a man with money. I'd hate to have her kidnapped."

Edan raised an eyebrow. "Is that it, or are you worried she might be seeing Fenton again?"

"She spends most of every Wednesday inside that church of hers, and I want to know what she's doin'."

"So it's the handsome Reverend Thomas you're worried about."

"I'm damn well not worried about anybody!" Kane shouted. "Just do what I say and watch her."

With a look of disgust, Edan stood. "I wonder if Houston has any idea what she's getting herself into."

Kane turned back to the window. "A woman'll do a lot to get her hands on millions."

Edan didn't respond before he left the room.

Houston, dressed in the hot, padded suit of Sadie, handled her team of horses with ease as she made her way to the Little Pamela mine. She'd discussed it with Reverend Thomas and decided it was all right to talk to Jean about the forthcoming wedding. Houston still liked to think Jean was safe in her ignorance of Sadie's identity, but Reverend Thomas had, in a patronizing way, again told Houston the secrecy was long gone.

Now, as Houston travelled to the mine, she began to feel an almost overwhelming urge to talk to Jean. Jean always seemed so quiet and sensible, and even though she'd never met Kane, she was his cousin.

Houston got through the guarded gate with no trouble or challenge and went straight to the Taggert house.

Jean was waiting for her. "No problems?" she asked, then stopped and stared at Houston. "I'm glad you finally know," she said softly.

"Let's get the food distributed and we can talk," Houston said.

Hours later they were back at Jean's little house. Houston pulled a packet of tea from her pocket. "For you."

They were silent as Jean prepared the tea, then when they were both seated, Jean spoke. "So, we're to be related by marriage."

Houston held the chipped mug in her hands. "In five days. You will be there, won't you?"

"Of course. I'll pull my Cinderella gown from the closet and come in my glass coach."

"You needn't worry about any of that. I made all the necessary arrangements. Jacob Fenton has given permission for any Taggert to be allowed to come and go. My dressmaker is waiting and Mr. Bagly, the tailor, has been given instructions. All you have to do is bring your father, Rafe and Ian."

"That's all, is it?" Jean asked, smiling. "My father will be no problem, but Rafe is another matter. And unfortunately, Ian is just like his uncle."

With a sigh, Houston looked down at her mug. "Let me guess. First of all, you have no way of knowing whether Rafe will like the idea of attending the wedding or not because he is completely unpredictable. He could laugh and be happy to go, or he could possibly shout and refuse to attend."

For a moment, Jean gaped. "Don't tell me Kane is a *real* Taggert."

Houston stood and walked to gaze sightlessly out the single window, not speaking for several long minutes.

"Why are you marrying him?" Jean asked.

"I really don't know," she answered, pausing again. "Leander and I were the perfect couple," she said softly, almost as if in a dream. "In all the years we were engaged, in essence, since we were both children, I don't think we ever once disagreed. We had some . . . problems as we grew up," she thought of Lee's anger when she'd refused to let him make love to her, "but nearly always we agreed. If I wanted green curtains, Leander wanted green curtains. There was almost always perfect harmony between us."

She looked at Jean. "And then I met Mr. Taggert. I don't think he and I've yet had a harmonious conversation. I find myself yelling at him as if I were a fishwife. The day after I agreed to marry him I broke a water pitcher over his head. One minute I'll be furious with him, and the next I want to put my arms around him and protect him, then the next minute I find I want to lose myself in his strength."

She sat down, her face in her hands. "I am so confused. I don't know what anything means anymore. I loved Leander for so long, was so sure of my love for him, but right now I know that if I were offered a choice, I'd keep Kane."

She looked up. "But why? Why would I want to live with a man who makes me furious, who makes me feel like a street woman, who runs after me like a satyr, then pushes me away and says 'there'll be more of that later, honey' as if I'd been the forward one? Some of the time he ignores me, some of the time he leers at me. Sometimes he charms me. He has no respect for me; he treats me as if I were a backward child one minute, and the next he hands me unspeakable amounts of money and tells me to accomplish the work of ten people."

Houston stood quickly. "I think I must be insane. No woman in her right mind would go into a marriage like this. Not with her eyes open. I could see being so in love with a man that you'd not see his faults. But I see Kane Taggert as he really is: a man of towering vanity, a man of no vanity. Whatever you can say about him, there is a contradiction."

She sat down again, heavily. "I *am* insane. Completely, thoroughly insane."

"Are you sure?" Jean asked quietly.

"Oh, yes, I'm sure," Houston answered. "No other woman would—."

"No, I mean about being so in love with him you'd not be able to see his faults. I've always thought—or hoped—that if someone loved me they'd know all my bad points and still love me. I wouldn't want a man who thought I was a goddess, because when he found out that I have an awful temper, I'd be afraid he wouldn't love me anymore."

With a puzzled look, Houston gaped at Jean. "But loving someone means . . ."

"Yes? What *is* being in love with someone?"

Houston stood, looked out the window absently. "Wanting to be with a person. Wanting to stay with him through sickness and health, wanting to have his children, loving him even when he does something you don't like. Thinking he's the grandest, most noble prince in the world, laughing when he's said something that hurts you for the fifth time in one hour. Worrying whether he'll like what you're wearing, if he'll be proud of you, and feeling your insides melt when he does approve of you."

She stopped and was silent for several long moments.

"When I'm with him, I'm alive," she whispered. "I don't think I was ever alive until I met Kane. I was just existing, moving, eating, obeying. Kane makes me feel powerful, as if I could do anything. Kane . . ."

"Yes?" Jean asked softly. "What is Kane?"

"Kane Taggert is the man I love."

Jean burst out laughing. "Is it really such a catastrophe, being in love with one of us Taggerts?"

"The loving will be easy, but the living with might be somewhat difficult."

"You'll never be able to imagine half of it," Jean said, still laughing. "More tea?"

"Is all of your family like Kane?"

"My father takes after his mother's side of the family, I'm happy to say, but Uncle Rafe and Ian are true Taggerts. I thought this Kane, because he had money . . ."

"It probably makes him worse. Who is Ian's father? I don't remember meeting the boy."

"You haven't. He's worked in the mines for years now even though he's only sixteen. He looks like Rafe: big, handsome, angry. His father was Lyle, Rafe's brother. Lyle was killed in a mine explosion when he was twenty-three."

"And Kane's father . . . ?"

"Frank was the oldest brother. He was killed in an accident long before I was born and, I believe, even before Kane was born."

"I'm sorry," Houston said. "It must be hard for you to have to take care of so many men."

"I have help from charitable young ladies," she said, rising. "It'll be dark soon. You'd better go."

"Will you please come to my wedding? I'd very much like for you to be there and, besides, you'll see me in something a little cleaner." Houston grinned, showing off her blackened teeth.

"To tell you the truth, I somehow think I'll feel more comfortable around Sadie than the Society Princess, Miss Chandler."

"Don't say that!" Houston said seriously. "Please don't."

"All right. I'll do my best."

"And you'll go to my dressmaker's tomorrow? She needs all the time she can get to make the dress. Here's the address."

Jean took the card. "I'll look forward to it. And I'll do my best with Uncle Rafe and Ian. But I make no promises."

"I understand that from the bottom of my heart." On impulse, she clasped Jean to her. "I'll look forward to seeing you again."

On her way back to town, Houston mused on her talk with Jean. It made perfect sense that she was in love with Kane and, with the knowledge, she laughed aloud. All those years with Lee, and she'd never really been in love with him. She knew that now.

Of course, she couldn't tell anyone. It would make her seem like a woman whose love was given lightly. But it wasn't; she was sure of that. Kane Taggert was the man she loved and would always love.

She used the reins to urge the horses to move faster. She still had to wash and change her clothes. Then make arrangements for . . . A secret little smile shaped her lips as she thought of her plans for Friday night. She'd ask Leander to invite Kane and Edan to Lee's men's club and she'd ask Kane for the use of his house for a farewell dinner with her girlfriends. Just a quiet little get-together—like the one Ellie had before she got married.

Now, if Houston could only persuade that strongman she'd seen on the billboard on Coal Avenue to do what she wanted . . .

Houston was so busy musing on her plans that she didn't keep her usual vigil. Behind her, hidden by the trees, was a lone man on horseback.

Edan wore a frown as he followed her back into town.

Chapter 12

With only days left until the wedding, Houston found herself quickly running out of time. Kane's dinner on Wednesday was a great success.

"I broke my engagement to John today, Mr. Taggert," Cordelia Farrell said shyly.

"That's good news," Kane laughed as he grabbed her shoulders and kissed her heartily on the mouth. Cordelia was embarrassed but pleased. "You can do lots better 'n that ol' man."

"Thank you, Mr. Taggert."

For a moment, Kane looked puzzled. "How come ever'body calls me *Mr.* Taggert?"

"Because, Mr. Taggert," Houston said smoothly, "you've never asked *anyone* to call you Kane."

"All of you can call me Kane," he said quietly, but, looking at Houston, his eyes turned hot. "Except you, Houston. You've only called me Kane once and I liked it when you did."

Houston knew his meaning was clear to everyone and her throat went dry at the embarrassment of what he'd said.

Sarah Oakley picked up a pillow and threw it at Kane's head.

He caught it and everyone waited with breath held. Who could guess how Kane was going to react?

"Sometimes you're not a gentleman . . . Kane," Sarah said daringly.

But Kane grinned at her. "Gentleman or not, I see you took my advice and bought yourself a new dress. All right, Houston, you can call me Kane."

"At this moment, I much prefer Mr. Taggert," she said haughtily, and everyone laughed together.

All day Thursday was given over to preparing Kane's house for the wedding on Monday. Kane and Edan locked themselves in Kane's study and ignored the furniture movers, the deliveries, and the arrivals and departures of most of Chandler's tradesmen.

Friday and Saturday were more of the same, with Houston explaining and reexplaining their roles to all the people involved in the wedding. There were men and women to prepare and serve food, men to build tables for outside. There were the men who set up the enormous open-sided tents Houston'd had made in Denver. On Sunday, there were thirty-eight people doing nothing but arranging flowers.

Jean Taggert sent a message that Rafe was going to come but young Ian was balking, and could she bring a covered dish perhaps?

When Houston read the message, she was in the kitchen, and before her on the table were two butchered cow carcasses and 250 pounds of potatoes that had just been delivered. And under the cows were three enormous wheels of cheese and 300 oranges—and she was praying the oranges weren't on the bottom.

Through all the turmoil, Houston was pleased that Kane stayed out of her way and left her to her work. He complained that he was so far behind in his own work, from lollygagging about with her, that he'd never catch up.

Only once did he give her any trouble, and that was when Leander asked Edan and him to spend the evening at Lee's men's club.

"I ain't got time to do that!" Kane bellowed. "Don't those men ever work? Lord knows but I'll have little enough time after the weddin', what with a woman always underfoot and—." He stopped and looked at Houston. "Maybe I didn't quite mean it that way . . ." he began.

Houston just looked at him.

"All right," he finally said, with disgust in his voice. "But I don't see why you women can't have your little tea party at your house." He turned on his heel and went back to his office.

"Damned women!" he muttered.

"What horrible imposition has Houston placed on you now?" Edan asked, with a hint of a smile.

"We're to spend the evenin' at Westfield's fancy club. We're to leave here by seven and not to return before midnight. What happened to the good ol' days when women obeyed and respected their husbands?"

"The first woman disobeyed the first man; the good ol' days are a myth. What does Houston want to do tonight?"

"A fancy tea party for her lady friends. I want you to stay here and watch her."

"What?"

"I don't like all those women bein' here alone. Houston's hired servants to fill the house after the weddin', but tonight only a bunch of unprotected women will be here. She's set up the dinin' room for her little party and there's a door in there that's covered with cloth, you know, the one with the flowers painted on it, and—."

"You expect me to hide inside a closet and spy on a ladies' tea party?"

"It's for their own good, and I damn well pay you enough to do a little work for me."

"A little work—," Edan sputtered.

Hours later, Houston saw Edan and noticed a bruise on his right cheek.

"How did you hurt yourself?" she asked.

"I ran into a stone wall," he said tightly and walked away.

At six, the house began to clear of workers and at six forty-five Houston's friends began to arrive, each bearing a beautifully-wrapped gift.

Kane, still complaining about the injustice of having to leave his own house, climbed into the wagon beside a solemn Edan, and rode away.

Altogether, ten women plus Blair arrived at the Taggert house, and their gifts were placed on the eighteenth-century table in the dining room.

"Is everyone gone?" Tia asked.

"At last," Houston said, closing the double doors behind her. "Now, shall we get down to business?"

Edan sat inside the closet on an uncomfortable chair, a full bottle of whiskey in his hand. Damn Kane! he thought again and wondered if he could get away with murder. Any judge would surely let him off for killing a man who'd forced him to spend an entire evening watching a bunch of women drink tea.

Absently, he drank the whiskey and watched the women through the silk in the door panel. Miss Emily, a pretty, fragile, elderly lady, was banging her fist on the table.

"The third annual meeting of The Sisterhood will now come to order."

Edan held the bottle to his lips but didn't drink.

Miss Emily continued. "First, we'll hear a report from Houston on the coal camps."

Edan didn't move a muscle as Houston stood and delivered a detailed report on the injustices inside the coal camps. He'd followed her a few days before and knew of her innocent little forays to deliver fresh vegetables into the camps, but now Houston was talking of strikes and of unions. Edan'd seen men killed for less than what she was saying.

Nina Westfield began to talk of starting a magazine that the women would secretly deliver to the coal miners' wives.

Edan set the whiskey bottle on the floor and leaned forward.

There was mention of Jacob Fenton—fear of him and what he'd do if he found out about the women delivering information to the coal miners.

"I can talk to Jean Taggert," Houston said. "For some reason, Fenton seems afraid of all the Taggerts. They were given permission to attend the wedding."

"And Jean visits stores in Chandler," Miss Emily said. "I know your Kane," she said to Houston, "used to work for the Fentons, but something else is going on. I thought perhaps you might know."

"Nothing," Houston said. "Kane explodes at the mention of Fenton's name, and I don't think Marc knows anything."

"He wouldn't," said Leora Vaughn. "Marc only spends money; he's uninterested in where it comes from."

"I'll talk to Jean," Houston repeated. "Someone is stirring up a great deal of trouble. I don't want to see anyone hurt."

"Maybe I can get into the coal camps, too," Blair added. "I'll find out what I can."

"What other business is there?" Miss Emily asked.

Edan leaned back in his chair. "The Sisterhood," he breathed. These women, under the guise of lace dresses and gentle manners, were talking about wars.

The rest of the meeting was involved with various charities, of helping orphans and sick people—all the things ladies *should* do.

When the meeting was over, Edan picked up the whiskey and felt that at last he could breathe again.

"Refreshments?" Meredith Lechner asked, laughter in her voice, as she opened a large, yellow-wrapped box and pulled out a bottle of homemade wine. "Mother sent these in memory of a few meetings when she was a girl. Daddy will be told our wine cellar was robbed."

Edan didn't think he could have been further shocked, but his mouth fell open when each woman was handed a full bottle of wine and a long-stemmed glass from a wall cabinet.

"To the wedding night!" said Miss Emily, glass aloft. "To wedding nights everywhere, whether they're preceded by marriages or not."

With laughter, the women downed full glasses of wine.

"Mine first!" said Nina Westfield. "Mother and I had an awful time finding these in Denver. And then Lee almost looked in the box this afternoon."

Houston opened a blue box and withdrew a transparent black garment dripping with four-inch-wide black lace.

Edan saw that it was ladies' underwear, but not the kind for ladies.

In disbelief, he watched the women drink their bottles of wine and open presents amid shouts of laughter and boisterous comments. There were two pairs of high-heeled red shoes, more transparent underwear, and some pictures the women passed from one to another and nearly collapsed with laughter over. Chairs were discarded and the women began to dance about the room.

Miss Emily sat down at the piano that Edan hadn't noticed and started banging away.

Edan's chin hit his chest as he watched the women dance with skirts raised, legs kicking.

"It's the cancan," Nina said, out of breath. "Mother and I sneaked away from Daddy and Lee when we were in Paris and saw it."

"Can anyone try it?" Houston asked, and soon eight women were tossing their skirts over their heads to the tune of Miss Emily's playing.

"Rest!" Sarah Oakley called. "And I brought a bit of poetry to read to you."

When Edan was a boy, he and his friends had shared a copy of what the prim Miss Oakley was now reading from: *Fanny Hill.*

The women giggled and laughed as they slapped Blair and Houston on the back repeatedly.

When Sarah finished, Houston stood. "Now, my dear, dear friends, I have the pièce de résistance upstairs. Shall we go?"

Several minutes passed before Edan could move. So much for a ladies' tea party. With a jolt, he sat upright. What in the world could be upstairs? What could be more than what they'd already done? He knew that he'd as soon die as not find out what was going on.

As quickly as possible, he left the house, circled it, and saw light in the northeast corner sitting room. Ignoring thorns, he began to climb the rose trellis.

All that had happened before hadn't prepared him for what he now saw. The room was totally dark except for a large candelabra blazing with light, set behind a translucent silk screen. And between the screen and the light was a well-muscled man, scantily clad, moving his body into poses to show off his muscles.

"I've had enough of this," Miss Emily said and, with Nina on the other side, moved the screen away.

For a moment, the strongman looked bewildered, but the now-drunk women began clapping their hands and cheering, so he grinned and put more enthusiasm into his posing.

"Not nearly as big as my Kane," Houston shouted.

"I'll take him on," the strongman shouted back. "I can lick anybody."

"Not Kane," Houston said stubbornly, which made the man work harder at showing his biceps.

Edan slipped down the rose trellis to the ground. Kane'd wanted Edan to protect the ladies. Who was to protect the men from the ladies?

On Saturday morning, Kane slammed his office door for the fifth time in one hour. "Of all the days for Houston to be sick," he growled as he sat down. "You don't think she's gettin' afraid of tomorrow's weddin', do you?" he asked Edan.

"More likely something she ate—or drank," Edan answered. "I heard there were several young women of Chandler spending the day being 'indisposed'."

Kane didn't look up from his papers. "Probably just restin' for tomorrow."

"What about you?" Edan asked. "Any nerves?"

"Not a one. Real simple matter. People do it every day."

Edan leaned forward, took the paper Kane was looking at and turned it right side up.

"Thanks," Kane mumbled.

Chapter 13

The day of the wedding was so beautiful that it seemed to have been specially created for that momentous occasion. Opal woke the Chandler household at five o'clock and began the careful packing of the two wedding dresses and veils.

Houston heard her mother downstairs but she lay in bed for several minutes before she rose. She'd slept little during the night, mostly tossing and turning. Her mind was too alive with thoughts of the approaching day to sleep. She thought of Kane and prayed that in the years to come he'd learn to love her.

When Opal came to wake her, she was more than willing for the day to begin.

The three women were ready to leave for the Taggert house by ten o'clock. They travelled in Houston's carriage, with Willie behind them driving a borrowed wagon, the bed covered with muslin, the dresses concealed.

Waiting for them at the house were a dozen young women, all members of The Sisterhood.

"The tables are ready," Tia said.

"And the tents," Sarah added.

"And Mrs. Murchison has been cooking since four," Anne Seabury put in, as she took one end of the wrapped wedding dresses.

"And the flowers?" Houston asked. "Were they all put in place according to my plan?"

"I think so," one of the women said.

Miss Emily stepped forward. "Houston, you'd better look at them yourself. Someone will make sure that husband of yours stays in his office, and you can take a turn through the house."

"Husband," Houston murmured to herself as Nina ran ahead to hold Kane prisoner in his office. Everyone was going to try to insure that the bride wasn't seen before the wedding.

When she'd been assured that it was safe, Houston left her mother and Blair in the hall as she walked through each downstairs room and, for the first time, got to see the reality of the decorations that she'd planned.

The small drawing room was furnished with three long tables bearing gifts for the two brides from all over the United States. Kane had as much as said that he had no true friends in the moneyed world he dealt with in New York, but, if their gifts were any indication, it was obvious that those men considered him one of their own.

There was a little Italian inlaid table from the Vanderbilts, silver from the Goulds, gold from the Rockefellers. When the gifts had started arriving, Kane'd said that they damn well should send presents since he'd sure as hell sent enough to their kids every time they got married.

Other gifts came from Leander's relatives, and the people of Chandler had done their best to come up with the most ingenious "twin" gifts possible. There were twin brooms, twin barrels of popcorn, twin books, twin bolts of fabric. The gifts ranged from duplicate papers of dressmaker's pins to identical oak chairs from the Masons.

The room was decorated with tall potted palms set before mirrors, and the mantel dripped with red roses and purple pansies.

Houston moved to the large drawing room. This was where the close friends and relatives would mingle before and after the ceremony.

Along the baseboards, doorways, and the ceiling had been tacked the delicate twining smilax vine. Yard upon yard of the vines graced the room, weaving around the fireplace, around windows.

Set before each window were pots of ferns that filtered the morning sun and made lacy shadows on the floor. The hearth was draped with pink carnations, and entwined in the vines here and there were more carnations.

As quickly as possible, Houston finished her inspection tour of the rest of the downstairs and hurried upstairs where the others waited.

There were five hours before the ceremony, but Houston knew that there'd be a million and one last-minute details to take care of.

During the last few days, she'd spent a great deal of time downstairs, but the upstairs was still new to her. The eastern branch of the U-shaped house was guest quarters, and today Blair would be dressing in one of the suites. The center section contained Edan's rooms on one side of an aviary and hallway, and a nursery, bath, and nurse's room on the other side.

Next to the nursery was the long wing that belonged to Houston and Kane. He had a bedroom at the back, relatively small, but overlooking the gardens. Houston's room, separated from his by a marble bathroom, was by far the largest, with pale panelled walls that were set with carvings of swags and garlands to outline the paintings that had yet to be hung.

Next to her room was a large pink and white marble bath and a dressing area with walls covered in pink moiré, and beyond that a sitting room and private dining room for when she and Kane were dining alone.

"I shall never get used to this house," Tia said as she returned from an inspection of the rooms beyond the bedroom. "And look at this rooftop garden."

"Garden?" Houston asked, walking toward the double doors where Tia stood. She opened one and stepped outside into a lovely tangle of potted trees and flowers. Stone benches hid themselves amid the greenery. This had not been here the last time she saw the railed roof of the loggia that was outside her bedroom.

"Look at this," Sarah said, holding out a large white card that was attached to an enormous fig tree. Most of the plants were protected from the Colorado sun by an overhead lattice work that made a very pretty shade.

Houston took the card.

I hope you like it, I wish you all the best in your marriage.

Edan

"It's a gift from Edan," Houston said and felt that the garden was a symbol of her happiness today.

Before Houston could say another word, the door burst open and Mrs. Murchison entered as if a storm were behind her.

"There's too many people in my kitchen!" she yelled toward Houston. "I don't know how I'm supposed to cook with all of them in there. And Mr. Kane's got too much to do already, what with losin' a day's work as it is."

"Losing . . ." Meredith said, aghast. "Do you think Houston has nothing else to—?"

Houston cut her friend off. Mrs. Murchison was under Kane's spell and no doubt she'd defend the man to the death. "I'll go down the back stairs," Houston said, ignoring the fact that Sarah was unwrapping her wedding dress. It still needed pressing and there were last-minute stitches to be taken.

Once she was downstairs, there were more catastrophes to be seen to. Several times, she heard Kane shouting from within his office, and someone pushed Houston inside the scullery when Kane stormed past on his way outside to the gardens. She envied him his freedom, and at the same time wished she could be with him. Tomorrow, she thought. Tomorrow, they'd be able to walk together in the garden.

It was only two hours before the service when she finally made it back upstairs.

"Houston," Opal said, "I think you should begin dressing now."

Houston removed her clothing slowly, thinking that when she disrobed the next time . . .

"Who in the world is that woman?" Anne asked as Houston stepped into a chemise of cotton so fine that it was a mere whisper against her skin. The top had tiny, worked buttonholes that were inserted with pink silk ribbon, and the bottom was hand-embroidered with tiny rosebuds.

"I have no idea," Tia said, joining Anne to look over the

railing of the garden, "but she must be the tallest woman I've ever seen."

Sarah began tightening the laces on Houston's pink satin, hand-featherstitched corset. "I think I'm going to have to take a look," Sarah said. "Maybe she's one of Lee's relatives."

"I've seen her before but I have no idea where," Anne said. "How odd of her to wear black to a wedding."

"We have work to do," Opal said in a way that made Houston's head come up. "No one need interest herself in the private matters of any one of the guests."

Houston was quite sure that something was wrong. Ignoring her mother's stern look, she went to the edge of the rooftop garden where Tia stood. Instantly, she knew who the woman was. Even from upstairs, she looked tall and elegant.

"It's Pamela Fenton," Houston whispered, and turned back toward the bedroom.

For a moment, no one spoke.

"Probably wearing black in mourning," Sarah said, "because she lost him. Houston, which one of these petticoats do you want on first?"

Mechanically, Houston continued dressing, but her thoughts were on the fact that Kane was in the garden and the woman he once loved was walking toward him.

A knock on the door was answered by Anne. "It's the man who works with Kane," she told Houston. "He wants to see you, and he says it's urgent and he has to see you immediately."

"She couldn't possibly go . . ." Opal began, but her daughter had already snatched a dressing gown from a chair back and was on her way to the door.

Kane was standing at the far edge of his garden, looking out over the city of Chandler, smoking one of his cigars, one foot on a stone bench.

"Hello, Kane," Pamela said softly.

He waited a moment before turning to face her, and when he did look at her, his eyes were calm, not showing what he felt. He looked her up and down. "The years have treated you kindly."

"On the outside." She took a deep breath. "I don't have much time so I'll say what I came to say. I still love you; I've never stopped loving you. If you'll walk away with me now, I'll follow you to the ends of the earth."

Quickly, he took a step toward her but stopped and walked back. "No, I can't do that," he said quietly.

"You *can!* You know you can. What do you care about any of these people? What do you care about the people of Chandler? What do you care about . . . her?"

"No," he repeated.

She moved so they were standing close. He was a couple of inches taller than she, but with her heels they were equal. "Kane, please, don't make this mistake. Don't marry someone else. You know you love me. You know I—."

"You love me so much that you left me alone," he said angrily. "You married your rich lover and . . ." He stopped, turned away from her. "I *won't* leave with you today. I'll not hurt her like that. She doesn't deserve it."

Pam sat down on the bench. "You're going to cast me aside merely because you don't want to hurt Houston Chandler? She's young. She'll find someone else. Or is she in love with you?"

"I'm sure you know the gossip. She's still in love with Westfield, but she agreed to console herself with my money. Unfortunately, I go along with the money."

"Then why? Why do you feel obligated?"

He looked at her with blazing eyes. "Have you forgotten me so completely? *I* keep my bargains."

His meaning was clear. "I thought you would have found out by now," she said softly.

"You mean found out why you left me alone with $500 to pay me for services rendered? I made an effort not to find out."

"When I told my father that he had to allow us to marry because I was carrying your child, he had me forcibly put on a train to Ohio. Nelson Younger owed my father a great deal of money, and the debt was paid when he married me."

"I was told—," Kane began.

"I'm sure you were told that I'd run away rather than marry you. No doubt my father said a few words about his daughter dallying with the stable lad, but she'd certainly not marry him. You were always so easy to get to. That pride of yours was so easily wounded."

Kane was silent for a while. "And the child?"

"Zachary is thirteen now, a wonderful boy, handsome, strong, as full of pride as his father."

Kane stood quite still, looking out over the acres of garden.

"Leave with me now, Kane," Pam whispered. "If not for my sake, then for your son's."

"My son's," Kane said under his breath. "Tell me, was this man you married good to 'im?"

"Nelson was quite a bit older than me, and he was pleased to have a child whether Zach was his or not. He loved Zach." She smiled. "They used to play baseball together every Saturday afternoon."

Kane looked back at her. "And Zachary thinks of this man as his father?"

Pam stood. "Zach would learn to love you as I do. If you and I told him the truth . . ."

"The *truth* is that Nelson Younger was Zachary's father. All I did was plant the seed."

"Are you rejecting your own son?" Pam asked with anger.

"No, I'm not. You send the boy to me and I'll take 'im. Sight unseen. It's you, Pam, I'm rejectin'."

"Kane, I don't want to beg. If you don't love me now, you could learn to again."

He took both her hands in his. "Listen to me. What happened to us was a long time ago. I don't guess I knew until now how much I'd changed. If you'd been here a few months ago, I'd have run with you to the altar, but it's different now. Houston—."

She pulled away from him. "You say she doesn't love you. Do you love her?"

"I hardly know her."

"Then why? Why turn away a woman who loves you? Why turn your back on your own son?"

"I don't know, damn you! Why do you have to show up on my weddin' day and make me miserable? How can you ask me to humiliate a woman who's been so . . . kind to me? I can't go off and leave her standin' at the altar."

Tears began to run down Pam's face as she sat down on the bench. "Nelson was kind to me also and loved Zachary so much. I tried to find you to tell you what'd happened, but you seemed to have vanished. Years later, when I began to see your name in the papers, I couldn't find the courage to write—or maybe I couldn't bear to hurt Nelson. When he died, I wanted to find you. I felt so guilty, like I was running from Nelson's deathbed to my lover's arms, but I'd waited so very long. Then Zachary became ill and, by the time he could travel to Chandler, you were engaged. I told myself it was over between us, but at the last minute, I had to see you, had to tell you."

He sat beside her, put his arm about her shoulders and pulled her head down. "Listen, love, you always were a romantic. Maybe you don't remember our fights, but I do. The only place we were good together was in a haystack. Two thirds of the time we were mad at each other. Over the years, you've forgotten all the bad parts."

Pam blew her nose on a lace-edged handkerchief. "Is Miss Chandler any better?"

"When I do somethin' she doesn't like, she hits me over the head with whatever's handy. You always ran off and hid and worried whether I still loved you."

"I've grown up since then."

"How could you? You've lived with an old man that spoiled you, just like your father did. No one's ever spoiled Houston."

Pam pulled away from him. "And is she good in bed? Is she also better at that than I am?"

"I have no idea. There's a little fire in her but she's clumsy with it. I'm not marryin' her for sex. That's always available."

Pam put her arms around his neck. "If I begged you—," she began.

"It wouldn't help. I'm gonna marry Houston."

"Kiss me," she whispered. "Remind me. Let me remember."

Speculatively, Kane looked at her. Perhaps he wanted to know, too. He put his big hand to the back of her head and his lips on hers. It was a long kiss and he put all he had into it.

And when he moved away, they were smiling at each other.

"It *is* over, isn't it?" Pam whispered.

"Yes."

She stayed close to him. "All those years with Nelson, I believed I was in love with you but I was in love with a dream. Perhaps my father was right."

He removed her arms from his neck. "Any more talk of your father and we may come to blows."

"You aren't still angry at him, are you?"

"This is my weddin' day and I want happiness, so let's not talk about Fenton. Tell me about my son."

"Gladly," Pam said and began talking.

It was an hour later when Pam left Kane alone in the garden to finish his cigar. When he was done, he flung the butt to the ground, looked at his pocket watch and knew it was time to return to dress for the wedding.

He hadn't taken but a few steps when he came face to face with a man who, if Kane had been able to see them together, he would have known was the image of himself in about ten years' time.

Kane and Rafe Taggert stared at each other silently, rather like dogs meeting for the first time. Immediately, they each knew who the other was.

"You don't look much like your father," Rafe said with a hint of accusation in his voice.

"I wouldn't know. I never met the man—or any of his kin," Kane answered, pointing out the fact that no Taggert had ever contacted him in all the years he was growing up in Fenton's stable.

Rafe stiffened. "I hear there's blood on your money."

"I hear you don't have any—bloody or not."

They glared across the space separating them. "You ain't much like Frank, either. I'll be leavin' now." He turned away.

"You can insult me but not the lady I'm marryin'. You'll stay for the ceremony."

Rafe didn't look back, but he gave a curt nod before walking away.

"I want to talk to you," Edan said from the doorway, his eyes grim.

The many women around Houston began to protest, but she put up her hand and silently followed Edan. He led her into his bedroom.

"I know this isn't proper, but it's the only place in the house that's not crawling with people."

Houston tried to not let her emotions show because she had the distinct impression Edan was angry with her.

"I know today's your wedding, but I've got something to say. Kane knows all too well that the personal safety of the people connected to a man as wealthy as he is is often in jeopardy." He looked at her. "What I'm saying is that Kane's had me follow you a couple of times in the last week."

Houston could feel color leaving her face.

"I don't like what I've seen," he continued. "I didn't like that a young woman, unprotected, was going into a coal camp, but this Sisterhood of yours—."

"Sisterhood!" Houston gasped. "How . . . ?"

Edan grabbed a chair and put it behind her.

Feebly, Houston sat down.

"I didn't want to do it, but Kane insisted that I . . . ah, hide in a closet and be there during your tea party in case you needed protection."

Houston was looking at her hands and didn't see Edan's slight smile at the words "tea party." "How much does he know?" she whispered.

Edan took a seat across from her. "I was afraid of that," he said heavily. "How could I tell him that you're marrying him because of his connection to Fenton? You're using him and his money to further your crusade against the evil of coal. Damn! but I should have known better. With a sister like yours who'd steal her own sister's—."

Houston stood. "Mr. Nylund!" she said through clenched teeth. "I will *not* listen to you impugn my sister, and I have no idea what you're talking about when you say Kane is connected to the Fentons. If you believe my purposes are evil, we'll go now and tell Kane everything."

"Wait a minute," he said, standing, grabbing her arm. "Why don't you explain—?"

"Don't you mean that I should try to convince you that I'm innocent, that I'm not leading Kane Taggert down the aisle only to be slaughtered? No, sir, I do not answer such accusations. Tell me, did you plan to use your knowledge of me as blackmail?"

"Touché," he said, visibly relaxing. "Now that we've both shown our anger, could we talk? You'll have to admit that your actions aren't exactly beyond suspicion."

Houston also tried to relax, but it was difficult. She didn't like to think of how he'd come to know of The Sisterhood.

"How long have you been doing your Wednesday masquerades?" Edan asked.

Houston walked to the window. On the lawn below were workers looking as if they were preparing for the siege of an army. She looked back at Edan. "What we women do, we've done for generations. The Sisterhood was founded by my father's mother before there even was a Chandler, Colorado. We are merely friends who try to help each other and anyone else we can. Right now, our major concern is the treatment of the people in the coal camps. We do nothing illegal." Her eyes fastened on his. "Nor do we use anyone."

"Why the secrecy then?"

She looked at him in disbelief. "Look at your own reaction to your knowledge, and you aren't even a relative. Can you imagine how the husbands and fathers would react if they found out their delicate women spent their free afternoons learning to drive a four-horse wagon? And some of us have . . ." She stopped talking.

"I see your point. But I see theirs, too. What you're doing is dangerous. You could be—." He stopped. "You say you've been doing this for three generations?"

"We take on different problems at different times."

"And the . . . ah, tea parties?"

In spite of herself, Houston blushed. "It was my grandmother's idea. She said she went to her own wedding night knowing nothing and terrified. She didn't want her friends or her daughters to have the same experience. I think perhaps the pre-wedding celebration has evolved slowly into what you"—she swallowed—"saw."

"How many women in Chandler belong to The Sisterhood?"

"There're only a dozen active members. Some, like my mother, retire after they're married."

"Do you plan to retire?"

"No," she answered, looking up at him, because, of course, her participation could depend on him.

He turned away from her. "Kane won't like your driving the wagon into the coal fields. He won't like your being in jeopardy."

Houston moved to face him. "I know he wouldn't like it, which is truly the *only* reason I haven't told him. Edan,"— she put her hand on his arm—"this means so much to so many people. It took me months of work to learn how to act like an old woman, to be able to really become Sadie. If I stopped now, it would take more months to train someone else and, in the meantime, so many miners' families would go without the little extras I give them."

He took her hand. "All right, you can get off your pulpit. I guess it's safe enough, even though it goes against everything I believe."

"You won't tell Kane? I'm quite sure he won't be understanding in the least."

"I'm sure that's an understatement. No, I won't tell him if you swear to only deliver potatoes and *not* get involved with the unions. And about this seditious magazine you women want to start—."

She stood on tiptoe and kissed his cheek to cut him off. "Thank you so much, Edan. You are a true friend. Now I must go dress for my wedding." Before he could speak, she was at the door, but paused, her hand on the knob. "What did you mean about Kane's connection to the Fentons?"

"I thought you knew. Jacob Fenton's younger sister, Charity, was Kane's mother."

"No," she said softly. "I didn't know." She left the room.

Houston was in her bedroom only minutes when Sarah Oakley said, as she held out Houston's wedding dress, "I just saw the oddest thing."

"What was that?"

"I thought it was Kane in the garden wearing his old clothes, but instead it was a boy who looks like him."

"Ian," Houston said with a smile. "He *did* come."

"If there's anything left of him," Nina said, looking over the rail. "Two of the Randolph boys and Meredith's two brothers started laughing at him and your Ian attacked them."

Houston's head came up. "Four against one?"

"At least that many. Now they've gone behind a tree and I can't see them."

Houston took her hands off the wedding dress Sarah was still holding and went to the window. "Where are they now?"

"There," Nina pointed. "See the commotion in the shrubs? That's one heck of a fight going on."

Leaning far out the window, Houston surveyed the garden area. Most of the scene was hidden from the house by trees.

"I'll send someone to stop the fight," Sarah was saying.

"And humiliate a Taggert?" Houston said, going to the closet. "Not on your life." She again pulled on her dark blue satin dressing gown.

"What in the world are you planning, Houston?" Sarah gasped.

"I am going to stop a fight and save a Taggert from a fate worse than death: humiliation. There's no one in the back."

"Just a few dozen waiters and guests and . . ." Nina said.

"Houston, dear, aren't there some fireworks downstairs? If someone were to light them it would create a diversion," Opal said softly. She knew from experience that it was useless to tell her daughter that she needed to get dressed. Not when one of her girls wore that expression.

"I'm on my way," Nina called, running out the door as Houston put her foot out the window and onto the rose trellis.

The east lawn was alive with the explosive noise of fireworks, with early guests all looking that way, as Houston made her way diagonally across the stretch of west lawn and into the trees.

Deep in the shade of a grove of black walnut trees, Ian Taggert uselessly fought the four stout boys on top of him.

"Stop that!" Houston said in her sternest voice.

Not one boy paid her the least attention.

She moved into the flailing arms and legs, grabbed an ear and pulled. Jeff Randolph came up swinging but stopped when he saw Houston. She motioned him to stand back while she went after George and Alex Lechner, pulling up both boys by their ears.

Only Steve Randolph remained on top of Ian and when Houston touched Steve's ear, he came up flying, an uncomprehending mass of rage. The three boys standing in the background gasped when Steve sent a fist sailing toward Houston's jaw. She ducked and, seeing no other way, decked young Steven with a right. Months of handling a four-horse wagon had given her quite a bit of strength in her arms.

For a moment, no one could move as Steve slowly fell across Ian's legs.

Houston recovered first. "Steve!" she said, kneeling, slapping the boy's face. "Are you all right?"

"Damn!" Ian breathed. "I ain't never seen no lady punch like that."

Steve groaned, sat up, rubbed his jaw and looked at Houston in wonder. In fact, all five of the boys were gaping at her.

She stood. "I don't appreciate such behavior on my wedding day," she said regally.

"No, ma'am," four of the boys mumbled.

"We didn't mean nothin', Miss Blair-Houston. He—."

"I want no excuses. Now, you four go back to your parents and, Steven, put some ice on your jaw."

"Yes, ma'am," he called over his shoulder, all of them getting away as quickly as possible.

She held her hand out to Ian to help him up. "You may come with me."

He ignored her hand. "I ain't goin' into *his* house if that's what you mean," he said angrily.

"Perhaps you're right. For this fracas, I'm using a rose trellis as a staircase. Any boy who'd lose a fight probably couldn't climb a trellis."

"Lose a fight!" He was as tall as she was and, at sixteen, already big, showing promise of reaching Kane's size. He almost put his nose to hers. "In case you cain't count, there was four of 'em on me and I woulda won if you hadn't come along and interrupted."

"But you're afraid to enter your own cousin's house," she said, as if it were an observation. "How odd. Good day to you." She started briskly toward the house.

Ian began walking beside her. "I ain't afraid. I just don't wanta go inside."

"Of course."

"What's that mean?"

She stopped. "I agree with you. You aren't afraid of your cousin, you just don't want to see him or to eat his food. I understand perfectly."

She watched emotions play across his face.

"Where's this damned rose trellis of yours?"

She stood rooted to where she was and looked at him.

He stopped glaring. "All right then, where's the rose trellis you're usin' as a staircase?"

"This way."

Kane was just returning to the house when he was halted by the extraordinary sight of his wife-to-be, wearing only a garment he knew no lady wore outside her own house, climbing down the rose trellis.

More than a little curious, he stepped behind a tree to watch her and saw her fling herself into the midst of a pile of wrestling boys who were as big as she was. He was halfway there to help her when he saw her flatten a boy with a championship right.

The next minute, she was arguing in her own cool way with a big, sullen-looking boy. "Might as well give up," Kane said aloud, laughter in his voice. He'd already learned that when Houston looked like that, a man might as well give in because that delicate little lady was going to get her own way.

He laughed again when he saw the boy start up the rose trellis ahead of Houston. But as Kane watched, he saw Houston's gown snag and saw her struggle to free herself. Around the corner three men and a woman were walking and, in another minute, they'd see her.

Quickly, he ran across the lawn and put his hand on her ankle.

When Houston looked down and saw Kane, she nearly fainted. What in the world would he think of the woman he was going to marry? She knew quite well what Leander or Mr. Gates would say if they saw her now, in public, wearing her bedroom clothes, and climbing a rose trellis.

As Houston looked down at Kane, she said the only thing she could think of. "My hat isn't on straight."

She hoped that the sound he made was a chuckle.

"Honey, even I know that ladies don't wear hats with their bathrobes."

Houston was paralyzed. He didn't mind!

"Unless you want ever'body to see you like that, you'd better get inside."

"Yes," she said, recovering herself and climbing to the top while he watched. Once on the balcony, she leaned over the side. "Kane," she called to him, "your wedding gift is in your office."

He grinned up at her. "See you real soon, baby."

With that he stuck his hands in his pockets and went away whistling, nodding at the people he passed.

"Houston," Opal said from behind her. "If you don't get ready now, you're going to miss your own wedding."

"I'd rather die," she said with great feeling and returned to her bedroom.

Ten minutes later, Kane was unwrapping the package Houston'd put on his desk. Inside were two boxes of cigars and a note.

These are the finest Cuban cigars made. Each month two more boxes of the best cigars available in the world will be delivered to Mr. Kane Taggert.

It was signed with the name of a cigar store in Key West, Florida.

Kane was just lighting one when Edan entered. He held out the box to him. "From Houston. How in the world do you think she got these here in time?"

Edan took a moment to enjoy the cigar. "If I'm learning anything in life, it's to not underestimate that lady."

"Any woman who'd buy cigars like these is indeed a lady. Well," he said heavily, "I guess I better go get dressed. You wanta come help me tie things?"

"Sure."

Chapter 14

The wedding dress was of Houston's own design, simple but elaborate in its simplicity. It was of ivory silk satin cut in a long, gentle princess style with no horizontal seams from the high neck to the tip of the twelve-foot train. About the waist, extending over her breasts and flowing down her hips, was an intricate Persian design done in thousands of hand-applied seed pearls. The sleeves from shoulder to elbow were huge, their size further emphasizing the tiny waist of the dress. The tight cuffs that extended from elbow to wrist carried a repeat pattern done in pearls.

Houston stood very still as her friends attached the veil to her head. It was a five-yard-long froth of handmade Irish lace called Youghal, a bold design of wild flowers set off by spiked leaves. The complicated pattern of the lace complemented the satin smoothness of the dress.

Tia held out Houston's teardrop-shaped bouquet of orange blossoms and white rosebuds, made to reach from her hands to just graze the floor as she walked.

Opal looked up at her daughter with tears glistening in her eyes. "Houston . . ." she began but could say nothing else.

Houston kissed her mother's cheek. "I'm getting the best of men."

"Yes, I know." She handed Houston a little corsage of pink rosebuds. "These are from your sister. She thought that she'd wear red roses and you could wear pink. I guess she's right that you don't have to dress alike."

"Our veils are different," Houston said as Sarah pinned the flowers over the veil just above Houston's left ear.

"Ready?" Tia asked. "I believe that's your music."

Blair was standing at the head of the double stairs waiting for her sister. Solemnly, they embraced.

"I love you more than you know," Blair whispered. There were slight tears in her eyes as she pulled away. "I guess we should get this spectacle over."

The polished brass rails of the staircase were covered with fern leaves and at regular intervals hung clusters of three calla lilies. Beneath the arch of the stairs was a twelve-piece string orchestra now playing the wedding march.

With heads held high, both twins walked slowly down the stairs, one curving east, one curving westward. Below them, in silence, the guests looked up at the beautiful women. Their tightly-fitted dresses were identical except for the lace veils, which varied in pattern and type of lace. The color of rosebuds at the sides of their heads also distinguished one twin from the other.

When the women reached the main hallway, the crowd pulled back and the twins walked straight ahead, down the short corridor outside the library door.

Once outside the door, they paused and waited for the six organs placed around the enormous room to begin playing. Inside, seated, but now rising, were the close friends and relatives of the couples.

As Houston looked down the aisle, she saw Jean Taggert standing between her uncle and her father. And ahead of the guests, on a raised platform that was canopied in greenery and roses, stood the men—in the wrong places.

Houston should have known it was too good to be true that all her plans would come about without anything going wrong. As it was now, she was walking up the aisle toward Leander. Quickly, she glanced at Blair to share the joke, but Blair was looking straight ahead—toward Kane.

Houston's stomach began to turn over. This wasn't just a simple mistake. With a pang, she thought of the flowers that Blair had sent her. Could Blair have arranged this so she'd not have to marry Leander? Did she want Kane?

The thought was ridiculous. Houston smiled. No doubt

Blair was making a noble sacrifice and taking on Kane so Houston could have Lee. How sweet, but how wrong she was.

Still smiling, Houston looked toward Kane. He was staring at her intently and Houston was glad that he recognized her.

At least for a moment she was happy, but when his face darkened and he turned away, the smile left Houston's face.

He couldn't believe she'd arranged this switch so she could marry Leander, she thought. But of course he could.

As they drew closer to the platform, Houston tried to think of how to get out of this gracefully. Miss Jones thought she'd covered every possible situation that a lady could get herself into, but she'd never thought that a lady would find herself marrying the wrong man.

As the twins stepped onto the platform, Kane kept his head turned away, and Houston couldn't help feeling a pang of resentment that he was going to do nothing to change positions. Didn't he care if he got one twin or the other?

"Dearly beloved, we—."

"Excuse me," Houston said, trying to keep her voice low so that only the five of them could hear. "I'm Houston."

Leander understood instantly. He looked at Kane, who was still facing straight ahead. "Shall we exchange places?"

Kane didn't look at either woman. "Don't much matter to me."

Houston felt her heart sink. Leander wanted Blair and Kane would take her, too. Quite suddenly, she felt as useful as a fifth wheel on a wagon.

"It matters to me," Leander said, and the two men traded places.

Behind them, during the discussion, the audience had begun to twitter, but when Kane and Lee switched places, there was full-fledged laughter. Even though the people tried to cover their amusement, they weren't successful.

Houston stole a glance at Kane and saw the anger in his eyes.

The service was over quickly and, when Reverend Thomas said to kiss the brides, Lee enveloped Blair with gusto. But Kane's kiss was cool and reserved. He wouldn't look her in the eyes.

141

"Could I speak to you in your office, please?" she asked. "Alone?"

He gave her a curt nod and released her as if he couldn't bear to touch her.

The four of them walked out of the room very fast and, once outside the library, people descended. Kane and Houston were quickly separated, as one guest after another wedged his way close to the bride. There was much giggling about the mix-up at the altar. Not one person could resist the temptation to remind everyone how Lee never could seem to make up his mind about which of the twins he wanted.

Jean Taggert pulled Houston aside. "What happened?"

"I think my sister thought she was doing me a favor by giving me Leander. She was going to sacrifice herself by taking the man I love."

"Have you told Blair that you love Kane? That you wanted to marry him?"

"I haven't even told Kane. Somehow, I felt that he might not believe me. I'd rather show him how I feel over the next fifty years." In spite of herself, tears sparkled in her eyes. "At the altar, he said he didn't care whether he married me or my sister."

Jean grabbed Houston's arm and pulled her away from an approaching relative. "When you marry a Taggert, you have to be strong. His pride's been wounded and he's liable to say or do anything when he's hurt. Find him now and tell him what your sister did, or tell him it was just an error in planning—anything—but don't let him brood in silence. He'll build everything into a mountain of anger, and then there'll be no hope of reaching him."

"I asked him to meet me in his office."

"Then why are you standing here?"

With the beginning of a smile, Houston deftly flung the long train twice over her left arm and marched down the hall to Kane's office.

He was standing in front of a tall window watching the people outside, an unlit cigar in his mouth. He didn't look around when she entered.

"I'm very sorry about the mistake at the altar," she began. "I'm sure it was just a flaw in my planning."

"You didn't want to marry Westfield?"

"No! It was a misunderstanding, that's all."

He took a step toward his desk. "I gave up somethin' today because I couldn't bear the idea of humiliatin' you." He gave her a cold look. "I never could abide a liar." He tossed a piece of paper at her.

Houston bent to pick it up. It was a note, laboriously hand-lettered, that said, I'll be wearing red roses in my hair today. The name of Houston Chandler was at the bottom.

"Damn you, *Lady* Chandler! I played fair by you, but you—." He turned away from her. "Keep the money. Keep the house. You worked for it hard enough. And you won't have me to put up with. Maybe you can get Westfield to take that virginity that you're so protective of." He started toward the door.

"Kane," she called after him, but he was gone.

Heavily, she sat down on one of the oak chairs in the room.

A few minutes later, Blair came into the room. "I guess we should get out there and cut the cake," she said hesitantly. "You and Taggert—."

All Houston's rage came to the surface and she came out of the chair toward her sister with anger in her eyes. "You can't even call him by his name, can you?" she said furiously. "You think he has no feelings; you've dismissed him and therefore you think you have a right to do whatever you want to him."

Blair took a step backward. "Houston, what I did, I did for you. I want to see you happy."

Houston clenched her fists at her sides and moved closer to Blair, prepared to do battle. "Happy? How can I be happy when I don't even know where my husband is? Thanks to you, I may never know the meaning of happiness."

"Me? What have I done except try everything in my power to help you? I tried to help you come to your senses and see that you didn't have to marry that man for his money. Kane Taggert—."

"You really don't know, do you?" Houston interrupted. "You have humiliated a proud, sensitive man in front of hundreds of people, and you aren't even aware of what you've done."

"I assume you're talking about what happened at the altar?

I did it for you, Houston. I know you love Leander and I was willing to take Taggert just to make you happy. I'm so sorry about what I've done to you. I never meant to make you so unhappy. I know I've ruined your life, but I did try to repair what I'd done."

"Me, me, me. That's all you can say. You've ruined my life and all you can talk about is yourself. *You* know I love Leander. *You* know what an awful man Kane is. For the last week or so, you've spent every waking moment with Leander, and the way you talk about him is as if he were a god. Every other word you say is, 'Leander.' I think you did mean well this morning: you wanted to give me the best man."

Houston leaned forward. "Leander may set your body on fire, but he never did anything for me. If you hadn't been so involved with yourself lately, and could think that I do have some brains of my own, you'd have seen that I've fallen in love with a good, kind, thoughtful man—admittedly he's a little rough around the edges, but then, haven't you always complained that my edges are a little too smooth?"

Blair sat down, and the look of astonishment on her face was almost comical. "You love him? Taggert? You love Kane Taggert? But I don't understand. You've *always* loved Leander. For as long as I can remember, you've loved him."

Houston began to calm down as she realized that what Blair had done, she'd done out of love for her sister, out of wanting Houston to have the best. "True, I decided I wanted him when I was six years old. I think it became a goal to me, like climbing a mountain. I should have set my sights on Mt. Rainier. At least, once I'd climbed it, it would have been done. I never knew what I was going to do with Leander after we were married."

"But you do know what you'll do with Taggert?"

Houston couldn't help smiling. "Oh, yes. I very much know what I'm going to do with him. I am going to make a home for him, a place where he'll be safe, a place where I'll be safe, where I can do whatever I want."

To Houston's amazement, Blair rose from her chair with a look of fury on her face. "I guess you couldn't have bothered to take two minutes to tell me this, could you? I have been through Hades in the last weeks. I have worried about you, spent whole days crying about what I've done to my sister, and here you tell me that you're in *love* with this King Midas."

"Don't you say anything against him!" Houston shouted, then managed to calm herself. "He's the kindest, gentlest man and very generous. And I happen to love him very much."

"And I have been through agony because I was worried about you. You should have told me!"

Houston took a moment to answer. Maybe she had been aware of Blair's agony of the last few weeks, but part of her was too angry to care. Maybe she'd wanted her sister to suffer. "I guess I was so jealous of your love match that I didn't want to think about you," she said softly.

"Love match?!" Blair yelled. "I think I'm Leander's Mt. Rainier. I can't deny that he does things to me physically, but that's all he wants from me. We've spent days together in the operating room, but I feel there's a part of Leander I don't know. He doesn't really let me get close to him. I know so little about him. He decided he wanted me, so he went after me, using every method he could to get me."

"But I see the way you look at him. I never felt inclined to look at him like that."

"That's because you never saw him in an operating room. If you'd seen him in there, you would have——."

"Fainted, most likely," Houston said. "Blair, I am sorry that I didn't talk to you. I probably knew that you were in agony, but what happened *hurt*. I had been engaged to Leander for, it seemed to me, most of my life, yet you walked in and took him in just one night. And Lee was always calling me his ice princess, and I was so worried about being a cold woman."

"And you're no longer worried about that?" Blair asked.

Houston could feel the color in her cheeks rising. "Not with Kane," she whispered, thinking of his hands on her body. No, she didn't feel cool when he was near.

"You really do love him?" Blair asked, sounding as if loving Kane were the most impossible task on earth. "You don't mind the food flying everywhere? You don't mind his loudness or the other women?"

Houston caught her breath. *"What* other women?" Right away, she saw that Blair was hesitating about answering, and

Houston had to use all her control to calm herself. If Blair thought she was going to once again decide what her sister should or should not do . . . "And Blair, you'd better tell me."

Houston saw her sister trying to decide and she advanced on her. "If you even consider managing my life again as you did today at the altar, I'll never speak to you again. I am an adult, and you know something about *my* husband, and I want to know what it is."

"I saw him in the garden kissing Pamela Fenton just before the wedding," Blair said all in one breath.

Houston felt a little weak, but then she saw the truth of the matter. Was this what Kane was referring to when he said he'd given up something today? "But he came to me anyway," she whispered. "He saw her, kissed her, but he married me." Nothing else could have made her happier than this. "Blair, you have made me the happiest woman alive today. Now, all I have to do is find my husband and tell him that I love him and hope that he will forgive me."

A horrible thought came to her. "Oh, Blair, you don't know him at all. He's such a good man, generous in a very natural way, strong in a way that makes people lean on him, but he's . . ." She buried her face in her hands. "But he can't stand embarrassment of any kind, and we've humiliated him in front of the entire town. He'll never forgive me. Never!"

Blair moved toward the door. "I'll go to him and explain that it was all my fault, that you had nothing to do with it. Houston, I had no idea you really wanted to marry him. I just couldn't imagine anyone wanting to live with someone like him."

"I don't think you have to worry about that anymore, because I think he just walked out on me."

"But what about the guests? He can't just leave."

"Should he stay and listen to people laughing about how Leander can't decide which twin he wants? Not one person will think that Kane could have his choice of women. Kane thinks I'm still in love with Lee, you think I love Lee, and Mr. Gates thinks I'm marrying Kane for his money. I think Mother is the only person who sees that I'm in love—for the very first time in my life."

"What can I do to make it up to you?" Blair whispered.

"There's nothing you can do. He's gone. He left me money and the house and he walked away. But what do I want with this big, empty house if he's not in it?" She sat down. "Blair, I don't even know where he is. He could be on a train back to New York for all I know."

"More than likely, he's gone to his cabin."

Both women looked up to see Edan standing in the doorway. "I didn't mean to eavesdrop, but when I saw what happened at the wedding, I knew he'd be in a rage."

Houston wrapped the train of her wedding dress about her arm. "I'm going to him and explain what happened. I'm going to tell him that my sister is so in love with Leander that she thinks that I am, too." She turned to smile at Blair. "I can't help but resent the fact that you thought that I was low enough to marry a man for his money, but I thank you for the love that made you willing to sacrifice what has come to mean so much to you." Quickly, she kissed her sister's cheek.

Blair clung to her for a moment. "Houston, I had no idea you felt this way. As soon as the reception is over, I'll help you pack and——."

Houston pulled away with a little laugh. "No, my dear managing sister, I am leaving this house right now. My husband is more important to me than a few hundred guests. You're going to have to stay here and answer all the questions about where Kane and I've gone."

"But Houston, I don't know anything about receptions of this size."

Houston stopped at the door beside Edan. "I learned how in my 'worthless' education," she said, then smiled. "Blair, it's not all that tragic. Cheer up, maybe there'll be an attack of food poisoning, and you'll know how to handle that. Good luck," she said and was out the door, leaving Blair alone with the horror of having to manage the reception of hundreds of people.

Outside the office, Edan caught her arm and led her into the storage closet beside the north porch. He was smiling at her.

"You certainly do make a habit of spying on me," she snapped, pulling away from him.

"I've learned more in two weeks of spying on you than I have in the rest of my life, total. Did you mean what you said about loving Kane?"

"Do you think I'm a liar, too? I'm going to get dressed now. It's a hard climb to the cabin."

"You know where it is?"

"I know the general whereabouts."

"Houston, you really can't go rushing off up the side of a mountain after him. I'll go get him, explain what happened and bring him back."

"No, he's mine now—at least legally—and I'm going after him alone."

Edan put his hands on her shoulders. "I wonder if he realizes how lucky he is. What can I do to help you?"

She moved toward the door. "Could you find Sarah Oakley and ask her to come upstairs and help me change?" She paused and looked at Edan speculatively. "On second thought, maybe you could find Jean Taggert for me. She's the especially pretty lady in the violet silk dress and hat."

"Especially pretty, is she?" he asked, laughing. "Good luck, Houston."

Chapter 15

Jean helped Houston dress in record time. She fully agreed
with Houston in her need to go after Kane.

When Houston was dressed, they went through the west
wing to the housekeeper's rooms and down that remote
staircase. Hidden among some trees, Edan was waiting with a
horse laden with four bags of food.

"That should keep you for a few days," he said. "Are you
sure you want to do this? If you got lost—."

"I've lived in Chandler all my life and I know this area."
She gave him a hard look. "I'm not the bit of fluff people
think I am, remember?"

"Did you put the wedding cake in there?" Jean asked
Edan.

"In its own sweet little tin box," he said in a way that made
Houston glance from one to the other and begin to smile.

"You must go, and don't worry about anything here. Just
think about your husband and how much you love him," Jean
said as Houston mounted.

Houston sneaked away from the wedding as secretly as she
could, considering that she was surrounded by over six
hundred guests. The few people who saw her were so
astonished that they could say nothing. She'd pulled her hat
veil down over her face and she hoped that would confuse
some people, but it didn't.

As she reached the western end of the garden, she nearly
ran over Rafe Taggert and Pamela Fenton walking together.

She wasn't sure if it was shock or surprise, but her horse's front feet came off the ground.

Rafe looked at her with amusement. "No doubt you're the twin that married a Taggert, and now you're runnin' away."

Before she could speak, Pam answered. "If I know Kane, his pride was hurt at the altar and he ran away somewhere to lick his wounds. You aren't by chance going after him, are you?"

Houston wasn't sure how to act toward this woman who had been loved by her husband. With all the coolness she could muster, her chin quite high, she said, "Yes, I am."

"Good for you!" Pam said. "He needs a wife with your courage. I always insisted that he come to me. I hope you're prepared for his anger. It's quite frightening at times. I wish you all the luck in the world."

Houston was so astonished at Pam's words that she couldn't reply. She was torn between feeling anger at the idea of someone else knowing *her* husband, and gratitude that Pam was giving her some good advice. And, too, Pam seemed to have given up her hold over Kane. Was Kane the one in love; would Pam not have him?

"Thank you," Houston murmured as she reined her horse away from them.

She encountered no one else and breathed a sigh of relief when she was past the city limits of Chandler and heading for the country.

The first part of the journey was very easy and she had time to muse on what must be happening at Kane's house. Poor Blair! She really had meant well. She had thought Houston wanted Leander, so she was willing to make a supreme sacrifice and spend her life with a "villain" like Kane Taggert. Perhaps that's what Kane had sensed, that he was the medicine to be taken by Blair because Houston'd been wronged by her sister.

Of course, what Kane didn't understand was that none of the guests would think anything about what had happened, except as something to tease about. They would tease Leander because they had known him since he was a child. If Kane had stayed and laughed, all would have been forgotten—but Kane had yet to master the art of being able to laugh at himself.

She rode to the foot of the mountain as quickly as possible and started up the trail that she and Kane had used before. When she reached the place where they'd picnicked, she dismounted and drank some water. Above her was what looked like an impregnable piece of mountain. But Kane'd said that his cabin was up there and, if he was there, she was going to find him.

As she removed her jacket and tied it to the horse, she tried to see a path through the scrub and piñon trees. It was only after several minutes of walking about, looking at the mountainside from several angles, that she saw what could have been a trail of sorts. It went straight up the mountain, over terraced rock, and disappeared into the trees.

For a moment, Houston wondered what in the world she was doing in such a place as this on her wedding day. Right now, she should be wearing a satin dress and dancing with her husband. A thought which brought her back to the present. Her husband was at the top of this mountain—maybe. Edan could be wrong, and Kane could be on a train to Africa for all anyone knew.

After giving the horse some water, she tightened her hat on her head to give her some protection against the sun and remounted.

The way up was worse than it had looked. At times the trail was so narrow that the tree branches clawed at her legs, and she had difficulty forcing the horse to travel the narrow path. The plants that grew out of rock weren't like the soft, cared-for plants in town. These trees had to fight for life every day and they refused to bend or give way for a mere human.

A Crown of Thorns cactus caught the side of her divided skirt and tore it, leaving several long thorns in the cloth. Houston paused while she pulled thorns and fat cockleburs off her clothing and a few from her hair. So much for looking her best when she arrived, she thought, as she pushed strands of hair under her hat.

At one point, the trail took a sharp right, and the sky became hidden by the overhanging trees and rock formations. All about her were mushrooms of bizarre structure and unreal colors. Some were tiny and yellow, some as big as her foot and brilliant red. Large patches of five-inch-tall grasslike mushrooms stood upright on the forest floor.

Always, she was climbing upward, and the air was thinning as the area around her became more and more like a rain forest, rather than the semiarid region that surrounded Chandler. Twice, she had to stop and look for the trail, and once she followed a path for a mile, only to have it end abruptly in a sandy-bottomed cavelike rock formation that had a natural window at the top. The place had an odd feeling about it: half frightening, half like a place where one should attend church services.

She walked her horse out of the rocks and back onto the path, where she again tried riding.

An hour later, she had her first good luck: she found a piece of Kane's wedding suit caught on a sharp edge of rock. Her relief at finding out for sure that he was indeed at the top of the trail was great. With renewed spirit, she urged her reluctant horse upward.

She might have made it perfectly well except that it began to rain. Cold, cold sheets of water came from the sky, then, as the water collected on the overhead rocks, it flooded down on top of her, making visibility impossible. She tried to keep her head down and her eyes on the nearly invisible trail in front of her at the same time.

Flashes of lightning began to make the horse shy and dance about on the skinny little path. After quite a while of fighting both the rain and the horse, she dismounted and led the animal as she gave most of her attention to searching through the deluge for the way.

At one point, the trail ran along a little ledge, sheer rock above and below her. Houston took one step and soothed the frightened horse, took another step and calmed the horse. "If you weren't carrying the food, I'd let you go," she said in disgust.

At the edge of the cliff ledge, the lightning flashed and she saw the cabin. For a moment, she stood perfectly still and looked through the rain dripping off her nose. She had begun to doubt the cabin's existence. And now what did she do? March up to the door, knock and, when Kane answered it, tell him she thought she'd drop by and leave her calling card?

She had half a mind to turn around and leave, when all hell broke loose. The idiot horse she'd had to practically drag up the mountain called out, was answered by another horse, and so proceeded to run toward the cabin. Never mind that Houston was standing in the animal's way. She screamed as she fell into the mud and began rolling down the side of the mountain, but the blast of a shotgun aimed in her direction covered her voice. "Get the hell out of here if you wanta keep your skin," Kane bellowed over the rain.

Houston was hanging over the edge of the drop-off, clutching the roots of a little piñon tree and trying to find a place to stick her dangling feet. Surely he wasn't so angry that he'd shoot her?

Now was not the time to ask questions. She was either going to slide to her death or take a chance on Kane's temper.

"Kane!" she screamed and felt her arms giving way.

Almost immediately, his face appeared over the side. "My God," he said in disbelief as he stretched out his hand to grab her wrist.

Quite easily, he hauled her to the top, stood her on the ground and stepped back from her. He didn't seem to believe she was there.

"I came to see you," Houston said with a wet, crooked smile, as she began to weave about on her feet.

"Nice to have you," he said, grinning. "I don't get much company up here."

"Maybe it's your welcome," she answered, nodding toward the shotgun in his hand.

"You wanta come in? I gotta fire inside." His voice was highly amused—and, Houston hoped, pleased.

"I'd like that very much," she said, then squealed and jumped toward him as above her a tree limb gave a loud crack.

She was standing quite near him and, as he looked down at her, his eyes were questioning. It was now or never, Houston thought, and there was no sense in being shy or coy. "You said you'd be there for the wedding if I'd show up for the wedding night. You fulfilled your part of the bargain, so I'm here for mine."

With breath held, she watched him.

Kane's face went through several emotions before he threw back his head and laughed loud enough to be heard over the rain and the thunder. The next moment, he swept her into his arms and carried her toward the cabin. At the doorway, he stopped and kissed her. Houston clung to him and knew the arduous climb had been worth it.

Inside the little one-room cabin was a stone fireplace that filled one whole wall, and a warm, cheerful fire blazed within it.

Kane held up a blanket. "I ain't got any dry clothes up here so this'll have to do. You get out of them things while I find your horse and pen it up."

"There's food in the bags," she called as he left.

Alone, Houston began to undress, peeling the soaking garments from her cold, clammy skin. She couldn't help glancing at the door every few minutes. "Coward!" she said to herself. "You've propositioned the man and now you have to live up to your boasts."

By the time Kane returned, Houston was wrapped in the scratchy wool blanket with only her face sticking out. After a quick, smiling look of understanding, Kane put the food on the floor.

The only furniture in the room was a big bed made of pine, covered with an odd assortment of blankets that didn't look overly clean. Against one wall was a mountain of stacked canned goods, mostly peaches like she'd found in the kitchen of his house.

"I'm glad you brought food," he said. "I guess I left in too much of a hurry to get any. I don't guess Edan'd believe it, but even I get tired of peaches after a few cans."

"Edan packed the food, and your cousin, Jean, had him put in some wedding cake."

Kane straightened. "Ah, yes, the wedding. I guess I ruined the day for you, and women like weddings so much." He began to unbutton his shirt.

"Many women have weddings like the one I planned, but few have a day such as this one turned out to be."

As he pulled his wet shirt out of his pants, he smiled at her. "Your sister did all that at the weddin', didn't she? You didn't have nothin' to do with it, did you? I realized that after I got all the way up here."

"No, I didn't," she answered. "But Blair didn't mean any

harm. She loves me and she thought I wanted Leander, so she tried to give him to me." As Kane began to remove his pants, Houston looked back at the fire. This was her wedding night, she thought, and her body warmed considerably.

"Thought?" Kane asked, and when she didn't answer, he persisted. "You said she *thought* you wanted Westfield. She doesn't think so anymore?"

"Not after what I said to her," Houston murmured, looking into the fire. Behind her, she could hear him rubbing himself with a towel, and she was greatly tempted to look around. Was he really as well built as the strongman she'd hired for The Sisterhood meeting?

With a swift movement, Kane knelt before her.

He was wearing only the towel about his hips, looking for all the world like a Greek god of old. The smooth, big muscles under deeply bronzed skin were indeed better than those of the man she'd hired.

Whatever Kane'd been about to say was forgotten as he looked at her. His breath caught in his throat. "You looked at me like this once before," he whispered. "That time you hit me with a water pitcher when I touched you. You plannin' somethin' like that this time?"

Houston just looked at him and let the blanket slide from her head, then down her neck, off her shoulder to hang just above her breasts. "No," was all she could think to say.

The heat of the fire was warm on her skin but nothing compared to the feel of Kane's hand on the side of her face. His fingers tangled themselves in the wet hair that flowed down her back. His thumb ran across her lower lip as he watched her.

"I've seen you dressed up a lot, but you've never been prettier than you are right now. I'm glad you came up here. A place like this is where people should make love."

Houston kept her eyes on his as his hand travelled down her neck and onto her shoulder. When he started to move the blanket away from her breasts, she held her breath, and realized that she was praying that she'd please him.

Very gently, as if she were a child, he put one arm around her shoulders and lowered her to the cabin floor. She tensed as she thought, this is it.

Kane parted the blanket so that her nude body was entirely exposed to him.

Houston waited for the verdict.

"Damn," he said under his breath. "No wonder Westfield made a fool of himself over a body like that. I've found that them curvy dresses you ladies wear are usually stuffed with cotton."

Houston had to laugh. "I please you?"

"Please me?" he said, as he held out his hand. "Just look at that. It's shakin' so bad I can't hold it still." He put his hand on the soft skin of her stomach. "It ain't gonna be easy for me to wait, but any lady'd climb all the way up here to spend the night with me deserves the best—not no quick tumble on the floor. You just sit there and I'll make us somethin' to drink. You like peaches? No!" he said as Houston began to pull the blanket about her. "You can just leave that on the floor. You get too cold you can crawl in my lap and I'll warm you."

Growing up in Duncan Gates's house had not given Houston much opportunity to learn to like the taste of liquor. But Kane took a can of peaches, poured out the juice, mashed the peaches to a pulp and mixed it with a generous amount of rum.

He handed her the concoction in the can. "It ain't a fancy glass, but it works."

Houston took a sip. She felt quite awkward wearing absolutely nothing while sitting in front of a man. But by the time she'd finished the drink, which didn't taste at all like the few sips of liquor she'd drunk before, she was feeling as if it were the most normal thing in the world to have no clothes on.

Kane took a seat across from her and watched her. "Better?" he asked as he handed her another drink.

"Much."

She was only halfway through the second can of drink when Kane took it from her. "I don't want you drunk, just relaxed."

He put his arms around her and pulled her close to him. The drink inside Houston made her feel less inhibited than she ever had been in her life. Her arms twined about his neck and she put her lips on his.

"What did you tell your sister about you and Westfield?"

"That Lee might set her body on fire, but he did absolutely nothing for me."

"Not a good asker?"

"The worst," she said as his lips came down on hers.

His hands played along her body as he kissed her, touching her skin and sending fire through her. Some small part of her brain was aware that Kane was holding back part of himself, that he was more reserved than she was, but she didn't listen.

As his hands roamed about her body, Houston moved so she was closer to him, stretching out her body to give him freer access.

He kissed her face, her neck, his mouth running down to her breasts. When he took the pink crest in his mouth, she arched against him, and he used his hands to caress her waist and hips.

"Slow down, love," he murmured. "We have all night."

All the sensations were so new to Houston. Always, when Lee'd touched her, she'd felt like withdrawing, pulling away from him rather than wanting to explore and discover everything at once. As Kane touched her, she felt more and more wonderful, and all the fears that Lee'd instilled in her, that she was frigid, were fast disappearing.

Her hands began to explore his skin, to feel the warmth of it. The firelight made his flesh glow, and Houston so much wanted to touch all of him.

Kane pulled her closer to him, lying down with her in his arms. He removed the towel from his hips and Houston moved her hips closer to his, a little afraid of the feel of his swollen manhood.

Kane's control began to break. His breath in her ear was ragged and quick, and his gentle kisses turned hot and demanding. Houston met his force with her own.

"Houston, sweet, sweet Houston," he said as he laid her down on the blanket-covered floor and lay on top of her.

Eagerly, she clutched his body to hers. When he entered her, she gasped and quick tears of pain came to her eyes. Kane lifted himself and looked at her, and held himself back until he saw by her face that the pain was receding. He kissed her neck with little nibbling kisses, running his tongue along her ear until she moved her face and sought his mouth.

Slowly, Kane began to move inside her, and after the first

few painful movements, Houston began to arch toward him in clumsy little circles. Kane put his hands on her hips and began to guide her, slowly, carefully, gracefully.

Houston put her head back and gave all her thoughts and feelings over to the new and delicious sensations Kane was sending through her body.

She began to move in a rhythm as old as time itself, and inside her she felt all the emotions she'd kept pent up, at last finding a release.

Her breath came faster and harder as she began to feel herself building into an explosion.

Kane began to move faster and she moved with him. Higher and higher her passion climbed, until she thought she might burst.

And when she did explode, she was sure she might die from the experience. "Kane," she whispered. "Oh my dear, dear Kane."

He pulled away from her just enough to look at her, and his face wore an unusual expression, one she couldn't understand.

"I didn't please you?" she asked, as her body began to tense again. "Do you think I'm frigid, too?"

He put his hand to the side of her head and kissed her softly. "No, sweetheart, the last thing I think you are is frigid. I'm not sure I know anythin' about you at all, except that you're the prettiest woman I've ever seen and you do the damnest things, like come all the way up the side of a mountain just to spend the night with me, and then my prim little lady-wife turns out to be a hot little . . . Maybe we shouldn't go into that."

He kissed her forehead. "I'm goin' outside into the rain and wash this blood off, and when I get back, let's eat. I need my strength if I'm gonna make love to you all night."

As he stood, Houston stretched, her fair skin tawny in the firelight.

As Kane watched her, an unusual thought entered his head: he didn't want to be alone, not even for the length of time it took him to go outside.

He reached out his hand to her. "Go with me," he said, and there was a plea in his voice.

"Anywhere," Houston answered.

Chapter 16

Houston walked out into the rain with her husband and wasn't even aware of the cold. Her mind was occupied with the fact that she wasn't frigid. Maybe the problem had been Leander, maybe she had been too close to him, or felt too much like his sister, to want to climb into bed with him. But whatever the reason, she was now released from her fear that there was something missing inside her.

Kane pulled her into his arms. "You look dreamy," he said. Rain was dripping down his face and onto hers. "Tell me what you're thinkin'. What does a lady think after havin' the local stableboy make love to her?"

Houston pulled away from him and stretched her arms up toward the sky. On impulse she began dancing slowly, as if she wore her satin wedding dress, holding the skirt out and moving gracefully with it. "This lady feels wonderful. This lady doesn't feel at all like a lady."

He caught her wrist. "You aren't regrettin' that your weddin' night wasn't in a silk-sheeted bed? You don't wish some other man—."

She put her fingers to his lips. "This is the happiest night of my life, and I don't want to be anywhere else or with anyone else. A cabin in the woods with the man I love. No woman in the world could ask for more than that."

He was watching her with an odd intensity, a slight frown on his face. "We better go in before we freeze to death."

Calmly, he started back to the cabin, Houston beside him,

159

but suddenly he turned and grabbed her to him, their cold, wet skin sticking together as he kissed her.

Houston melted against him, letting him feel her joy and happiness.

With a smile, he lifted her into his arms and carried her into the cabin. Once inside, he grabbed a blanket, wrapped her in it, and began rubbing her cold body.

"Houston," he said, "you're not like any lady I ever met. I thought I had a pretty clear idea of what marriage to one of the Chandler princesses would be like, but you 'bout busted all my ideas."

She turned around in his arms, her nude body wrapped in the blanket, his bare skin glowing in the firelight. "Am I different in a good way or a bad one? I know you wanted a lady; am I not being one?"

He took a while to answer, looking at her speculatively, as if judging what he should tell her. "Let's just say that I'm learnin' a lot." He grinned. "I'll bet Gould's wife never followed him up the side of a mountain." He began kissing her neck, but stopped abruptly. "Would it be too much to hope that you know how to cook?"

"I know the rudiments, enough to direct a cook, but I don't know how to prepare a meal from scratch. You don't like Mrs. Murchison?"

"I'm happy to say that she ain't here at the moment. What I want to know is whether you can make somethin' to eat out of those bags of food."

She wiggled her arms out of the blanket and put them around his neck. "I believe I could arrange that. I never want this night to end. I was so afraid that you'd be angry with me for coming up here when I hadn't been invited. But I'm glad that we're here now and not in Chandler. This is so much more romantic."

"Romantic or not, if we don't eat soon, I'm gonna shrivel away to nothin'."

"We can't let that catastrophe happen," Houston said quickly and rolled out from under him.

Kane thought for a moment that his bride had just made a bawdy joke, but he dismissed that as an impossibility.

With the blanket loosely wrapped around her, falling off

one shoulder, Houston took the bags Kane handed her and began unpacking them. He'd once again wrapped the towel about his hips as he piled more wood on the fire. She saw right away that whoever had packed the food had done an excellent job. She withdrew lidded tins, tied porcelain boxes, and muslin-wrapped packages. A note fell out of the second bag.

My dear daughter,
I wish you all the happiness in the world in your marriage, and I think you're perfectly right in following your husband. When you return, don't be surprised to hear that Kane carried you away with him.

Very much love,
Opal Chandler Gates

Kane looked up from the fire to see Houston with tears in her eyes as she clutched a piece of paper. "Is somethin' wrong?"

She handed him the note.

"What's this mean, that I carried you away?"

Houston began unwrapping food. "It means that when we return to Chandler, your reputation as the most romantic man in town will be further enhanced."

"My *what?*"

"Yes," she said as she unwrapped a package of Vienna rolls. "It started when you carried me out of the Mankins' garden party and was added to later when people began repeating the story of how you ran the cowboys who accosted me out of town. And then there was the romantic dinner party you gave at your house with the pillows and candles."

"But it's because I ain't got any chairs, and I spilled food all over you, and was I supposed to stand around and let those cowboys bother you?"

Houston opened a can that contained creamed lobster soup. "Whatever the true reason, the result is the same. By the time we return, I expect adolescent girls to stare at you on the street, and to tell each other that they hope they marry a man who drags them away from their own weddings to a lonely mountain cabin."

For a moment, Kane said nothing, but then he grinned and came to sit by her. "Romantic, am I?" he said, kissing her neck. "I don't guess anyone'll see that it's the lady I married that's keepin' me from lookin' like a fool in front of ever'body. What's that gray stuff?"

"Pâté de foie gras," she said, spreading some on a cracker with a little pearl-handled knife Opal'd included. She put it in his mouth for him.

"Not bad. What else you got?"

There was a piece of Stilton cheese, an artichoke which Kane thought was a waste of time to eat, tomatoes, soft-shell crabs, chicken croquettes, Smithfield ham, sirloin steak in onion gravy, and fried chicken.

When Houston saw the chicken, she laughed. It hadn't been on the menu that she'd planned for the wedding. No doubt Mrs. Murchison had prepared it especially for her dear Mr. Taggert. Houston wondered how many other people had been involved in packing the food for her "secret" runaway.

"What in the world is this?" Kane asked.

"I thought the wedding might be a good place to introduce a few foreign foods to Chandler. That is a German pretzel, and some Italian pastries were served, but I don't think any were packed for us."

As Houston talked, she unwrapped more food: a cloth bag filled with fruit, a tin of Waldorf salad, a big round box filled with slices of several different pies, gingerbread, a bag of peanut candy, one of fudge. There were three loaves of bread, a box of sliced meats, cheese, and onions, a jar of olives, another of mustard.

"I don't think we'll starve. Ah! Here it is." She showed Kane the inside of a metal box that contained a large section of wedding cake.

He took the little knife from the bed, cut a piece of cake and fed it to her from his fingertips. Houston held his hand and licked away every last crumb. He put his hand to the side of her face and kissed her lingeringly.

"A body could starve to death with you around," he murmured. "Why don't you feed me before you seduce me again?"

"Me!" she gasped. "You're the one who . . ."

"Yes?" he said as he picked up a piece of fried chicken. "I did what?"

"Perhaps I won't pursue that line of thought. Would you pass me that can of soup?"

"Did you find my weddin' present to you? In that little leather trunk?"

"The one in the sitting room?" When he nodded, she said she hadn't had time to look at it. "What's in it?"

"Wouldn't that spoil the surprise?"

Houston continued eating for a moment. "I think that wedding gifts should be given on the day of the wedding. And since we are here, and the trunk is there, I'd like another gift."

"You ain't even seen what's in that trunk and, besides, how can I buy you somethin' up here?"

"Sometimes, the most precious gifts aren't purchased in a store. What I want is something personal, something very special."

Kane's face showed that he had no idea what she was talking about.

"I want you to share a secret about yourself with me."

"I already told you all about myself. You wanta know where I have money hidden in case some of my investments fall through?"

Delicately, she cut herself a piece of Camembert. "I was thinking more in the line of something about your father or mother, or perhaps about your hatred for the Fentons, or maybe about what you and Pam talked about in the garden this morning."

Kane was too stunned to speak for a moment. "You don't ask for much, do you? Anythin' else you want, like maybe my head on a platter? How come you wanta know things like that?"

"Because we're married."

"Don't you go puttin' your lady face back on. A lot of married people are like your mother and that sober ol' man she married. She calls him *Mr.* Gates out of respect, like you used to do to me. I'll bet your mother never asked Gates questions like you're askin' me."

"Well then, maybe I'm just terribly curious. After all, it was my curiosity that made me want to see your house, and that led to now, and . . ." She let her voice trail off and the blanket slide down another two inches.

Kane looked at the sliding blanket with amusement. "You sure do catch on fast. All right, I guess there is somethin' I better tell you 'cause Pam says it's gonna be all over town in just a few days."

He paused a moment, looking down at the food. "You ain't gonna like this too much, but there ain't much I can do to change it now. You 'member that I told you that Fenton kicked me off his land when I was a kid 'cause I'd been messin' around with his daughter?"

"Yes," she said softly.

"I always thought that somebody'd snitched on us and told Fenton, but today Pam said she was the one that told him." He took a deep breath, looked at her with an air of defiance, and continued. "Pam told her old man that she was expectin' my kid and she wanted to marry me. Fenton, bein' the bastard he is, sent her away to marry some ol' man that owed him money, and told me Pam never wanted to see me again."

"Is that the reason you hate Mr. Fenton?"

He looked her in the eye. "No, it ain't. I just learned all this today. The point of all this storytellin' is that Pam's come back to Chandler to live, and with her is her thirteen-year-old son who also happens to be my son. And accordin' to Pam, he looks enough like me to set a few tongues waggin'."

Houston took her time in replying. "If everyone will know this shortly, it's not really a secret, is it?"

"It was damn well a secret to me until a matter of hours ago," he said with some anger in his voice. "I didn't know I had a kid somewhere."

When needed, Houston's stubbornness could match his. "I asked for a real secret, not something that next week everyone will know and be discussing over tea. I want to know something that only you know about yourself, something that even Edan doesn't know about you."

"How come you wanta know about me? How come you can't just put the furniture away and sleep with me?"

"Because I've come to love you and I want to know about you."

"Women are always sayin' they love you. Two weeks ago you were in love with Westfield. Damn it! All right, I'll tell you somethin' that's none of your business, but you'll probably like hearin' it. This mornin' Pam came to me and told me she'd been in love with me all these years, and she wanted me to leave with her, but I turned her down."

"For me?" Houston whispered.

"Ain't you the one I married? With no thanks to that idiot sister of yours, I might add."

"Has something happened between you and Blair that makes you two snarl at each other?"

"One secret to a weddin' day," he said. "You want another secret, you gotta work for it. And the best way you can work is to get that food off this bed and take that blanket off and come rub up against me."

"I'm not sure I can stand such torture," she said, as she frantically removed food and tore the blanket away at the same time.

"I like obedient women," he said, holding out his arms to her.

"I have been trained to be the most obedient of women," she whispered, putting her lips up to be kissed.

"As far as I can tell, you ain't obeyed me once yet . . . except maybe here in this cabin. Damn it, Houston, but I never thought you'd be like this. Maybe you're more like your sister than I thought."

She pulled away from him. "You thought I was an ice princess, too?"

With a smile, he pulled her back to him. "Honey, what happens when you apply heat to ice?"

"Water?"

"Steam." He moved his hand down to her firm backside and pulled her between his legs, covering her body with his.

Houston loved the sensation of being close to him, of feeling his skin against hers. She'd been warned that the wedding night was very painful, but this night had been all the joy she'd hoped it would be. Perhaps it was Kane, and the fact

165

that she felt approval coming from him, rather than the criticism that she'd always received from the other men in her life, but now she felt free to react in any way she truly felt.

Kane began to stroke her body, her legs, the back of her, and his touch made her feel beautiful in a way that no compliment or pretty dress ever had. She closed her eyes and gave herself to the lovely sensations of the darkened room, the sound and warmth of the fire, and this man's big, wide, hard hands going up and down her body, curving over surfaces that she'd not even been aware that she owned until this night. He stroked her hair, spreading it out on the pillow, running the back of his fingers along her cheekbones.

When she opened her eyes to look at him, she saw a softness in his face that she'd never seen before. His eyes were dark and hot-looking.

"Kane," she whispered.

"I'm right here, baby, and I'm not about to go away," he said as he began touching her again.

As she closed her eyes again, his hands became more insistent as he clutched her hips, burying his thumbs in her soft flesh. Her breath came faster as he moved to put one of his big, hard thighs across her smooth soft ones. His hands were on her breasts as his mouth sought hers and she opened to him like a flower to a bee.

Crushing her to him, his mouth clinging to hers, he put his hands on her buttocks and raised her to meet him.

Houston gasped at the first thrust, but there was no pain as she began to move with him. He pulled her closer and closer until their skin was as one person's, fusing them in this act of love.

Instinctively, Houston wrapped her legs around his waist and clutched his neck as he lifted her from the bed, supporting her weight with his arms and on his knees.

He shoved her against the rough cabin wall and increased the passion of his thrusts as Houston threw her head back and loudly exclaimed her pleasure. And when the last hard, fiery thrust came, Houston screamed.

For a moment, Kane held her suspended and she clung to him as if for her life.

After several long minutes, he eased both of them down to the bed, and snuggled her so close she could barely breathe. "A screamer," he murmured. "Who would a guessed that a lady would be a screamer?"

Houston was too exhausted to reply before she fell asleep in his arms.

Chapter 17

When Kane woke the next morning, it was full daylight. After a few long moments of grinning at Houston's nude body cuddled next to his, he caressed her bare rump.

"Time to get up and fix me some breakfast."

"Ring the bell on the table and the maid will come," she murmured as she buried her face deeper into his warm chest.

With one eyebrow raised, he looked at her. "Oh, good mornin', Mr. Gates and Leander. So nice to see you."

Houston reacted at once, sitting up poker-straight in the bed, grabbing the sheet, and wrapping it about her so that only her face could be seen.

It took her only seconds to realize that Kane was teasing. "What a terrible trick to play!" she accused, but Kane had started to laugh at the sight of her covered so primly, and all of it done so quickly. She tried her best to not laugh with him, but found it impossible.

"I guess I don't have to worry 'bout Westfield anymore," he said as he left the bed and began to rummage in the food that had been packed for them.

Houston lay back in the bed and watched him with a great deal of interest. His body was indeed better than that of the strongman she'd invited to The Sisterhood meeting, strong muscles, wide shoulders tapering to a small rear end atop heavy thighs—thighs that could rub on hers and make her body sing.

Casually, Kane turned to glance at her, but when he saw

168

her expression, he dropped the food he was holding, stood and held out his hand to her.

She took it and he pulled her out of the bed and drew her close.

"I hadn't planned to spend much time up here, but maybe you wouldn't mind it if we spent a few days alone together, like a honeymoon, except not in Paris or some place like that."

"I've been to Paris," she whispered, moving her hips closer to his and gently rubbing against him. "And I can honestly say that here is better than there. Now, what were you saying about breakfast?"

With disbelief on his face, Kane pushed her away. "If there was one thing that I learned as a kid, it was that toys are precious and you don't wear them out on the first day."

"I'm a toy to you?"

"A grown-up toy. Now, get some clothes on and let's eat. I thought I might show you some old minin' ruins around here. I just hope I'm man enough to spend all day with you."

"I think you are," she said through her lashes as she coyly glanced down at the part of him that showed no qualms about "wearing her out."

Quite firmly, he took her shoulders in his hands and turned her around. "I got a extra shirt and pants over there and you go get dressed—and I want every button done up and nothin' left hangin' out to drive me crazy. You understand that?"

"Completely," Houston said, her back to him; she was grinning so hard that her skin was stretching.

When they were dressed and had eaten, Kane led her up the side of the mountain. Chandler was at 6200 feet elevation and now they were at about 7500 feet, making the air cold and crisp. Kane didn't seem aware of the fact that Houston wasn't used to the climbing or that her riding boots weren't made to grip the slippery rock, but led her straight up, past overhanging rock that looked as if it were about to fall on them.

"Is it much farther?" she asked once.

Turning, Kane held out his hand to help her over a particularly difficult rock. "How about a rest?" he asked as he began to remove the pack of food from his back.

"I would appreciate it very much," she said as she took the

canteen he offered and drank deeply of it. "Are you sure there's a mine up here? How could they get the coal out?"

"Same way they get all coal out, I guess. What do I know about coal mining?" He was looking at her intently and, when he seemed satisfied that she was going to live, he turned away.

"Do you come up here often?"

"Whenever I can get away. Look through there at those rocks. Ever see anythin' like 'em?" Down through the mist of the valley she could see a razorback formation of rock that rose straight out of the ground, looking unnatural and dangerous. "What do you think caused somethin' like that? It's like some giant tried to pull the rock out of the ground, got it halfway up and stopped."

Houston was eating one of the pretzels that Kane had put in the pack. He'd already declared them to be one of nature's best foods, and she was to have them always on hand. "I think that perhaps a geologist would have a better explanation. Wouldn't you love to have had the opportunity to go to school and learn things such as why those rocks are shaped like that?"

Very slowly, Kane turned to look at her. "You got somethin' to say, say it. My schoolin's got me by enough to earn me a few million dollars. It ain't good enough for you?"

Houston studied her pretzel. "I was thinking more in the line of people less fortunate than you."

"I give as much to charity as anybody else does. I do my part." His jaw was set in a hard line.

"I just thought that perhaps now was a good time to tell you that I've invited your cousin Ian to live with us."

"My cousin Ian? That ain't that sullen, angry-lookin' kid that you saved from the fight, is it?"

"I guess you could describe him like that, although I rather thought he had a look of your . . . determination."

Kane ignored her last remark. "Why in the world would you volunteer to take on a problem like him?"

"He's very intelligent, but he had to quit school to help support his family. He's only a boy, yet he's been working in the coal mines for years. I hope you don't mind my asking him without consulting you first, but the house is certainly big enough, and he *is* your own first cousin."

Standing, Kane began to strap the pack on his back. As he started to walk again, this time on flatter ground, he said, "It's fine with me, but keep him away from me. I don't like kids much."

Houston started to follow him. "Not even your own son?"

"I ain't even met the kid; how am I supposed to like 'im?"

She struggled to throw her leg over a fallen tree blocking the way. Kane's pants that she wore were so large on her that they snagged on branches and caught debris inside them. "I thought perhaps you'd be curious."

His voice came from behind a clump of white-barked aspens. "All I'm curious 'bout right now is whether ol' Hettie Green's gonna sell me some railroad stock she owns."

Panting, Houston tried to catch up with him, but caught her shirt on a tree branch. Fighting to free herself, she called to him, "By the way, did you get your apartment building from Mr. Vanderbilt?"

Kane turned back to help her, gently freeing her shirt and then her hair from the rough branches. "Oh, that. Sure. Though it wasn't easy, what with bein' out here 'n' all. For what I'm spendin' in telegrams, I could own that company."

"You *don't* own Western Union?" she asked, wide-eyed.

Kane seemed to have no idea that she was teasing him. "Not much of it. Someday they're gonna hook up the telephones all over the country. Damn thing is useless as it is. Cain't call nobody outside Chandler. And who wants to talk to anybody in Chandler?"

She looked up into his eyes and said softly, "You could call your son and say hello."

With a deeply-felt groan, Kane turned around and started walking again. "Edan was right. I shoulda married a farm girl, one that'd mind her own business."

As Houston practically ran to keep up with him, stumbling over fallen branches, slipping once on an enormous mushroom, she wondered if she'd gone too far, but for all Kane's words, his tone was not angry.

They walked for what must have been another mile before they came to the abandoned mine opening. It was situated on the very steep side of a hill, overlooking a broad panorama of the valley below it.

The mine went back into the earth for only about twenty

feet before it collapsed. Houston picked up a piece of coal from the ground and studied it in the sunlight. When looked at closely, coal was beautiful: glossed with an almost silver quality, and Houston could readily believe that coal, with pressure and time, could become diamonds.

She looked out over the valley at the steep mountainside below. "Just what I thought," she said, "the coal is worthless up here."

Kane was more interested in the view, but gave a cursory glance to the pieces of coal on the ground. "Looks like all the rest of the stuff to me. What's wrong with it?"

"Nothing is wrong with the coal; in fact, this is high grade ore, but the railroad can't get up here. Without the railroad, coal is worthless—as my father found out."

"I thought your father made his money from sellin' things."

Houston rubbed the coal in her hand. She liked the slick feel of it and the angles made by the way the coal fractured. Many of the miners thought coal was pure and kept a piece in their mouths to suck on while they worked. "He did, but he came to Colorado because he'd heard of the wealth of coal here. He thought the place would be full of rich people dying to buy the two hundred coal stoves he nearly lost his life bringing across the 'Great Desert,' as they used to call the land between St. Joseph and Denver."

"Makes sense to me. So he sold the stoves and got started in the mercantile business."

"No, he nearly went bankrupt. You see, the coal was in Colorado all right, you could mine it with a shovel, but the railroad hadn't arrived yet, so there was no economical way to market it. Ox carts couldn't carry enough to make a profit."

"So what did your father do?"

Houston smiled at the memory of the story her mother'd told her so often. "My father had grand dreams. There was a little settlement of farmers at the foot of this mountain we're on now, and my father thought it was an ideal place for a town—his town. He gave each of the farmers one of the coal stoves if the farmer'd promise to buy all his coal from Chandler Coal Works in Chandler, Colorado."

"You mean he named the town after himself?"

"He most certainly did. I'd like to have seen the faces of

the people when he informed them that they were now living in the town of Mr. William Houston Chandler, Esquire.''

"And all these years I thought the town'd been named for him because he'd done somethin' like save a hundred babies from a burnin' buildin'.''

"Mrs. Jenks at the library says my father was honored by the town for his many contributions.''

"So how come his money wasn't made in coal?''

"My father's back gave out after one year. He shoveled coal, loaded it and hauled it to the growing population, but after a year he sold the mine to a couple of farmers' brawny sons for a pittance. A month later, he returned to the East, bought fifty-one wagonloads of goods, married my mother and brought her and twenty-five couples back to settle in the glorious town of Chandler, Colorado. Mother said that chickens were roosting on the mantel of the building that someone dared to call the Chandler Hotel.''

"And the comin' of the railroad made the farmers' sons rich,'' Kane said.

"True, but by then my father was dead, and my mother's family had already remarried her to the highly respectable Mr. Gates.'' Houston moved to look inside the mine, while Kane stayed outside.

"I guess a person gets funny ideas sometimes. This whole town thinks of your family as some sort of royalty, but the truth is, the town is named after your father only because he was enough of a braggart to want to own a town. Not much of a king, was he?''

"He was a king to my sister and me—and to my mother. When Blair and I were children, the town decided to declare my father's birthday as a holiday. Mother made an effort to tell everyone the truth, but after great frustration, she realized that the townspeople *wanted* a hero.''

"And how does Gates figure in this?''

Houston gave a deep sigh. "Mr. Gates's reputation could never be of the most sterling quality because he runs a brewery, so when Queen Opal Chandler and her two young princesses were on the marriage block, he offered everything he owned. Mother's family accepted with enthusiasm.''

"He wanted a real lady, too,'' Kane said softly.

"And he was willing to enforce his rigid beliefs of what a

173

lady should be on the three women under his roof," Houston said through a tightened jaw.

Kane was silent for a moment. "I guess the grass always looks greener on the other side of the fence."

Houston moved to stand close to him and take his hand in hers. "Did you ever think that if you'd been raised as a son, instead of in the stables, you'd be spoiled like Marc is, instead of a man who knows the value of work?"

"You make it sound like Fenton done me a favor," he said, aghast.

"Did."

"What?!"

"Fenton *did* you a favor. I was correcting your grammar. It was part of our agreement."

"You're changin' the subject. You know, I oughta send you to New York to do business for me. You'd destroy some of those men."

She put her arms around his neck. "Could I perhaps destroy you instead?"

Chapter 18

As Houston put her arms around his neck, she saw by his expression that he seemed to be fighting something within himself, almost as if he didn't want to kiss her but couldn't keep from it.

He put his hand to the back of her head and came down on her lips as if he were a dying man. Houston clung to him, loving the feel of his big body next to hers, the power of him taking over her body.

"Kane," she whispered from somewhere deep within her throat.

He pulled away to stare down at her, his dark eyes black with desire. "What have you done to me? It's been years since what's between my legs ruled what's between my ears. But right now, I think I could kill any man that tried to take you away from me."

"Or any woman?" she asked, her lips against his.

"Yes," was all he could manage to say before he began to tear the big shirt off her.

Before, Houston had felt that Kane was withholding something in his lovemaking, that part of him was remaining aloof, not with her but somewhere else. But now he was different, no more reserve of coolness, no more holding back and watching.

With all the passion of a charging bull, Kane swept her into his arms and carried her into the opening of the abandoned mine shaft. As Houston glanced at his impassioned face, she thought, this is the man who has made millions in a few short years. This is the Kane Taggert I knew was inside. This is the man that I love—the man whom I want to love me.

Kane seemed to have no thoughts as he lowered her to the ground, his lips reclaiming hers while his hands clawed the rest of her clothes from her body, exposing her soft skin to his touch. He was ravenous as his mouth tore its way down her body.

No more was he the kind, patient, considerate lover, but in his place was a man starving with want of her. Houston thought she'd responded to him previously, but now her mind left her and she became one mass of raw, pulsating feeling.

Kane's mouth on her flesh was like a fire travelling up and down, seeping into her very bones until she was sure she'd be consumed by him.

His strong fingers clutched at her waist and pulled her close to his skin, so hot it felt as if the fire in her were searing him also. He rolled to his back, holding her and moving her body as if she were of no more weight than a child.

In one swift, fluid motion, he lifted her and set her down on his manhood. Houston gave such a half-scream, half-moan of pleasure that it echoed off the back walls of the mine and swirled about them.

Her head was thrown back, there was sweat on her neck that dampened the tendrils of her hair about her shoulders and, as she put her hands on his shoulders, she let the emotion of their lovemaking take over. She had no thoughts; at that moment she only felt—as she'd never felt anything in her life before.

Kane's hands dug into her skin as he lifted her, as she lifted herself to the frenzy of movement that their passion inspired.

Once, she opened her eyes and saw him, saw the expression on his face, his mouth partly open, his eyes closed and the deep, consuming pleasure she saw there refired her own feelings.

The pace increased.

"Kane." She thought she had whispered, but again the sound reverberated about them, swirling in the cool air, wrapping around them.

Kane didn't answer but lifted her up and down with

lightning speed, and when he brought her down for that last, blinding thrust, Houston felt her body tighten as her back arched and her thighs gripped Kane's hips.

An earthshaking shudder passed through her and when it was done, she fell forward against his sweaty chest. Kane's arms held her so tightly that her ribs threatened to break, but she curled her arms against his chest, kept her legs inside his and tried her best to be even closer to him.

They lay together, the only movement being Kane's hand gently stroking her hair.

"Did you know it's started to rain?" he said softly after a while.

Houston was oblivious to anything but his body next to hers and the extraordinary experience she'd just been through. She managed to shake her head but didn't look up.

"Did you know that it's about forty degrees out there, and that I'm layin' on hundreds of those sharp little pieces of coal that you find so fascinatin', and that my left leg died 'bout an hour ago?"

Smiling, her face buried in his warm skin, Houston shook her head.

"I don't guess you have any plans of movin' within the next week or so, do you?"

Laughter was building inside Houston as she kept her face hidden and shook her head.

"And it doesn't matter to you that my toes are so cold that if I knocked 'em against somethin' they'd probably fall right off?"

Her negative response only made him hold her closer. "Could I bribe you?"

"Yes," she whispered.

"How 'bout if we get our clothes on, and then we stay in here and watch it rain, and I let you ask me questions? That seems to please you the most, as far as I can tell."

She raised her head to look at him. "Will you answer them?"

"Probably not," he said as he gently pushed her off him, but stopped midway to kiss her lingeringly, softly, and caress her cheek. "Witch," he murmured before turning away and reaching for his pants.

When he moved, Houston saw that pieces of coal were sticking to his broad back, and she began to brush them away. By some odd chance, her breasts grazed his skin repeatedly.

Kane turned around and grabbed her wrists in his. "Don't start that again. There's somethin' about you, lady, that I don't think I can resist. And you can stop lookin' so pleased with yourself." Even as he spoke, his eyes travelled down her bare body. "Houston," he half groaned as he released her and turned away, "you ain't like what I expected at all. Now, get dressed 'fore I make a fool of myself . . . again."

Houston didn't ask him what he meant about making a fool of himself *again,* but her heart raced with pleasure as she pulled on the loose clothing she'd borrowed from him. There were several buttons ripped from the shirt and the torn places made her smile.

She was barely dressed before he pulled her into his arms, and sat her on his lap as he leaned back against the wall of the mine tunnel.

The soft rain outside came down slowly, as if it never meant to stop, and Houston snuggled back into Kane's arms.

"You make me happy," Houston said as she moved his arms closer about her.

"Me? You didn't even get the present I got for you." He paused. "Oh, you mean just now. Well, you don't exactly make me sad, either."

"No, it's you who makes me happy, not the presents and not even the lovemaking—although that does help."

"All right, tell me how I make you happy." There was caution in his voice.

She was silent for a moment before she spoke. "When Leander and I had just become officially engaged, we were going to a dance at the Masonic Temple. I was looking forward to the evening very much and, I guess as a reflection of my mood, I had a red dress made. Not a deep, subdued red, but a brilliant, scarlet red. The night of the dance, I put on the dress and felt as if I were the most beautiful woman in the world."

She paused to take a breath and to remind herself that she was here in Kane's arms and safe now. "When I walked down the stairs, Mr. Gates and Leander stared at me, and I stupidly thought they were in awe of the way I looked in that red dress. But when I reached the bottom, Mr. Gates started shouting at me that I looked like a harlot and to go back upstairs and change. Leander stepped in and said he'd take care of me. I don't think I ever loved him more than at that moment."

Again, she paused. "When we arrived at the dance, Leander suggested that I keep my cloak on and tell people that I'd caught a chill. I spent the entire evening sitting in the corner and feeling miserable."

"Why didn't you tell both of 'em to go to hell and dance in your red dress?"

"I guess I've always done what people expected of me. That's why you make me happy. You seem to think that if Houston's climbing down the trellis in her underwear, then that's what ladies do. Nor do you seem to mind that I make very unladylike advances toward you." She turned her head to look at him.

After a quick kiss, he turned her back around. "I don't mind the advances, but I could do without your public appearances in your underwear. I don't guess you remember the puppies, do you?"

"I'm not sure I know what you're talking about."

"At Marc Fenton's birthday party—I guess he was about eight—I took you into the stables and showed you some black-and-white spotted puppies."

"I do remember! But that couldn't have been you, that was a grown man."

"I guess I was about eighteen, so that would make you . . ."

"Six. Tell me about it."

"You and your sister came to the party together, wearin' white dresses with pink sashes and big pink bows in your hair. Your sister went runnin' into the back and started playin' tag with the other kids, but you went and sat down on a iron bench. You didn't move a muscle, just sat there with your hands folded in your lap."

"And you stopped in front of me with a wheelbarrow that had obviously once been full of horse manure."

Kane grunted. "Probably. I felt sorry for you there all alone, so I asked you if you wanted to see the pups."

"And I went with you."

"Not until you'd looked me up and down real hard. I guess I passed 'cause you did go with me."

"And I wore your shirt, and then something awful happened. I remember crying."

"You wouldn't get near the pups, but stood way back and looked down at 'em. Said you couldn't get your dress dirty, so I gave you a shirt of mine to put on over your dress—which you wouldn't touch until I swore three times that it was clean. And what you remember as the great tragedy was that one of the dogs ran behind you and bit your hair ribbon and pulled it undone. I never saw a kid get so upset. You started cryin' and said that Mr. Gates would hate you and when I said I'd retie it you said that only your mamma could tie a bow properly. That's what you said, 'properly'."

"And you did tie it properly. Not even Mother knew that it'd come untied."

"I was always braidin' the horses' manes and tails."

"For Pam?"

"You're damned curious 'bout her. Jealous?"

"Not since you told me you turned her down."

"That's why you shouldn't tell women secrets."

"Would you like me to be jealous?"

Kane considered this. "I wouldn't mind it. At least you know I turned Pam down. I ain't heard nothin' like that about Westfield."

She kissed the hand that was idly fondling her breast, knowing quite well she'd told him about Leander several times. "I turned him down at the altar," she said softly.

Kane tightened his arms a bit. "I guess you did at that. Course, he ain't got near as much money as me."

"You and your money! Don't you know anything else? Like kissing, perhaps?"

"I have unleashed a monster," he laughed but showed no reluctance in obeying her wish.

"Behave yourself," he said when he at last turned her back around. "I ain't got as much stamina as you have. Don't forget that compared to you I'm an old man."

With a giggle, Houston wiggled her bottom in his lap.

"And I'm gettin' older by the minute. Now sit still! Gates was right to lock you two women up."

"Will you lock me away?" Houston whispered, leaning her head into his neck and chin.

He took so long to answer that she turned to look at him. "I might," he finally answered, then, in an obvious attempt to change the subject, he said, "You know, I ain't talked so much about stuff other'n business in years."

"What did you talk to your other women about?"

"What other women?"

"The others. Like Miss LaRue."

"I don't 'member ever talkin' to Viney about anything."

"But the nice part is afterward, lying like this together, and talking."

He ran his hand down her body. "I guess it is pretty nice at that. But cain't say as I've ever done it before. I guess after we . . . I guess I just went home. You know, I don't even 'member wantin' to lay around like this. Fat waste of time," he said, but he made no attempt to move away from her. Houston snuggled closer to him.

"Cold?"

"No, I'm the warmest I've ever been."

Chapter 19

Houston looked up at Kane from the cabin bed, watching him dress, and knew that her short honeymoon was over. "I guess we have to go," she said sadly.

"I have a couple of men comin' this mornin' and I can't afford to miss 'em." He turned to look back at her. "I wish I could spend more time up here but I can't."

There was sadness in his voice, too, and Houston decided to help rather than fight him. Quickly, she got out of bed and began to dress in her riding clothes. Kane had to help her with the ties to her corset.

"How in the world can you breathe in that blasted thing?"

"I don't think breathing has anything to do with it. I thought you liked the curves of women. With no corseting, we'd soon all have twenty-seven- and twenty-eight-inch waists. Besides, the corset supports a woman's back. They're really quite healthful."

Kane merely grunted and finished shoving food into the cloth bags. She could tell that his mind was already back on his work.

Silently, the two of them prepared for the journey down the mountain. Houston wasn't sure what was on Kane's mind, but she knew she'd never been happier in her life. Her fear that she was frigid was gone, and ahead of her was a lifetime with the man she loved.

As they were leaving the cabin, Kane paused to look back at the little room. "I sure never had a better time in that place," he said before shutting the door and walking toward the saddled horses.

Houston started to mount by herself, but Kane grabbed her by the waist and hoisted her into the saddle. She tried to hide her surprise as she looked at him. Was this the man who had left her to climb boulders all alone?

Kane ducked his head. "You look like a lady again in that suit," he mumbled.

They were silent as they started down the treacherously steep slope, and several times Kane slowed for her.

It wasn't until they were near Chandler, and they began to slow their horses to a crawl, that Houston spoke.

"Kane, you know what I've been thinking the last few days?"

He gave her a bawdy wink. "I sure do, honey, and I've enjoyed ever' minute of your thoughts."

"No, not that," she said impatiently. "I thought I'd invite your cousin Jean to live with us."

When she looked at Kane, she saw that his mouth was open.

"I doubt whether she'll accept a direct invitation because all you Taggerts are much too prideful, but I've purposely held off hiring a housekeeper and thought she might like to have the job. That would get her out of the coal camps and, besides, don't you think she and Edan would make a lovely couple?"

Kane was still gaping at her.

"Well, what do you think?"

He managed to shut his mouth and stop staring at her. "When I told Edan I was thinkin' about gettin' married, he asked me if I was ready to let a woman in my life. He 'bout laughed his fool head off when I said I didn't plan to let marriage change my life. I'm beginnin' to see why he was laughin'. Who else you gonna invite to live at my house? The town drunk? But I tell you, I draw the line at preachers. I like preachers even less 'n kids. Course, it don't matter who *I* like——." He broke off as Houston, her back rigid, urged her horse ahead.

For a moment, he didn't move but watched her, then, in a spurt of speed, he caught up with her. "You ain't gonna get mad, are you, honey? You can invite whoever you want to live in that big house. It don't matter none to me." It was the first time in his life that he'd ever tried to coax a woman out of a bad mood and he was awkward at it.

He grabbed her horse's bridle. "I ain't even seen this woman. What's she look like? Maybe she's so ugly that I won't be able to stand lookin' at her." He was sure that he saw the faintest glimmer of a smile on her lips. So . . . humor was the way.

"Jean was wearing violet chiffon over purple satin, with tiny brillants at the shoulder and—."

"Wait a minute!" he interrupted. "You mean that little black-haired, green-eyed wench with the curvy backside and the great ankles? In fact, I saw her get out of the carriage and her calves ain't bad either."

Houston glared at him. "You were looking at other women on our wedding day?"

"When I wasn't watchin' you climbin' up and down the rose trellis. Come to think of it, you sure looked mighty good in your underwear." He moved his hand to caress her arm.

In the distance was the civilization of town and the people who would make demands on their time. Now was their last chance for privacy.

As if reading her thoughts, Kane dragged her off the horse and into his arms and they came together as if it were to be their last night alive.

And when they entered the Taggert house two hours later, there was dirt on their clothes, cockleburs in their hair, and their faces were flushed. Kane was holding Houston's hand until Edan appeared.

Edan took one look at them and, when he'd recovered his speech, he said to Houston, "I see you found him. Kane, there are four men waiting for you and half a dozen telegrams. And Houston, I think those servants you hired are in a state of war."

Houston felt Kane give her hand one last squeeze, and then he disappeared down the hall. She started up the stairs to her bedroom to change clothes. Reality had come back to them.

Ten minutes later, Kane came to say he had to leave on urgent business and would be back as soon as it was finished. He was gone for three days.

Chapter 20

Within four hours after Kane had left, Houston knew that being a wife was what she was meant to do. Blair could have her ambition, her need to reform the world, but Houston just wanted to manage a household for the man she loved.

Of course, running Kane's house was rather like directing an army during wartime, but she'd been trained for her position as General of the Army.

The first thing she did was write a note to Jean Taggert begging her to spend a few days helping with the housekeeping arrangements. Then Houston wrote a letter to Jean's father telling him that she planned to ask Jean to stay and be her housekeeper. Houston prayed that Sherwin Taggert would want his daughter to get out of the coal camp.

When she gave the notes to a new footman to deliver, Houston had her first taste of what was upsetting the servants so badly. The footman seemed to think it was beneath him to go to a coal camp, and, being American, he didn't hesitate to express his opinion.

Houston very calmly asked him if he wanted his job or not, and, if he did, he was to do what she asked and to not belittle the relatives of the man who was feeding him. When that was settled, and the footman on his way, Houston went downstairs and began sorting out the duties of the other people she'd hired. Most of the people she'd chosen were now sitting on the bare floors, refusing to do anything until they knew exactly the limits of their responsibilities. Houston saw immediately why Miss Jones had strongly recommended that experienced servants be hired.

By the morning of the second day, Houston had seven maids cleaning the house, four footmen bringing furniture down from the attics, and three assistants helping Mrs. Murchison in the kitchen. Outside, she had a coachman, two stableboys, and four young, strong-backed boys to help in the gardens.

It was while she was in the garden introducing herself to Mr. and Mrs. Nakazona and trying to explain to them as best she could, since neither spoke the other's language, that the boys were to be under the Japanese family's rule, that she saw Ian's face in an upstairs window.

This morning, while helping her dress, Susan had informed Houston of the awful brawl Rafe Taggert had caused after the wedding guests left. Susan had just happened to hear some of it. Young Ian had boasted that he hated his cousin Kane and would never live in his house. Rafe had said that it was an empty boast since no one had asked Ian to live there. Ian'd said that Houston had but he'd die before he accepted.

It was at that point that Rafe and Ian had had the fight, which the larger Rafe easily won. Rafe'd said Ian was going to stay with his cousin and receive all the benefits that money can buy, even if Rafe had to beat Ian every day for the rest of his life, and he'd said he'd find Ian if he tried to run away.

So, for the last few days, Ian had been holding himself prisoner in the room where Houston had left him. Mrs. Murchison had been the only one to see him when she took trays of food and books to him.

"Books?" Houston'd asked.

"The boy seems to love them," Susan said. "Mrs. Murchison says he reads all day long and that it isn't good for him. She thinks he should join the boys' baseball team and get outside some."

Now, when Houston had most of the other people under control, she turned her thoughts to Ian. If the boy was going to live with them, he was going to be part of their family.

Upstairs, she knocked on his door and, after several minutes, he told her to come in. From his flushed face, Houston had an idea he was hiding something, and she thought she saw the edge of a book sticking out from under the bed.

"You're back," he said as if it were an accusation.

"We returned yesterday," she said, and was sure he knew that. "Do you like your room?"

The big, light, airy room was twice as big as the Taggert house at the mine camp, but there was no furniture in it except for a bed covered with a dirty blanket—evidence of Ian having lain on it for days.

"It's all right," Ian mumbled, looking at the toe of his heavy work boot.

The Taggert pride, Houston thought. "Ian, could you help me this afternoon? I have four men hired to help me arrange furniture, but I think I'm going to need a supervisor, someone to make sure that they don't hit the edges on the doors as they bring it down, that sort of thing. Could you help me?"

Ian hesitated, but he agreed.

Houston was curious as to how Ian'd handle his new responsibility, and she was sure he'd be a little tyrant. But he surprised her. He was careful, observant, and very serious. Only at first, when he used his size and adolescent strength to establish his authority, did he show any anger. By late afternoon, he was so completely in control that Houston merely had to point to where she wanted a piece of furniture placed.

She was watching Ian with amazement, as he skillfully guided a large desk down the main staircase, when Edan spoke from behind her.

"Kane was like that. People like those two have never been children. Your footmen sense that, and that's why they're willing to obey a kid."

She turned to face him. "Do you know how to play baseball?"

Edan's eyes sparkled. "Sure do. You thinking of starting a team?"

"I almost have enough men. I think I'll call Vaughn's Sporting Goods and order some equipment. You think I could learn to hit a ball with that stick?"

"Houston," he said, as he turned back toward Kane's office, "I think you could do anything you set your mind to."

"Dinner at seven," she called after him. "And we dress for dinner."

She could hear Edan's laughter as he went back to the office.

The meal was pleasant and Edan's quiet patience with Ian seemed to melt some of the boy's tense anger.

But the next day was different. When it was time for dinner, Houston was dressed in pale green silk faille with a green net overlay embroidered with cut-steel bugle beads, a large pink cameo at her waist. She hadn't seen Kane since he'd returned that afternoon, and he hadn't changed out of the heavy work clothes he'd worn on his business trip. But she wasn't about to start an argument with him. Let him come to the table and be the only one in his dirty canvas.

Edan, looking strikingly handsome in his dark dinner clothes, was waiting for her at the head of the stairs, and Ian, wearing one of Edan's new suits that was only a little too big, was standing in a shadow of the hallway.

Houston, without saying a word, took Edan's offered arm, then held out her other arm for Ian. For several long moments, he didn't move, but when Houston just stood there, as stubborn as he was, Ian came forward and took her other arm.

There was more than enough room for the three of them to walk down the stairs together.

"Ian," Houston said, "I can't thank you enough for helping me the last couple of days."

"I need to earn my keep," he mumbled, looking away from her in embarrassment, but he was pleased with her thanks.

"Where the hell is everybody?" Kane shouted from the bottom of the stairs, then looked up and saw them. "You all goin' somewhere? Edan, I need you." As he said this, his eyes were on Houston alone. The other two didn't exist as far as he was concerned.

"We're going in to dinner," Houston said, as she forcibly held Ian's arm to her. He'd tried to jerk it away when Kane appeared. "Would you join us?"

"Somebody has to earn a livin' around here," he snorted as he turned on his heel and returned to his office.

During dinner, as course after course was brought into the

room, Houston led the conversation to what Ian had been reading over the last few days. This was a topic that hadn't been mentioned last night.

Ian nearly choked on a piece of tenderloin. His Uncles Rafe and Sherwin had encouraged his reading, but he'd learned to read in secret for fear of being thought of as a sissy. "Mark Twain," he said with an air of defiance when he'd cleared his throat.

"Good," Houston said. "Tomorrow, I'm arranging for a tutor to come and give you lessons. I think that will work out better than going to school, since you'd be quite a bit larger than the other children. And besides, I rather like having you here."

Ian gaped at her for a moment. "I ain't goin' to no school to be laughed at and called names. I'll go back to the coal mines and—."

"I perfectly well agree with you," Houston interrupted. "And tomorrow, we'll have you fitted for your own clothing. Ah, the sorbet. I think you'll like this, Ian."

Edan was laughing at the expression on Ian's face. "You might as well give in, boy. Nobody wins an argument with this lady."

"Except *him*," Ian said.

"Especially not him," Edan answered.

They were just starting dessert when Kane came in. Houston had persuaded Ian to tell them the story of *Huckleberry Finn*, but when Kane entered he stopped talking and looked down at his plate.

"Sure is takin' a long time to eat," Kane said, putting his foot on a chair and helping himself to a handful of grapes from the arrangement in the center of the table.

The look Houston gave him made him sit down in the chair. She nodded to a footman, who set a place in front of Kane and served him. After a moment of surprise, Kane began to eat the chocolate charlotte with gusto, so much gusto that the others started watching him. Kane put his spoon down and looked a bit like he wanted to run from the room.

Ian was surreptitiously watching his cousin and Edan was concentrating on his food.

Houston had left the head of the table for Kane and was sitting next to Ian, across from Edan, but Kane didn't take the head seat, sitting next to Edan instead. Houston caught Kane's eye and held up her fork, and he began to follow her directions on how to eat with some semblance of manners. To start the conversation again, she told of getting the gardeners to work and how well the Japanese family had taken to having help.

Kane told of how he'd met the Nakazonas, and Edan added to the conversation with a story of bringing in the plants from all over the world, and Ian asked what the tree was outside his window. It was stilted, but it did resemble conversation and, best of all, it was pleasant. When the meal was finished, the four of them went away smiling.

Kane and Edan went back to work after dinner while Ian and Houston went to the small drawing room. Houston embroidered pillow cases while Ian read and, after using some persuasion, she got him to read aloud to her. He had a good voice and a flair for reading dialogue. Edan joined them for a while.

At bedtime, Houston went up alone, Kane being firmly ensconced inside his office, cigar smoke seeping out from under the door. Sometime during the night, he crawled into bed with her, pulled her close to his big, warm body and went to sleep immediately.

Houston woke to the heavenly sensation of Kane's hand roaming over her legs and hips. She turned her face toward him before even opening her eyes, and he fastened his lips onto hers as he began to make love to her gently, slowly, languidly.

It wasn't until their passion was spent that Houston at last opened her eyes.

"Wanted to make sure it was your husband?" Kane asked, smiling down at her. "Or would any man do, this early in the mornin'?"

She decided to answer his teasing with some of her own. "How would I know about other men? Should I try to find out?"

A frown crossed his face as he rose.

She put her arms around him, her bare breasts against his

back. "I was only teasing; I have no desire for any other man."

He pulled away from her. "I got to get to work and earn enough money to feed that army you hired."

Houston lay in bed and watched him until he disappeared into his bathroom. There was a part of him that she knew nothing about.

A knock on the door gave her no more time to think.

"Miss Houston," Susan said. "Miss Jean Taggert is downstairs with her father and all their belongings in a wagon, and they want to speak to you."

"I'll be right down," she called, reluctantly getting out of bed, wishing that Kane had stayed with her. He was already at work by the time Houston was dressed.

Downstairs, she led Jean into the small drawing room. "I'm so glad you've decided to accept my offer," Houston began. "I really do need a housekeeper."

Jean waved her hand. "You don't need to continue the lie. I know why you're offering me the job, and I know more than you do that you'll have to teach me everything, and that I'll be more of a hindrance than of any use. But more important than my pride is getting my family out of the coal mines. Rafe blackmailed Ian into leaving, and my father has blackmailed me. I've come to ask for more charity than you've already offered. I'll work myself into a stupor for you, if you'll let my father live here with me."

"Of course," Houston said quickly. "And, Jean, you're family, you don't really have to be my housekeeper. You can live here as a guest, with no duties or obligations except to enjoy yourself."

Jean smiled. "I'd go crazy in two weeks. If my father is welcome, then I'll stay."

"Only if you sit at the table with us for meals. It's a big table and almost empty. Now, may I meet your father?"

When Houston saw Sherwin Taggert, she knew why Jean wanted to get him out of the mines. Sherwin was dying. Houston was sure that Jean knew it, and that her father did also, but it was also apparent that no one was going to mention the fact.

Houston found Sherwin to be a gentle, polite man and,

191

within minutes, he had the rest of the staff running to make him comfortable. There was some argument as to where the elder Taggert would stay, but Jean won when she put her father in the downstairs housekeeper's rooms with a door leading outside to the gardens and placed near the stairs that led to the upstairs room Jean chose.

At luncheon, Kane stayed in his office, but Edan joined the growing group who sat down to meals. Ian relaxed visibly when he saw his uncle and Jean, and the meal became very pleasant. Sherwin told a funny story of a happening in the mine and, while everyone was laughing, Kane came into the room. Houston introduced him to his relatives, and he looked about for a seat. Since Jean was seated next to Edan, Kane stood still for a moment until Houston motioned for a footman to pull out the chair at the head of the table.

Through the rest of the meal, Kane sat quietly, saying very little but watching everyone, and especially watching the way Houston ate. She ate slowly, prolonging the meal and giving Kane plenty of time to see which fork she was using.

Toward the end of the meal, Houston turned to Ian. "I have some good news for you. Yesterday, I sent a telegram to a friend of my father who lives in Denver and asked him if he'd like to move to Chandler and be your teacher. Mr. Chesterton is a retired British explorer. He's been all over the world, up the Nile, to the pyramids, to Tibet; I doubt if there's anywhere he hasn't been. And this morning, he agreed to come here. I think he'll make you a marvelous teacher, don't you?"

Ian could only stare at her. "Africa?" he said at last.

"That among others." She pushed back her chair. "Now, who'd like to play baseball? I have equipment, a playing field chalked out on the north lawn, and a book of instructions. Unfortunately, I have no idea what a word of it means."

"I think Ian could show you some of the basics," Sherwin said, eyes twinkling. "And I imagine that Edan knows a few rules, too."

"You'll join us, Edan?" Houston asked.

"I'd love to."

"And you, Jean?"

"Since I have no idea how to even begin running a house

like this, I may as well make myself useless on a baseball diamond."

"And Kane?" Houston asked her husband as he began to pull back from the group. He wore a puzzled expression.

"I have some work to do, and, Edan, I need you to help me."

"I guess that leaves me out of baseball," Edan said, rising. "I'll see you at dinner."

Once in Kane's office, Edan watched his friend pace the floor and look out his window at the others on the baseball field. Edan wondered if Houston had purposely put the diamond outside Kane's office. Twice, Edan had to repeat questions before Kane answered them.

"She's really pretty, isn't she?" Kane asked.

"Who?" Edan asked, pretending ignorance as he looked through the morning's batch of telegrams, studying the offers for land, factories, stocks, whatever Kane was buying or selling at the moment.

"Houston, of course. Damn! Look at that Ian. Playing! At his age, I was working fourteen hours a day."

"And so was he," Edan said. "And so was I. Which is why he's playing now," he said as he dropped the telegrams on the desk. "Everything here can wait for a few hours. I think I'll go out and enjoy the sunshine, and listen to something else besides money."

He paused at the door. "You coming?"

"No," Kane said, his eyes on the papers. "Somebody better stay here and . . ." He looked up. "Hell, yes, I'm comin'. How far can a body hit that ball with that bat? I'll put a hundred on it that I can beat you and anybody else out there."

"You're on," Edan said, leading the way out the door.

Kane took to baseball like a child to candy. It took three swings before he first hit the ball—and no one had the nerve to tell him of the three-strikes-and-you're-out rule—but when he hit it, the ball flew through the air and smashed a second-story window. He was disgustingly pleased with himself and from then on proceeded to give everyone advice.

Once, Kane and Ian almost went after each other with bats, but Houston managed to separate them before it became bloody. To her consternation, both men turned on her and told her to mind her own business. She retreated to Sherwin's side.

"Ian will feel at home now," Sherwin said. "He and Rafe argued all the time. He misses the discussions."

Houston groaned. "Discussions are what Kane calls them, too. You don't think they'll hurt each other, do you?"

"I think your Kane has too much sense to let it go that far. It's your turn to bat, Houston."

Houston didn't care for trying to hit the ball that came flying at her, but she very much enjoyed it when Kane put his arms around her and snuggled up against her to show her how to hold the bat. Ian shouted that Kane was giving the opposing team an unfair advantage and, while Kane was shouting at his young cousin, Houston slammed the ball past second base.

"Run!" Jean shouted. "Run, Houston, run."

Houston took off as fast as she could, holding her skirt up almost to her knees. Edan, on first, just stood there grinning at her with delight, but Kane tore across the field, grabbed the ball and went running for Houston. She looked up, saw him coming and thought that, if he hit her, she'd never survive the impact. She started running faster, hearing in the background everyone shouting at Kane to stop before he hurt Houston.

He caught her at home base, grabbing her by the ankles and slamming her face down into the dirt. But she stretched out her arm and touched the plate.

"Safe!" Sherwin yelled.

Kane jumped up and started yelling at his smaller uncle and Ian, on the same team as Kane, joined in the shouting. Sherwin just stood there quite calmly.

Jean helped Houston up and examined her for cuts and bruises. Houston looked fondly at her shouting husband and said, "He does like to win, doesn't he?"

"Not any more than you do," Jean said, looking at a huge tear in Houston's skirt, and the dirt on her face.

Houston touched her husband's arm. "Dear, since we've beaten you so badly today, perhaps we could stop now for refreshments, and you can try again tomorrow."

For a moment, Kane's face darkened, then he laughed,

grabbed her in his arms and twirled her around. "I've beat ever' man on Wall Street at one time or another, but you, lady, I ain't never beat at nothin'."

"Stop bragging and let's get something to eat," Edan said. He turned to Jean and held out his arm. "May I?"

The two couples walked toward the house together, Sherwin and Ian behind.

Chapter 21

It was as if the baseball game broke the ice with the entire family. Kane stopped staying in his office during meals, and Ian stopped being quiet. Kane told Ian he was a dreamer and didn't know anything about the real world. Ian, who considered Kane's words a dare, suggested—in language that made Houston threaten to make him leave the table—that Kane show him some of the "real" world.

Kane began to introduce Ian to the world of business, showing him stock-market reports and teaching him how to read a contract. In only days, Ian was talking in terms of thousands of dollars being paid for land in cities he'd only read about.

One day, Houston saw Sherwin doodling on a scrap of paper. Later, she saw that it was a very accurate rendition of one of the Colorado mockingbirds. She ordered, from Sayles, a large, portable watercolor kit and presented it to Sherwin with an elaborate lie, saying that she'd found it in the attics, and did he know anyone who'd want it? She was afraid of the Taggert pride and thought he might refuse the paints.

Sherwin had laughed so knowingly that Houston'd blushed. He'd accepted the paints and kissed her on the cheek. After that, he spent most of his time in the garden painting whatever took his fancy.

Twice, Houston visited Blair at the new Westfield Infirmary for Women, staying for hours and getting to know her sister again after all the years of separation. And one day, Leander called her to ask about hiring servants for Blair and him. Lee was cautious and hesitant about talking to her, and she remembered the time he'd tried to speak to her in the church when the engagement had been announced, and how rude she'd been.

"Lee," she began, "I'm glad the way things worked out. I'm really happy with Kane."

He was slow to answer. "I never meant to hurt you, Houston."

She smiled into the telephone. "*I* was the one who insisted that Blair trade places with me. Maybe I knew that the two of you were better as a couple than we were. Shall we forget it and be friends?"

"That would be my fondest wish. And, Houston, that man you married is a good one."

"Yes, he is, but what makes you say so?"

"I have to go, and thanks for the advice on the housekeeper. Blair's even worse than I am at these things. I'll probably see you in church on Sunday. 'Bye."

She frowned at the telephone in puzzlement, then shrugged and went back to the library.

It was three weeks after they were married that Houston told Kane that she was now ready to decorate his office. She had thought perhaps he might object, but she wasn't prepared for the violence of his objections. In expressing his opinion of her tampering with his private space he used words she'd never heard before—but it didn't take much intelligence to understand them.

Edan and Ian stood in the background and watched with interest to see who was going to win this battle.

Houston had no idea how to handle this, but she was determined. "I am going to clean and put proper furniture in this room. Either you let me do it now, when you can supervise and voice your approval, or I'll do it when you're asleep."

Kane leaned over her in a threatening manner and Houston bent backward, but she didn't relent.

Kane slammed from the room so hard the door nearly came loose from its hinges. "Damned women!" he shouted. "Can't let any man alone, always changing everything, can't stand for a man to be happy."

As Houston turned to look at Edan and Ian, they both gave her weak smiles and left the room.

Houston'd had an idea that the room was dirty and messy, but when she got into it, she found it to be a pigsty. It took six people an hour and a half to clean all of it, including the marble lions' heads on the fireplace. When it was clean, Houston had the footmen remove Kane's cheap oak desk and replace it with a partners' desk, William Kent style, built in 1740. There were three chair openings in the big, dark desk, two for the partners, one for a visitor. She placed two comfortable leather chairs at the desk and, for Kane, an enormous chair upholstered in red leather. When she'd first seen this chair in the attic, she had known where it was meant to go, and who was to sit in it.

When the desk was in place, Houston sent all the servants away except Susan, and they started sorting out the contents of the cabinets. She knew it would be useless to try to file the documents that were jammed in every available place, so she had Susan bring hot irons and they ironed the wadded papers and placed them neatly in the desk drawers.

Flanking the fireplace were two glass-doored wall cabinets, both filled with papers and, in one of them, four whiskey bottles and six glasses that hadn't been washed within the last four years.

"Boil these," Houston said, holding them out as far as she could. "And see that Mr. Taggert has fresh glasses in here every morning."

In the glass cabinets she placed a collection of small brass statues of Venus.

"Mr. Kane will like those," Susan giggled, looking at the exquisite, plump, nude women.

"I think they were bought with him in mind."

On the north wall were two cabinets concealed in the panelling, and Houston gasped when she opened the first one. Mixed in with the papers were stacks of money, some tied together, some wadded into balls, some loose that floated to the floor when the door was opened.

With a sigh, Houston began to sort it out. "Tell Albert to call the hardware store and have them send me a cashbox immediately, and get another couple of hot irons and we'll see if we can get this to lie flat."

With her eyes wide in astonishment, Susan went to do as she was bid.

When Kane saw his office, he looked at it for a long time, noting the draperies of deep blue brocade, the collection of statues of pretty women, and the red chair. He sat in the chair. "At least you didn't paint the room pink," he said. "*Now*, will you let me get back to work?"

Houston smiled as she passed him and kissed him on the forehead. "I knew you'd be pleased. Whether you admit it or not, you like pretty things."

He caught her hand. "I guess I do," he said as he looked up at her.

Houston left the room feeling as if she were floating, and grinned all through her fitting at her dressmaker's.

Two days later, they gave their first dinner party and it was a major success. Houston invited only some of her friends whom Kane had already met so he'd feel comfortable, and Kane turned out to be a charming host. He poured champagne for the ladies and escorted everyone on a grand tour of his house.

It was only later, during the entertainment, that Houston wanted to disappear. She'd hired a travelling clairvoyant to come after dinner and perform. Kane fidgeted in his chair for the first ten minutes, then started talking to Edan, who sat next to him, about a piece of land he wanted to buy. Houston nudged him once and he turned to her and said, much too loudly, that he thought the man was a fraud and he refused to sit there another minute.

In front of everyone, he got up and left the room. Houston, her back rigid, signalled to the psychic to continue.

Later, after their guests had departed, Houston found her husband at the bottom of the garden. She followed winding dirt paths downward to the flat, grassy bottom. The steep hill, the house on top of it, was at her back, while before her stretched a secret, magic place of shadowy trees and plants, with only the sound of birds around them.

"I didn't like that man, Houston," Kane said, not turning from where he stood leaning against a tree, smoking a cigar. "There's no such thing as magic, and I couldn't sit there and pretend there is."

She put her fingers to his lips to stop his words, then slipped her arms around his neck. He bent to kiss her, bending her entire body to fit with his.

"How'd a lady like you get hitched up with a stableboy like me?"

"Just lucky, I guess," she answered before kissing him again.

One of the things that Houston liked best about Kane was his lack of knowledge about what was right and what was improper. There were people not far from them, servants who could easily decide to take an evening stroll, gardeners who could come searching for a forgotten tool—but none of this bothered Kane.

"You wear too damn many clothes," he said as he began unbuttoning her dress, slipping the satin off her shoulders as he progressed.

When she was standing in her underwear, her dress a heap at her feet, he slipped his arm under her knees and carried her across the lawn, through a tangle of flowers to a marble pavilion containing a statue of Diana, goddess of the hunt.

He placed her on the grass at the foot of the goddess and carefully removed her clothing, piece by piece, kissing each part of her body as it was exposed.

Houston was sure she'd never felt so good in her life, and her passion was very slow to build since she wanted to prolong this time together forever.

He stroked and caressed her body until she was dizzy. The world seemed to be spinning and twirling about, and her fingers began to tingle.

When at last he moved on top of her, he was smiling, as if he knew what her thoughts were. She clung to him, pulling him closer and closer until they were one person.

He continued to move slowly, prolonging her ecstasy, slowly bringing her to new heights of passion.

"Kane," she whispered repeatedly, "Kane."

When at last he exploded within her, she shivered, her whole body shuddering with the force of her own release.

He lay on top of her, bronze skin in the moonlight, sweat glistening on his skin, and held her close to him. "What have you done to me, woman?" she thought she heard him whisper.

Slowly, he moved off her. "Warm enough? You want to go inside?"

"Never," she said, snuggling against him, the mountain air cool on her damp skin. She looked up at the statue above them. "You know, don't you, that Diana is the Virgin Goddess? Do you think she'll resent our intrusion?"

"Probably jealous," Kane snorted, running his hand up and down the smooth skin of her waist and hip.

"Why do you think Jacob Fenton paid Sherwin for working in the mines when it's obvious that he's too weak to actually earn his salary?"

The groan Kane gave as he rolled away from her was heartfelt. "I can see that the honeymoon is over. Or, with you, maybe it's still on, since you only started these questions after we got married. I reckon you can get dressed by yourself. I got some business to finish before I can go to bed." With that, he left her alone.

Houston was torn between wanting to cry and being glad that she had asked Kane what she had. There was something deep between the Fentons and the Taggerts, and she was sure that Kane could never be truly happy until he was rid of what bothered him.

The next night, Houston woke shivering and somehow knew that her sister's life was in danger. She'd heard her mother's often-repeated story of how one afternoon when Houston was six years old she'd dropped her mother's best teapot and started crying that Blair was hurt. They'd finally found Blair by the side of an arroyo, unconscious, her arm broken from having fallen from a tree. Blair was supposed to have been attending a dancing lesson.

But the odd bond between the twins had not appeared since then—until now. Kane called Leander, then held Houston for over two hours until she stopped shaking. Somehow, Houston sensed the danger was over, stopped shaking, and fell into a deep sleep.

The next day, Blair came to Houston's house and spent the afternoon telling her what'd happened that had indeed endangered her life.

It was four days later that Zachary Younger burst into their lives. The Taggerts were just sitting down to dinner when the boy, a footman running after him, stormed into the dining room and yelled that he'd heard that Kane was his father, and that he already had one father and didn't want another one. He left in the next breath.

Everyone seemed to be stunned except Kane. He sat down while the others remained standing and asked the maid what kind of soup they were having tonight.

"Kane, I think you should go after him," Houston said.

"What for?"

"Just to talk to him. I think his heart was broken when he found out that the man he thought was his father wasn't."

"Pam's husband *was* the boy's father as far as I can tell. And I sure as hell didn't tell him any different."

"Perhaps you should explain that to the child."

"I don't know how to talk to no kid."

Houston looked at him.

"Damned woman! In another year, I'll be broke 'cause I'll have spent all my time doin' whatever fool things you dream up for me to do."

As he started out the door, Houston touched his arm. "Kane, don't offer to buy him a single thing. Just tell him the truth and invite him to meet his cousin Ian."

"Why don't I invite him to live here and help you think up things for me to do?" He went out the door muttering about "starvin' to death."

Kane walked out the door slowly, but Zach was moving even slower. He caught up with him. "You like to play baseball?"

Zach turned, his handsome young face full of fury. "Not with you I don't."

Kane was taken aback by the boy's anger. "You ain't got no reason to be mad at me. From what I hear, your father was a good man and I never said otherwise."

"The people in this nothing town say *you're* my father."

"Only in a manner of speakin'. I didn't even know you existed until a few weeks ago. You like whiskey?"

"Whiskey? I . . . I don't know. I never drank any."

"Come on inside then. We'll have some whiskey and I'll explain to you about mothers and fathers and pretty girls."

Houston was nervous all afternoon as Kane and his son spent hours locked together in his office. And when at last

Zachary left, he looked at Houston from under his lashes, his face red, his mouth smirking.

"Zachary was certainly looking at me oddly," she said to Kane.

Kane studied the fingernails of his left hand. "I explained to 'im about makin' babies, and I guess I got carried away."

Houston's jaw dropped a fraction.

Kane grabbed an apple. "I got to work tonight 'cause Zach is comin' over tomorrow to play baseball with me and Ian."

He gave her a sharp look. "You sure you're all right? You look a little green. Maybe you oughta rest a while. Takin' care of this house might be too much for you." He kissed her cheek before he returned to his office.

It was four days later that Kane decided to visit Vaughn's Sporting Goods and see what other game equipment was available. His and Edan's team had been soundly beaten by the team of Ian and Zachary. Ian, having spent most of his young life inside a coal mine, was awed by Kane and not yet sure enough of himself to accuse Kane of not playing by the rules. After all, it *was* Kane's bat.

Zach had no such qualms. He made Kane follow every rule to the letter and would not let his father be what Kane called "creative." So far, Kane'd had to forfeit every game because he refused to follow any rule that someone else had made. He wanted to rewrite the baseball rule book.

Now, he and Edan were in the sporting goods store choosing tennis equipment, bicycles, and an entire gymnasium set of Indian clubs and pulleys.

On the other side of the counter was Jacob Fenton. He rarely left his house now, preferring to stay at home and read his stock reports and curse the fact that his only son wasn't interested in business in the least. But lately, his future had brightened, because his daughter, whom he'd dismissed as worthless long ago, had returned to his house with her young son.

Young Zachary was all that a man could hope for in a son: eager to learn, interested, extremely intelligent, and the boy even had a sense of humor. In fact, Zach's only flaw was his growing attachment to his father. On afternoons when he should have been at home studying how to manage the coal mines he'd someday inherit, he was at his father's playing games. Jacob had decided to fight fire with fire and buy the boy all the sporting equipment he could find.

Kane, his arms full of tennis racquets and two pairs of fifteen-pound dumbbells, turned a corner and came face to face with Jacob Fenton. Kane stood there staring, his face rapidly starting to show his rage.

Jacob had no idea who this big, dark man was except that he looked vaguely familiar. The suit the young man wore obviously cost him some money.

"Excuse me, sir," Jacob said, trying to pass.

"Don't recognize me out of the stable, do you, Fenton?"

Jacob realized that this man reminded him of Zachary. And he knew quite well why Taggert's face showed hatred. He turned away.

"Wait a minute, Fenton!" Kane called. "You're comin' to my house for dinner two weeks from today."

Jacob paused for a moment, his back to Kane, and gave a curt nod before briskly leaving the store.

Kane was silent as he put his purchases on the counter and Edan handed the storekeeper a long list of equipment. "Send all this to my house," he said, not bothering to identify himself before he walked outside and climbed into his old wagon.

When Edan was beside him, he clucked to the horses. "I think I'll get me somethin' better to drive around in than this ol' wagon."

"Why? So you can impress Fenton?"

Kane looked at his friend. "What's in your craw?"

"Why are you inviting old man Fenton to dinner?"

Kane's jaw stiffened. "You damn well know why."

"Yeah, I know why: to show him that you've done better than he has, to show off your pretty house and your pretty silverware and your pretty wife. Have you ever thought what Houston's going to say when she finds out that you want her just as much as you want a new carriage?"

"That ain't true and you know it. Houston's a lot of trouble sometimes, but she does have her compensations," Kane said, smiling.

Edan calmed his voice. "You said before that after Houston had served her purpose and sat at the foot of your table with Jacob Fenton as your guest, you were going to get rid of her and go back to New York. I believe you said that you were going to buy her off with jewelry."

"I gave her a whole trunkful of jewels and she ain't even opened it yet. She seems to like other things instead of jewels."

"She damn well likes you and you know it."

Kane grinned. "She seems to. Who knows, though? If I didn't have any money—."

"Money! You bastard! You can't see what's in front of you. Don't invite Fenton. Don't let Houston know why you married her. You don't know what it's like to lose the ones you love."

"I don't know what the hell you're talkin' about. I ain't plannin' to lose nothin'. All I'm gonna do is have Fenton over for dinner. It's what I've worked for most of my life, and I'm not gonna deny myself the pleasure."

"You don't even know what pleasure is. Both of us have worked because we had nothing else. Don't risk everything, Kane, I'm begging you."

"I ain't givin' up nothin'. You don't have to come if you don't want to."

"I wouldn't miss your funeral, and I won't miss this."

Chapter 22

As Houston adjusted the *une fantaisie* in her hair, she found that her hands were shaking badly. The last two weeks had been nerve-racking. When Kane had come home and told her that he planned to invite the Fentons to dinner, she'd been very happy because she saw this as a way to close the rift between the two men.

But her happiness had soon turned to despair. She'd never known Kane to be so concerned about anything before. He repeatedly asked her if whatever she was planning for the dinner was of the best quality. He inspected the engraved invitations, had Mrs. Murchison cook the entire elaborate dinner beforehand so Kane could inspect each dish. He stood over the footman's shoulder as the man polished the hundred-year-old Irish silver. He went through Houston's closet and said that she had nothing really good enough to wear to this dinner, and insisted that she wear a dress of white and gold and even chose the fabric himself from the selection that the dressmaker brought to the house. He had new clothes made for everyone and hired two tailors to come to the house the night of the dinner to help the men dress. He even had new uniforms made for all the servants, and Houston had to talk him out of forcing the footmen to wear their hair powdered, as he'd seen in one of Houston's fashion magazines that the Prince of Wales' servants did.

By the end of the two weeks, everyone was praying for this evening to be over. So far, Sherwin and Jean had turned coward and said they weren't feeling well enough to attend. Ian, his courage boosted from his past days of association with Zach, said he wouldn't miss the fireworks for the world. And besides, Fenton, as the mine owner, was his image of the Devil. He was looking forward to sitting, as an equal, at the same table with his enemy.

If the President had been coming to visit, no more care could have been taken—and no group of people could have been more nervous than this household. Houston feared that one of the maids would pour a bowl of soup in Fenton's lap and Kane would try to murder the girl on the spot.

But what was making Houston's hands shake was that Kane had promised to tell her what was between him and Fenton. It seemed that she'd wanted to know forever, but now she had an urge to tell Kane she didn't want to know.

Adding to her fear was a telephone call yesterday from Pamela Fenton. Pam had begged Houston to call the dinner off, saying that she had a bad feeling about what was going to be said. She said that her father's heart wasn't strong and that she was afraid of Kane's temper.

Houston had tried to talk to Kane, but all he had said was that Houston didn't understand. She had told him she was willing to try to understand if he'd explain things to her.

And that was when he'd said that he'd tell her everything before the dinner party.

Now, sitting before the mirror, inspecting herself, she found herself shaking.

She gasped when she saw Kane behind her.

"Turn around," he said, "I have something for you."

She turned back toward the mirror and, as she did so, Kane slipped a cascade of diamonds about her neck. They fitted high on her neck like a tall collar, with looping strands falling over her collarbone. There were long, double-strand earrings to match.

He stepped back to look at her. "Good," he said, and took her hand in his and led her to his bedroom.

Without saying a word, very aware of the cool diamonds around her throat, she sat down in the blue brocade chair in front of an inlaid round table.

Kane went to a panel in the wall, slid aside part of the

molding and released a little handle. The panel moved back to expose a safe built into the wall.

"Very few people in the world know the whole of the story I'm about to tell you. Some people know parts of it and have guessed at the rest of it, but they've been wrong. I've only been able to piece it together after years of work."

From the safe he removed a leather portfolio, opened it, and handed Houston a small photograph. "This is my mother."

"Charity Fenton," she whispered, looking at the pretty woman in the picture, very young, both her eyes and hair dark. She looked up to see surprise on Kane's face. "Edan told me who she was."

"He told you everything he knows." He gave her a photograph of four young men, all looking nervous and out of place in the photographer's studio. Two of the men looked like Kane. "These are the four Taggert brothers. The youngest is Lyle, Ian's father, next is Rafe, then Sherwin, then my father, Frank."

"You look like your father," she said.

Kane didn't reply but put the rest of the contents of the portfolio on the table. "These are originals or copies of all the documents that I could find pertaining to my parents or to my own birth."

She only glanced at the papers, blinking once at a copy of a family tree that showed a Nathaniel Taggert who'd married a twelve-year-old French duchess, but soon looked up as she waited for him to continue and tell her the story behind the papers, to explain his many years of hatred for his mother's family.

He walked to the window, staring down at the garden. "I don't guess you know anything about Horace Fenton, since he died long before you were born. He was Jacob's father. Or at least Jacob thought Horace was his father. The truth was that Horace gave up tryin' to have his own kids, so he adopted the newborn baby of some people travellin' to California after they were killed by a stampede of horses. But Jacob was only a few years old when Horace's wife finally had a little girl, and they named her Charity because they felt so lucky.

"From what I could find out, there's never been a kid more

spoiled than Miss Charity Fenton. Her mother took her travellin' all over the world, her father bought her ever'thing she even thought she wanted."

"And how was Jacob treated?" Houston asked.

"Not bad. Ol' Horace spoiled his daughter, but he taught his adopted son how to survive—maybe so Jacob could support Charity after her father died. Jacob was trained to run the empire that Horace'd built.

"I'm not sure how they met. I think Frank Taggert was elected to present some grievances to Fenton about the sawmill—that was before the coal mines were opened—and he met Charity. Anyway, they took to each other pretty fast, and she decided that she wanted to marry Frank. I don't guess it crossed her little spoiled mind that her father would ever deny her anything.

"But Horace not only refused to let his daughter marry a Taggert, he locked her in her room. Somehow, she managed to escape and spend two days with Frank. When her father's men found her, she was in bed with him, and told her father she was gonna have Frank Taggert even if her life depended on it."

"How terrible for her," Houston whispered.

Kane took a cigar from a drawer by the bed and lit it. "She got him, though, because two months later she told her parents she was pregnant."

"With you," Houston said softly.

"With me. Horace kicked his daughter out of the house and told her she was no daughter to him. His wife went to her bed and stayed there until she died four months later."

"And that's why you hate the Fentons, because you are rightfully an equal heir with Jacob, but you were sent to the stables."

"Equal, hell!" Kane exploded. "You ain't heard half the story. Charity moved down to the slums where the Taggerts lived, the only place they could afford on what Fenton paid 'em, and hated it. Of course, nobody would talk to her since she was one of the Fentons, but, from what I heard, her uppity ways didn't help none.

"Two months after she married Frank Taggert—and I have the marriage certificate there—he was killed by some fallin' timbers."

"And Charity had to go home to her father."

"He was an unforgivin' bastard. Charity'd tried to make it without him, but she nearly starved. I talked to a maid that used to work for Fenton, and she said that when Charity returned she was filthy, thin and heavily pregnant. Horace took one look at her and said that she'd killed her mother and that the only way she could stay was as a servant. He put her to work in the scullery."

Houston rose to stand beside her husband and put her hand on his arm. She could feel him trembling with emotion. Kane's voice quietened. "After my mother put in fourteen hours of scrubbin' Fenton's pots, she went upstairs, gave birth to me, and then very calmly hung herself."

Houston could only gape at him. "No one helped her?"

"No one. Fenton had put her in an attic room far away from the other people in the house, and if she did call out, no one could have heard her."

"And what did Horace Fenton do?"

"He was the one that found her. Who knows? Maybe his conscience bothered him and he went to make up to her, but he was too late. She was already dead.

"Not many people could tell me much of what happened after that, so I had to piece it together. Horace arranged for a wet nurse for me, then spent a day closeted with a battery of lawyers and twenty-four hours after Charity had hung herself, he put a pistol to his head and fired."

Houston sat down. There was nothing for her to say. She thought of Kane having to live with this tragedy all his life. "And so you were raised by the Fentons."

"I damn well wasn't 'raised' by anybody," he shouted. "When Horace Kane Fenton's will was read two days after his suicide, it was found out that everything he owned had been left to Charity's son."

"You?"

"Me. Jacob didn't own a cent of it. He was left as guardian to Kane Franklin Taggert, aged three days."

"But I don't understand," Houston said. "I thought . . ."

"You thought that I was born penniless. Jacob didn't leave the room for hours after the will was read, and when he and the lawyers did leave, he'd managed to bribe every one of them—and to forge a new will that said he inherited everything."

"And you?"

"People were told that Charity's baby had died at birth, and I was sent to spend the first six years of my life on one farm after another. Jacob was afraid that if I stayed with one family, I might find out some of the truth of my birth."

"Or that the Taggerts might find out about your being alive. I can't imagine Rafe letting his nephew be cheated out of his inheritance."

"Money gives power, and none of the Taggerts ever had any."

Houston walked across the room. "And Jacob didn't want to give up everything he'd worked for all those years. He must have thought of Horace as his father, yet at the last minute he was disowned as if he meant nothing. And everything was given to an infant."

"Are you takin' his side?!"

"Certainly not. I'm just trying to ascertain why he would do such a dreadful thing. What if he held the money in trust for you, and when you came of age, you decided to throw him out?"

"I wouldn't have done that."

"Of course, he had no way of knowing that. So what now? Will you prosecute him?"

"Hell, no. I've known about this for years."

"You aren't planning to take the money back, are you? Right now, your own son is living with the Fentons, and you wouldn't send him out of his home, would you?"

"Wait just one damned minute before you start takin' Fenton's side in all this. All I ever wanted to do was have Fenton someday sit down at *my* table, which was bigger than his, and to have a first-class lady at its head."

Houston looked at him for a long moment. "Perhaps you should tell me the rest of the story. Why are you having Mr. Fenton to dinner, and where do I fit into this?" she asked quietly. For some reason, she could feel fear creeping over her body.

Kane turned his back to her. "All those years that I worked in the stables, all the times I cleaned Fenton's boots, I thought

I was gettin' above myself when I imagined myself in that big house of his. Pam and I started foolin' around, and the next thing I know, she's packed up and gone and left me $500 and a fare-thee-well-it-was-a-pleasure. Ol' Jacob pulled me into his office and screamed that I'd never get what he'd worked so hard for. At the time, I thought he meant Pam.

"I took the money and went to California, and after a few years, when I'd made some money, I began to wonder about what Fenton meant when he threw me out. I hired some men to search out the answers for me. It took a while, but I finally learned the truth."

"And you planned revenge on Mr. Fenton," Houston whispered. "And I was part of your plan."

"In a manner of speakin'. At first, all I wanted was enough money so I wouldn't have to worry about bein' a stableboy again, but after I learned the truth about what'd been stolen from me, I began to imagine havin' Fenton to a dinner party at my house, and my house would be five times as big as his. And sittin' at the foot of the table would be Pam, the daughter he said I wasn't good enough for."

"But you couldn't get Pam."

"I found out that she was married and had a kid—I didn't know that the kid was mine—so I had to give up the idea of her. Of course, I had to build my house in Chandler because, if it was any place else, nobody would know that the stableboy had made good. And I wanted Fenton to be able to see it every day. So I started thinkin' who would do as well as Pam at my table, and I knew that the only real ladies in this town were the Chandler twins.

"I hired somebody to find out about you two, and I saw right away that Blair wouldn't do. Fenton might laugh that all I could get was a woman nobody else would have."

"You had to have a real, true, deep-down lady," Houston whispered.

"That I did. And I got one. I was a little upset when I first asked you and you turned me down, but I knew you'd come around. I got more money 'n Westfield'll ever have, and I knew you'd marry me."

He removed his watch from his pocket. "It's time to go downstairs. I been waitin' for this for a long time."

He took Houston's elbow and escorted her to the stairs.

Houston was too numb to speak. She'd been asked to marry him because he wanted an instrument for revenge. She'd thought he wanted her because he needed her, that he'd come to like her, if not love her, over the past months, but the truth was, he was only using her.

Chapter 23

Houston sat through the dinner feeling as if her skin had turned as icy as the diamonds around her neck. She moved and spoke as if in a dream. Only her years of training helped her as she led the conversation and directed the servants in serving the meal.

On the surface, nothing seemed to go wrong. Pam seemed aware of the tension and helped as best she could. Ian and Zach talked of sports, Jacob looked at the food on his plate, and Kane watched it all with a look of pride on his face.

What had he planned to do with me after I'd served my usefulness, she kept wondering. Did he plan to go somewhere else, now that he'd done what he wanted to in Chandler? She remembered every complaint he'd made about trying to do business in this boring little town. Why hadn't she ever wondered *why* he'd built this house? Everyone in town had asked that question while it was being built, but after Houston had been swept away by him, she'd stopped asking questions.

He'd marched into town and gone straight up to Jacob Fenton and announced his arrival, asking the older man how he liked his house. Why hadn't Houston realized that everything in Kane's life was ruled by his feelings for the Fentons?

And Houston had only been a part of the revenge.

That's all she was to the man she'd given her heart to, a tool to be used in the game he wanted—had—to win.

214

And the man she'd chosen to love was the sort of man who could dedicate his life to an unholy emotion such as revenge.

The food she ate stuck in her throat, and she had to force herself to swallow. How could she have been so wrong about a man?

When at last the long meal was finally over, Houston rose, preparing to lead Pam into the small drawing room, leaving the men to their cigars.

The two women talked about ordinary matters—clothing, where to buy the best trims, the best dressmakers in town—and did not say anything about the meal they'd just been subjected to. But twice, Houston caught Pam looking at her in a speculative way.

Kane led Jacob Fenton into his office, where he offered the man one of the cigars that Houston had given him and hundred-year-old brandy in a glass of Irish crystal.

"Not bad for a stableboy, huh?" Kane began, looking at Fenton through a haze of cigar smoke.

"All right, you've shown me your big house. Now what do you want?"

"Nothin'. Just the satisfaction of seeing you here."

"I hope you don't expect me to believe that. A man who would go to so much trouble to show me what he's done in life isn't going to stop with a dinner party. But I warn you that if you try to take away what's mine, I'll—."

"You'll what? Bribe more lawyers? All three of those bastards are still alive, and if I wanted to, I could pay them more than you own just to tell the truth."

"That's just like a Taggert. You always take what you don't own. Your father took Charity, a sweet, pretty little thing, and subjected her to horrors that caused her to hang herself."

Kane's face turned red with his rage. "Horace Fenton caused my mother's death, and you stole everything I owned from me."

"You owned nothing. It was all mine. I'd been running the business for years, and if you think I was going to stand back and see it all turned over to a squalling baby, I'd have seen it dead first. And then you, a Taggert, wanted to take my daughter away from me. You think I was going to peacefully let you do to my daughter what your father did to my sister?"

Kane advanced on the smaller, older man. "Take a good look at this place. *This* is what I would have done to your precious daughter. *This* is how I would have treated her."

Jacob stubbed out his cigar. "Like hell you would have. Did you ever think that maybe I did you a favor? It's your hatred of me that's made you rich. If you'd won Pamela, and received the money from *my* father, you probably would never have worked a day in your life."

He started for the door. "And, Taggert, you try to take back from me what you think you own and I'll prosecute that pretty wife of yours for illegal entry into the coal camps."

"What?" Kane gasped.

"I wondered if you knew," Jacob smiled. "Welcome to the world of the rich. You never can be sure whether people want you or your money. That sweet little lady you married is up to her ears in sedition. And she's using every connection you have, including yours to me, to start what may develop into a bloody war. You'd better warn her that if she doesn't slow down, I'll stop honoring her relationship to the Taggerts. Now, good night, Taggert." He left the room.

Kane sat alone for a long time in the room. No one bothered him as he drank most of a bottle of whiskey.

"Miss Houston!" Susan said as she burst into the drawing room where Houston was pacing the floor. "Mr. Kane wants you to come to his office right away. And he looks awful mad."

Houston took a deep breath, smoothed the front of her gown and started down the hall. Jacob had bid her a pleasant good evening and left two hours ago with his daughter. Houston had done nothing but think since the Fentons had left. Never before had she thought about where her life was leading her. Always before, it had seemed that she'd taken what life had handed her. Now, it was time to make some of her own decisions.

He sat at his desk, his jacket off, his shirt open halfway down his chest, a nearly empty bottle of whiskey in his hand.

"I thought you were working," she said.

"You ruined it all, you and your lying ruined it all."

"I . . . I have no idea what you're talking about," she said, sitting down in one of the leather chairs across the desk from him.

"You not only wanted my money, you wanted my connections to the Taggerts. You knew that Fenton would let you do your illegal work because of your relationship to me. Tell me, did you and your sister think up this whole scheme? How were you plannin' to use Westfield in all this?"

Houston stood, her back rigid. "You're making no sense to me. I only learned of your mother's name the day of our marriage. I couldn't have used something I knew nothing about."

"I told Edan once that you were a good actress, but I had no idea how good a one. You almost had me believin' what you were sayin' about marryin' me for love, but all the time you were usin' my name to get into the coal camps."

Involuntarily, Houston gasped.

Kane stood and leaned across the desk toward her. "I worked all my life for this night and you destroyed it. Fenton threatened to prosecute my lovin' wife and tell the world about how you've been usin' me. I can see the headlines now."

Houston did not back down from his stare. "Yes," she said softly, "I do go into the coal camps, but it has nothing to do with you, since I was doing it long before I met you. You are so obsessed with your money that you think everyone wants it." She moved away from the desk.

"In the last few months," she continued, "because of you, I've learned a great deal about myself. My sister said that I'm the unhappiest person she's ever known, and she's been afraid that I might take my own life. I never realized that she was telling me the truth, because until I met you I'd never experienced happiness. Until I began to spend days with you, I never questioned why I didn't, as you said, 'Tell 'em all to go to hell' and dance in my red dress. But with you, I've learned how good it feels to do things for myself, to not always be trying to please other people.

"And now, I feel I can make some of my own decisions. I don't want to live with a man who'd build a house like this and marry a woman he didn't want to marry, all in an attempt to repay some old man who was trying to protect what was rightfully his. I can understand, and almost forgive, Mr.

Fenton's actions, but I can't understand yours. You may think I married you for your money, but I married you because I fell in love with you. I guess I loved a man who lived only in my imagination. You aren't that man. You're a stranger to me, and I don't want to live with a stranger."

Kane glared at her for a moment, then stepped back. "If you think I'm gonna beg you to stay, you're wrong. You been a lot of fun, baby, more than I expected you to be, but I don't need you."

"Yes, you do," Houston said quietly, trying to control the tears gathering in her eyes. "You need me more than you could possibly know, but I can only give my love to a man who is worthy of my respect. You're not the man I thought you were."

Kane walked to the closed door and opened it, making a sweeping gesture with his arm to let her pass.

Houston, somehow, managed to walk past him and out into the night. She never once thought of packing clothes or taking anything with her.

A carriage stood outside in the drive.

"You're walking out, aren't you?" Pamela Fenton asked from inside the carriage.

Houston looked up at the woman with such a ravaged face that Pam gasped.

"I knew something awful had happened. My father has the doctor with him now. He was shaking as if his bones would break. Houston, get in. I have a house here now, and you can stay with Zach and me until you have things settled."

Houston only stared at the woman, until Pam climbed down from the carriage and half pushed her, half pulled her into the vehicle. Houston had no idea where she was. All she thought of was that now everything was over, that all she'd had was gone.

Kane burst into the large upstairs sitting room that Ian and Edan shared. Edan was alone, reading.

"I want you to find out anything you can about Houston goin' into the coal camps."

"What do you want to know?" Edan said, slowly putting his book down.

218

"When? How? Why? Anything you can find out."

"She dresses up as an old woman every Wednesday afternoon, calls herself Sadie, and drives a wagonload of vegetables into the camp. Inside the food she hides medicines, shoes, soap, tea, anything she can get in there and gives it to the miners' wives. Later, Jean Taggert returns the scrip the women pay Houston."

"You've known all this and haven't bothered to tell me?" Kane bellowed.

"You sent me out to watch her, but you never bothered to ask me what I found out."

"I've been betrayed on all sides! First, that lying little bitch, and now you. And Fenton knew everything that was goin' on."

"Where's Houston, and what have you said to her?"

Kane's face hardened. "She just walked out my front door. She couldn't face the truth. As soon as she knew I was onto her little scheme of usin' me and my money to get what she wanted, she ran out. Good riddance. I don't need the money-grubbin'—."

Edan grabbed Kane by the shoulder. "You stupid son of a bitch. That woman's the best thing that ever happened to you, and you're too goddamn stupid to see it. You have to find her!"

Kane shrugged away. "Like hell I will. She was just like all them others; she was just a higher-priced whore."

Kane never even saw the right that plowed into his face and sent him sprawling. Edan stood over the big dark man as Kane rubbed his jaw.

"You know something?" Edan said. "I've about had it, too. I'm tired of hiding away from the world. I spent my twenties closeted inside ugly rooms with you, doing nothing but working to make money. And for what? The only thing you ever bought was this house, and you did that because you wanted revenge. Houston told me once that I was as bad as you, hiding away, staying at your beck and call, and I've come to think she's right."

Edan stepped away and rubbed the knuckles of his hand. "I think it's time I found my own life. Thanks to you, I've been paid for the years I've dedicated to your goals, and I have a few million stashed away. I'm going to take them and do something with my life."

He put out his hand to shake, but Kane ignored him.

Later, Kane saw Ian, Jean and Sherwin get into the wagon with Edan, which meant that only the servants were left, and he didn't wait until morning before he fired them.

Chapter 24

Houston wasn't even aware of her surroundings as she stood in the middle of Pam's bedroom.

"First, we'll put you in a tub of hot water, then you can tell me what's going on."

Houston stood completely still as Pam left to fill the tub. She wasn't sure she was fully aware yet of what had happened tonight. She'd fallen in love with a man who was using her.

"It's ready now," Pam said, pushing Houston into the pink tiled bathroom. "You get undressed while I call and see how my father is. And Houston! don't just stand there looking as if the world were about to end."

Through years of training, Houston obeyed as well as any trained animal, and when Pam returned, she was lying in the big tub, up to her neck in suds.

"Dr. Westfield finally calmed my father down," Pam said. "He's too old to go through nights like this one. Whatever did Kane say to him? The only thing that I know of that could upset him so badly would be something about Zachary. If Kane thinks that he's going to take my son away from me, he'd better be prepared to fight—."

"No," Houston said tiredly. "He's not after his son. Nothing so noble."

"I think you should tell me."

Houston looked up at this woman whom she really didn't know, a woman who was once the love of her husband's life. "Why are you helping me? I know you still love him."

221

Pam narrowed her eyes for a moment. "So he told you, did he?"

"I know he . . . refused your invitation."

Pam laughed. "That's tactful of you. I guess he didn't bother to also tell you that I, too, realized we'd never make it together? We came to a mutual understanding that if we married we'd probably kill each other within three months. Now, tell me what happened between you and Kane. It's all family, if that's what you're thinking, and it's going to come out sooner or later."

If Kane decided to take the Fenton money that was legally his, it would indeed all come out, Houston thought. "Do you know who Kane's mother was?" she asked softly.

"I have no idea. I don't think I ever considered that he had a mother, probably because he seemed too self-sufficient to need something as simple as a mother. I guess I assumed he'd arrived on earth all by himself."

Houston sat in the hot water and told the story of Charity Taggert slowly, trying not to color the tale with her own viewpoint.

Pam had pulled up a pink upholstered brass wire chair. "I had no idea," Pam said at the end of the story. "You're saying that everything my father owns is legally Kane's. No wonder he's so angry at my father, and no wonder my father is shaking with fear. But, Houston, you didn't walk out on Kane tonight because he wasn't born a pauper. What else happened?"

It was more difficult for Houston to tell about herself, to admit that she was second choice to Pam and that, now that she'd fulfilled what Kane needed her for, she was useless to him.

"Damn him!" Pam said, standing and pacing the floor. "He would feel completely justified in telling you that he'd married you for what he thinks he needs. He is the most spoiled man I ever met in my life."

Houston, showing the first signs of life, rolled her head upward to look at Pam.

"He likes to imagine that his life was one of great misery, but I can tell you that *he* was the real ruler of our household when he lived there. People look down on me for having fallen in love with the stable lad, but that's only because they never had someone in their stables like Kane Taggert."

She sat down in the seat again, leaning forward, her face angry. "You know him. You've seen his temper and the way he orders everyone about. Do you think he was ever any different, merely because he was supposed to be someone's servant?"

"I don't guess I really thought about it," Houston said. "Marc did say that Kane was a tyrant."

"Tyrant!" Pam gasped, getting up again. "Kane ran everything. More than once, my father had to miss business appointments because Kane said he couldn't have a carriage or a horse, that the animals weren't ready to travel. At dinner, we ate what Kane liked because the cook thought his tastes were more important than Father's."

Houston remembered the way Mrs. Murchison had succumbed to Kane's teasing and how the woman adored him.

"He was always a handsome boy and knew how to get whatever he wanted out of women. The maids cleaned his rooms, they did his laundry, they took meals to him. He didn't run Fenton Coal and Iron, but he ran our household. I can't imagine what he would have been like if he'd known that all the money was legally his. Perhaps my father did him a favor. Maybe living in the stables taught him some humility, because he certainly wasn't born with it."

Pam fell to her knees by the tub. "You have my permission to stay here as long as you want. If you want my two cents, I think you were right to leave him. He can't marry a person in order to enact some plan of revenge. Now, get out of that tub while I fix you a toddy that will help you sleep."

Again, Houston did as she was told, drying herself with one of Pam's pink towels and slipping into Pam's chaste nightgown.

Pam returned with a steaming mug in her hand. "If this doesn't make you sleep, it'll make you not care that you're awake. Now, get into bed. Tomorrow has to be better than today."

Houston drank most of the concoction and was asleep very soon. In the morning, when she woke, the sun was already high in the sky and she had a headache. Draped over the end of the bed was her underwear and a dressing gown. A note from Pam said that she had to go out and for Houston to help herself to breakfast downstairs and to tell the maid if she needed anything.

"Edan," Jean Taggert was saying, "I can't thank you enough for all you've done tonight. There was no need for you to stay up with me."

They were standing in the corridor of the Chandler Hotel. Both of them looked tired. After they'd left Kane's house, they'd come to the hotel. Ian had gone to bed immediately, but Sherwin had been extremely upset by the night's happenings and, in his weakened state, he'd begun coughing and couldn't catch his breath. He gasped that he was afraid that Jean and Ian would have to return to the coal fields.

Edan called Dr. Westfield, and Lee was there in minutes, already dressed from having just seen to Jacob Fenton. Edan also roused the hotel staff and had hot water bottles and extra blankets brought. He sent a bellboy to get the druggist out of bed to fill a prescription for Sherwin.

Jean was able to stay by her father throughout the night and try to reassure him that she and Ian would not return to the mines, while Edan tended to all the necessary details.

Now, with the sun just coming up, Sherwin asleep at last, they stood outside his door.

"I can't thank you enough," Jean said for the thousandth time.

"Then stop trying. Would you like some breakfast?"

"Do you think the dining room is open at this hour?"

Edan grinned at her as he pushed a loose strand of hair out of her eyes. "After last night, this hotel is so afraid of me that they'll do anything for me."

He was right. A weary-looking clerk escorted them into the dining room, removed two chairs from a table by the window and went to drag the cook out of bed. Unfortunately, the cook lived four miles out of town and it took him a while to get there. Neither Jean nor Edan noticed that breakfast took over two hours to arrive.

They talked about when they'd grown up, Jean telling about taking care of all the men in her life, of her mother dying when Jean was eleven. Edan told of his family, of their deaths in the fire and of how Kane had taken him in.

"Kane was good for me. I didn't want to love anyone again. I was afraid that they'd die, too, and I didn't think I could bear being left alone again."

He put down his napkin. "Are you ready to go? I think the business offices should be open by now."

"Yes, of course," she said, rising. "I didn't mean to keep you from your work."

He caught her by her elbow. "I didn't mean me, I meant us. You and I are going to a realtor to buy a house today. It'll have to be something large to have room for all of us."

She moved out of his grasp and turned to look at him. "All of us? I don't know what you mean, but Ian, Father and I couldn't possibly live with you. I'll get a job in town, perhaps Houston can help me, and Ian can go to school and work afterwards, and Father—."

"Your father would hate himself for being a burden to you both, and Ian is too big to go to school with the others and he'd be better off with his tutor. And you couldn't earn enough to support them. Now, come with me and help me find a big house, and you can be my housekeeper."

"I couldn't possibly do that," she said, aghast. "I can't be a housekeeper to an unmarried man."

"Your father and cousin will be there as chaperones in case I try to molest you and, then again, from what I've seen of married life in the last few months, I rather like the idea. Come on, Jean, close your mouth and let's go shopping. We'll probably have to buy furniture and food and all sorts of things before we can get out of this hotel. Do you think the staff will volunteer to help us if they know their help will get rid of us faster?"

Jean was too stunned to say another word as Edan led her upstairs to her father's room to tell him where they were going. In the end, Ian, Jean and Edan went to the realtor's.

Houston sat at Pam's dining table, listlessly poking at a bowl of oatmeal.

Pam burst into the room, pulling off long, white chamois gloves. "Houston, the entire town is on fire with gossip about last night," she said without a greeting. "First of all, after you left, it seems that Kane and Edan had a brawl in an upstairs bedroom. One of the maids said that the fight went on for hours and, when it was over, Edan left the house in a storm."

"Edan left, too?" Houston asked, wide-eyed.

"Not only Edan, but also the other Taggerts: Jean, Ian and Sherwin. And when they were gone, Kane marched downstairs and fired all the servants."

Houston leaned back in her chair and gave a great sigh. "He said he was tired of all of us taking so much of his time. I guess he can work all he wants now . . . or go back to New York and work there."

Pam unpinned her Strada hat, fluffing the ostrich plumes atop the white Italian straw. "I haven't told you the half of it. Edan and Jean took up residence at the Chandler Hotel and kept the staff up all night, waiting on Sherwin who was, as far as I could find out, near death's door, and this morning they bought a house together."

"Edan and Jean? Is Sherwin all right?"

"Gossip says he's fine and, yes, Edan and Jean bought that enormous Stroud place at the end of Archer Avenue, across from Blair's hospital. And after they signed the papers— Edan paid cash for the house—Jean went back to the hotel and Edan went to The Famous and bought, I hope I get this right, three ladies' blouses, two skirts, a hat, two pairs of gloves, and assorted underwear. That nasty little Nathan girl waited on him, and she kept after the poor man until he admitted that the secret woman he was buying the clothes for was approximately the exact same size as Miss Jean Taggert. If Edan doesn't marry her after this, her name won't be worth much in this town."

She paused for a moment. "And, Houston, you might as well know that the Chandler Chronicle is hinting that there's another woman involved in everything that happened last night."

Houston picked up her coffee cup. The local paper didn't faze her. Mr. Gates had complained for years that the paper was nothing but a gossip rag consisting of reports on the most bizarre deaths from around the world and inane articles about where each English duke's family was wintering. He stopped delivery of the paper after it carried a half-page story in which an Italian man declared Anglo-Saxon women to be the best kissers in the world.

"Wherever did you hear all this?" Houston asked.

"Where else but Miss Emily's Tea Shop?"

Houston almost choked on her coffee. The Sisterhood! she thought. She had to call an emergency meeting to let them know that Jacob Fenton knew about the women disguising themselves and illegally entering the coal camps. All the man had to do was get angry enough at Kane and he could have the women arrested.

"May I use your telephone?" Houston asked. "I have some calls to make."

Chapter 25

Houston called her mother first and interrupted Opal in a fit of crying. After Houston'd managed to calm her mother without giving her too much information, she persuaded Opal to . help her call some of the members of The Sisterhood. The only suitable meeting place, where they were sure of not being overheard, seemed to be the upstairs of the teashop.

"At two o'clock, then," Houston said as she hung up and began calling the others who were on the telephone system.

When the women finally met in Miss Emily's parlor, they all looked askance toward Houston. She was sure they were dying to hear the truth of what had happened last night when everyone left Kane's house. She walked to the front of the women who stood waiting.

"Last night, I found out some very important information," she began. "Jacob Fenton knows about our going into the coal camps. I'm not sure exactly how much he knows, but I called this meeting to discuss it."

"But the guards don't know, do they?" Tia asked. "Is it only Fenton himself who knows? Has he told others? How did he find out?"

"I don't know any of those answers. All I know is that he's aware that we disguise ourselves and go into the camps . . . and he's threatened to prosecute me."

"You?" Blair gasped. "Why you, particularly? Why not all of the drivers?"

Houston looked at the floor. "It has to do with my husband and Mr. Fenton, but I don't believe that I will be arrested."

"I don't think we can chance it," Blair said. "You'll have to stop driving."

"Wait a minute!" Miss Emily said. "Fenton must have known about this for a long time. He didn't just learn about it yesterday and come storming to your house to threaten you. Is that right, Houston?"

She nodded.

"It's none of our business, of course, but am I safe in saying that a great deal happened at the Taggert house last night, and that it's likely that Fenton's declaration of his knowledge of you was only part of what happened?"

Again, Houston nodded.

"My guess is that Fenton has decided that what we do isn't all that harmful, and so he allows us to go safely into the camps. If I'm correct, and I do know Jacob, he's probably had a few laughs about the silly women dressing up and enjoying themselves. I say that we continue the visits. For myself, I feel better knowing that, in a way, we're protected."

"I don't like it!" Meredith said.

"And how do you propose secrecy?" Sarah asked. "It doesn't matter about Fenton, anyway. He overlooks half of what goes on at the camps. Remember last year when that union official was found beaten to death? The official verdict was 'death by person or persons unknown'. Surely, Fenton knew who did it, but he keeps his hands clean. Do you think he's going to prosecute the daughters of the leading citizens of Chandler? My father, after removing some of my hide, would go after Fenton with a shotgun."

"If we're an object of humor, and we're protected by the mine owner himself, then what's the use of all the secrecy?" Nina asked. "Why don't we wear lace dresses and travel in pretty carriages and just distribute the goods?"

"And which miner will let his wife accept charity from the rich town women?" Miss Emily asked. "I think we should keep on with things just as they are. Houston, I want you to consider this very seriously: do you think Fenton'll press charges against you or the other women?"

And risk exposing that he'd stolen everything from a three-day-old baby, Houston thought. "No," she said. "I don't think I'll be arrested. I say that we proceed as always. The few men who know what we do have a vested interest in keeping our secrets. If that's everything, I say we adjourn and go home."

"Just a minute," Blair said, standing. "Nina and I have something to say."

Together, Blair and Nina told of an idea they'd been working on for weeks, of a ladies' magazine that, in code, informed the miners of what was going on throughout America concerning the organization of unions. They showed sample articles and talked of distributing the magazine as a gift to the women in the coal mines.

The women of The Sisterhood were hesitant at first to agree. They'd already experienced fear when they'd learned of Fenton's knowledge.

"Are we committed or not?" Miss Emily asked, and the women began discussing the new magazine.

Hours later, it was a quiet group who left Miss Emily's parlor, each woman thinking about the possibility of arrest of either herself or one of her friends.

"Houston," Blair said as the others left. "Could we talk?"

Houston nodded, but couldn't bring herself to tell her sister what'd happened. Blair just might start blaming herself again, and Houston didn't need more misery right now.

"You want to tell me what happened last night?" Blair asked when they were alone. "The gossip says that you left him. Is that true?"

"True enough," she said, refusing to cry. "I'm staying with Pamela Younger, Jacob's daughter."

Blair looked at her sister for a long time but offered no advice nor any comment. "If you need me, I'm here to listen, but in the meantime you'll need something to keep you busy. The first issue of Lady Chandler's Magazine will have to be submitted to the Coal Board for approval and I want it to be as safe and innocuous as possible. I need articles on how to clean clothes, how to take care of your hair, how to dress like a duchess on a coal miner's salary, that sort of thing. I think you'll do a great job of writing them. Can you go with me now and we'll buy you a typewriter? I'll show you how to use it this afternoon."

Houston hadn't thought about how she'd spend her time when she didn't have Kane to care for, but now she realized that, if she didn't do some work, she'd sit at Pam's and curse herself for being such a fool as to love a man like Kane Taggert. "Yes," she said, "I'd like to be busy. I've had some ideas about how the miners' wives could brighten up the cabins and how they could add a little beauty to their lives."

Blair put Houston to work with so much to do that Houston didn't have time to think about anything. As soon as Houston got one article completed, Blair had an idea for another one. Pam was so interested in Blair's magazine that she converted her kitchen into a stain-removal center and tried to find a really effective way to clean velvet. The entire house reeked of ammonia by the end of the day, but Houston was able to report that "two tablespoons of ammonia and two of warm water rubbed well into the velvet with a stiff brush" did the job. Blair said she might make it the headline story. Pam smiled at this, but Houston knew her sister was being sarcastic.

The writing gave Houston a perfect excuse to stay inside and not face the townspeople. Pam left the house often, telling no one where she was going, and was able to keep Houston up to date on the gossip, reporting that Kane stayed alone in his big house with no servants and no friends.

"And no relatives. That should make him happy," Houston said. "Now, he can work uninterrupted, with no interference."

"Don't be bitter, Houston," Pam said. "Regretting what could have been makes a person miserable. I know. What do you think of including this dye recipe in the first issue? A pennyworth of logwood and a pennyworth of soapbark. I've renewed my black felt hat with it twice, and it worked quite well."

"Yes, of course," Houston said absently, as she scrubbed away the ink that filled the typewriter keys. Blair had told her that when Remington first issued the typewriter, the keys were constantly jamming together. When the owners looked into the matter, they found that the typists were too fast for the mechanics of the machine, so they decided to make the keyboard as difficult as possible to use. They placed the most frequently used keys all over the board so the typist would have to reach constantly, and thus she'd be slowed down. By chance, the top letters spelled QWERTY.

Two weeks after Houston left Kane, the railroad car that he'd had made for Opal arrived, causing a great stir in the town. With tears running down her face, Opal went to Houston and talked about what a wonderful man she'd left, and how could she do such a thing, and a woman wasn't a woman without a baby and, with Houston not even having a husband, it was all too horrible to contemplate.

Houston managed to tell her mother that it was Kane who didn't want her, not the other way around. It wasn't quite the truth but, somehow, lies to one's mother, to placate her, were acceptable.

Houston returned to her typewriter and tried not to think of what was past.

Opal Chandler Gates slowly made her way up Hachette Street toward the Taggert Mansion. She was supposed to be shopping downtown this morning, and Mr. Gates had never questioned why she was wearing her new fox-trimmed suit with the little matching fox hat, but then men rarely understood the importance of clothing. Today, she had to look her best, for today, she was going to beg Kane to take Houston back—if he'd indeed thrown her out as Houston'd intimated.

Houston could be so rigid, Opal thought. She was so much like her father in that. Bill would be friends with someone but, if that person broke his trust, Bill would never, *never* forgive him. Houston had a tendency to do that. Opal knew that after what Leander had done to Houston, he could disappear for all Houston cared.

And now, something had to be done about Kane. Opal was sure that Kane had done something dreadful, something clumsy and awkward and stupid. But then, that was one of Kane's most appealing characteristics: he was as rough as Houston was polished. They were perfectly suited, and Opal meant to see them together again.

At the big front door of the house, she knocked but there was no answer, so she opened it and went inside. The hall echoed with emptiness and the lonely feeling of an unoccupied house.

Opal ran her finger along a table in the hall. It was amazing how much dust could collect in two short weeks.

She called Kane's name, but there was no answer. She'd only been in the house once before and didn't know her way around very well. It took quite a while to walk through both the downstairs and the upstairs. While she was upstairs, in Kane's bedroom, she looked out at the gardens and saw him walking across the lawn.

She practically ran down the stairs and across the grass that badly needed mowing. Following a twisting path downward, she found him at the bottom, standing near a tree, smoking one of his lovely, fragrant cigars, and staring into space.

He turned to look at her as she approached. "And what brings you here this mornin'?" he asked cautiously.

Opal took a deep breath. "I hear you got angry and tossed my daughter out of your house."

"Like hell I did! She walked out on me! Said somethin' about she didn't respect me."

Opal sat down on a stone bench under the tree. "I was afraid of that. Houston's just like her father was. Would you tell me what happened? Houston won't tell me a word. That's also just like her father."

Kane was silent as he looked back into the garden.

"I know it's private, and if it has anything to do with . . . well, the bedroom, I know Houston is probably a little frightened, but I'm sure that if you're patient—."

"Frightened! Houston? You're talkin' about the woman that married me? She ain't afraid of nothin' in bed."

Opal fidgeted with her gloves, her face red. "Well, then, perhaps it was something else." She waited. "If you're worried about secrecy, I assure you—."

"Ain't nothin' much secret in this town. Look, maybe you can understand what made her so mad, I can't. You know I used to work in Fenton's stables? Well, all the time I worked there I was never allowed upstairs in his house, and I always used to wonder what it'd be like to be master of a big house like that. And later, when I wanted to marry Fenton's daughter, he said I wasn't good enough for her. So I left and started makin' money, yet in the back of my mind was this dream that someday I'd have him to dinner at my house, which was bigger than his, and I'd have a lady-wife sittin' at the end of the table."

It took Opal a few moments to realize that this was the end of his story and she was going to have to piece together the rest of it. "My goodness," she said after a moment. "Do you mean that you built this enormous house and married my daughter to fulfill your dream?"

There was no answer from Kane.

Opal smiled. "Well, no wonder Houston left when she found out. She must have felt quite used."

"Used! She was damn well usin' me, too. She married me for my money."

Opal looked at him seriously, all smiles gone. "Did she? Do you have any idea how hard Mr. Gates worked to keep her from marrying you? In fact, many people advised her not to marry you. But she did. And as for money, neither she nor Blair have to worry about money. They aren't rich, but they have enough to buy all the dresses they need."

"Considerin' Houston's dress buyin', that's a fortune," he mumbled.

"Do you think Houston wants more, the kind of riches only you can give her?" Opal continued. "Does she strike you as greedy?"

Kane sat down on the bench.

Opal put her arm about his big shoulders. "You miss her, don't you?"

"I've only known her a few months, but I guess I . . . got used to her. Sometimes I wanted to strangle her because she was always makin' me do things I didn't wanta do, but now . . . Now, I miss steppin' on her hairpins. I miss havin' her interrupt me and Edan. I miss Edan. I miss baseball with Ian and my son. I miss—." He stood, his face angry. "Damn her! I wish I'd never met her. I was a happy man before I met her and I will be again. You go tell her I wouldn't have her back if she came crawlin'."

Kane started up the path toward the house, Opal hot on his heels.

"Kane, please, I'm an old lady," she called after him, trying to keep up.

"Ain't nothin' old about a lady," he shouted over his

shoulder. "I shoulda stayed with prostitutes," he mumbled. "They only want money."

Opal only caught up with him when he was inside his office, papers in his hand. "You have to get her back."

"Like hell I do. I don't *want* her back."

Opal sat down, fanning herself, out of breath. Surreptitiously, she adjusted her new health corset that was boned with thin blades of steel. "If you had no hope of getting her back, you'd be on a train to somewhere else."

Kane sat in his red leather chair, silent for a moment. "I don't know how to get her back. If she didn't marry me for my money, I don't know how I won her in the first place. Women! I'm better off without her." He looked at Opal through his lashes. "You think she'd like a present?"

"Not Houston. She has her father's morals. Apologies and declarations of love won't do it either. She is so rigid. If there were some way to make her move back in and give you a little time, perhaps you could convince her that you didn't just marry her in order to repay Mr. Fenton—who really can't be blamed for not allowing his daughter to marry the stableboy."

Kane opened his mouth but closed it again. His eyes lit. "I do have a way, but . . . No, it wouldn't work. She'd never believe I'd do such an underhanded, dirty trick."

"It sounds perfect. Tell me."

Kane hesitantly told her and, to his disbelief, Opal thought the idea splendid. "Ladies!" Kane muttered.

Opal stood. "Now, I must go. Oh yes, dear me, I almost forgot. The reason I came was to tell you that the train car arrived and I couldn't possibly accept it. It's really too expensive a gift. You'll have to take it back."

"What in the world would I do with a pink train? You can travel in it."

Opal smiled fondly at him. "Dear Kane, we all have our dreams; unfortunately, if they come true, sometimes they aren't as nice as the dream. I'd be scared to death to travel."

"Well then, park it somewhere and have it for your tea parties. Are you sure this thing with Houston'll work? I don't know if I *want* her to believe that I'd do somethin' like that."

"She'll believe you, and I think that's a very good use for the train, but you could have it redone in another color."

"If you don't accept that thing, I'll move it to your front yard."

"Since you're blackmailing me . . . ," she said, eyes twinkling.

Kane groaned as she kissed his cheek. "I feel that everything will go well now. Thank you so much for the train, and we'll have you and Houston to dinner next week. Good-bye."

Kane sat for a long time, muttering about women in general and ladies in particular.

Chapter 26

Houston had to stifle a yawn as she hurried down Lead Avenue, trying to get her errands done before it started to rain. She was tired after the turmoil at Pam's house last night that had kept all of them up late.

Zachary had gone to see his cousin Ian at the new house Edan had bought and asked him to go to Kane's to play baseball. Before Ian was half through expressing his opinion of Kane, Zach put his head down and rammed the older, larger boy in the stomach. They fought a bloody battle for thirty minutes before Edan found them and separated them.

When Zach returned to Pam, his collar clutched by Edan, Jacob was there visiting. He saw his precious grandson covered in dried blood, his face scratched, bruises forming. And touching him was someone connected with Kane Taggert.

Another war began.

Pam, worried about her son's health, wasn't concerned with who and why, but Jacob was. Immediately, he began attacking Edan.

"Your fight's not with me," Edan said, then left the house.

Jacob started demanding answers from Zach, and when the older man realized that Zach'd been defending his father, Jacob's anger knew no bounds. His wrath turned to Pam and included comments on her fitness as a mother and allusions to how she came to have Zach in the first place.

For the first time, Houston saw Pam's temper, and Houston

understood why Kane had turned her down the day of the wedding. Both Pam and her father said things they couldn't possibly mean; neither seemed to have any control. If Kane and Pam had tried to live together . . . Houston didn't like to think of what could have happened.

Zachary entered the fight, torn between protecting his mother and wanting to be on the man's side. Both Pam and Jacob started yelling at him.

"That's not the way to handle a Taggert," Houston whispered to herself.

She stepped into the middle of the red-faced, screaming people. "Zachary," she said, in a voice that was at once cool and commanding. Startled, they all stopped to look at her.

"Zachary, you will come with me and we will wash you. Mr. Fenton, you will call your carriage and return to your home. You may send flowers of apology later. And you, Pamela, may go upstairs to your room and bathe your wrists with cologne and lie down."

She stood there quite still, her hand outstretched to Zachary, until Pam and Jacob moved to obey her. Meekly, the boy took her hand and followed her into the kitchen. He was much too old to allow a woman to wash his face and hands, but he sat there quietly and let her tend to him as if he were four. After a few minutes, he began telling her about the fight.

"I think you were perfectly right to defend your father," Houston said.

Zach's mouth dropped open. "But I thought you didn't like him anymore."

"Adults fight differently than children do. Now, put on a clean shirt and you and I will visit Ian."

"That bas—," Zach began but cut himself off. "I never want to see him again."

"You *will* see him again," she said, leaning forward until they were nose to nose.

"Yes, ma'am," was Zach's answer.

Houston and Zachary spent hours with Edan and the rest of the Taggerts. Houston felt as if she'd stepped into the middle of someone's honeymoon, as Jean and Edan kept giving each other looks when they thought no one else was looking.

Sherwin took over the boys and had them both in the back garden pulling weeds and moving rocks. By the time Houston and Zach returned home, he was too tired to be angry at anyone, and he and Ian had a date tomorrow to play baseball with some of the town boys, all of whom Houston had called and invited.

When at last she'd climbed into bed, after having heard Pam's three apologies and four thanks, she was exhausted. On the table by the bed was a vase of two dozen red roses from Jacob Fenton to "Lady" Houston.

Now, she was still tired as she ran to catch the streetcar before the rain began again.

She was nearly at the corner, approaching the Chandler Opera House, when thunder cracked, the skies opened and the rain began—and a hand pulled her into the alleyway. Houston's scream was covered by the thunder.

"You'll have ever'body in here if you don't be quiet," Kane said, his hand over her mouth. "It's just me, an' all I wanta do is talk to you for a minute."

Houston glared at him through the rain that was running down her face.

"This is the same place that I pulled you in that first time, you remember? I asked you why you'd defended me to that bad-tempered little woman. This is sorta like an anniversary, ain't it?"

His face softened as he spoke and, as he let his hand on her mouth relax, Houston let out a scream to wake the dead. Unfortunately, the rain covered her scream, and the people within hearing distance had moved indoors.

"Damn you, Houston!" Kane said, replacing his hand. "What's wrong with you? All I wanta do is talk. I'm gonna take my hand away and if you scream I'll stop you. You understand me?"

Houston nodded, but the moment he released her, she pivoted on her left foot and started out of the alleyway. Kane, with a curse of disbelief, made a grab for her and the stitching at the waistband of her dress tore away.

Houston turned back to him, her face furious as she looked down at her dress, now attached only for a few inches at the front. "Can't you ever listen to what a person says? I don't want to talk to you. If I did, I'd be living with you," she shouted above the rain. "I want to go home. I don't care if I never see you again."

As she again turned to leave, Kane reached out for her. "Houston, wait. I have somethin' I wanta say."

"Use the telephone," she said over her shoulder.

"You little bitch," Kane said through clenched teeth. "You're gonna listen to me, no matter what I have to do."

He made a grab for her, succeeded in pulling the rest of her skirt away and they both fell into the mud that was about three inches of soft ooze from several days of rain. Houston fell on the bottom, burying her face in the wetness, while Kane, on top, remained relatively clean.

Houston managed to lift the upper half of her body out of the sucking mud. "Get off of me," she said, her lips closed to prevent the mud from entering her mouth.

Kane rolled to one side. "Houston, honey, I didn't mean to hurt you. All I wanted was to talk to you."

Houston turned so she was sitting up in the mud, but didn't try to rise as she used her skirt, now completely torn loose and hanging about her hips, to wipe some of the filth from her face. "You never mean to hurt anyone," she said. "You just do whatever you want, no matter who gets in your way."

He was grinning at her. "You know, you look pretty, even like that."

She gave him a hard look. "What is it you have to say to me?"

"I . . . ah, I want you to come back to live with me."

She continued wiping her face. "Of course you do. I knew you would. You lost Edan, too, didn't you?"

"Damn it, Houston, what do you want me to do, beg?"

"I want absolutely nothing from you. Right now, my only wish is to go home and take a bath." She started to rise, struggling over the suction of the mud and her torn skirt.

"You can't forgive nobody for nothin', can you?"

"Like you can't forgive Mr. Fenton? At least, I don't use others to get what I want."

Even through the rain, Houston could see Kane's anger staining his face. "I've had enough," he said, advancing on her and pinning her against a wall. "You're my wife and by law you're my property. I don't care if you respect me or love me or whatever else you think you gotta have, you're returnin' to live with me. And, what's more, you're gonna do it right now."

She looked at him with as much dignity as she could manage, considering the state of her face. "I'll scream all the way through town, and I'll leave your house at the first opportunity."

He leaned toward her, bending her backward.

"You know that brewery your stepfather owns? A year ago, he had some money problems that he didn't tell nobody about. Two months ago, in secret, he sold the place to an anonymous buyer, somebody that lets him remain manager."

"You?" Houston whispered, her back against the wet brick wall.

"Me. And last month, I bought the Chandler National Bank. I wonder who'd be hurt if I decided to close the place?"

"You wouldn't do that," she gasped.

"You just said that I do whatever I want, no matter who gets in my way. And right now, I want you to move back into my house."

"But why? I never meant anything to you. All I ever meant to you was something to further your revenge on Jacob Fenton. Surely, someone else would be better—."

He ignored her words. "What do you say? Will you martyr yourself to save the whole town? My house and my bed bein' the stake you'll burn at, of course."

Suddenly he grabbed her chin in his hand, his fingertips roughly caressing her damp, gritty skin. "Can I still make you burn? Can I still make you cry out in pleasure?"

He bent his head as if he meant to kiss her but stopped a breath away from her lips. "You ain't got any choice at all as far as I can see. You either come home with me right now or I foreclose on a whole lot of people. Are your uppity morals more important than the food in people's mouths?"

She blinked at the water in her eyes, whether from tears or the rain she wasn't sure. "I'll live with you again," she said, "but you have no idea how cool the Lady of Ice can be."

He didn't answer her but lifted her into his arms and

carried her to his waiting wagon. Neither spoke on the way up the hill to the Taggert mansion.

Houston didn't have a great deal of difficulty remaining cool to her husband, and only once was she tempted to falter. She remembered too well why he'd married her and what a fool she'd been to think she was in love with such a selfish man. At least Leander had been honest when he'd told her what he wanted of her.

Houston did the bare minimum of what was required of her to run the house and no more. She rehired the servants but planned no entertainments, and she spoke to Kane only when necessary and refused to react when he touched her—which had been the most difficult part.

The first night she was in his house had been the worst. He'd come to her bedroom and slowly pulled her into his arms. Houston had refused to let her body betray her. She'd stood as rigid as a steel pole and thought about Sunshine Row at the mining camp. It was probably the most difficult thing she'd ever done in her life, but she wasn't going to fall into bed with him after the way he'd used her. Nor had she let her reserve break when he'd moved away from her and looked at her with the eyes of a sad puppy. She thought he'd used his good looks to advantage to get what he wanted.

The next morning he came to her room and lifted a small chest from the floor. Houston knew that it was his wedding gift to her, and she'd always known what was in it, but she'd waited for him to present it to her. And now, when he dumped about a million dollars' worth of jewels in her lap, all she could think about was that they were so cold—about as cold as her insides felt.

Kane stood back and watched for her reaction.

"If you mean to try to buy me—," she began.

He cut her off. "Damn it, Houston! Was I supposed to tell you about Fenton *before* we were married? I had a hard enough time as it was, what with you tryin' to get Westfield even when we were standin' at the altar." He waited a moment. "You ain't gonna deny that you wanted Westfield?"

"It doesn't seem to matter what *I* want. You are an expert at getting your own way. You wanted a house to impress Mr.

Fenton, you wanted a wife to impress him. It doesn't matter that the house cost millions and the wife is a human being with feelings of her own. It's all the same to you. You have to have your own way, and look out, anyone who tries to thwart you."

Kane left the room without another word.

The jewels glowed in Houston's lap and, without another glance, she turned the blanket down to cover them as she stepped out of bed.

She spent the days in her sitting room reading. The servants came to her to ask questions, but otherwise she stayed alone. Her only hope was that Kane would see that she didn't want to live with him and would release her.

A week after she'd returned, he came storming into her room, papers from the bank in his hand.

"What the hell are these supposed to mean?" he shouted. "The account of Mrs. Houston Chandler Taggert has been charged for bath powder, two yards of ribbon, and for paying the telephone bill of the Taggert household."

"I believe I'm the only one who uses the telephone, therefore I should pay the expenses."

He sat down in a chair across from her. "Houston, have I ever been stingy with you? Have I ever complained about how much you spend? Have I ever done or said anything that makes you think that I'd ever withhold money from you?"

"You have accused me of marrying you for your money," she said coolly. "Since your money is so precious to you and not to me, you may keep it."

He started to speak, but closed his mouth. After a long moment of looking at the bills, he said softly, "I'll be goin' to Denver tonight, and I'll be gone for about three days. I'd like you to stay in the house. I don't want you doin' anything to get in trouble, like tryin' to start a riot at the coal mines."

"And what will you do to innocent people if I do? Will you throw three families into the snow?"

"If you haven't noticed, it's still summer." He walked to the door. "You don't know me very well at all, do you? I'll tell the bank to send your bills to me. Buy whatever you want." With that, he left her alone.

As soon as he was gone, she went to the window to look at

Chandler below. "You don't know me very well, either, Kane Taggert," she whispered. "You'll not be able to keep me chained inside this house."

Three hours later, after she saw Kane drive away from the house, she called Reverend Thomas and told him to prepare a wagon because, tomorrow, Sadie would visit the Little Pamela mine.

Chapter 27

Houston, dressed as Sadie, eased the wagon up the hill toward the coal mine and, as she maneuvered the horses around a long, deep rut in the road caused by the recent heavy rains, she thought she heard a sound in the back of the wagon. Last summer, a cat had been caught under the canvas that was tied down so tightly, and she was sure that was what was making noise now.

She flipped the reins to the horses and concentrated on getting up the hill. At the gate, she prayed the cat, or, by the sound, several cats, would be still long enough for her to get past the guards. She'd hate to have the men's curiosity aroused so they'd feel compelled to search her wagon.

She breathed a sigh of relief when she was past the guards and into the camp. She'd called Jean this morning and, in between Jean's breathless announcement that Edan had asked her to marry him, Jean had said that Rafe was now working the graveyard shift and would be at home when she brought her wagon. Rafe didn't know about Houston, but he was willing to introduce Sadie to another woman who'd help her with the distribution of the vegetables and the contraband goods. Jean didn't know whether the new woman was aware of Sadie's true identity or not.

Houston pulled the wagon over in front of the Taggerts' company house and halted just as Rafe came out the door.

"Mornin' to you," Sadie called as she struggled to get her fat old body down from the wagon.

Rafe nodded in her direction, looking at her so hard that Houston kept her head down, the sloppy hat shading her face. "I hear you're gonna find me somebody else to help me get rid of this stuff. Now that Jean's gone to be a lady, I don't guess I'll get to see much of her." Sadie began to untie one corner of the canvas. "I got me some cats caught under here and I got to get 'em out."

She glanced up at Rafe as she tossed the canvas back and picked up a head of cabbage, meaning to brag a bit on her fine produce. But when she looked back at the wagon, her knees buckled under her and she grabbed the side of the wagon for support. Under the head of cabbage was Kane Taggert's face and he gave her a lusty wink.

Rafe grabbed Sadie with one hand and looked into the wagon at the same time.

Kane sat up, food falling over the side of the wagon. "Are you deaf, Houston? Couldn't you hear me callin'? I thought I was gonna pass out, since I couldn't breathe. Damn it, woman! I told you not to go into the mines today."

Rafe looked from one person to the other before he took Houston's chin and held her face up to the light. If you were looking for it, you could see the makeup. Over the years, Houston'd become an expert at keeping her face down and she'd soon learned that people rarely look at each other critically. They saw at first glance that she was an old woman and they never questioned that first impression.

"I didn't believe it," Rafe said under his breath. "You'd better get inside and start talkin'."

Kane stood beside her, gripped her elbow painfully and half pushed her inside the little house of Rafe's.

"I told you not to do this," Kane began. He looked at his uncle. "You know what the ladies of Chandler are doin'? There's three or four of 'em that dress up like this and they carry illegal things inside the food."

Houston jerked away from Kane's grasp. "It's not as bad as you make it sound."

"What's more, Fenton knows about the women and he can prosecute 'em at any time. He must hold half the leadin' citizens in the palm of his hand, and they don't even know it."

Rafe looked at Houston for a moment. "What sort of illegal goods?"

"Nothing much," she answered. "Medicines, books, tea, soap, anything we can fit inside the vegetables. It's not what he makes it seem. And as for Mr. Fenton, since he does know and hasn't done anything about it, perhaps he's protecting us, seeing that nothing interferes with our trips. After all, we hurt no one."

"No one!" Kane gasped. "Honey, someday I'm gonna explain to you about stockholders. If Fenton's stockholders found out about you, and how you're takin' profit out of their greedy little mouths, they'd string all of you up. But before Fenton swung, he'd use all you women, and all the daddies and husbands he could, to get himself off. I'm sure Fenton loves what you're doin', 'cause he knows that, any time he wants it, he has power over Chandler's leadin' citizens—just so long as his investors know nothin' about nothin'.' "

"Just because you'd blackmail a person, doesn't mean that other people would do the same thing. Perhaps Mr. Fenton—."

She stopped, because Rafe was shoving her out the door. "I think you better go tend to your wagon. The woman that's gonna help you lives next door. Just knock on the door and she's ready." With that, he shut the door behind her.

"How long's this been goin' on?" Rafe asked Kane. "And what's she do with the money she's paid for the food?"

Kane didn't know all the answers to his uncle's questions, but between them they were able to figure out most of the story. Rafe agreed with Kane about why Fenton allowed the women into the mine camp.

"He'd sell 'em out in seconds," Rafe said. "So what're you plannin' to do now? You gonna let her keep on drivin' the wagon and risk gettin' hurt someday? If the guards found out that she'd played 'em for the fool for a couple of years, they'd act first and ask who was protectin' her later."

"I told her she wasn't to go into the mines today and you see how she obeyed me. The minute she thought I was out of sight, she bought a load of vegetables to bring up here."

"*She* paid for 'em?"

Kane pulled out a chair and sat down. "She ain't too happy with me right now, but she'll come around. I'm workin' on her."

"If you wanna talk about it, I can listen," Rafe said as he took a seat across from his nephew.

Kane had never talked to anyone in his life about his personal problems, but lately, things were changing rapidly. He'd told Opal some of his problems and now he wanted to tell his uncle. Maybe a man could help him.

Kane told Rafe about growing up in Fenton's stables, about his dream of building a bigger house. Rafe nodded in understanding, as if what Kane said made perfect sense to him.

"Only thing was, Houston got real mad when I told her why I'd married her, and she walked out the front door. I got her to come back but she ain't exactly happy about it."

"You say that you'd planned to have her sittin' at your table, but what about afterward?"

Kane started looking at his fingernails. "I didn't want a wife and I thought she was in love with that Westfield that jilted her, so I was sure she'd be glad to see the last of me after the dinner with Fenton. I thought I'd give her a box of jewelry and then I'd go back to New York. Damnest thing was, though, I gave her the jewelry, but she didn't even look at it."

"So why don't you just leave her and go back to New York?"

Kane took a while to answer. "I don't know, I kinda like it here. I like the mountains, and it ain't hot here in the summer like it is in New York and—."

"And you like Houston," Rafe said, grinning. "She's a pretty little thing, and I'd rather have a woman like her than the entire state of New York."

"So how come you ain't married?"

"All the women I like won't have me."

"I guess that's the same with me. When I didn't really care whether Houston married me or not, and thought somebody else'd do just as well, she kept tellin' me that she loved me, and now, when I don't think I could live very well without her, she looks at me like I was a pile of horse manure."

The two men were silent for a moment, the air heavy with their feelings of injustice.

"You want some whiskey?" Rafe asked.

"I need some," Kane answered.

As Rafe turned away to get the whiskey, Kane, for the first time, looked around at the house. He calculated that the whole place would fit into his dressing and bathing area. The house was dirty in a way that no cleaning could remedy. There was no light to speak of in the room, and the air gave off a smell of the deepest poverty.

On the mantelpiece were a tin of tea, two cans of vegetables and what looked to be half a loaf of bread wrapped in cloth. Kane was sure that that was all the food in the house.

Quite suddenly, Kane remembered the rooms above the stables where he'd grown up. He'd sent his sheets and clothes to the Fenton laundress to be cleaned and, when he'd grown up, he'd coaxed the maids into cleaning his rooms. And there'd always been food in abundance.

What was it that Houston had said she was taking to the miners? Medicines, soaps, tea? Whatever she could hide in a head of cabbage. Never had Kane actually had to worry about food. And no matter where he'd lived, he'd never lived like this.

As he looked up at a corner where the roof obviously leaked, he wondered how his mother, raised with all the finest in life, had survived in a house like this as long as she did.

"Did you know my mother?" Kane quietly asked, as Rafe set a tin cup of whiskey on the table.

"I did." Rafe was watching this man who was his relative, both familiar and unknown at the same time. Sometimes Kane moved in a way that made Rafe think it was Frank sitting in front of him—and then he had a way of looking at people that made him think of pretty little Charity.

Rafe took a seat at the table. "She lived with us for just a few months, and it was hard on her, but she was a game little thing. We all thought Frank was the luckiest man on earth. You should have seen her. She worked all day cleanin' and cookin' and then, just before Frank got off his shift, she'd doll herself up like she was ready to meet the President."

Kane stared at his uncle for a moment. "I heard she was a spoiled brat and snubbed all the other women and they hated her."

Rafe's face showed his anger. "I don't know who told you that, but he's a damned liar. When Frank was killed, she just didn't care about livin' anymore. She said she was goin' home to have the baby because she knew Frank would want the best for his child, and she wanted to share her baby with her father. The bastard!" Rafe said under his breath. "The next thing we heard was that Charity and the baby had died and her father had killed hisself in grief. Sherwin and me were glad that Charity's last moments had been happy, and that her father had accepted her back right away. None of us knew about you, or knew that Charity had killed herself, until years later."

Kane wanted to ask why Rafe hadn't done anything about it when he found out, but he put his mug to his mouth and drank instead. He'd told Houston that money gave a man power. What could any of the Taggerts have done when they could barely scratch out a living? And besides, he hadn't done so badly on his own.

"I was thinkin'," Kane said, looking down at his cup. "You and me got off to a bad start, and I was wonderin' if there was anything I could do to help . . ." Even as he said the words, he knew he shouldn't have. Houston said that he used his money and used people. He looked at his uncle and saw that Rafe was holding himself rigid, waiting for Kane to finish his sentence. "Ian likes to play baseball a lot and so does Zach, and now I don't get to see them too much, so I was wonderin' if maybe I could start a baseball team with the kids here. I'd buy all the equipment, of course."

Rafe relaxed. "The kids'd like that. Maybe you can come on Sunday mornin' when they're not down in the mine. You think Fenton'll agree?"

"I sorta think he will," Kane said, finishing his whiskey. "I guess I better go look for my wife. The way she's feelin' about me right now, she just might leave me here."

Rafe rose. "You better let me find her, and I guess you'll have to ride home in the back of the wagon. If the guards saw you leave when you didn't enter, they'd get suspicious, and then the other ladies that drive wagons could get in trouble."

Kane nodded. He didn't like the idea but he knew the sense of it.

"Kane," Rafe said as he stood by the door. "If I could give you some advice about Houston, it'd be to just be patient with her. Women have odd ideas about things that men can't begin to understand. Try courtin' her. You did somethin' that won her in the first place, so maybe you can repeat it if you try courtin' her all over again."

"She don't much like presents," Kane muttered.

"Maybe you're not givin' her the right presents. One time, a girl was real mad at me, and what made her come 'round was when I gave her a puppy. Just a little mutt, but she loved it. She was *real* grateful, if you know what I mean." With a smile and a wink, Rafe left the cabin.

Houston waited all the way back to Kane's house for his explosion, but it never came. He climbed onto the wagon seat with her after she was out of sight of the guards and, although Houston never said a word, he talked to her about the scenery and some about his business. A few times she started to reply, but she stopped herself. Her anger at him was too deep, and she couldn't soften toward him. He'd soon realize that she could never love him again, and he'd have to release her from being his prisoner.

At home, he said good night to her politely and went to his office. The next day, he came to her sitting room at lunch time and, without a word, took her hand and led her down the stairs to the kitchen, where he picked up a picnic basket from Mrs. Murchison. Still holding her hand, he led her down the paths of the garden to the very bottom—to the statue of Diana where they'd once made love.

Houston stood rigid while he spread the white linen cloth and the food, and he had to pull her to make her sit on the cloth. All through the meal, which she just nibbled at, Kane talked to her. He told her more about his business, telling her what a difficult time he was having without Edan to help him.

Houston didn't reply to anything he said, but her silence didn't seem to bother him.

After they'd finished eating, Kane turned around and put his head in her lap and continued talking. He told her about talking to Rafe about his mother. He told her about how dingy Rafe's house had been and how his own quarters, when he was growing up, hadn't been nearly as bad.

"You think there's somethin' I could do to get Uncle Rafe away from the mines? He's not a young man any longer, and I'd like to do somethin'."

Houston didn't speak for a moment. She'd never heard

such a question from Kane. "You can't offer him a job because he'd think it was charity," she said.

"That's what I thought. I don't know what to do. If you have any ideas, will you let me know?"

"Yes," she said hesitantly, and into her mind's eye came the picture of Rafe walking with Pamela. They made a striking couple.

"I have to go back to work now," he said, startling her by kissing her quickly and sweetly as he rose. "Why don't you stay here and enjoy the garden?"

He left her alone and Houston wandered about looking at the plants, and in the rose garden she borrowed a pair of clippers from a gardener and snipped a few blooms. It was the first time since she'd arrived that she'd done anything that wasn't absolutely necessary. "Just because the master is horrible is no reason to hate the house," she said to herself to justify carrying the roses inside.

When Kane came to dinner, the house was full of freshly cut flowers, and he did little more than grin at Houston all the way through the meal.

The next day, Blair came to luncheon, talked about her friend from Pennsylvania, Dr. Louise Bleeker, who'd come to help in the clinic, and asked if Houston was all right. For some reason, Blair no longer seemed to hate Kane.

"Things aren't much better," Houston said, toying with her meal. "And you?"

Blair hesitated. "Lee will get over it, I'm sure."

"Over it?"

"He's a bit angry with me right now. I, ah . . . made a journey in the back of his buggy. But let's talk about you."

"Let's talk about the magazine. I have two new articles for you."

On Sunday, Kane roused Houston from bed, remaining far back from her, not getting too close to her sleepy form inside the warm bed. He tossed on the bed a dress of deep rose zephyr-gingham that was trimmed with narrow bands of black velvet ribbon. "Wear that and get dressed as fast as you can," he ordered before leaving the room.

Minutes later, he returned wearing corduroy trousers, a bright blue flannel shirt and navy suspenders. He stood for a moment looking at Houston in her underwear, the tight corset pushing her breasts up above the lace-edged chemise, her legs encased, from the knee down, in black silk stockings with little butterflies going up one side, and wearing tiny black leather high-heeled shoes.

He gaped at her for a moment, then turned and left the room as if, if he stayed any longer, he might not live through it.

Houston dropped the robe she'd grabbed but not bothered to cover herself with and let out a sigh. She told herself that it was a sigh of relief and not the sigh of regret that it sounded like.

He didn't tell her where they were going when he lifted her into the buggy that he'd given her, but started driving. Houston didn't ask him where they were headed, but her face showed her surprise when they turned up the road to the Little Pamela mine.

The guards allowed them to pass without so much as a challenge or a question and, once through the gate, people came out of the houses and began following them. Houston started to wave to a few women she knew.

"They don't know you when you're clean," Kane warned her.

She couldn't help looking around, as more and more people began following them, and there were enormous smiles on the children's faces.

"What have you done?" she asked.

"There," he answered, pointing. In front of them was the only open area in the camp, the mine mouth in the background. In the center of the dirt field were wooden crates.

Kane halted the buggy and two boys with black-rimmed eyes held the horse as he helped Houston down. When they were standing on the inside of the circle of people who had gathered around the boxes, Kane grinned and said loudly, "Go to it, boys."

As Houston watched the boys tear into the crates, Rafe walked up behind them.

"The boxes came two days ago, and I didn't think you'd mind if I told 'em what was inside. They've been dancin' around and nervous with excitement since then," Rafe said, as he put his hand on his nephew's shoulder.

Houston looked at that hand on her husband's shoulder

with astonishment before turning back to see what the boys had found in the crates. They withdrew baseball equipment: uniforms, bats, gloves, balls, catchers' face masks.

Kane turned to Houston, his face showing his expectation.

Had he done all this just to impress her, she wondered. She looked about the circle of parents who looked on their sons adoringly. "And what did you get for the girls?"

"Girls?" Kane asked. "Girls can't play baseball."

"No? What about tennis, archery, bicycling, gymnastics, fencing?"

"Fencing?" Kane said, his face turning to anger. "I guess nobody can please you, can they, Miss Ice Lady? Nobody's up to your standards, are they?" he asked before turning away and walking toward the boys, who were swinging bats and tossing balls in the air.

Houston moved away from the crowd. Perhaps she had been a little too hard on him. Perhaps she should have said something nice about his trying to help the boys. It was what she'd always wanted to happen and, when it did, she was ungrateful.

At least, she could make the best of the day and not stand sulking in a corner. She stepped forward and spoke to a little girl near her and began explaining some of the rules of baseball. Within minutes, Houston had a crowd around her of women and girls, and even some men who had never seen the game before. By the time Kane and Rafe had organized the boys into teams, Houston had started a cheering section to applaud the boys' progress, no matter how inept it was.

Two hours after they arrived, a four-horse wagon came barrelling into the midst of the people. Everyone stopped dead still, thinking that it must mean that a disaster had occurred.

The driver, red-faced and sweating, was Mr. Vaughn, who owned the sporting goods store. "Taggert!" he yelled at Kane as he controlled the sweaty horses. "This is the last time that I make an order like this for you. I don't care if you buy my whole store, I ain't workin' on Sunday for nobody."

"Did you bring everything?" Kane asked, moving to the back of the wagon that was covered with canvas. "And stop bellyachin'. With the prices I've paid you in the last months, I *do* own your store."

The crowd laughed, enjoying the power money gave a man to say what he wanted to anyone. But Houston was watching the back of the wagon.

"Well, look at this," Kane said, pulling out a tennis racquet. "I don't think we can hit a baseball with this." He turned to a little girl standing by him. "Maybe you could use this."

The child took the racquet but didn't move. "What is it?" she whispered.

Kane pointed to Houston. "See that lady there? She can show you how to use it."

Houston walked straight to her husband, put her arms about his neck and kissed him, much to the delight of the people around them. When he wouldn't let her go, Houston pushed at him.

"I guess I finally found the right present," he said to someone over her shoulder as he pressed her close.

As Houston moved away from him, she heard Rafe laugh.

The rest of the afternoon, Houston didn't have much time to think as she organized games of tennis and showed girls how to use the archery equipment. There were balls, hoops and sticks, jump ropes, jacks, dolls, paper dolls. She had her hands full just trying to portion out the goods fairly, and the mothers helped her soothe the girls who thought they weren't getting their fair share.

Before Houston knew it, it was sundown, and Kane came to her and put his arm about her shoulders. As she looked up at him, she knew that she still loved him. Perhaps he wasn't the man she had first thought he was, perhaps he was capable of living his life for the sole purpose of revenge, and maybe today was only a show of his hatred for Jacob Fenton, but at the moment, she didn't care. She'd promised to love him for better or worse and his obsession with revenge was part of the worse. As she looked up at him, she knew that she'd always love him, no matter what he did, no matter what dreadful motives he had for the things he did. She would stand by him and love him even if he took everything the Fentons owned.

"You ready, honey?" he asked.

"Yes," she said and meant the word from the bottom of her heart.

Chapter 28

Kane didn't look at Houston as they left the coal camp and drove past the sullen guards. He held the reins tightly and kept his eyes on the road ahead.

Houston looked at nothing else but him, wondering how she could have so little pride as to admit to being in love with a man who used her. But as she looked at him, she knew that she couldn't help herself.

At the foot of the hill, just before the road turned back to the main highway, Kane stopped the wagon. The sun was going down in a riot of pinks and oranges, setting the horizon on fire. The cool mountain air was growing cooler, the air was fragrant with the scent of sage, the road was littered with the silvery pieces of coke from the ovens, and blowing in the gentle breeze were feathery seedpods.

"Why are we stopping?" she asked, as he came around to her side of the wagon and lifted his arms to her.

"Because, love," he said, pulling her down into his arms, "I don't think that I can wait any longer to make love to you."

"Kane . . ." she began to protest, "we can't stop here. Someone might come along."

She said no more because he was holding her in his arms, drawing her closer to him, his hands beginning to caress her back. Houston leaned into him with all the fervor she felt.

He drew back from her, touching her cheek with a rare gentleness. "I missed you, honey," he whispered. "I missed you a lot."

The next minute, all gentleness was gone as his mouth swooped down on hers and hungrily caught her lips under his own.

Houston was as eager for him as he was for her. Her body melted against his, her curves fluidly conforming to the hard planes of his body.

The next minute, he pushed her away and looked at the expression of rapture and desire he saw on her face. With a look of fortitude, he moved away from her and went to the back of the wagon and removed the piece of canvas. After he'd spread it on the ground, behind the privacy of piñon trees and juniper shrubs, he held his hand out to her.

Slowly, Houston walked toward him, watching him, her mind a blank except for thoughts of the pleasure to come.

His hands were shaking as he began to undress her, slowly working the tiny buttons loose one by one. "I've been thinkin' about this for a long time," he said softly. The dim evening light made shadows of his lashes across his face, making him look younger and very vulnerable. "You asked me once about other women. I don't guess I ever even thought about a woman once I was outta bed with her—in fact, I don't think I thought about her while I was *in* bed with her. And worst of all, I sure as hell never told a woman all the things I've told you in the last few months. Are you a lady or a witch?"

As his hand slid inside her dress, touching her skin, finding her breast and sending the warmth of his touch throughout her body, Houston put her arms around his neck, pressed her lips to his. "I'm a witch who's in love with you," she whispered.

Kane grabbed her to him so close that she felt her ribs giving way, and only a squeal of protest made him loosen his grip.

There was no more talk as Kane attacked her with all the pent-up desire that he had stored. And Houston responded in the same manner.

With exuberance, they both began tearing at each other's clothes, and the still night air was filled with the sound of bits of fabric tearing when a reluctant button refused to slide through the hole.

Houston wasn't given time to remove her hose and high

heels before Kane was on her, his hot mouth running over every bit of skin that he could find. She dug her nails into his flesh and pulled him closer and closer until they were one person.

As she started to open her mouth, Kane closed it with his own. "You scream here, Ice Lady, and you'll get us some unwanted visitors."

Houston had no idea what he was talking about and had no intention of wasting her time finding out. Yet every few minutes, Kane would clamp down on her mouth with whatever was handy and Houston kissed whatever he placed there.

She had no idea of time or of how long they were there, because her thoughts were taken up with Kane's body that was sometimes on top of hers, sometimes under, beside, sitting and, even once, she thought, standing. Her hair was plastered to her face with sweat, hanging down her back in wet tendrils—and everywhere she was surrounded by Kane's skin: hot, damp, and moving, delicious skin that was hers for the tasting and the touching. Her long-stored desires, her nearness to losing the man she loved, made her insatiable. They came together, then broke apart, reunited and at last came together for the last final, paralyzing thrust.

They slept for a few minutes, locked together, their skin fused.

Kane roused after a while and pulled the end of the canvas over them and snuggled his jacket about Houston's bare upper body. He looked at her for a moment in the moonlight, at her sleeping face, smoothed back her drying hair. "Who woulda thought that a lady like you . . ." he whispered, before trailing off, pulling her to rest on his shoulder and lying back on the canvas.

Houston woke an hour later to Kane's hand running up and down her body, his thumb playing with the pink tip of her breast. She smiled at him in a dreamy way.

"I got all a man can ask for," Kane said, moving to his side. "I got a naked woman in my arms and she's smilin' at me." He put his big thigh between hers. "Hey, lady, you wanta get tumbled by the stableboy?"

She rubbed her hips against his. "Only if he's very gentle and doesn't frighten me with his barbarian ways."

Kane gave a grunt as his mouth followed his hand. "When

a man wants somethin', he uses a gun or a knife, but, honey, the weapons you use scare me to death."

"You look terrified," she said, as she took his ear lobe between her teeth.

This time they made love leisurely, taking their time, and not feeling frantic or rushed, and when they were finished, they lay still, in each other's arms, and slept. Sometime during the night, Kane rose and unhitched the horses from the wagon. When Houston sleepily asked him what he was doing, he said, "Once a stableboy, always a stableboy," before coming back to the canvas that was their bed.

Before the sun came up, they stirred and wakened and began to talk. Kane lay on his back, Houston draped around him, and talked about how much pleasure he'd had in seeing the children with the toys that he'd given them. "Why do some of the boys look like raccoons?"

It took Houston a while to understand what he meant. "They work in the mines and haven't yet learned how to wash the dust out of their eyes."

"But some of those boys were just babies, or at least not much older. They couldn't . . ."

"They do," Houston answered, and they were silent for a moment. "You know something I'd like to do for all the mines instead of just one?"

"What?"

"I'd like to buy about four wagons, something like a big milk wagon, but inside would be shelves of books, and the wagons would travel to all the camps and would be a free lending library. The drivers could also be librarians or teachers, and they could help the children, and the adults, too, to choose books."

"Why don't we hire men to drive the wagons?" Kane asked, with a twinkle in his eye.

"Then you like the idea?"

"It sounds fine to me, and a few wagons have to be cheaper than that train I bought your mother. How's she doin' with that thing, anyway?"

Houston smiled at him in the growing light. "She says that you gave her the idea. She had it moved to her backyard and now she uses it for her own personal retreat. I hear that Mr. Gates was so angry that he could barely speak."

As the sun lightened the sky, Kane said they should return home before the morning traffic started. All the way home, Houston sat close to him and, several times, he stopped and kissed her. Houston told herself that the Fentons didn't matter and that she would love Kane no matter what he did to take his revenge.

At home, they took a bath in Houston's big, gold-fixtured tub and ended with more water on the tile floor than inside the tub. But Kane absorbed most of it when he covered the floor with twenty-one thick white Turkish towels, then laid Houston on the floor and made love to her. Houston's maid, Susan, nearly walked into the room, but Kane slammed the door in her face and they laughed together as they heard the girl run across the hardwood floor of Houston's bedroom.

Afterward, they went downstairs to the biggest breakfast two people ever ate. Mrs. Murchison came out of the kitchen and personally attended them, grinning and smiling and obviously pleased that Kane and Houston were reconciled.

"Babies," she said, on her way out the door. "This house needs babies."

Kane nearly choked on his coffee as he looked at Houston with terror on his face. She refused to look at him but smiled into her own cup.

Just as Mrs. Murchison reentered the room bearing a platter of pan-fried beefsteaks dripping brown gravy, they heard the rumble. It felt as if it came rolling under their feet, something deep and dark and evil. The glasses on the table rattled and, from upstairs, they could hear the sound of breaking glass.

With a scream, Mrs. Murchison dropped the platter.

"What the hell was that?" Kane asked. "An earthquake?"

Houston didn't say a word. She'd heard that sound only once before in her life but, once heard, it was never, never forgotten. She didn't look at Kane or the servants, who were already running into the dining room, but went straight to the telephone and picked it up.

"Which one?" was all she said into the receiver, not bothering to tell the operator who she was.

"The Little Pamela," she heard before the cold instrument slipped from her hand.

"Houston!" Kane yelled into her face as he grabbed her

shoulders. "Don't you dare faint on me now. Was that a mine?"

Houston didn't think she'd be able to speak. There was a knot of fear closing her throat. Why did it have to be *my* mine, she kept hearing inside her head as her mind's eye saw all the children. Which boys who'd played ball yesterday were now dead?

She looked up at Kane with bleak eyes. "The shift," she whispered. "Rafe was on the last shift."

Kane's hands tightened on her shoulders. "It was the Little Pamela then?" he whispered. "How bad?"

Houston's mouth opened but no words came out.

One of the footmen stepped out of the group of now-silent servants gathered in the hall. "Sir, when the explosion is bad enough to smash windows in town, then it's very bad."

Kane stood still a minute, then went into action. "Houston, I want you to get every blanket and sheet in this house and load it into the big wagon and bring it to the mine. You understand me? I'm gonna get dressed and go on up there ahead of you. But I want you to come as soon as possible, you understand that?"

"They'll be needin' rescuers," the footman said.

Kane gave him a quick look up and down. "Then get out of them fancy duds and get on a horse." He turned back to Houston. "Alive or dead, I'll get Rafe out." After a quick kiss, he bounded up the stairs.

Houston stood still for a moment before she began to move. She couldn't change what had happened but she could help. She turned to the women left standing near her. "You heard the master. I want every sheet and blanket put into the wagon within the next ten minutes."

One of the maids stepped forward. "My brother works at the Little Pamela. May I go with you?"

"And me," said Susan. "I've mended a few broken heads in my time."

"Yes," Houston answered as she hurried up the stairs to change out of her lacy morning gown. "I'm afraid we'll need all the help we can get."

Chapter 29

Kane had never had much experience with disasters; his battles had usually been on a one-to-one basis, so he was unprepared for what met him at the site of the Little Pamela mine. He heard the screams of the women from far away and he thought that, as long as he lived, he'd never get the sound out of his head.

The gate to the camp was open and unguarded, only a woman sitting there rocking her baby and crooning to it. Kane and the four men with him slowed as they entered the camp, and as more women, some of them running, some of them just standing and crying, came into view, the men dismounted.

As Kane walked past one woman, she grabbed his arm in an iron grip.

"Kill me!" she screeched in his face. "He's gone and we have nothing! Nothing!"

Kane was unable to stop her from pulling him inside the shack. Rafe's cabin was a mansion compared to this place. Five filthy children, wearing little more than rags, stood in a corner clutching at one another. Their gaunt faces and big, sad eyes told of their constant hunger. He hadn't seen these children when he'd come yesterday, but then, he didn't remember being in this part of the camp where the houses were hovels of tarpaper and flattened tin cans.

"Kill us all," the woman screamed. "We'll be better off. We'll starve now."

On the board that seemed to serve as a table was a half loaf of old bread, and Kane could see no more food in the house.

"Sir," the footman who'd entered behind Kane said. "They'll need help with the bodies."

"Yes," Kane said softly and left the hut, the woman crying loudly behind him. "Who are these people?" he asked, once they were outside.

"They can't afford to pay the rent for the company houses at two dollars a room, so the company rents them land at a dollar a month and they build their own houses out of whatever they can find." He nodded toward the slum area of shacks of corrugated tin, powder cans, and Kane thought he saw pieces of the crates that yesterday had contained the baseball equipment.

"What will happen to the woman if her husband is dead?"

The man's mouth turned grim. "If she's lucky, the company will pay her six months' wages, but then she and the kids are on their own. Whatever happens, the company will say that the explosion was caused by the miners."

Kane straightened. "At least we can help now. Let's go get this woman some food."

"Where?" the man asked. "Four years ago, there was a riot and the miners attacked the company store, so now there's always only a bare minimum of goods, including food, in any one camp." His mouth twisted. "And the town won't help, either. We tried to get City Hall to help us when the last mine went up, but they said we had to go through 'channels'."

Kane started walking toward the center of the camp where the mine was. Before the mouth of the mine lay three sheet-draped bodies; two men carried another body to the open doors of the machine shop, where he could see Blair and two men at work. Kane walked to the stand beside Leander. "How bad is it?"

"The worst," Leander said. "There's so much gas in the mine that the rescuers are passing out before they reach the men. We can't tell exactly what happened yet, or how many are dead, because the explosion went inward instead of outward. There could be tunnels of men still trapped in there alive. Somebody get her, will you?" Lee called as he jumped on the elevator that would take him down into the mine.

Kane caught the woman in question as she ran toward a

burned body that was being hauled from the mine. She was a frail little thing, and he picked her up in his arms. "Let me take you home," he said, but she only shook her head.

Another woman came up to them. "I'll take care of her."

"Do you have any brandy?" Kane asked.

"Brandy?" the woman spat at him. "We ain't even got any fresh water." She helped the woman Kane was holding to stand.

Two minutes later, Kane was on his horse and tearing down the side of the mountain toward Chandler. He passed Houston on the way up and she called to him, but he didn't slow his pace.

Once in town, he kept going at full speed, nearly running over a half-dozen pedestrians who all shouted questions at him. Most of the citizens of Chandler were standing outside looking up toward the mountain that held the Little Pamela mine and speculating on what had happened.

Kane thundered through town and up Archer Avenue until he came to Edan's house. Across the street, the new West-field Infirmary was alive with activity. He hadn't seen Edan since the night they'd parted so bitterly.

Edan was walking across the front porch, a saddled horse waiting for him, when Kane skidded to a stop, reining his horse so hard the animal's front feet came off the ground.

Kane dismounted and ran up the steps all in one motion. "I know you ain't got much use for me anymore, but I don't know who else has got the brains to help me organize what I want to do, so I'm askin' you to forget your feelin's at the moment and help me out."

"Doing what?" Edan asked cautiously. "I'm planning to go help at the mine. Jean's uncle is up there and—."

"He happens to be *my* goddamn uncle, too!" Kane exploded in Edan's face. "I've just spent the last hour up there and they got more rescuers than they know what to do with, but they don't have much food and no water, and the explosion flattened a bunch of the houses—if you can call those shacks that. I want your help in gettin' together some food and shelter for the people, for the rescuers, and for the women that're standin' around screamin'."

Edan looked at his former employer for a long hard minute. "From what Jean could find out on the telephone, it's going to take a long time to get all the bodies out. We'll have to rent wagons to haul everything up to the mine, and we ought to try to get a train for . . . for the bodies. Today, we'll need food that doesn't have to be cooked."

Kane gave Edan a brilliant smile. "Come on, we got to get to work."

Jean had just come onto the porch, her face ghostly white.

Edan turned to her. "I want you to call Miss Emily at the teashop and tell her to have all her sisters meet me at Randolph's Grocery as soon as they can get there. Be sure you talk to Miss Emily herself, and be sure you say 'sisters'. Jean! This is very important, do you understand me?"

Jean nodded once before Edan gave her a quick kiss and mounted his horse.

Once in town, Kane and Edan separated and went to anyone who they knew owned a freight wagon. Most of the owners volunteered their services and, throughout Chandler, there was a feeling of togetherness as their concern for what had happened in the camp drew them together.

Six young ladies met them in front of Randolph's and Kane took only seconds telling them what was needed before the women took over, sweet Miss Emily bellowing orders in the voice of a gunnery sergeant.

As the wagons pulled up in front of the store's big back doors, the women loaded cases of canned beef, beans, condensed milk, crackers and hundreds of loaves of bread. When a crowd of curious people began to gather, Miss Emily put them to work helping to load the cases of food.

Edan saw to the filling of a water wagon.

Pamela Fenton came running down the hill, holding her hat on, Zachary in front of her. "What can we do?" she asked loudly over Miss Emily's orders.

Kane looked down at his son and a feeling of thankfulness spread through his body. This child of his would never be exposed to the constant danger of the mines. He put his hand on the boy's head and turned to Pam. "I want you to get as many friends as you can to help you and find every tent in this town. Go up to my house and find out what Houston did with those big tents she had for the weddin'. Then, I want every one of those tents taken up to the mine."

"I don't think Zach is old enough yet to see what's

happened up there," Pam said. "Sometimes those explosions can be——."

Kane's temper had played no part in the day's happenings, but now he let it loose. "It's *you!*" he yelled into her face. "It's you Fentons that caused all this. If the mines weren't so dangerous, and your father would part with his precious money, none of this would have happened. This boy is *my* son and, if the boys up there can die in the mines, he's not too delicate to see the deaths that your father caused. Now, woman, you get busy and do what I say or I'll remember who you are and remember that right now my dearest wish is to see your father dead."

When Kane stopped, he was aware that all the many townspeople around him had stopped to stare at him, pausing, frozen in motion, as they gaped.

Edan stepped down from a wagon, the first one to move. "Are we going to stand here all day? You!" he yelled at a young boy. "Load that case of beans and you, move that wagon before that horse runs into the back of the other one."

Slowly, the people began to return to their duties, but Kane's mind was on the deaths that had been caused by Jacob Fenton. In spite of what he'd said to Pam, he wouldn't allow Zach to travel on any wagon to the site of the mine disaster until he was ready to drive one himself.

It was nearly sundown when Kane climbed into a seat and started the trip up to the Little Pamela mine. Zach was beside him, and the boy didn't speak until they were well on their way.

"Did my grandfather really kill the people? Was it really his fault?"

Kane started to tell his son just what he thought of Fenton, of how the man wanted money so badly that he had cheated Kane out of what was his, but something inside him made him stop. Whatever else the old man was, he was Zachary's grandfather, and the boy had every right to love him.

"I think sometimes that people get confused about money. They think that money can give them everything that they want in life, and so they go after it any way that they can. It doesn't matter whether they have to cheat or steal to get it, or even that they may take the money away from someone else, they think that gettin' the money is worth all they have to do."

"My mother said that you're richer than my grandfather. Does that mean that you stole it, too? Did you cheat people?"

"No," Kane answered softly. "I guess I was lucky. All I had to do was give up my life to get the money."

They were quiet as they travelled the rest of the way to the mine, and Kane experienced again the horror of first entering the scene of the explosion.

By the mouth of the mine lay eight bodies, undraped, before they were taken away to the machine shop where Blair, another female doctor, and two male doctors were working.

Houston, her hair straggling about her cheeks, her dress soiled, came to the back of the wagon as Kane let down the board.

"This is wonderful of you," she began, as she lifted a case of condensed milk and started to hand it to a waiting woman. "You really have no part in this. You——."

Kane took the heavy case from her. "I live here too, and in a way these mines belong to me. Maybe if I'd collected on Fenton, I could have prevented this from happening. Houston, you look tired. Why don't you take the wagon back and go home and rest?"

"They need everyone. The rescuers are succumbing to the gas and they're having difficulty reaching the men."

"Here! Give me a drink of that," said a familiar voice behind them, and Kane turned to see his uncle Rafe downing a mug of water.

Houston was sure that she'd never seen Kane's smile so big or showing so much gladness before. He thumped his uncle on the back so hard that the mug went flying across the ground. Rafe said a few well chosen words about Kane's exuberance, but Kane just stood and grinned until Rafe stopped cursing and winked at Houston before he went back to the mine mouth.

Kane went to the mine where he saw Leander, blackened from the smoke of the explosion, just coming up from the inside. He handed Lee a dipper of water. "Many more?"

Lee drank the water greedily. "Too many." He held up his hands and looked at them in the fading light. "The bodies are burned and, when you touch them, the skin comes off on your hands."

There was nothing Kane could say, but his thoughts went to the man who was responsible for all this.

"Thanks for the food," Lee was saying. "It's been more help than you know. Tomorrow, more people will be here, the press, relatives, the mine inspectors, government people, and the curious. Food is something that sometimes gets overlooked. I better get back now," he said, turning away.

Kane made his way through the growing number of people, found Houston and his son and put them on one of the empty freight wagons. "We're going to organize the rest of the food," was all he said as he started down the hill. When Houston's head nodded against his shoulder, he put his arm around her and held her so she could sleep the rest of the way into Chandler.

Houston and Zach slept for a few hours in the back of the wagon while Edan and Kane wakened townspeople and purchased goods to be taken to the mine. In the morning, they went to the high school and asked that the children be dismissed for the day so they could help gather the needed goods.

The students purchased vegetables, jam, fruit; they talked their mothers into cooking the food and boiling hundreds of eggs. They collected clothes, dishes, firewood, and carried everything to receiving stations.

And all day, the news came down from the mountain: twenty-two bodies found so far, so burned, bloated, and mutilated as to make identification almost impossible. Twenty-five more bodies were expected to be found by the rescuers who were working in two shifts. So far, one rescuer had died.

At midday, Kane drove a heavily laden wagon to the mine and, as he unloaded bundles of blankets and hundreds of diapers, he saw the rescuers coming to the surface and more than one of them vomited on the ground.

"It's the smell," said a man beside Kane. "The bodies down there smell so bad the men can't stand it."

For a moment, Kane stood there staring, then he grabbed someone's saddled horse and tore down the mountainside—heading for Jacob Fenton's house with all the speed he could muster.

He hadn't been up the drive to that house since he'd left years before, but the familiarity was so strong that he felt that he'd never been away. He didn't wait to knock on the door but rammed his foot through the leaded-glass panel and walked through the door that barely stayed on its hinges.

"Fenton!" he bellowed as servants came running from every part of the house, two footmen grabbing his shoulders to restrain him, but he shrugged them off as if they weighed nothing. He knew the arrangement of the downstairs of the house well enough and soon found the dining room, where Jacob sat eating alone, at the head of the table.

They looked at each other for a moment, Kane's face red with his rage, his body heaving.

Jacob waved his hand to dismiss the servants. "I don't imagine you came here for dinner," he said, calmly buttering a roll.

"How can you sit there when the people you've killed are on that mountain?" Kane managed to get out.

"There I beg to differ with you. *I* have not killed them. The truth is, I have done everything in my power to keep them alive, but they seem to have a suicidal bent. Could I offer you some wine? This is a very good year."

Kane's mind was full of the sights and sounds of the last few days. His ears seemed to ring with the sound of women's crying, and he wasn't aware of it, but he hadn't eaten in nearly two days. Now, the smell of the food, the cleanliness of the room, the quiet, all went together to make him sway on his feet.

Jacob stood, poured a glass of wine and, as he pulled out a chair for Kane, he set the glass before him. Kane didn't notice that Jacob's hand was trembling as he held the wine.

"Is it very bad?" Jacob asked, as he walked to a sideboard and removed a plate, which he began filling.

Kane didn't answer as he sat in the chair, looking at the wine. "Why?" he whispered after a moment. "How could you kill them? What is worth the death of those people? Why couldn't you have been satisfied with taking all the money that was left to me? Why do you have to have more? There are other ways of making it."

Jacob put a full plate of food in front of Kane, but the younger man didn't touch it. "I was twenty-four when you were born, and all my life I had thought that I was the owner of what I'd grown up with. I loved the man I thought was my father . . . and I thought that he cared for me."

Jacob straightened his shoulders. "At that age, one tends to be idealistic. The night Horace killed himself, I found out that I was nothing to him. His will stated that I could remain your guardian until you were twenty-one years old, and then I was to turn everything over to you. I was to walk out with the clothes on my back and nothing more. I don't think you can imagine the depth of the hatred I felt that night for the squalling infant that had ruined my entire life. I don't think I had a rational thought as I sent you away to a farm woman to wet-nurse and then bribed the lawyers. That hatred kept me going for years. It was all I could think of. If I signed a paper, I knew that somewhere there was a four-year-old child who actually owned what I was buying or selling. I sent for you once when you were young, so I could see for myself that you weren't worthy of what my father had left you."

Jacob sat down, across the table from Kane. "The doctor says that at most I have only a month or two to live. I haven't told anyone, but somehow I wanted to tell you the truth before I died."

He picked up his full glass of wine and sipped it. "Hatred hurts the one who hates more than it does the hated. All those years that you lived here, I'd see you and I was sure that you were trying to take everything that I owned. I lived in fear that you'd find out the truth and take what was mine and my children's. And when you wanted Pam for your wife, it seemed that all my fears had come true. Later, I thought that I should have seen your marriage to my daughter as a solution, but at the time . . . I don't think that I had any rational thoughts then."

He drank deeply of the wine. "There you are, Taggert, a dying man's last confession. It's all yours; you can take it if you want. This morning, I told my son the truth about who owns my property because I don't have the strength or the inclination to fight you any longer."

Kane sat back in the chair and, as he looked at Fenton and saw the gray tinge under his skin, he realized that he no longer hated the man. Houston had said that his hatred of Jacob Fenton had spurred him on to achieve what he had, and perhaps she was right. In fact, she had pointed out the injustice of Horace cutting Jacob out of his will.

Kane took a drink of the wine that was in front of him and looked at the food. "Why did you have to starve the miners to make your money?"

"Starve the miners?" Jacob gasped, his eyes bulging. "Doesn't anyone in the world understand that I barely break even with the miners? The only money I make is in Denver at the steel mills, but everyone looks at the poor mistreated miner and accuses me of being Satan."

He stood and began to pace around the room. "I have to keep the coal mines under lock and key or the unionists will come in and incite the miners to demand more money, fewer hours. You know what they want? They want to elect a check weighman. Look, I know as well as anyone that the scales are fixed, and that the miners dig more coal than they're credited for, but if I were honest and paid them what they earned, I'd have to charge more per ton for the coal, and then I'd not be competitive, and I'd never get more contracts and then they wouldn't have any more jobs. So who gets hurt the most if I let them hire honest weighmen? I can hire coal miners by the hundreds, but I don't think they can get jobs so easily."

Kane looked at the older man for a moment. He understood about business, and he knew that sometimes compensations had to be made. "What about the mine safety? I hear you use rotten timbers and—."

"Like hell I do. The miners have their own pride system. You can ask your uncle if I'm not right. They brag about how they can tell just how far they can go before the roof caves in. I have mine inspectors in there all the time, and they find that the men won't take the time to shore up as they go."

Kane picked up the fork by the plate of food in front of him and slowly began to eat, but then found that he was ravenous and began to shovel it in. "You don't pay them for the time they spend shoring, do you? They're paid by the tonnage they get out, aren't they?"

Jacob took a chair across from Kane and put another thick slice of beef on his plate. "I hire them as subcontractors and it's up to each man to fulfill his part of the contract. Did you know that I pay men to inspect the miners' hats? The idiots open the cap to light cigarettes and send the whole place up. The inspector has to check that the caps are welded shut to prevent them from killing each other."

Kane, his mouth full, was gesturing with his fork. "One minute, you treat 'em like children and lock 'em up and the next minute, they have to be subcontractors and take the responsibility for their own . . . what's it called when you have to work and don't get paid for the work?"

"Dead work," Jacob supplied. "I do the best I can and still keep the miners working. I'd like to buy my coal from someone else and just make steel, but I can't see putting so many people out of work. Every time something like this happens," he motioned in the general direction of the Little Pamela, "I say that I'm going to close the mines. There's a vast amount of competition to supply coal to the mills in Denver, and I could close all seventeen mines around Chandler and they wouldn't even be missed. But you know what would happen to this town if I closed the mines? It'd be a ghost town in two years."

"So, according to you, you're just doin' the whole town a favor."

"I am, in a way," Jacob said righteously.

"I imagine you're payin' your stockholders, ain't you?"

"Not as much as I'd like, but I do the best I can."

Kane was cleaning the bottom of the second plate of food with a piece of bread. "Then you'd damn well better start doin' better. I happen to have a little money of my own and I just might decide to use it to bring a few lawsuits against the principals of Fenton Coal and Iron, and I think that all production—steel and coal—might be shut down while this thing was in court."

"But that would ruin Chandler! You couldn't—."

"I somehow think that the owners of FC&I might have enough self-interest to keep that from happening."

Jacob looked at Kane for a long time. "All right, what do you want?"

"If the men need inspectors to protect them from themselves, I want inspectors, and I want the kids out of the mines."

"But the children's small bodies can do things that the adults can't!" Jacob protested.

Kane merely gave him a look and went on to the next point, trying to remember everything that Houston had told him about the problems in the mines. Jacob protested every aspect of Kane's complaints; from libraries, "reading just makes them discontented"; to church services, "and pay preachers for every religion? We'd have religious wars if we tried to make them all go to the same service"; to better housing, to which Jacob said that the miners living in the shacks were really healthier because of all the fresh air coming through the cracks in the walls.

They talked and argued through the afternoon, with Jacob constantly refilling Kane's wineglass. By about four o'clock, Kane's words began to slur and his head rested against his chest. When he finally nodded off to sleep in the midst of telling Jacob that perhaps unions weren't as bad as Jacob seemed to think, the older man stood and looked down at Kane's big body sprawled in the chair.

"If I'd had a son like you, I could have conquered the world," he murmured before leaving the room and sending a servant for a blanket to cover Kane.

It was full night when Kane woke, stiff and sore from sleeping in the chair, and for a moment he didn't know where he was. The room was dim, but on the table he could make out the outline of a cloth-wrapped package and knew without a doubt that the package contained sandwiches.

With a smile, he stuffed the food into his pocket and left the house. Somehow, he felt lighter than he had in years, and as he rode back to the mine, he felt new hope that from now on his life was going to be different.

At the mine, Reed Westfield, Leander's attorney father, was just entering the elevator to go back into the tunnel to continue the rescue operation. Kane caught the man with Reed by the collar. "Go get somethin' to eat. I'll go on this trip."

As the machinery started, Kane told Reed a quick story of how all that Jacob Fenton owned was legally Kane's.

"I don't want that hangin' over the man's head any longer, and I don't need the money. I want you to draw me up a paper sayin' that I turn everything over to him and whoever he wants to leave it to, and I want it done soon because the old man is dyin'."

Reed looked at Kane through weary eyes and nodded. "I have an office full of clerks with nothing much to do. Is tomorrow morning soon enough?"

Kane did no more than nod because, as they reached deeper into the mine, his face contorted at the smell.

Chapter 30

On the third day after the explosion, a total of forty-eight bodies had been taken from inside the mine, and seven were still unaccounted for. In the afternoon of the second day, four bodies had been found on their knees, their hands cupped over their mouths. They'd survived the major explosion, but the afterdamp, the gases, had killed them.

In town, the businesses were draped with black and flags were flown at half-mast. As the hearses drove through the streets in an unending stream, the people walked about with bare, bowed heads.

The fiancé of Sarah Oakley had been killed as he walked home from helping with the rescue of the miners. Too tired to watch where he was going, or to be aware of his surroundings, he didn't see or hear the train before it overtook him, killing him instantly.

Leander and Kane, with help from Edan, had demanded, and received, the promise of a rescue station to be built on land that had been donated by Jacob Fenton. No one dared say so but everyone was of the opinion that Kane had gone to Fenton's house and demanded the gift of the land.

Houston spent the day attending funerals and trying to comfort widows and seeing that children had enough to eat.

"I think this is what you want," Reed Westfield said, handing Kane a piece of paper as they stood before the mine entrance. "After this is settled, we can draw up a longer form, but I believe that should hold up in court."

275

Kane scanned the document and quickly saw that it said that he gave all rights to the holdings of the Fentons to the trust of Jacob Fenton, to dispose of however he wished.

"If you'll sign it, I'll witness it and file it. I have a copy here that you can give Fenton."

Kane smiled at Reed. "Thanks," he said, as he took the fountain pen from Reed and signed the paper. He held the copy up. "I think I'll take this to him right now. Maybe it'll make up to him for parting with that land, and I might mention that he ought to start a program to train men in mine rescue."

Reed returned Kane's grin. "I think the man might have remained richer before you gave him the rights to his property."

As Kane rode down the hill toward Chandler, he looked about the camp and thought of the horror of the last few days. There was still much to do, and he had some ideas about how to prevent future explosions and how to act if there were more disasters. He planned to talk to Edan about his ideas, and Leander would be a good one, too, and even Fenton. When Kane thought of Jacob's approaching death, he felt some sadness. After all, he had grown up seeing the man most of his life until he was eighteen. And now, the owner of the mines would be Zachary, after Marc, that is. Somehow, Kane thought, everyone seemed to forget Marc.

As he rode up the drive to the old Fenton house, he saw that the front door was standing open. The jamb had been repaired from where he'd kicked it in the day before and the glass replaced, but now it was wide open.

He dismounted, and called into the house as he entered, but there was no answer. Jacob's office was at the back of the house, and Kane clearly remembered that the last time he'd been in this room was when Jacob had thrown him out for wanting to marry Pam. As he put the paper on the desk, he wondered how different his life would have been if he'd married Pam and not had the opportunity to make his own fortune. For one thing, he wouldn't be married to Houston.

With that thought, he again wondered if Houston would have married him if he hadn't had a few million in the bank.

He called out again, but there was still no answer so he started to leave the house through the kitchen, a way that was

276

very familiar to him. The kitchen was also empty and the back door was standing open. As he reached the door, he saw the narrow stairs leading to the upper floor.

When he'd been growing up, he'd always wanted to see the upstairs of the house, had even imagined owning the house one day.

He laughed as he thought of the house he'd built because he was angry at not being able to see the upstairs of the Fenton house.

With his hand on the bannister, curiosity overrode his common sense and he bounded up the stairs two at a time. Hurriedly, like a thief afraid of getting caught, he went down the hall and looked into the bedrooms. They were very ordinary, with heavy, ornate, dark furniture and heavy, depressing curtains and wallpaper. "Houston has much better taste," he mumbled and then laughed at his snobbery.

He was still smiling when he came to the head of the front staircase, but his smile vanished instantly.

At the foot of the stairs, in a crumpled heap, lay Jacob Fenton—obviously dead.

Kane's first thought was that he'd come too late and now Jacob would never know that at last he was the legal owner of all he'd worked so hard to have. And, too, Kane felt sadness. All those years that Kane had worked in New York, all he could remember were the times he'd polished Fenton's boots, but right now what he remembered were the times he'd given Jacob a hard time, embarrassed him in front of guests, argued with him about when he could and could not have his own horses, and all the times Kane'd tickled the cook and talked her into putting onions into the gravy, both of them knowing that onions gave Jacob such indigestion that he didn't sleep all night.

Slowly, Kane started down the stairs, but he'd only taken one step when Marc Fenton and five of his young friends burst into the hall. By the state of their clothes and their loud voices, they looked as if they were just returning from all night on the town.

"If Taggert thinks that he's gonna take *my* inheritance away," came Marc Fenton's slurred voice, "he's gonna have to fight me. Nobody in this town will believe Taggert over me."

The two women, wearing yellow satin, one with a red feather boa, the other with four peacock feathers in her hair, and the three men, all shouted agreement with Marc.

"Where's the whiskey, love?" one of the women asked.

As a group, the people stopped to stare at the body of Jacob Fenton lying at the foot of the stairs. It was Marc who looked up and saw Kane standing at the head of the stairs.

"I came to see your father—," Kane began but Marc never gave him a chance to finish.

"Murderer!" Marc screeched and started up the stairs in one leap.

"Wait a minute!" Kane shouted, but no one paid him the least attention as the three other men jumped him also. All five men went rolling down the stairs and Kane thought that since he was the only one who was sober, he would probably be the only one who was hurt. In spite of the fact that it was four against one, Kane was winning the fight.

But then one of the women slammed Kane over the head with a heavy brass statue of David preparing to slay the giant.

The four men unsteadily got to their feet and looked down at the unconscious form of Kane.

"What do we do now?" one of the women whispered.

"Hang 'im!" Marc shouted, starting to pick up Kane, but when he made no progress, and none of the others offered to help, he looked up, pleading, "He killed my father."

"There ain't enough whiskey in the world to get me drunk enough to hang a man as rich as he is," one of the men said. "While he's out, let's take him to the jail. Let the sheriff deal with him."

There was some argument from Marc, but he was too drunk to put up a great deal of fight, and so the four of them struggled to heave Kane's big body into the back of a buckboard that had been left standing outside the house. Not one of them seemed to give the body of Jacob another thought as they left him on the floor, the doors of the house wide open.

"Here, drink this," Edan was saying as he held Kane's head.

With a groan, Kane tried to sit up, but the pain in his head made him lean back against the cold stone wall. "What happened?" He looked up to see Edan, Leander and the sheriff hovering over him.

"It was all a mistake," Lee said. "I told the sheriff about the paper and why you went to Fenton's."

"He was dead?" Kane asked. "He looked like it from where I stood." Kane's head came up sharply, causing him more pain. "The last thing I remember is Marc Fenton and some drunks pullin' me down the stairs."

Edan sat down on the cot where Kane was stretched out. To his right were the bars of the jail. "As far as we can tell, the servants found Jacob Fenton dead about three minutes before you walked into the house. For some reason, they all decided to go get help and so left the body alone and the house open. Then Marc and his friends came in from an all-night spree and saw you standing at the top of the stairs and thought you'd pushed him down. You're lucky, because Marc wanted to hang you from the front porch."

Kane rubbed the knot on the back of his head. "Hangin' couldn't hurt more than this does."

"You're free to go, Mr. Taggert," the sheriff said. "And I suggest that you get out of here before your wife finds out. Women take on so when their husbands are put in jail."

"Not Houston," Kane said. "She's a lady to the core. She'd be calm if they hanged me." Even as he said the words, a new thought came to him. How *would* Houston react if she thought he were a murderer? Hadn't he heard one time that all the property of murderers was confiscated by the state? Or was it that a person couldn't inherit from a person he'd killed?

"How many people know about this?" Kane asked. "The Fenton servants can testify that I'm innocent, but has that fact spread around town yet?"

"I called Lee the minute I saw young Fenton push you out of the wagon," the sheriff said, puzzled.

"Everyone is too concerned with the mine explosion to care much who gets thrown in jail," Leander said. "All the reporters are at the Little Pamela trying to figure out new ways to describe the bodies," he added with a grimace.

"What are you planning?" Edan asked, his eyes narrowed.

Kane was silent a moment. "Sheriff, you mind if I stay in here overnight? I'd like to play a little practical joke on my wife."

"Joke?" the sheriff asked. "Women don't usually appreciate a joke, no matter how good it is."

Kane looked up at Lee and Edan. "Can I count on you two keepin' quiet for twenty-four hours?"

Edan stood and, at the look on Lee's face, he said, "My guess is that he wants to see if Houston will stand by him if he tells her that he'll probably be convicted as a murderer. Am I right?"

Kane started studying the dust in a far corner of the room. "Somethin' like that."

Both Lee and the sheriff snorted.

"I ain't interferin' in love," the sheriff said. "Mr. Taggert, if you wanta set up residence in this jail, be my guest, but the city of Chandler is gonna bill you as if this were the finest hotel in San Francisco."

"Fair enough," Kane answered. "Lee? Edan?"

Leander merely shrugged. "It's up to you. I've known Houston for most of my life, and I never knew anything at all about her."

Edan looked at Kane for a long moment. "When Houston passes this test—and she will—will you give up your obsession of doubting her so we can get back to work? Vanderbilt has probably bought the eastern seaboard by now."

Kane drew his breath in sharply. "Well, he can sell it back to us starting tomorrow, as soon as I get out of this place," he said with a grin.

When the men were gone, Kane lay down on the cot and went to sleep.

Houston had a three-month-old baby in her lap, trying to get the child to sleep, and a two-year-old and a four-year-old in a bed beside her. They were some of the many children who'd lost their fathers in the last few days. Their mother was beside herself trying to figure out how she was going to support herself and her small children in the years to come. Houston and Blair and other members of The Sisterhood had been campaigning to get the local merchants to try to find jobs for the women, and Houston was one of the volunteers to help in an impromptu child-care center—something new that Blair had seen in Pennsylvania.

280

When the sheriff's deputy came to the little house and asked for her, she had no idea what he wanted.

"Your husband has been arrested for the murder of Jacob Fenton," the young man said.

It took Houston a moment to react, and her first thought was that Kane's temper had at last gotten the better of him. "When?" she managed to whisper.

"Sometime this mornin'. I wasn't there so I don't know much about it, but ever'body in town knows that he threatened ol' man Fenton's life, not that anybody blames him, 'cause we all know that Fenton's guilty as sin, but it ain't gonna help Taggert none. They hang you for killin' a bad man as well as a good one."

Houston gave him her iciest look. "I will thank you to not judge and condemn my husband before you hear the facts." She put the baby into the boy's arms. "Here, you may take care of the babies while I go see my husband."

"I can't do that, Blair-Houston, I'm on city time. I'm a deputy sheriff."

"I had the impression that you believed you were a judge. Check her diaper and see if she needs changing, and if the others wake up, feed them and entertain them until their mother returns in about two hours."

"Two hours!" she heard the boy wail as she left the cabin.

Houston's carriage was waiting outside for her and she made the trip to the jail in record time. The little stone building was built into a hill at the far edge of town. Most of the prisoners were drunks sleeping off Saturday night, and the real cases were usually taken to Denver to be tried.

"Good morning, Miss Blair-Houston," the sheriff said, getting to his feet and hastily putting his paper down.

"Mrs. Taggert," she corrected. "I'd like to see my husband immediately."

"Why, of course, Mrs. Westfield-Taggert," he said, removing the keys from a nail in the wall.

Kane was asleep on the cot and Houston saw the dried blood on the back of his head. She went to him, touched his face as she heard the cell door being locked behind her.

"Kane, darling, what have they done to you?" She began to kiss his face and he started to wake.

"Oh, Houston," Kane said as he rubbed his head. "What happened?"

"You don't remember? They say that you killed Jacob Fenton. You didn't, did you?"

"Hell, no!" he blurted, then paused as Houston went to her knees and put her head in his lap. "At least I don't think so. I . . . ah, I really don't remember too well."

With her cheek against his thighs, his hand in her hair, she was determined not to show her fear. "Tell me what you do remember."

He began his story slowly. "I went to see Fenton, and nobody was home so I went upstairs lookin' for him. When I got to the front of the house, there he was lyin' at the bottom of the stairs. Dead. The next minute, Marc Fenton and some others came in and started yellin' that I'd killed him. There was a fight, and I got hit over the head with somethin' hard, and I woke up here. I think there's talk of a lynchin'."

Houston looked up at him with fear in her eyes and after a moment she stood and began to walk about the cell. "That's a very weak story."

"Weak!" Kane gasped, then calmed. "Houston, honey, it's the truth, I swear to you."

"You were the only one in the house? There were no witnesses that he was already dead when you entered?"

"Not exactly that way. I mean, nobody saw me come into the house, I don't think, but maybe somebody saw Fenton dead earlier."

"That won't matter. If someone saw him die, that would make a difference, but you could have been hiding in a closet for hours for all they know. Did someone actually see him die?"

"I . . . I don't know, but Houston—."

She came back to sit on the bed by him. "Kane, everyone in town heard you say that you wished Jacob was dead. Unless you have an eyewitness to his death, we'll never prove that you're innocent. What are we going to do?"

"I don't know, but I think I'm beginnin' to worry. Houston, there's somethin' I wanta tell you. It's about the money."

"Kane," she said softly, looking up at him. "Why *were* you at Mr. Fenton's house? You weren't really planning to murder him?"

"Hell, no," he said quickly. "I had Mr. Westfield draw up a paper sayin' that I was releasin' all my claims to the Fenton property, and I was takin' the paper to Fenton. What I wanta talk to you about is my money. If they convict me, they're gonna confiscate everything I own. You'll not only be a widow, you'll be a pauper. Your only chance to save any of the money is to leave me right now before I go to trial. If you do that, Westfield can arrange for you to have a few million."

Houston was barely listening to the last part of what he was saying. Her face showed how stunned she was. "Why did you go to Fenton's?" she whispered.

"I told you," Kane said impatiently. "I wanted to give him a paper sayin' I had no hold on his property. Poor ol' man, he was dead when I got there and never saw the paper. But, Houston, what matters is that you have to save yourself and you've gotta do it now. If I'm taken out of here and lynched, it'll be too late."

Houston felt that she was in a dream. Ever since she'd found out that Kane had married her to enact a plan of revenge, she had never felt the same. She'd admitted that she loved him in spite of what he felt about her, but in her heart she'd always known that some part of her would withhold her complete love.

"You've given up your revenge, haven't you?" she asked softly.

"Are you on that again? I told you that all I wanted was to have him at my table at a house that was bigger than his. If I could afford it, what was wrong with it?"

"But you also wanted a lady-wife at the table, too. You married me because—."

"You married me for my money!" he shot at her. "And now you're gonna lose ever' penny of it when they hang me for a murder I didn't commit."

Houston stood. He hadn't said, in so many words, that he loved her, but he did. She knew it. She knew it with every fiber in her body. He had married her as part of a stupid plan of revenge, but in the end, he'd fallen in love with her and, because of that love, he could forgive an old man who'd wronged him.

"I have to go," she said. "I have a great deal of work to do."

283

If she'd looked at Kane, she would have seen the look of pain on his face. "I guess you gotta talk to Mr. Westfield about the money."

"Someone," she murmured, pulling at her gloves. "Perhaps Mr. Westfield isn't the right person." Absently, she kissed his cheek. "Don't worry about a thing. I know exactly what to do." With that, she called to the sheriff and he let her out.

Kane stood in the middle of the cell for a moment, unable to move. She had certainly jumped at the chance to get rid of him, he thought. He climbed on the cot to look out the window and, as he saw Houston speeding away in her shiny carriage, he had to blink his eyes to clear the water. Sunlight, he thought, stepping down.

Easy come, easy go, he told himself. He'd done all right without a wife before, and he'd do all right again.

"Sheriff," he called. "You can let me out now. I found out what I wanted to know."

"Not on your life, Taggert," the man answered, laughter in his voice. "The city of Chandler needs the revenue that I'm gonna charge you for a night's accommodations."

Without a word of protest, Kane went back to the cot. He didn't really care where he spent tonight.

Chapter 31

"You're sure you know what you're doing?" Houston once again asked Ian.

Solemnly, Ian nodded as he glanced back at the small wooden crate in the back of the wagon. Beside him sat Zachary, his eyes straight ahead and alive with excitement. He wasn't yet old enough to be fully aware of the dangers of what they'd planned.

"It isn't in any danger of going off by itself, is it?" Houston asked.

"No," Ian answered, but he couldn't help glancing back at the little wooden box that held the dynamite.

Houston's hands on the reins were white with the strain of holding them as tightly as she was.

It had taken nearly twenty-four hours to arrange what was going to happen tonight. She had known what she wanted to do, and right away she had also known that no adult would help her. When she'd asked Ian, she'd explained to him that he was taking a risk and could get into serious trouble if he was openly involved, but Ian had said that he owed Houston for all that he had now, and he was willing to risk anything. Much to Houston's chagrin, Ian'd asked young Zachary to come along, saying that they needed someone to hold the horses.

Tonight, at midnight, Houston had met Ian at the Little Pamela mine and, counting on the confusion caused by the mine explosion, they'd broken the chains on the dynamite shack and stolen enough to blow away about two city blocks. Against Ian's protest of the time it would take, Houston had rechained and relocked the shack.

Slipping about, neither of them very good at hiding the fact that they were doing something illegal, they managed to get the box into the waiting wagon. A few people said hello to Houston, but they'd seen her often in the last few days and thought nothing of her presence.

She and Ian were halfway down the mountainside when they met Zachary walking toward them. He'd climbed out his window, using a knotted rope, hours ago and had planned to walk all the way to the mine.

"You're to do nothing but stay with the horses, nothing more," Houston warned. "And, as soon as your father and I get on the horses, I want both of you out of there. Ian, can you get back into Edan's house all right?"

"Of course."

"And you, Zach?"

Zachary swallowed hard, because the rope had given way when he was still four feet off the ground. There was no way he could slip back into his house unnoticed. "Sure," he answered. "No problem at all."

Houston didn't relax as they neared the sleeping town. It was three o'clock when they reached the jail. Earlier, she'd hidden two saddle horses outside the jail, their bags laden with food, clothes and enough cash to carry them through a couple of months in hiding.

She stopped the wagon quite a distance from the jail and watched nervously as Ian removed the box of dynamite. She knew that he had trained in the mines as a shot-firer, but she wasn't convinced that he knew how to blow up the side of the stone jail.

Just as she opened her mouth to speak, Ian started talking. "I'll put a few sticks in the base of that wall that's in the hill, then, when it blows, the entire wall will come sliding down. It'll be like opening a very large window. Kane will have to jump down from the floorboards onto a horse, and then you'll be off. It couldn't be simpler."

"A very simple plan, for which we could all go to prison for the rest of our lives," she murmured.

Yesterday, when Kane had told her that he might be

hanged for a murder that he didn't commit—and, when Houston was honest with herself, she admitted that she didn't really care whether he was a murderer or not—she knew that something had to be done to get him released. The town's sympathy would be on Kane's side after the way he'd helped with the disaster, but the trial would probably go to Denver, and Fenton Coal and Iron was a powerful force in Denver. She did not think he'd have a fair trial and, with no witnesses except to say that Kane had been found at the top of the stairs with a dead Jacob at the bottom, she had no doubt that Kane would be found guilty.

After only a moment's soul-searching, she knew what had to be done. She had to get him out of the jail, and even if it meant that they had to spend the rest of their lives in hiding, she meant to do it. They'd go to Mexico, and she thought that she could get Blair to send them enough money to live on. As long as Kane kept a quiet profile and didn't call too much attention to himself, she thought they could get away from the American law. It was too bad that Kane was so well known in so many parts of the country, so they couldn't possibly hide in the United States.

Houston's only regret was that she wouldn't be able to say good-bye to her family and her friends. She probably wouldn't even be able to write to them, as her letters might lead to Kane's capture.

But she knew what had to be done, and she felt that as long as she had Kane she could be happy, no matter where they lived or in what hardship.

Now, in the darkness, she directed Zach to get the horses from their hiding places, to tighten the girths and to bring the horses closer to the jail.

Her hands were trembling as she helped Ian insert the sticks of dynamite into the chinks of the stone wall. When everything was set, she motioned Ian to let her stand on his shoulders so she could see inside the window.

"Tell him to put the mattress around his head," Ian said as he lifted her.

"We don't have enough dynamite to hurt him, do we?" she asked.

"The heels on those boots of yours hurt, so don't waste my time askin' damn fool questions."

Houston looked into the dark cell and saw Kane sprawled across the little mattress, parts of him hanging over the side. She tossed a pebble into the cell.

He didn't even move and it took six stones, one of them glancing sharply off his chest, before he woke.

"Kane!" she said as loudly as she dared.

"What?" he asked, sitting up. "Is that you, Houston? What're you doin' here in the middle of the night?"

She motioned for him to come to the window. "I don't have time to explain now but Ian and I are getting you out of jail. We're going to dynamite this wall away, so I want you to get into the farthest corner and put that mattress around as much of you as you can cover."

"You're what?" Kane gasped. "Dynamite! Listen, Houston, there's somethin' I have to tell you."

"Houston!" Ian said from below her. "Them little heels are killin' me. Are you gonna stay up there all night?"

"I have to go," she said. "Just get in the corner, and when the wall is gone, I have horses ready. I love you." With that, she bent and got off Ian's shoulders.

Kane stood by the window of the cell for several long moments. She hadn't run off to get the money, but instead, she'd set up a plan to blow the side of the jail out and rescue him. He put his hands in his pockets and started to whistle a little tune, smiling at the thought of Houston being so concerned about him.

It was while he was whistling that he heard an odd sound, like something on fire.

"Dynamite!" he gasped, grabbed the mattress and leaped into the corner of the room. Nothing could have prepared him for the noise of the explosion. It was as if the top of his head had been taken off—and the noise went on and on.

Houston, Ian and Zach hid behind a boulder as the wall to the jail came tumbling down. The dynamite removed the foundation to the two-story wall and the stones above it fell rather gracefully, leaving a clear view of the interior of the jail. Kane was huddled in a corner and, when the dust began to settle, he made no attempt to move.

"We've killed him," Houston cried and started running, Ian behind her.

"Probably just deafened him. Kane," Ian shouted above

the sound of the rock that was still falling, and when Kane made no response, Ian scrambled up the rock and into the three-walled cell.

Ian pulled the mattress off but Kane couldn't understand a word he said, so Ian had to use gestures. For some reason, Kane seemed to have been made stupid by the explosion, since he kept shaking his head at Houston, and Ian had to nearly push him onto the rock pile so he could get to the ground.

Houston waited on a horse and, as Kane got close to her, she saw that he kept putting his hands to his head as if he were in great pain. He seemed to want to say something, but Houston wouldn't give him time as Ian and Zach started pushing him onto the other horse.

"Go home, both of you," she ordered as she saw that people were rushing down the street toward them after hearing the explosion.

"Let's go," she shouted to Kane and he followed her down the south road of town and out into the dessert.

Houston rode as fast and as hard as she could spur her horse, looking back occasionally to Kane who followed her with a blank, odd look on his face.

The sun came up, and still they rode, slowing just enough to allow the horses to breathe. At noon, they stopped at a stage station, a desolate place in the middle of the barrenness between Colorado and New Mexico, and Houston paid an outrageous price for two fresh horses.

"He all right?" the station manager asked, nodding toward Kane as he leaned against the building and hit his head with his hand.

Houston handed the old man a twenty dollar bill. "You haven't seen us."

He took the money. "I mind my own business."

Houston tried to talk to Kane, but he just dumbly stared at her moving mouth and followed her only after she motioned him to do so.

What they ate during the day, they ate while on their horses, never stopping even after the sun set. Only once did Kane try to speak, but when he couldn't seem to hear himself, he made gestures that Houston finally realized meant that he wanted to know where they were going.

"Mexico," Houston shouted four times before he seemed to understand.

Kane shook his head, but Houston urged her horse on faster and ignored him. No doubt, he didn't want her to get into trouble with him, but she wasn't going to let him talk her into returning. If he was to live his life in exile, she was going to live with him.

Kane caught her horse's reins and pulled until she had to slow down.

"STOP!" he bellowed. "WE'LL STAY HERE FOR THE NIGHT."

Every word was at the top of his lungs and Houston blinked several times at the volume breaking the still night air.

Kane didn't say another word as he dismounted and led his horse over a small hill and into a grove of trees. Houston followed his lead as he unsaddled his horse and made a camp for the night. She wanted to go on longer, to put more distance between them and the posse from Chandler, but perhaps Kane had been hurt in the blast and needed rest. It would take a long time before the citizens could be organized, so perhaps they had time.

She had the saddle in her hands when she glanced toward Kane and saw that he was looking at her in a way that was almost frightening.

Very slowly, he took the saddle out of her arms, tossed it to the ground, and after one look that she couldn't interpret, he was upon her.

He was like a hungry animal and, after Houston got over her surprise, she reacted in kind. Buttons flew off her dusty riding suit like corn popping in a skillet. His mouth was all over her body at once, with his big, strong hands tearing away all that inhibited his contact with her skin.

"Kane," she half-cried, half-laughed. "Kane. My only love, my true love."

He didn't seem to need words as he pushed her nude body to the ground and thrust inside her with the strength of the dynamite they'd set off that morning. Houston felt as if she were like the stone wall crumbling and, as they moved together in a sweaty, fierce passion, she was sure that this was all she needed in life, and that what she'd done today had been right.

When at last they erupted together, Houston shivered with the force of her passion and the depth of her love for this man.

They lay together for a while, Kane holding her tightly in his arms, as if he never meant to let her go. And Houston clung to him just as tightly, afraid now when she thought how close she'd come to losing him, how close he'd come to being hanged.

After a long while, Kane stood and went to the horses to care for them. Houston started to help but he motioned her to lie still, tossing her a blanket to cover her from the cool night air.

Even when he built a fire, he wouldn't let her help. Houston started to protest that perhaps they'd be seen, but Kane shouted that she should trust him, and she did. She was glad to turn over the mastery of this wild escape to him, and she was glad to lie back and be waited on. He brought a plate of beans to her, with a tortilla and a cup of dreadful coffee. But Houston thought it was the most delicious meal of her life.

When they'd finished eating, Kane put out the fire, lay down beside her and pulled her into his arms. In minutes, both of them were asleep.

Chapter 32

When Houston woke, it was full light and Kane was holding her and smiling angelically.

"We have to go," she said, sitting up, shrugging off his hands and pulling on the remnants of her torn clothing. The front of her riding habit was missing so many buttons that it was decidedly indecent. "They'll be after us soon, and I don't imagine they'll stop to rest this long."

He caught her arm. "Hot after the murderer, right?"

"I really don't think this is any time for laughter."

"Houston, I want you to tell me what you have planned. Why are you runnin' toward Mexico?"

"I'll tell you as we get the horses saddled," she said and stood, waiting impatiently until Kane also rose. "I think we can hide in Mexico," she said, putting the saddle blanket on her horse.

"For how long?"

"Forever, of course," she answered. "I don't think that the law ever forgives one for murder. I think we can live there quite frugally, and I hear that people don't ask as many questions there as they do in this country."

He caught her arm. "Wait a minute. You mean that you're plannin' to live in Mexico with me? That if I'm an outlaw, you're gonna be one, too?"

"Yes, certainly, I'm planning to live with you. Now, will you please saddle your horse so that we can ride?"

Houston didn't say any more because Kane grabbed her

about the waist and twirled her around. "Honey, that's the best thing that anybody's ever said to me. You don't care about the money after all."

"Kane!" she said, exasperated. "Please put me down. They'll find us and you'll—."

She stopped because he planted a hearty kiss on her mouth.

"Ain't nobody comin' after us, unless it's the sheriff 'cause he's mad at you for tearin' up his jail. Oh, Houston, honey, I wish I could see that man's face."

Houston took a step back from him. What he was saying made no sense to her, but in the pit of her stomach was a little feeling of fear. "Perhaps you should explain that remark."

Kane drew three circles in the dirt with his toe. "I just wanted to see how you . . . ah, felt about the fact that I wasn't a rich man anymore."

She gave him a look that had stopped many a forward cowboy. "I would like to know about Jacob Fenton."

"I didn't tell you a single lie, Houston, it's just that I guess I didn't tell you all of it. I did find him dead at the foot of the stairs, and I was taken to jail for his murder, but the truth was that the servants had run out of the house and knew he was already dead. Although, I didn't ask if any of them actually *saw* him die. That was real clever of you to think of that."

"So why were you in jail when I got there? Why weren't you released immediately?"

"I guess I was, sorta. Houston, honey," he held out his arms to her. "I just wanted to know for sure that you liked me for myself and it wasn't my money you wanted. You know, when you walked out of that jail after I told you that I'd lose my money, I thought for sure that you were goin' to Westfield to see what you could get before I was hanged."

"Is that what you thought of me?" she said under her breath. "You think that I'm that low a human being that I'd leave the man I love alone to face a murder trial and not lift a finger to help?" She turned toward the horse.

"Houston, baby, sweetheart, I didn't mean nothin'. I just wanted to know for sure. I didn't have any idea you'd do somethin' as damn fool as . . . Well, I mean, I had no idea that you'd blow the jail to kingdom come and near kill me."

"You seem to have recovered well enough."

"Houston, you ain't gonna be mad, are you? It was just a little joke. Ain't you got any sense of humor? Why, ever'body in town will—."

"Yes," she said, glaring at him. "Go on. What will everybody in town do?"

Kane gave her a weak grin. "Maybe they won't notice."

She advanced on him. "Won't notice that I removed the entire side of a jail that had two-foot-thick stone walls? Perhaps they all slept through the explosion. Yes, perhaps they *will* just drive past the building and not even notice. And maybe the sheriff will forgo telling the story of the decade about how one of the Chandler twins stuck dynamite into the wall to rescue a husband who wasn't even charged with murder. Maybe every person for miles around won't be laying bets as to when I'll find out my error and whether *I'll* be charged with murder." She turned back to the horse, every muscle in her body aflame with anger.

"Houston, you have to understand my side of it. I wanted to know if it was me you loved or my money. I saw an opportunity to find out and I took it. You can't blame a man for tryin'."

"I most certainly *can* blame you. Just once, I'd like you to listen to me. I told you that I loved you—you, not your money—yet you never heard a word I said."

"Oh, well," he shrugged, "you said that you couldn't live with a man you couldn't respect, either, but you came back, and it didn't even take all that much persuadin'. I guess you just can't help yourself." He gave her a crooked grin.

"Of all the arrogant, vain men I have ever met, you are the worst. I am very, very sorry that I ever rescued you. I wish they had hanged you." With that, she mounted her horse.

"Houston, baby, you don't mean that," Kane said as he climbed onto his horse and began to ride beside her. "It was just a joke. I didn't mean no harm."

All day long they rode, and every minute, Kane was either presenting arguments to her or thinking of further excuses as to why she should be grateful to him for what he had done. He said that Houston could be more sure of her feelings for him now. He tried to make her see the humor of it all. He chastised her for using boys to help her and warned of the danger she'd placed them all in. He tried anything he could think of to get a reaction out of her.

But Houston sat on her horse as rigid as a human body could be. Her thoughts were on the people of Chandler. After the horror of the mine disaster, they'd want something to lighten their mood and they'd no doubt milk this story for every drop of humor. The sheriff would embellish it for all it was worth, and the Chandler Chronicle would probably run a series of articles on the whole affair, starting with the wedding and ending with . . . ending with a man who should have been hanged.

When Houston thought of Kane, her blood boiled, and she refused to listen to a single word he said. The fact that she had given him her love and he had doubted it so publicly, doubted her in such a spectacular, outrageous way was particularly humiliating.

She had her first taste of what was to come when they stopped at the stage station and traded horses. The old man asked if they were the couple from Chandler that he'd heard about. He could hardly recount the story for laughing so hard, and when they left, he tried to return the twenty dollars Houston had given him.

"That story was worth a hundred dollars to me," he said, slapping a grinning Kane on the back. "I owe you eighty dollars."

Houston put her chin in the air and went to her horse. She was doing her best to pretend that neither man existed.

Once they were on the trail again, Kane started talking to her with renewed vigor, but he lost a lot when he kept pausing to laugh.

"When I saw you standin' there, and you were sayin' that you were gonna bust me out and save me from the hangin' tree, I couldn't think of what to say, I was that stunned, and then when Ian started yellin' that the heels on them little boots of yours—," he had to pause to wipe the grin off his face. "Why, Houston, you'll be the envy of every woman west of the Mississippi. They'll all wish they had the courage and the bravery to rescue their husbands from the jaws of death and—."

He stopped to clear his throat and Houston glanced at him. He was unsuccessfully trying to control his laughter.

"When I think of the look on your face atop that horse. What're those women that wear horns on their heads? Lady Vikings, that's what you looked like, a lady Viking come to rescue her man. And the look on Zachary's face! If my head hadn't been hurtin' so much—."

He broke off because Houston kicked her horse's side and raced ahead of him.

Whatever Houston had expected, when she reached Chandler, it was worse. Ignoring Kane as best she could, she rode on the outskirts of the town to the north side so she would see as few people as possible on her way to Kane's house.

It was six o'clock in the morning when they rode up the hill to the Taggert house, but already there were about twenty couples who just "happened" to be strolling in front of the house. Most of the Taggert servants were in the front drive talking to the townspeople.

Houston held the front of her destroyed habit together and mustered as much dignity as she could and rode to the kitchen entrance, while Kane dismounted at the front and all the people ran to him.

"Probably wants to brag," Houston murmured. Somehow, she managed to get through the kitchen and Mrs. Murchison's smiles and unsubtle questions.

Upstairs, Houston dismissed Susan and drew her own bath. After a short time in the tub, she climbed into her bed and went to sleep. She heard Kane enter the room at some time, but she pretended to be fast asleep and he went away.

After nine hours of sleep and a huge meal, she felt physically better, but her mood was worse. When she walked in her rooftop garden, she could see the street and the extraordinary number of people who were strolling in front of the house.

Kane came into her room once to tell her that he was on his way up to the Little Pamela to see if any help was needed, and he asked Houston to go with him. She shook her head in refusal.

"You can't hide in here forever," he said angrily. "Why aren't you proud of what you did? I sure as hell am."

After he had left, Houston knew he was right, that she had to face the townspeople and the sooner she got it over, the better. She dressed slowly in a serviceable blue cotton, went downstairs and asked that her buggy be hitched.

It didn't take Houston but ten minutes to find out that Kane's prediction of how the people of Chandler would react was dead wrong. She was not being cast as a heroine who'd rescued her husband, but as a silly, flighty woman who went hysterical first and asked questions later.

She drove her little buggy through the back side of town and up the road to the Little Pamela. Perhaps at the mine they'd need so much help that they wouldn't have time to talk about her escapade.

No such luck. The victims of the disaster wanted something to laugh about and Houston's escapade was their target.

She did the best she could at holding her head high while she helped to clear the debris and tried to make arrangements for the relocation of the widows and orphans.

Her real complaint was that Kane was enjoying everything so much. At the wedding, he'd been hurt because the people believed that any woman would prefer Leander over him, but now he had very public proof that Houston was in love with him.

Houston kept thinking of all the times he could have told her that he wasn't really being charged with murder. He could certainly talk fast enough when he wanted to, so why was he so tongue-tied the night she informed him that she'd just inserted dynamite under his feet?

As the day wore on, and the people became more bold about asking her questions ("You mean you didn't ask the sheriff what his chances were or talk to an attorney? Leander was in on all of it. He could have told you. Or you could have . . ."), Houston wanted to hide. And when Kane walked past her, gave her a hearty punch in the ribs, a wink and said, "Buck up, honey, it was only a joke," she wanted to cry that it might be a joke to him, but to her the public humiliation was horrifying.

Toward evening, she saw Pamela Fenton standing nose to nose with Kane and, on the cool evening breeze, she heard the words, "At the wedding, you said that you wouldn't humiliate her. What do you think you've done now?"

The thought that someone was fighting her case was gratifying to her.

At home, she had dinner in her room and Kane made one more attempt to talk to her, but she just looked at him. He stormed out of the room, complaining that she had no sense of humor and was too damn much of a lady too damn much of the time.

Houston cried herself to sleep.

Chapter 33

The next day, Houston was arranging flowers in a large vase in the hall outside Kane's office. She was still angry, still too hurt and humiliated to speak to him, and she couldn't bear the thought of leaving the safety of her own house.

Kane had the door to his office open and with him were Rafe, Leander, and Edan. Kane'd called a meeting to discuss the possible consequences of the mine explosions. Kane had been concerned when he found out that the miners' widows would probably not be given any compensation.

Houston listened to the men discussing the future of Chandler and she felt a great deal of pride at what her husband was doing. She wondered how she could ever have believed that he would foreclose on the people whose mortgages the Chandler National Bank held. Yesterday, Opal'd had a long talk with Houston and told her why Kane had used blackmail to get Houston to come back to live with him.

"He loves you so much," Opal'd said, "and I don't see why you have to be angry with him now."

It might have worked, except at that moment she heard three women in the hall giggling like schoolgirls. They'd come to see Houston and "catch up on the latest news" was what they told the maid. Houston politely declined to see them, or anyone else.

Now, standing in the hallway, she listened with pride to the reforms her husband was planning, but then she heard Leander ask a question that caused her back to stiffen.

"Is this a bill from the City of Chandler?" Lee asked.

"Yeah," Kane answered. "The sheriff wants five hundred dollars cash to repair the jail. I think it may be the only bill I ever *wanted* to pay."

"Maybe you could have a grand openin' and Houston could cut the ribbon," she heard Rafe say.

There was a long silence. "If she ever speaks to him again," Edan said.

There was another pause.

Leander spoke next. "I don't think you ever know a person. I've known Houston most of my life, but the Houston I knew and the one who'd blow out the side of a jail aren't the same woman. A few years ago, I took her to a dance and she wore a very becoming red dress, but Gates had said something that had hurt her feelings and she kept clutching her cloak so every inch of that dress was covered. She was so nervous by the time we reached the dance that I said that if she wanted to keep wearing the cloak it was fine with me. Damned if she didn't spend the whole evening sitting in a corner looking like she was about to cry."

Houston's hand paused as she held a flower. It was odd how the same episode could be seen in two ways. Now that she looked back on it, maybe she had been silly to be so upset about a red dress. Now, she seemed to remember that Nina Westfield often wore just that shade of red that had caused Houston so much anguish that night.

Smiling, Houston continued with the flowers.

"If she was gonna break out of the mold, she could've done it with less danger to my hide," Kane said. "You don't know what it's like to have somebody tell you that they've just lit dynamite under your feet and there ain't nowhere you can run."

"You can stop bragging," Edan said. "You loved what she did and you know it."

Houston's smile grew broader.

Leander laughed. "Too bad you didn't get to see what happened after the explosion. Everybody thought another mine had gone up and we ran out of our houses in our underwear. When we saw the jail, with half of it blown away, we just stood there; not one of us could understand what had

300

happened. It was Edan who first remembered that you were in the jail."

A little laugh escaped Houston, but she got it under control.

"Listen," Edan said, "as soon as I saw that jail, I knew Houston was involved. While the rest of you've been worshipping at her feet over the years and telling yourselves what an ice princess she is, *I*'ve been following her around. Under her prim little exterior is a woman . . . Well, you wouldn't believe some of the things that woman does on a regular basis."

Houston had more difficulty controlling her laughter. Edan sounded half-appalled, half-admiring. She thought of the time he'd hidden and watched the pre-wedding party. The day he'd told her that he'd seen it, she hadn't allowed herself to think about anything except that he'd heard about their plans for the mines, but now she thought of the boxer, and the cancan, and, oh Heavens, *Fanny Hill*. At the time, she'd been terrified that Kane would find out some of the things that she did, such as The Sisterhood's stag parties, and infiltrating the mine camps, but, in the end, he'd caught her in nearly all of it and her life hadn't ended. The night she wore that red dress, he was sure that if she showed it to anyone, her reputation would be ruined and she wouldn't be a fit wife for Leander.

But look at what she'd done in the last few months! There was the time she had climbed down the rose trellis in her underwear. Then there was inviting all those people to live with them and telling Kane—who had to support them—about it later.

The more she thought, the more the laughter bubbled inside her. Before they were married, she was quite sure who was marrying Kane Taggert. He requested a lady, and she was sure that she could fill the bill. But when she began to remember the things she'd put him through, and all the times he'd said, with that special look of disbelief on his face, that he'd had no idea what he was getting when he married a real, true, deep-down lady, Houston could no longer control her laughter. It exploded from her in a sound that made the vase on the table tremble.

She grabbed the side of the table and kept on laughing as her knees grew weak.

Immediately, the men came running out of the room.

"Houston, honey, you all right?" Kane asked as he too[k] her arm and started to pull her upright. But it was like tryin[g] to get a piece of seaweed to stand.

"I covered my red dress because I didn't want anyone t[o] think I wasn't a lady," she cried, "but then I blew out the sid[e] of the jail." She put her hands over her stomach as she fell th[e] last few inches to sit on the floor. "Was my hat on straight?" she asked. "Was it on straight the night I challenged the boxe[r] to a muscle showdown?"

"What's she talkin' about?" Kane asked.

Edan was beginning a smile, and it broadened as he sai[d] "You lost it while you were dancing." He started to laug[h] "Houston, I took a bottle of whiskey with me that nig[ht] because I thought I'd be bored watching a ladies' tea party." By the time he finished, he was on the floor with Housto[n] "And Miss Emily!" he gasped. "I can't walk past her sho[p] with a straight face."

Houston was laughing too hard to speak clearly. "An[d] Leander! I was so careful all those years. I never let you kno[w] about Sadie or any of the other things."

Leander, smiling, watched. "You know what she's talkin[g] about?" he asked Kane.

Rafe answered. "This sweet little empty-headed lady th[at] looks too delicate to do anything but embroider, regular[ly] handles a four-horse wagon."

"I can drive twelve," she declared and that sent Edan an[d] her into new peals of laughter.

"And she has a right that can flatten boys as big as she is," Kane said with pride, "and she can leave her own weddin' [to] follow her pigheaded husband when he's made an ass [of] himself in front of the whole town, and she can pay m[y] mistress to get outta town and she can scream." He stoppe[d] when he said the last and began to look embarrassed.

Leander looked down at Houston on the floor, her arm[s] around Edan, both of them weak with laughter, and h[e] turned to Kane, saw the way the man was watching Housto[n] with a mixture of pride and love. "And to think that I calle[d] her an ice princess," Lee murmured.

Kane rocked back on his heels, his thumbs in his belt loop[s] and said, "I melted the ice."

Both Lee and Rafe shouted with laughter, as much at Kane's pride as at his words.

Rafe nodded down at Houston. "You better do somethin' with that piece of ice 'fore she melts and runs down into the cracks in the floor. I don't think you wanta lose her."

Kane stooped and lifted Houston into his arms. "I ain't ever lettin' this lady go."

Houston, still laughing, snuggled against him as he carried her toward the stairs.

"No sir," Kane said, "Ain't nothin' separatin' us. Not other ladies or kids of mine that she don't know about or the hangman. I guess that's why I love her so much. Ain't that right, Houston?"

Houston looked up at him with stars in her eyes.

He put his head toward hers and whispered so the others couldn't hear. "When I get you upstairs, you're gonna explain to me what a 'muscle showdown' is. And don't you start laughin' again. Houston!"

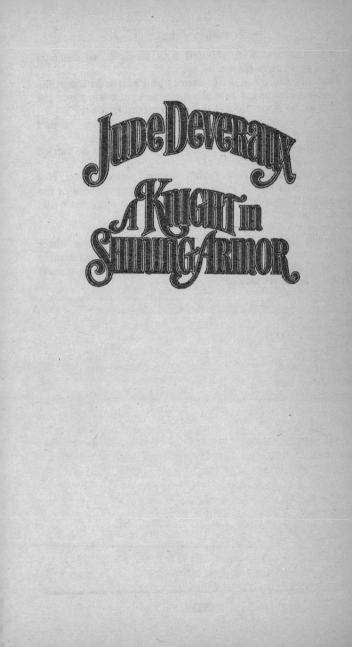

Jude Deveraux

A Knight in Shining Armor

A KNIGHT IN SHINING ARMOR

by
JUDE DEVERAUX

England
1564

Nicholas was trying to concentrate on the letter to
his mother, a letter that was probably the most
important document he'd ever write. Everything depended upon this letter: his honor, his estates, his
family's future—and his life.

But as he wrote he began to hear her. Softly at first,
but growing louder. It was a woman weeping, not
weeping as though from pain or even from grief but
from something deeper.

He gave his attention back to the letter but he could
not concentrate. The woman needed something but
he could not tell what. Comfort? Soothing?

No, he thought, she needed hope. The tears, the
weeping, were the tears of a person who no longer had
any hope.

Nicholas looked back at the paper. The woman's
problems were not his. If he did not finish this letter
and soon give it to the waiting messenger, his own life
would be without hope.

He wrote two more lines then stopped. The crying
increased. It wasn't louder, but it seemed to grow in
size until it filled the room.

"Lady," he whispered, "give me peace. I would give
my life to help you but my life is pledged."

He picked up the pen and wrote, with one hand
over his ear, trying to block out the woman's need.

England
1988

Dazed, numb, Dougless Montgomery walked back
toward the church. She was in a foreign country with
no money, no credit cards, no passport. But worst of
all, the man she loved had just walked out on her.

The heavy oak door of the church was standing
open and she walked inside. It was cool and damp and
dim in the church, and the tall stone walls made the
place feel calm and reverent.

She had to think about this, had to consider what to
do. She'd have to call her father, collect, and have him
send her money. She'd have to tell him that his
youngest daughter had once again failed at something,
that she couldn't even so much as go on holiday
without getting herself into trouble.

Tears started in her eyes as she imagined hearing
her oldest sister, Elizabeth, say, "What has our little
scatterbrained Dougless done now?" Robert had been
Dougless's attempt at making her family proud of her.
Robert wasn't like the other stray-cat men Dougless
had fallen for—he was *so* respectable, so very suitable, but she'd lost him. Maybe if she'd just held her
temper with his daughter Gloria . . .

Tears blurred Dougless's eyes as she looked toward
the end of the church. Sun was streaming through the
old windows high above her head, and sharp, clear
rays lit the white marble tomb in the arch to the left.
Dougless walked forward. Lying on top of the tomb
was a full-length white marble sculpture of a man
wearing the top half of a suit of armor and an

odd-looking pair of shorts, his ankles crossed, helmet tucked under his arm. "Nicholas Stafford," she read aloud, "Earl of Thornwyck."

She was congratulating herself on holding up so well under the awful circumstances, when suddenly everything hit her and her knees collapsed. She fell to the floor, her hands on the tomb, her forehead resting against the cold marble.

She began to cry in earnest, cry deeply from inside herself. She felt like a failure, completely, totally a failure. It seemed that everything she'd ever touched in her life had failed. Through her tears, she looked at the face of the man on the tomb. "Help me," she whispered, her hand on the marble hand of the sculpture. "Help me find my Knight in Shining Armor. Help me find a man who wants me."

She sat back on her heels, her hands over her face, and began to cry harder.

After a long while, she came to realize someone was near her. She turned her head and the sunlight hitting metal so blinded her she sat back on the stone floor with a thud. She put her hand up to shield her eyes.

Standing before her was a man. A man who appeared to be wearing . . . armor.

He stood utterly still, glaring down at Dougless. She stared up at him in openmouthed astonishment. She was an extraordinarily good-looking man, wearing the most authentic-looking stage costume she'd ever seen. There was a small ruff about his neck, then armor to his waist. But what armor! It looked almost as if it were made of silver, and there were many rows of etched flower designs filled in with a golden-colored metal. From his waist to mid-thigh he wore a type of shorts that ballooned about his body. His legs—big muscular legs—were in stockings that looked to be knitted of silk. He wore a garter tied above his left knee. His feet were covered with odd, soft shoes that had little cuts in them.

"Well, witch," he said in a deep baritone, "you have conjured me, what do you ask of me?"

"Witch?" she said, sniffing.

From inside his ballooned shorts, he pulled a handkerchief and handed it to her. Dougless blew her nose noisily.

"Have my enemies hired you? Do they plot against me more? Is not my head enough for them? Stand, madam, and explain yourself."

Gorgeous, but off his rocker, Dougless thought. "Listen, I don't know what you're talking about." She stood. "Now, if you'll excuse me—"

She didn't say more because he drew a thin-bladed sword that had to be a yard long and held the sharp point against her throat. "Reverse your spell, witch. I would return!"

It was all too much for Dougless. She burst into tears again and slumped against the cold stone wall.

"Damnation!" the man muttered, and the next thing Dougless knew she was being picked up and carried to a church pew.

She couldn't seem to stop crying. "This has been the worst day of my life," she wailed. The man stood scowling down at her like something out of an old movie. "I'm sorry," she managed to say. "I don't usually cry so much but to be abandoned by the man I love and attacked—at sword point no less—all in the same day, sets me off." She looked at the handkerchief. It was very large and had an inch-and-a-half border of intricate silk embroidery around the edge. "How pretty," she choked out.

"There is no time for trivialities. My soul is at

stake—as is yours. I tell you again: reverse your spell."

Dougless was recovering herself. "I don't know what you're talking about. I was having a good cry all alone, and you, wearing that absurd outfit, come in here and start yelling at me. I've a good mind to call the police—or the bobbies or whatever they have in rural England. Is it legal for you to carry a sword like that?"

"Legal?" the man said. He was looking at her arm. "Is that a clock on your arm? And what manner of dress is it that you wear?"

"Of course it's a clock and these are my traveling-to-England clothes. Conservative. No jeans or T-shirts. Nice blouse, nice skirt. You know, Miss Marple–type clothes."

He was frowning at her. "You talk uncommonly strangely. What manner of witch are you?"

Dougless threw up her hands in despair, then stood. He was a good deal taller than she was. He had black curling hair just reaching the stiff little ruff he wore, black mustache and a trim, pointed, short beard. "I am not a witch and I am not part of your Elizabethan drama. I'm going to leave now, and if you try anything fancy with your sword I'll scream the windows out. Here's your handkerchief. Sorry it's so wet but I thank you for its loan. Goodbye, and I hope your play gets great reviews." She turned on her heel and walked out of the church. "At least nothing else horrible can happen to me," Dougless murmured as she left the churchyard.

There was a telephone booth at the corner, within sight of the church door. She thought she'd better call her parents in Maine and ask for help.

Dougless leaned back against the booth. The tears

were starting again. She had the Montgomery pride but had no reason for being proud. She had three older sisters who were paragons of success: Elizabeth a research chemist; Catherine, a professor of physics and Anne, a criminal attorney. Dougless seemed to be the Montgomery jester, a source of endless material for laughter among the relatives.

As she was leaning there, her eyes blurred with tears, she saw the man in the knight-suit leave the church and walk down the path toward the gate. He looked at the ancient gravestones without much interest, then headed down the path toward the gate.

Coming down the lane was one of the little English buses, as usual doing about fifty miles an hour on the narrow street.

Dougless stood up straight. Somehow, she instinctively knew the man was going to walk in front of the bus. Dougless started to run. Just as she took flight the vicar came from behind the church, saw what Dougless saw and began to run also.

Dougless reached him first. She made her best flying tackle that she had learned from playing football with her Colorado cousins and landed on top of him, the two of them skidding across the graveled path on his armor as if it were a little rowboat. The bus swerved and missed the two of them by inches.

"Are you all right?" the vicar said, offering his hand to help Dougless up.

"I . . . I think so." Dougless stood and dusted herself off. "You okay?" she said to the man on the ground.

"What manner of chariot was that?" he asked. "I did not hear it coming. There were no horses."

Dougless exchanged looks with the vicar.

"Perhaps I'll get a glass of water," the vicar said.

"Wait!" the man said. "What year is this?"

"1988," the vicar said, and when the man lay back on the ground as if in exhaustion, the vicar looked at Dougless. "I'll get the water," he said and left them alone.

Dougless offered her hand to the man on the ground, but he refused it and rose to his feet.

"I think you ought to sit down." She motioned to an iron bench inside the low stone wall. He wouldn't go first but followed her through the gate, then wouldn't sit until she had, but Dougless pushed him to sit down. He looked pale and bewildered.

"You are dangerous, you know that? Listen, you sit right here and I'm going to call a doctor. You aren't well."

She turned away but his words halted her.

"I think perhaps I am dead."

She looked back at him. If he was suicidal, she didn't want to leave him alone. "Come with me," she said softly. "We'll find you some help."

He didn't move from the bench. "What manner of conveyance was it that nearly struck me down?"

She went to sit by him. If he was suicidal, maybe what he needed most was someone to talk to. "Where are you from? You sound English but you have a strange accent."

"I am English. What was the chariot?"

"All right," she said with a sigh. She could play along with him. "That was what the English call a coach. In America, it's a bus. It was going entirely too fast but it's my opinion that the only thing of the twentieth century the English have really accepted is the speed of motor vehicles. What else don't you know about? Airplanes? Trains? Look, I really need to go. Let's go to the rectory and have the vicar call a doctor.

Or maybe we'll call your mother." Surely the town knew of this crazy man who ran about in armor and pretended he'd never seen a watch or a bus.

"My mother," the man said and his lips formed a little smile. "I would imagine my mother is dead now."

"I'm sorry. Did she die recently?"

He looked up at the sky. "About four hundred years ago."

Dougless started to rise. "I'm getting someone."

He caught her hand. "I was sitting . . . in a room at a desk, writing my mother a letter when I heard a woman weeping. The room darkened, my head swam, and then I was standing over a woman—you." He looked up at her.

Dougless thought that leaving this man alone would be so much easier if he weren't so utterly divinely looking. "Maybe you blacked out and don't remember dressing up and coming to the church. Why don't you tell me where you live? I'll walk you home."

"When I was in the room it was the year of our Lord 1564."